W9-ASQ-791

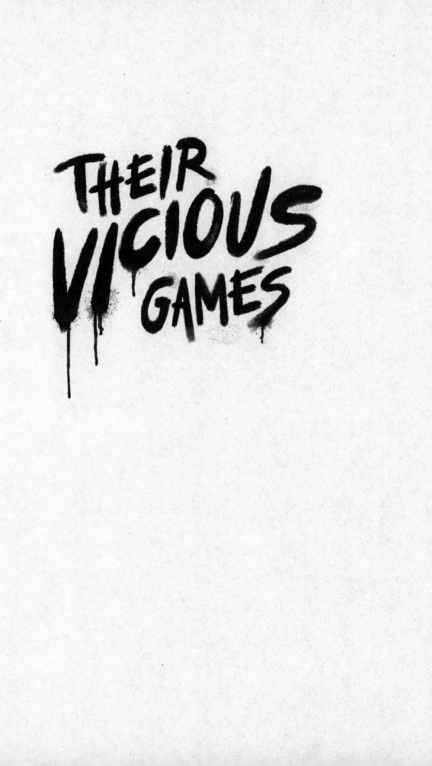

THEIR VICIOUS GAMES

JOELLE WELLINGTON

SIMON & SCHUSTER BFYR

NEW YORK LONDON TORONTO SYDNEY NEW DELHI

SIMON & SCHUSTER BFYR

An imprint of Simon & Schuster Children's Publishing Division
1230 Avenue of the Americas, New York, New York 10020

SIMON & SCHUSTER BOOKS FOR YOUNG READERS
and related marks are trademarks of Simon & Schuster, Inc.
For information about special discounts for bulk purchases, please contact
Simon & Schuster Special Sales at 1-866-506-1949
or business@simonandschuster.com.
The Simon & Schuster Speakers Bureau can bring authors to your live event.
For more information or to book an event, contact
the Simon & Schuster Speakers Bureau at 1-866-248-3049
or visit our website at www.simonspeakers.com.
Interior design by Laura Eckes
The text for this book was set in Adobe Garamond Pro.
Manufactured in the United States of America
First Edition
2 4 6 8 10 9 7 5 3 1
CIP data for this book is available from the Library of Congress.
ISBN 9781665922425
ISBN 9781665922449 (ebook)

❧ *To Alyssa.* ❧

Every story, every sentence, every word
I have crafted is for you.

CHAPTER

1

WHEN MY MOM PULLS ME CLOSE IN MY CAP AND gown and whispers into my ear, "I'm so proud of you, Adina," that's when I know—I've lost.

The realization hits me so hard that my head goes hazy with it and the crushing stench of terror. But I push down the bile and wrap my arms around her.

"Thanks, Mom," I whisper, burying my face in her neck.

She doesn't sound like she's lying, but I know she is.

I'm not Adina Walker, valedictorian, future Yale underclassman, destined for greatness. Not anymore.

I'm Adina Walker, college acceptance rescinded, unremarkable Edgewater graduate, destined for mediocrity.

Game over.

Life has never felt like a game to me, but I know that to everyone else, all my former classmates taking photos or filtering off the Green back to their drivers, that's all it has ever been. That's what makes losing it all hurt so bad—it meant nothing to *them*, but it meant everything to me.

I was six the first time I came to Edgewater, my tight curls tamed by bristle and grease into two puffs, dressed in a kilt and navy socks that slipped down my skinny, scab-laden legs. I stood on the Green, stuck between my mother and father as they rushed me past the blond and beautiful, toward the registration office. I asked my mother, "Are they royalty?"

My mother barely heard me, answering with a distracted, "Yes, of course," then she adjusted my little bow and said, "Stand up straight, Adina-honey." I did as she asked, all dressed up and shiny for my first day of first grade at the practically royal Edgewater Academy. I was precocious then, ready to make my mark.

But Edgewater Academy is a world of its own, unshifting and unmarkable, not changed by anything but the seasons in its two-hundred-plus years of existence. Positioned sixteen miles northwest of Lenox, Massachusetts, in the middle of nowhere, the only thing surrounding the campus's edges are the cliques of stately Queen Anne and shingle houses, and the Colonial Revival country mansion at the top of the hill and the back of the woods, where the Remingtons live. The only exit and entrance to the school is a parking lot, stuffed to the brim with the blinding chrome of luxury cars—Porsches and Mercedes and one Tesla. And while it still looks as royal and stately as it did when I was just a little girl, I know now that there is no place for me here, and there never was.

I know now that being welcomed amongst the crème de la crop doesn't mean they'll let you become one of them. It's royal in a different way, an immortal superficial beauty, covering a fractured ugliness.

An ugliness that was intent on eating me up and shitting me out.

Now as I pull away, Mom stares at me, like she's trying to read my mind, and I wonder if my pain is obvious. But before she can push me for more, I hear a sharp squeal and let go of her just in time to catch another person in my arms.

"We made it!" Toni cheers. She pulls back and flashes me a smile, all pearly whites and brown lipstick that's somehow immovable even in the heat. She tosses her long black hair—100 percent Brazilian sew in, pin straight—over her shoulders and turns just in time to look into the lens of Mom's phone.

I'm half a second late, so she only captures my profile while Toni beams in full.

"We made it," I agree, exhaustion straining my words instead of the excitement that laced hers.

Toni's smile falters just the tiniest bit and her arms tighten around me to the point of pain, but then she inhales shakily and forces the smile harder. Toni is dedicated to the fantasy of nothing being wrong, for both my sake and hers. She thinks it's all her fault. It's not.

I was the architect of my own failure. I lost my cool for just a second, and it cost me not just my acceptance to Yale but most of my friends and nearly my attendance at Edgewater Academy.

Only my parents' own strong standing as members of the faculty saved me from expulsion. After years of swallowing it all back, now it's all over because of a single *second* of lost control.

"We'll be by the car, sweetheart," Dad says as he finally breaks away from the other school administrators. They cut me side glances, staring without really staring. It's like they think I'll crack again and attack like a wild animal.

Never again. No matter how much I want to.

My parents wave goodbye to the other faculty, finally leaving Toni and me alone.

I guide us from the center of it all to the very edge of the Green, under the shade. We watch everyone left pose for pictures, laughing loudly about how they're going to summer in the South of France together, meet up to winter in Zermatt after first semester. Penthesilea Bonavich, freckled and redheaded sweet, off to Brown. Her perfect boyfriend, Pierce Maxwell Remington IV, going where all good Remington boys go. He's a Harvard man. Even Toni's twin brother, Charles, light-skinned so all the girls *want him*, is off to fuck the white girls of UPenn.

"Are you still going to the Remington luncheon?" I ask, turning away from all of them. That wasn't always the plan. Our families were supposed to go together to lunch after graduation. We'd celebrated everything together—Toni's pitch-perfect performances in the play, my academic awards—since we were kids, but after everything that happened, our parents are more . . . lukewarm to each other than they used to be.

"Um . . . yeah," Toni says reluctantly. "You know Pierce and Charles can't bear to be separated."

She looks onto the Green at our former classmates, all off to their own ivy-covered walks of life, and I nearly choke on my envy.

"Do you want to go?" I hear Toni ask distantly.

"No," I say, even though of course I do.

"Please, I don't think they'd mind. And *she* won't be there. It'll be me, Charles, Pierce, his brother, and Penthesilea. They won't mind three extra people, and you can ask Pierce about, you know, the . . ." Toni trails off.

But I know what she's going to say.

The Finish. She wants me to beg a Remington for entrance to the Finish.

"I think the invitations were already sent out. I heard some people talking about it," I say. We both know who the "some people" are, but we never clarify. "And I'm not the kind of girl that they'd invite anyway."

Not rich. Not white. Not flawless.

"You don't *know* that. All kinds of girls get invited," Toni insists, her hands tightening around mine. "You heard what they did last year for that girl from Phillips Exeter? She's at *MIT* and she's flourishing. She wasn't even accepted to MIT. She just, like, asked when she won. And then, the year before that, it was a scholarship girl from Taft, and now she goes to Cambridge. They're paying for *everything*, even her living expenses. Come on, Adina. They're the Remingtons. If they can do that, they can get you back into Yale, easy."

I know she's right. The Finish. Three tests. That's all it would take to get back into one of the most prestigious institutions in the world. There is no application. There is no entrance fee. No one even really knows what the selection process is or how it all works. But the girls who compete are handpicked, the best of the best, the cream of the crop, going head-to-head for the support of the Remington Family, and all that entails. Tuition. Influence. Power. *Admittance.*

And all on another level than the other families of Edgewater. The Remingtons know everyone, and everyone who doesn't know them wants to. There are libraries named for them, think tanks that defer to them, government officials begging for their approval. I've never known what it's like to have that much power.

For me, though, it would feel like begging, begging for something I already earned. That's one thing I can't do again. But if there was the right opportunity, if an invite was *offered* in such a way that I was just given a way to prove myself again . . . then, maybe.

"When would that even be possible, Toni? And don't say the luncheon, because I'm *not* going."

Toni leans in and whispers, "The bonfire."

I give her a warning look. *"Toni."*

"You can talk to him there. I'll even set you up at the luncheon. Mention you so that you're front of mind," Toni says. She's already eagerly forming a plan, more optimistic than I could ever be.

"She'll be there. They'll all be there," I warn.

Toni scoffs. "Fuck them, who cares."

She cares. I care.

I wasn't like Toni, whose parents were D9 chapter presidents and Ivy-educated descendants of the Black elite from the Gilded Age. I was the daughter of the help, in the eyes of everyone else.

Still, the idea of showing everyone up one more time before I fade into obscurity is more tempting than it should be. To be invited to the Finish and *win* would show them all that I wasn't the pitiful little upstart that cracked under pressure. And besides, I have nothing left to lose. With a long-suffering sigh, I say, "Come over at seven so we can get ready. Bring vodka."

I'll need a shot to be brave the way I'll have to be to go where I'm unwelcome one last time.

☠

"Do the shot and let's *bounce*," Toni insists, rocking back and forth in her excitement, a few hours later.

I grimace over my shoulder at her before I turn back to examine myself in my vanity. I look tired. I try to smile, to arch my neck, but give up quickly, reaching instead for the clear liquor next to the yearbook that I had a hand in making—the one that no one but Toni signed. I look at the pharmacy-developed photos of Toni and me tucked into the mirror frame as I pour. There were more but some are missing since March, ones that were full of the girls from the life I thought I had, a life that never quite belonged to me.

I throw the shot back and the burn wakes me up as it travels down my throat, not quite fire, but something close. Without the excuse of my former social calendar, I'm out of practice. I cough once, then twice, and Toni takes it as permission to swing a heavy fist at my back. I glare at her but her laugh softens everything inside me.

"You look nice," I say. She does, ethereal in all white to match her feathered lashes.

"I've got to look better than nice," Toni insists, her fingers curling into fists.

"Why? Do you have plans tonight?" I ask, surprised, leaning back against the vanity.

"I'm going to have sex with someone tonight. Maybe Franco," Toni declares.

I fight to keep from rolling my eyes. So, this is just another extension of Toni's crusade against her virginity. In some ways, it's nice that something feels semiregular.

"Well, you're going to be the prettiest girl there," I declare.

Toni scoffs to herself, like she doesn't believe me. "Not there," she says, and it's times like these that I remember the grit she buries under glitter. I recognize that kind of pain, one in conversation with mine.

Toni smiles through it, though, baring her teeth in a grin. No wonder they're secretly terrified of her.

"Finish your eyeliner," she commands. She pretends her mask didn't slip as she stows the half-sized bottle in her duffel and shoves it into the corner of my room, tucked carefully underneath three of my sweaters. It's unnecessary—my parents aren't in the habit of sneaking around my room, even after my massive fuckup—but I don't say anything.

I swipe the black liner on, the only makeup I know how to apply semiexpertly, before I grab a jacket and tug it around the champagne-colored corset top Toni wrapped me in earlier, declaring, "It picked you." She's right. There's something about its fine-boned elegance that draws me in, a borrowed thing that I want to make my own, like my life.

"Come here, your hair," she says, fluffing it.

There are girls who have touched my hair before. I remember even when I was just a kid, all of six years old, a girl burying her fist in my curls because she wanted to know if they felt like dog fur. But when Toni touches my hair, it feels reverent, like I'm loved, the way it was with my aunt's hand in my hair, with my grandmother's fingers twisting my ends, with every ancestor who has ever touched me and ever will.

"Dangly earrings. Gold, I think," Toni murmurs, pressing a quick kiss to the top of my head before breaking the moment. She bounces back, clapping her hands. "Oh my *God*, they're going to be so pissed. You look so good."

She cackles at the flash of my middle finger, and I grab the earrings, then my boots, holding them by the laces. We stomp down the stairs, into the living room, and I call, "Hey! We're going now!" without stopping as we move to the door. But my parents are right there on the couch, curled around each other, and their soft conversation creaks to a stop.

Dad looks over Mom's head with a little smile. Mom tries to echo it, but it looks more like a grimace. She's always been more readable.

"All right, girls. If you need me to drive you home—"

"We'll call," Toni promises.

"Are you sure, Adina? You don't have to prove anything to anyone."

She's wrong.

"I'm fine," I lie.

"Bye, Mrs. Walker. I've got her," Toni says proudly, and I roll my eyes but Toni locks arms with me and tugs me out the door.

"You're on aux, bitch," she insists as we climb into her car. "You have the best playlist for this moment."

This at least is the truth. I plug my phone in and scroll through my playlists until I land on "pov: you have the aux and you have something to prove." When I press play, Toni crows loudly.

"God, you always make me feel like I'm the main character in a *movie*. Fuck, just music-direct my life," Toni screeches over the bass.

"I live to create ambiance."

For a moment everything is okay. It always is, driving in cars like this, speeding through the dark, our way lit by the neon-blue glow of the dashboard and the sharp orange of the streetlights reflecting off Toni's silvery eyelashes. It's the palette of an A24 movie made flesh, and it feels powerful. I am the main character, whom things are taken from, won then irrevocably lost, but while the open ending isn't quite hopeful, at least it's still about me. I'm not an asterisk or a footnote in my own life. I don't have to hold my tongue here, because I'm the fucking *star*.

But as we drive through my neighborhood, if I look to the right or left beyond the lights, I see each cookie-cutter house. Every single one is the same, all two compact stories, wooden planks with navy-blue shutters and forest-green doors. Each lawn is perfectly manicured, modest, unassuming. And behind it are the boring lives of boring people.

When second cousins, aunts, or uncles twice removed learn that I go to Edgewater, they think of Gothic castles and uniforms and libraries and tweed. They think nihilism and wealth and Greek and blood so blue, it must be so much more special than the red of normal people. They think of a place that builds a genera-tion of leaders, who will leave the green pastures of Massachusetts for chrome towers. For most of my classmates, that *is* their future, so my family is right to think all those things. Just not about me.

Because I live here, outside the great iron gates in capital-*S* Sub-urbia. Suburbia is sticky lip gloss and the same silver-gray sedan at the end of every driveway. It's Chuck Taylors and blurry-eyed girls who stand on the edge of the local public school's football field in cheerleading uniforms. It's being stared at when they see you break the cookie-cutter mold in a plaid kilt, climbing out of a BMW that is not yours, wearing a gifted pair of diamond earrings that you cannot afford, and holding a purse that you borrowed. It's the way they see you in all these things that aren't yours, and *know* that they aren't yours, because they see that you're born from the same cookie-cutter house as theirs.

They know you're Of Suburbia.

Because Suburbia sticks to you, like the chemical sugar of Yankee Candles and Bath & Body Works, even though you left the store hours ago. For years I was able to disguise the scent under borrowed Dior perfume and by sticking close to the shadows of girls who winter in Aspen. But one slip and the smell surfaced.

Suburbia is forever.

But the Finish looms in my mind like the last life raft. I know if I don't try—no, if I don't *demand* otherwise—Suburbia *will* be my forever, roll credits.

When we pull into the parking lot at the edge of the forest next to Edgewater, we're one of three cars, meaning only the wealthiest are present, the kids who live in mansions walking distance away or who can afford the Uber Lux fare. It means that I'll be more outnumbered than I thought.

We begin the hike, Toni struggling in her heeled thigh-highs, but determinedly crunching over the path. I follow her shadow, eyes trained on her back.

When we pass through the hollow thicket of trees into the clearing, there's a brief moment where no one recognizes us. I catch sight of a few underclassmen, rising juniors still unsure of their new power, precocious rising freshmen, eager for their first night as fresh meat. The bonfire rages large enough that the crackles of the flames equal the thunderous bass that comes from the lone car parked just a little way away.

That's the last moment of anonymity that we get. Because the kids on the car—the coolest people at Edgewater—see us, and the mood shifts, the air threaded with a threat.

This is my last day at Edgewater.

I do not miss it. I don't think I ever will. And in that moment, I know for sure that it—and its occupants—won't miss me either.

There's only one last thing I need from it and then . . . I'm gone.

CHAPTER 2

TONI PRETENDS THAT NO ONE'S WATCHING US AS she swans through the clearing, head held high. I follow her shadow, gaze piercing through each person who *is* watching us, refusing to let them humble me. They don't matter anymore. Only one person's opinion matters.

"Aye, Tones!" Charles shouts, waving his twin sister over.

He must already be drunk. He has to be if he's calling Toni over. Toni and Charles prefer to act as if they don't know each other, especially after what went down this past spring. It works best for them. Toni is prim and proper and *theatrical*, good at everything she does, but she doesn't take well to being called an Oreo. To having her identity dismissed like Edgewater would prefer. Charles, on the other hand, is a future member of the North American Interfraternity Conference, to their parents' very Divine Nine chagrin. He'll never bark like a Que. It would be so disappointing if it wasn't so right. Charles's willingness to downplay certain parts of himself bought him social currency, as if the powers-that-be were *thankful* for his ability to "turn it off."

"Charlie," Toni drawls, pointedly. "Pass my friend a White Claw? None for me, I'm driving."

Charles does as he's commanded, tossing one to me. I crack it open and guzzle down half, ignoring the wary look he casts me. He's not so brainwashed that he'd be hostile, but he's definitely not willing to take the social bullet for me either. Not like Toni.

From the corner of my eye, I survey the area for a particular person until I find her.

Alpha Enemy Number One. Esme Alderidge.

She's pretending that she hasn't seen us, but I know she has. She's surprised by my audacity—the fact that I've shown up—and so to keep control of the situation, she won't give us her attention, not until she's good and ready, and hopefully before that my mission will be complete and we'll be long gone.

While she pretends to ignore us, Esme is regaling her circle with a tale about a house party that she threw when her parents were off in Dubai that some B-list New York influencer attended with her entourage. I was there for that one. Esme had been frantic in her en suite when they arrived, worried things didn't look cool or elevated enough after she'd sent an overeager DM inviting them in the first place. She doesn't tell it like that now. Now it's a story about how excited the influencer was to meet *her*.

Esme's easily the most overdressed of the group, her black hair slicked by an excess of gel so that it looks wet, the blunt edge of her bob severe at the nape of her neck. It just touches the diamond choker there that she once told me is worth fifty thousand.

She breaks it out for special occasions. But now every day is a special occasion, and only I know why. I know her secret. Her shame.

It's shaped like my fingernails, scarred into the back of her neck, hidden under the clasp.

"You sure you don't want anything harder?" Charles asks lazily, leaning back against the hood of the car.

"Ah, no—" I start, quickly tearing my gaze away from Esme and the sycophants formerly known as my *friends*, looking for my real target, but then I find myself looking through the windshield of the car, right into the backseat, at the glow of Penthesilea Bonavich. She has such perfect, clear skin and the perfect dusting of freckles across her perfect straight nose. The only thing wrong is her plump perfect mouth, downturned at the corners as she speaks softly to *him*.

Pierce Maxwell Remington IV.

Pierce Maxwell Remington IV has been my classmate for twelve years. He's the second son of the latest generation of the Remington Family, who own the land that Edgewater sits on. His father went to Edgewater, and his father before him, and so on for two hundred years back. There were oil paintings depicting the great actions of our benefactors staring over us every day. But for me, those looming eyes were more personal. The Remington presence at Edgewater was what made my presence there possible too. The scholarship that afforded my education was named after and funded by Pierce's great-great-aunt.

The Remingtons basically made me, at least I'm sure that's how they see it. Now I need the Remingtons to extend another offer and remake me.

Right now though, his head is bent toward his girlfriend, face nearly pressed into the swanlike curve of her neck. I can just see a flash of his blue eyes as he whispers to her. Penthesilea shakes her head, and then she says something that passes through the open car windows, but I only get a few words: ". . . tradition, Pierce, but I'm right here and I want to *go* with you. . . ."

Pierce and Penthesilea have been dating since fifth grade, when it wasn't even called dating. They'd kissed on the Green, on May Day, near the flagpole, and never stopped. It was more common to see them walking together than apart, both long-limbed and moneyed, pale in the winter and freckled in the summer. They seemed happy. Happier than anyone. Tonight—not so much. It sounds like a fight, an old one. I want to lean in, curious, but I deliberately turn my back. It's best if I can keep close without seeming like I'm eavesdropping, ready for any moment of opportunity that might reveal itself.

I tune back in to Toni and Charles's conversation.

"You think I can convince Mom to add another session?" Toni asks. "It's my last summer at camp and they're doing *Cabaret* the second session."

"No, it's too much to coordinate that, your move-in at Tisch, *and* me to UPenn," Charles says. He takes another long pull of Grey Goose, light eyes hazy.

I sneak a peek back at the car and see Pierce's eyes widen and the tendons in his neck strain against skin. He moves his hand down as if he's physically cutting Penthesilea off from saying any more, and then he climbs out of the car and stalks away from her. Away from *me*. Meanwhile, I can feel Esme's eyes looking my way more and more.

"This isn't working. I need to find a way to run into him," I hiss in Toni's ear.

Toni nods, guilt making tears well in her eyes.

I hurry away in the direction Pierce headed, clutching my White Claw and shaking off her misplaced remorse, determined before it's too late to at least attempt my Hail Mary plan for correcting everything that went wrong. What *I* did wrong—not Toni.

Even if she was involved, ultimately it was my fault. Everything that went down was because I broke the rules. For others, those rules were more like guidelines, but for me, they were absolute. Suburbia, for all its faults, was forgiving. Edgewater was not. I had no business testing those rules. Except, I did.

Rule one: Wealth is power. If you don't have it, keep your head down. I thought I'd gotten that one down to a science over the past twelve years.

Rule two: Knowledge is too—now *that* power I had in spades. But with knowledge comes the responsibility to know when to keep your mouth shut and when not to (see rule one). I chose not to and I chose wrong.

Esme has reminded me of how wrong I was every day since.

I can feel the weight of her stare again as I slip past. I want to glare back, not slink away with my tail tucked between my legs to avoid her ire. But here, and everywhere really, she has the upper hand and the rules are still in place, her entire clique ready to enforce them. The clique that Toni and I were once part of too.

☙ ☠ ❧

I'd spent my entire life at Edgewater under the radar, and Esme had liked that. She knew she wouldn't have to fight me too hard for attention. She could be the best at whatever she chose to be without worry of any of her "friends" eclipsing her. I'd chosen yearbook and student government, mockable electives in terms of social clout but good for college applications. I'd known her cruelty and her callousness, but always through the thin veneer of protection that being on her side allowed. All that attitude had always been directed at her enemies. And I was fine with that, ignoring what she did to others, because she became one of the few who didn't have anything to say about the neighborhood I'd grown up in. Nothing good, but not anything particularly bad, either. Where I came from every day didn't *matter* to her at all.

That all came to an end in mid-March. Spring was burning out our nostril hairs, pollen stinging violently at our eyes. It made Ivy

Day easier for some. When they didn't get into their top choice for one reason or another, the excuse of seasonal allergies hid their tears. But not me. I'd gotten into Yale, early action. All the acceptances that followed were my victory lap.

And then a month later, they were all gone.

Mistake one: I wasn't paying attention.

Esme had been deferred from Yale in the early action round. In the midst of my win, I hadn't been sympathetic enough. I hadn't downplayed anything. I'd been blinded by my own shine.

It started with a quiet, "You'll fill out their quota nicely," over lunch.

I didn't know how to respond, blinking at Esme as she said it through a wide smile. She'd been accepted to Dartmouth, after all. Johns Hopkins was her *safety*. But that wasn't enough for Esme—things were never enough if they didn't go her way, and worse if they went someone else's.

The table held their breath and only released it when Esme turned to Toni and congratulated her on Tisch—which Toni hadn't told anyone yet. Toni hadn't even had the chance to share her own good news. Esme took that from her, after finding out from Charles, whom she'd started hooking up with. She was reminding her whose side to choose. Not that Toni listened.

Then, isolation. I wasn't invited to Esme's second house upstate for spring break. I found out about it on the Monday after, when the other girls, including Toni, came in halfway through the day with handwritten notes from Mrs. Alderidge excusing them. I only forgave Toni for it after she explained that Esme had lied to her and told her that I was too sick to go and wouldn't be responding to text messages—that explained her Get well, bestie before she'd gone radio silent.

Cruelty that had never been aimed at me suddenly dogged my every step in the most subtle ways. "Dropped" invitations, "forgotten" hangouts, the biting laughter that stopped whenever I entered the room. Eventually, Esme kept laughing even when I sat right there in front of her, back rigid as she asked pointed question after question about my college application, about my family, about my parents' *income*, about fucking *Suburbia*.

"Toughen up, Adina," she'd say when she saw my expression falter as she got a rise out of me. "The girls and boys of Yale will be far more inquisitive. They won't be as nice as me. We have to find something."

"Find what?" I'd asked.

"Something that makes you interesting enough to have gotten in . . . besides the obvious."

The obvious.

Mistake two: I fought back.

"Don't listen to her," Toni said later that night, lying on her back on my bed, staring at me as I tore down every photo of our friend group, all except for the ones of just the two of us. "She's just feeling insecure."

"Insecure about what? She got into Dartmouth," I snapped. "I *earned* my spot at Yale. Why should I have to hide that?" I was frantic, moving with a frenetic energy that was unlike me. Control was all I'd known.

And Toni. Sweet, well-meaning, slightly nosy Toni said, "I don't think her parents are doing well. *Financially*, I mean. I heard her talking about it with Charles the other day, saying she'd have to hide her necklace before the Feds could find it. She played it off like she was joking, but also you know . . . *was* she? She *has* been nastier than usual."

Knowledge is power and right then I wanted some, badly.

Rumors are easy, especially at a place like Edgewater, where everyone knows or wants to know one another's business. I started with a "The Alderidges' donation this year was low. Yeah, lower than it usually is. Getting cheap, aren't they?" Dropped in the middle of a yearbook meeting, over a discussion with the layout editor. Then a whispered "I might've overheard in the main office that Esme's parents were late on her little sister's tuition payment for the semester. But . . . don't blame me, I'm just the messenger" in the bathroom. And finally, the most damning—"I hear they're going broke. Yeah, broke. And the Feds . . . yeah, the Feds. Heard there was something about embezzlement."

I didn't know for sure, of course, but "embezzlement" was a multimillion-dollar kind of word and one that *terrified* all the Edgewater kids, and none more than Esme Alderidge.

Mistake three: I miscalculated. Only three people had the potential to have heard Esme's joke. One was Esme, the other she was sleeping with, and the third—Toni.

So Esme set her sights on a new target to torment. First, it started with jokes. About Toni's hair, about her makeup, about her face, about her interests. She hadn't wanted to go to an Ivy. Toni'd always wanted to go to Tisch. She knew who she was, but Esme knew how to weaponize someone's joy against them with expertise. Suddenly, she had everyone buzzing that Toni only wanted Tisch because she hadn't been able to get into an Ivy.

Then the girls—Hawthorne, who was always at her right hand, and the rest—wouldn't talk to her. They even started inviting me to the table again, but Toni had made *my* days more than bearable when I'd been suffering Esme's ire, and I knew I owed her. Plus, *I* was the reason this was happening to her. So we stuck together.

Being ignored together for a few more months would be fine. It could have been fine.

But it escalated again. Direct this time. Food staining our book bags. Shitty photos paired with shitty captions making fun of us, "leaked" from finstas. Enough so that no one would talk about Esme anymore. It partially worked; at first all anyone talked about were the *jokes*. All Esme would say was, "It's a joke. Toni's an actress, she *likes* jokes, doesn't she?" But "embezzlement" was too big a word to drown out with jokes.

So it wasn't a joke, being cornered in that bathroom, Esme's voice running ragged as she screamed, "How dare you? What the fuck is wrong with you, spreading lies like that?" at Toni, even after Toni locked herself in the stall, sobbing, begging her, saying that it wasn't *her*.

"Are you so bored with your little virginal life that you have to listen to *my* personal business with your brother?" Esme growled. "Are you that needy and nosy that you have to use my name to get anyone's attention? That's what this is about, isn't it? Attention."

Toni's sobs echoed, and each hitch of breath felt like a punch in the chest, until I had to say something.

"Esme, that's enough," I warned, trying to cut the head off the beast, but three always rise from the Hydra's neck. Mistake number four: Esme never liked being told there was a line she couldn't cross.

She pressed herself up against the creamy stall door and slammed her fist into it with a snarl. "It was none of your business, Toni, and now the whole school is talking about it."

"I'll tell them. I'll tell them it was a joke. That I was *lying*—"

It wasn't Toni. It had never been Toni. And Toni knew. Of course Toni knew it was me, and still she didn't say a word. She proved to be a far better friend to me than I was to her as I stood there frozen.

"You were just waiting to tear me down, waiting for your opportunity, you *uppity*, social-climbing cunt."

I'm still not sure what was enough. The use of the word "uppity" and all its implications or calling her a cunt.

But it was enough.

"Maybe you're angry because it's not a lie," I said, and then Esme froze, like she couldn't believe what I'd just said. She looked back at Hawthorne, who stood by the door, ever her silent sentry. And

I continued. "Maybe you're angry because it's the *truth* and now everyone's going to know it. That you're not this spoiled *rich* girl anymore. Maybe you're just a spoiled regular girl now, pretending."

"You can shut the fuck *up*, Adina," said Esme savagely. I so rarely gave her a reason to say those words to me, but when I did, usually I'd shut up.

Not this time.

In for a penny, in for a pound.

"No, you're being cruel. You're taking out your anger at Toni because it's true. You really are broke, aren't you? When I told everyone, I wasn't sure, but I'm glad for the confirmation," I said, and then I laughed, almost in disbelief.

Esme had never taken kindly to being *laughed* at.

I watched her face drain of color. And then that pallid expression twisted into a mask of wrath and she *lunged*.

Like a bomb, the escalation happened in seconds and the fallout was massive. Because even if she didn't have all her money anymore, Esme still had her power. Everyone listened to her, and just like that my acceptance to Yale and every other backup school was up in smoke, and my attendance at Edgewater hanging on by the thread of my parents' employment there.

There would be no history degree. No Manuscript Society. No law school. No internship on the Hill or at the NAACP. No way up and *out*.

Not unless I succeed tonight.

Shaking off the memories in Esme's glare, I slip into the trees, just far enough to be hidden in the shadows. I pretend to look at my phone, but I'm really surveying the party, looking for where Pierce went while I was distracted by self-pity.

"Hey."

"Fuck. Shit. Motherfuck—" I blurt out, jumping and spinning around all at once.

"You have a mouth."

"Yeah, I do, use it to talk and stuff too," I say sharply, breathing through the sudden adrenaline rush. I right myself, ready to confront whatever asshole junior is hiding here, but then I see—

The man of the hour.

Pierce smiles his million-dollar smile, his canine tooth flickering white in the moonlight. One part of his lip lifts higher than the other. "I'm sorry for scaring you."

"You didn't scare me. I was just . . . surprised," I correct. A lengthy pause fills the silence, long enough for it to get awkward. "The alcohol is in the trunk."

"I know. It's my car," Pierce laughs.

"Oh. Right. Yeah. The Tesla." Shit, it's probably weird that I know he owns a Tesla. "You're the only one at Edgewater who owns a Tesla. That's how I know. That it's yours."

Pierce nods like I'm not being a weirdo.

It's fine, right? The Remingtons are weirdos. No. Rich people aren't weirdos. They're *eccentric*.

He's not popular in the same way that Esme is. He's so popular that he only has two friends and no one thinks it's odd. Sure, the wealthiest of the bunch were probably his playmates when he was a child, but now he'd only claim two of them—Penthesilea and Charles.

"I've seen you around before," Pierce declares, surprising me again.

"I'm Adina Walker. Professor Walker's daughter. Maybe you saw my picture on her desk?" I suggest.

Pierce hums doubtfully. "I've never been to Professor Walker's office hours."

I sigh internally, but I can't let it show. "We've been in the same grade since we were six."

Pierce hums again. "No . . . that's not what I'm thinking of." Christ.

And then he snaps his fingers in recognition. "Oh, right, you're on the school website, on the Diversity page."

Mother*fucker*.

He says it like it's just a light observation, like he doesn't hear himself, but it's so ridiculous, I don't know whether to laugh or cry. I swallow it back. Greater goals, and all that. Time to pivot.

"Yeah, I'm also the girl that Esme regularly curses to eternal damnation."

"Oh, is that you?" Pierce laughs to himself, shaking his head, and he slides around me, leaning against the tree trunk next to me. "Between you and me, Esme says a lot, and very rarely is it more than bullshit."

He's so direct and matter-of-fact that it shocks me into laughter. He looks pleased with himself suddenly, and it's an attractive look on him. Everything's attractive about him. It's *almost* enough to make me forgive his absent-minded ignorance, embarrassingly enough.

This is the first time I've been close enough to him to notice that he's *tall*, more than a head taller than me. My shoulder brushes against his bicep, and I have to crane my neck to see his eyes. I clench my hands behind me, back digging into the bark, and I wonder what part of me he is looking at—my eyes, the bridge of my nose, my lips, my shoulders, my tits.

"I was joking, you know. I do remember you, and not from the Diversity page or Esme's drivel. We had gym together in eighth grade. You got a bloody nose during the volleyball unit, so I took you to the infirmary," Pierce says proudly. "No one could ever remember where it was, but I do because I was born in there. My mom went into premature labor during a board meeting."

"You're a Remington. It was practically destiny," I deadpan.

"Yeah," Pierce agrees wholeheartedly, not recognizing the joke, because even if I recognize the whole story of the Remingtons as mythos, it's not mythos for Pierce. It's real. I don't believe in fate. Not for people like me. People like me have to *make* their own destiny.

"So now that you're finally leaving the infirmary you were born in behind, you're going to Harvard, right?" I ask.

"Yeah, we all do. Well . . . almost all of us," he amends. "I'm just ready to get out of here. I've known all these people my entire life. Esme . . . Charles . . . even *Pen*. God, Pen."

He looks almost lost, tilting his head back as he lets out a long sigh.

"You want?" I ask, offering him a sip of my White Claw.

He grabs it and drains it, tossing the can to the ground, crushing it underfoot. Well then.

"Thanks," he mutters, a second too late, a little awkwardly.

"So . . . Penthesilea . . . *Pen* won't be joining you at Harvard then?" I say slowly, attempting to gauge the situation.

"Nope. Pen's going to Brown. Pen . . . is *Pen*. She's the best, you know? Literally the best. But it's going to be hard, me at Harvard, her there."

"They don't seem that far apart though, are they? How many miles would you say there are between Cambridge and Providence?" I know the answer. It's fifty miles. Only fifty miles.

Pierce nods like he didn't quite hear my tone. "Too many to count. She applied to Harvard too, you know. And she didn't get in. She was so upset."

"Well, that wasn't your fault," I say lamely, but Toni's words float back up in my mind. He could probably get her in with a phone call.

I wonder why he didn't.

Pierce sighs righteously. "I know that, but she's angry."

I've never seen Penthesilea angry a day in my life. When our paths happened to cross, she'd show me courtesy, but it was removed. She exists in a perpetual state of content, her plush mouth curled upward, jovial sunshine in her eyes. She's *too* nice, *too* kind, *too* sugary-sweet. It's almost clinical, like the aftertaste of cotton candy.

"That . . . sucks," I say, trying to muster up some sympathy.

Pierce laughs to himself, a self-deprecating but low sound that does something to me despite myself. "It does, doesn't it?" he murmurs, conspiratorially, like we're sharing more than his girlfriend's secrets. "She's afraid, I think. Everything is going to change. But . . . maybe it should."

"Yes, hopefully for the better," I agree.

"Where are you going?" Pierce asks, just like I've been waiting for him to.

"Uh . . . nowhere," I admit.

Pierce straightens. "What do you mean?"

"I got into Yale, in December, my top choice. Early action. But, um, that fight with Esme happened and I was almost expelled and . . . and my acceptance there and everywhere else got rescinded," I explain.

Pierce leans in.

"Esme got your acceptance *rescinded*?" he whispers. When I nod, he whistles through his front teeth. "She's an asshole, isn't she? Just a spoiled, pretentious brat."

"You're in the same tax bracket."

Fuck, I shouldn't have said that.

Pierce lets out one of those charming laughs out of the movies, like he should be speaking with a transatlantic accent. "You have a smart mouth, Adina," he says finally, and then, "I like that."

It stops me short, this sudden victory and the turn I can feel it taking.

His grin widens in that way, and I tilt my head as I stare up at him. Pierce Maxwell Remington IV is blond and perfect. The last boy I kissed didn't have lips like his, a perfect Cupid's bow. His skin wasn't perfectly smooth like Pierce's, the product of good genes, hyaluronic acid, and an expensive dermatologist who probably doesn't take insurance. The last boy was kinder too, but tonight I don't need kind. I don't want it. Tonight, I want *this.*

"You are interesting, Adina Walker," Pierce declares, like it's fact, like anything he says becomes one. "You deserve better than the lot you've been handed."

"I think I'll decide what I deserve," I whisper, because this is a boy who has the key to the world in his palms, and I *deserve* that too—the boy or the key, I'm not sure, maybe both.

I reach up, sliding my hands over his shoulders, and I pull him in. His long fingers come up immediately, pressing just a little too hard on my scalp as he spins and presses me back up against the tree.

I gasp, arching into him as his lips find mine. I hum loudly into his mouth as his fingers drag down to my jaw, tilting my head up and just to the left. We get lost in the heat, hands tugging at clothes, pressing closer to each other. Goose pimples erupt over my shoulders and it's too much, and not enough, as he pushes me tighter against the tree, and practically consumes me.

"Wait . . . wait . . . ," I whisper, mouth wet against his jaw. His hands tighten on my hips, but he stops.

"What?" he mutters, breath wet against my neck.

There is something in the woods. I stand on my toes, looking over his shoulder, searching, but the bonfire is only a flickering pinprick in the distance. Shoving aside my paranoia, I turn back to him, cupping his jaw, pulling his face closer to mine.

And then I hear her, far away: "Can't believe you showed your fucking face, Toni."

"Fuck," I whisper, easing away from Pierce.

"What?" he asks, bewildered and sweaty, and still beautiful.

Esme's starting in on Toni, which means time is running out. I don't regret kissing him, but I know I will if I don't speed this up and shoot my shot.

"I wanted to ask you about something," I blurt out.

He blinks away his confusion. "Yeah? What is it?"

But before I can find the words, that same snide voice rings out, louder than it needs to be, loud enough to draw every eye and every ear. "You get away with a lot of shit because we like your brother, but not every invitation for him includes a plus-one or, worse, plus-two."

"Toni," I whisper, and I know instinctively I don't have time. Stumbling past him, I shake out my hair, preparing for the inevitable confrontation. Before I do, though, I stop and look behind me.

Pierce stares at me with a strange sort of awe. It's powerful and awful, all at once. I grab his shirt, tugging him in, and press one last kiss to his jaw before whispering, "Sucks that we'll never have that Harvard-Yale rivalry tension." Then before I can register if he gets the hint, I take off, darting through the trees, adjusting the borrowed corset and trying not to think about his hands on my skin or his nose at my ear or the way he sputtered into my curls every time they got into his mouth. I put away my devastation about the Finish for now, refusing to mourn something that, unlike my initial acceptance, was never quite mine anyway.

CHAPTER

3

RETURNING TO THE CLEARING, I CUT THROUGH THE crowd, shoving past the crew team at the edge, until I'm back at the car. Pen is still in the backseat, but she's hanging out the window, her lips twisted downward into a frowning pout.

Charles is standing, one hand outstretched toward Esme and the other out toward Toni, like he's prepared to shove them apart.

"Calm *down*, Esme, it's not that serious," Charles insists.

"What makes you think that there are no rules," Esme spits, ignoring him, eyes only for Toni, "that I'll let you get away this time? You made it clear whose side you're on. You and your poor townie trash friend aren't wanted here."

There's a remarkable silence as I realize that that's me. *I'm* the poor townie trash.

Esme has always been a wordsmith. Each one cuts deeper, a jab directly at my Suburbia bruise meant to gut a bitch, and I feel *gutted*.

"That's . . . that's enough," Toni says, but she's crumbling like wet paper under the weight of Esme's fury. Her gaze darts around, search-ing for a life preserver, and when it catches on me, she swallows.

Esme follows her gaze and finally deigns to address me directly. "Bringing this girl, who can barely afford a pack of gum let alone Edgewater's tuition, like it's a redemption tour. I did you a *favor*, Adina Walker," she hisses. "You wouldn't have been able to afford Yale without selling your fucking kidney."

"You should be a little less worried about what I can afford and more about when the Feds are finally going to show up to your house. Your parents aren't built for jail. Might cry if they break a nail," I retort. I learned to spit venom from the best.

Esme's mouth puckers, and I can hear her breath hitch in the back of her throat, once, then twice. I meet her eye, waiting patiently as she sputters. Esme's acrylics look like claws, just like they did on that March day, but I don't back down.

"Careful, Esme. I kicked your ass once," I say quietly.

Shame spreads liquid red under her creamy foundation and she sneers.

"Esme, enough, save it," Hawthorne says, grabbing her hand.

Esme stares, breathing heavily through her nose, but doesn't move. Hawthorne squeezes once, and then shockingly Esme turns on her heel and storms away, tugging Hawthorne and her other lackeys after her.

Toni looks shocked. Charles is staring after Esme like he's never seen her before, like he doesn't want to be seen with her.

Almost against my will, my shoulders curl in on themselves,

and I take a step back, as if Esme is still there, like we're sharing the same breath still. So much for my last chance.

"Well," Charles says, clearing his throat. "This isn't dinner theater, assholes!"

The surrounding crowd shatters with his bark, and then the air is filled with gossip.

"Can we go home?" I ask, voice aching with my plea as I reach for Toni.

Toni starts to nod frantically, and then she stops midbreath. I look back and freeze.

"Impressive takedown," Pierce says. Awe remains in his eyes, the same look he gave me after we stopped hooking up and I took off.

"It was very dramatic," the figure to Pierce's left says. I know him as well as anyone can know a Remington.

Graham Remington is Pierce's one year older, much more disappointing, brother.

We all knew by grade seven that Graham wasn't going to be the bright Remington heir, though I assume that his parents knew from birth, since they named him *Graham* instead of giving him the spot in the Pierce line of succession. Where Pierce is fair, tall, and beautiful, Graham is weathered, short, and regular. He isn't ugly by any means, but decidedly just cute. What really solidified it, though, was that he "settled" for Yale.

"Was it?" I challenge. "Esme is a bully."

"Yeah, yeah. You're the little defender that could," Graham

says, his eyes veined with redness—he's *so* high. "God, Esme looked like she was going to either claw your eyes out or shit herself. No in between."

Graham toasts his liquor bottle to me, and my lips curl back against my will.

"You handled her remarkably," Pierce says, meditative.

"She thinks that her money and status make her untouchable," I say quietly.

Pierce hums once more. "Do you agree?"

He asks it casually, but suddenly it feels important. Like there's another question underneath, a question I thought I had no chance of being asked after how this night has gone. I know the answer I want to give, but I can't let my eagerness ruin it now.

"In a way. Life is a competition. You win or you lose in every situation you face, right? In that situation, with Esme, like your brother said: I won. But that's almost never the case. Not with people like Esme. We're not on the same playing field."

When he looks at me again, his gaze is just that bit sharper, that bit more meaningful, and then he says, "We could be."

My breath catches in my chest.

The Finish.

"Four, *don't*," Graham warns. "Adina—Adina, isn't it? She's a good girl."

I *was* a good girl. Except for one moment. Now I'm a desperate girl.

"Maybe good girls should get to win sometimes too," I say.

Graham snaps, with more authority than I thought he could possess, "What are you even doing, Four? She doesn't have what it takes."

I don't know what happens in the Finish. The only girls who have ever gone were girls like Esme. Girls who have more than me, but less than what being associated with a Remington could get them, because there are levels to this sort of thing. Access and wealth.

What I do know is this: Girls who win go to school, with all the resources the Remingtons can provide, and do the impossible. One girl became a House rep, another a Fortune 500 CFO, another the provost at Duke. Each of them went on to *be* someone.

I want to be someone. I don't just want to go to Yale, I want to dominate it. I could take it further. Be greater than them.

And this boy—given everything—has no right to tell me otherwise.

"I do have what it takes," I say evenly, swallowing my frustration. I take another step toward Pierce. I tilt my head back just the tiniest bit, the same way I did when his eyes went half-lidded. "More than any of them. More than *you*, even."

Pierce lights up, eyes bright with a feverish enthusiasm. "You accept and you don't get to back out. You get it, right?"

He sounds serious but I am too. Besides, my mother didn't raise a quitter.

Before I can accept, the back door of the car swings open and Penthesilea finally slips out.

There's a strange lull that falls over everything, dampening the tension in the air. Penthesilea is backlit by the light of the bonfire. The golden headband in her hair sparkles, and she's wearing soft girl clothes, a white button-down tucked into sunflower-yellow corduroy shorts.

"What's going on?" she asks, her voice lilting and measured. "Is there something wrong?"

No one says anything. Pierce's good mood dips. He's not looking at me anymore, and I know that I'm losing him. He walks up to her, hands reaching out, "Pen, hey, it's just bullshit—"

Penthesilea looks at me directly. "Adina, are you all right?"

She knows my name.

Only then does a hot curl of liquid shame curdle in my belly.

I just hooked up with this girl's boyfriend in the woods. I'm relying on the strange intimacy between me and him now to get an invitation to my own future. Pierce's arm hooks around her waist and he drops his chin atop Penthesilea's hair.

"I—" I start and stop. "I'm *fine.* Toni, *please.*"

Toni steps forward immediately, grabbing my hand even though I can't look away from Penthesilea. I can still feel her boyfriend's hands on my hips. I can still feel the sear of his lips on the curve of my neck.

Toni pulls me away, and we march through the Red Sea of students, right past Esme as she sneers, "Later, nobodies."

I flip a middle finger at her because I *can,* because the Finish, a brief, beautiful life raft, has vanished back into smoke and mirrors and the glittering of Esme's collar.

CHAPTER

4

YAWNING MYSELF INTO THE WORLD OF THE LIVING, I squint down at Toni's fist knotted into the front of my sleep shirt. Slowly, I untwist each knuckle until she releases me with a soft grunt.

I slump off the bed and shift from side to side, stretching my arms above my head until my back cracks. I don't bother to tiptoe out of the room and downstairs. Nothing could wake Toni except for the smell of coffee beans; she sleeps like the dead.

Downstairs, Dad is already sitting at the table, and Mom is standing at the skillet.

"Budge over, she's my guest," I mutter, taking over the bacon.

"Can she be called a guest when she has a drawer?" Dad asks.

I snort. "I mean, assign her chores too, then. I bet she doesn't know how to do laundry yet and she has to learn."

Mom rolls her eyes. "How was the party?"

Pierce's mouth. Charles's horror. Esme's vitriol. Penthesilea knowing me by name.

And nothing to show for it.

"Bad," I say honestly. "Esme." I flip the bacon onto the platter, letting the grease catch on the paper towel laid out for me.

"Oh, I'm sorry, honey," Mom says. I can tell she means it, but also wants to say *I told you so.* "I thought you said she'd calmed down a bit."

I lied.

"She did. I guess she wanted to get in one last parting shot." I sigh. "I'm not going to miss a single one of them."

"Well, *one* of them might miss you," Dad says. "You've got mail." He gestures toward the front hall with his coffee cup.

I frown. "It's a Sunday." I pass the spatula to Mom and flip the switch on the coffee maker to wake Toni, the old thing rumbling to life as I walk out of the kitchen. I make my way toward the narrow table on which our keys sit, where I see a perfectly wrapped brown package with a crisp white envelope on top. I open it with the jagged edge of a house key.

Then I choke over air.

Maybe we'll get that Harvard-Yale rivalry after all. Or maybe I'll convince you that Harvard is the better option.

Affectionately,
Pierce Maxwell Remington IV

"'Affectionately'?"

I spin around, glaring at Toni, but Toni is still ogling the note. "You're up," I accuse.

"You're trying to distract me," Toni retorts. "Is it . . . you know."

She can't even say it, too afraid to jinx it.

"I don't know," I mutter. I snatch up the box and march back into the kitchen, Toni on my heels.

"He said 'affectionately,'" Toni says again, stunned.

"Who said 'affectionately'?" Dad calls. He looks wary already, like he can sense something coming that he doesn't want to deal with.

"Pierce Maxwell Remington IV!" Toni crows.

Mom pauses by the stove. She's looking right at me, and I can see *hope* there, in her eyes, where she's tried to keep disappointment hidden. She knows what this could be, and I can tell she feels guilty for feeling so hopeful. She's already done so well not blaming me, *not* asking me, *not* pushing me toward the Finish, but now that it's being offered to me, she can't hide her excitement very well. All she wants is for me to do better than she did. It's all any parents want.

"Pierce is a good boy," she says.

I grab the scissors off the table and slide them along the seam of the wrapping. I flip the package open to reveal a beautiful dark wooden box. It still smells like wood polish and gleams in the kitchen's strange yellow morning light. I brush my fingers over another crisp, starch-white card, with graceful calligraphy swooping across the front to perfection.

Toni snatches it up and reads it, "'Adina Walker. Welcome to the Finish.'"

For once in her entire life, she can't find words. She looks up at me, eyes so wide that her pupils look like saucers.

I'm shaking so hard, I nearly drop the box.

I can smell the pancakes burning and Mom yelps when she realizes, flipping a pancake off the hot skillet and turning the flame down low.

"Adina, this is *it*," Toni says.

Still, I don't open the box. If I open it, there's no turning back. This is the decision.

The promise of Yale, success, a *job*, a way out of *Suburbia*, this place that won't let me be more.

Or nothing.

I open the box.

An envelope rests on the velvet lining, and the melody to Vivaldi's "Storm" tingles out, tinny.

I break the wax seal with the Remington crest, expecting to find more of Pierce's handwriting, but this is a far more elaborate script that I don't recognize, on official paper, the heavy, sturdy kind I associate with letterhead. It reads:

Welcome to the Finish

For two centuries, the Remington Family has had a well-vested interest in the health and diversity of our region. Through the formation of Edgewater Academy, originally an all-boys school, we have shown a dedication to the youth and their future. But there came a time when we were reminded—by a Remington woman herself—that we had been neglecting a key demographic in Lenox and beyond. A demographic equally as poised and ambitious, striving to accomplish better in our world, despite an uneven playing field.

In pursuit of the furthering of women's education and placement in society, the Remington Family established the Finish—a two-week program led by the esteemed Remington matriarchs—in which we annually select twelve girls of already outstanding rank, with the intent of cultivating the poise, skill, and survival instincts needed to succeed at new heights. These skills are then put to the test in three distinct competitive events, evaluating for initiative, strategy, and finally mettle.

Among these twelve, the best of the best, a final girl will rise and be rewarded with opportunity and the full financial

*and emotional support of the Remington
Family, in perpetuity.*

*Candidate Adina Walker, you have
been nominated and selected from a sizable
and impressive pool of candidates to compete
in the Finish. We challenge you to prove
your vigor, your valor, and above all, your
ambition. If you choose to accept this offer,
you will arrive at Remington Estate on
Sunday, June 3, promptly at noon.*

There is no signature. My hands are shaking and I ball them into fists to steady myself.

A way to even the playing field.

"The Remingtons are a strange bunch. They keep to themselves. But I've heard . . . rumors. That the competition can get out of hand," Dad says, his natural skepticism overshadowing his positivity.

My mind is already focused on the game at hand, though. I can go to Yale again. I can create the destiny I want again. All I have to do is win.

CHAPTER

5

I PACK LIGHT, AS THE ITINERARY BURIED BENEATH the fanfare indicated. It didn't reveal much about what I'll be doing beyond two cocktail parties and a dressier affair toward the end of it all.

Jeans, a few blouses, a nice pair of slacks that I bought for college interviews. Pajamas. Sweats. Three dresses, two of them wrap dresses and the last an old formal dress from Toni. Today I wear my nicest blouse, tucked into a borrowed tartan skirt. Toni slipped it to me as she tried to drill in some of the upper-crust manners that have been trained into her from birth during the week that we'd had together between graduation and the Finish.

"You're going to do so well, Adina," Dad says firmly as he turns down the long, winding driveway that leads up to the Remingtons' estate.

"And even if you don't win, we're still so very proud of you,"

Mom affirms. "We've only ever asked you to do your best."

"Thanks," I say softly. Cynicism and hope war within me in equal measure.

Through a break in the thicket of woods, I catch a glimpse of the Remington Estate. We curl up and around it as we get closer, revealing more and more of the bleached white wood and pale, craggy stone. At the top of the hill are the wrought-iron gates, twice the size of a large man, wide open. There aren't any other midsized sedans waiting at the entrance, only a Rolls-Royce that's already driving back the way we just came and an enormous black Escalade, the kind celebrities travel in.

I paste myself to the window, staring as a girl I don't recognize climbs out of the Escalade. She's Chinese and moves with the air of someone that has money, but not New England money with country homes and horses. This girl is chrome and skyline. She looks powerful, like she's just walked out of *Blade* (1998), all black vinyl and oddly placed buckles and . . . is that a harness?

"This place is huge," Mom murmurs, calling my attention back to the mansion. Even with all these years at Edgewater, none of us has ever been to the actual Remington Estate.

"So fucking cool," I whisper to myself. My parents are too in awe of the Remington Estate to call me out on my language.

The girl turns back to the Escalade and waves for someone in the front seat. Then she stands there in her vinyl and doesn't look up from her phone once as her driver climbs out and goes around to the trunk, pulling out three suitcases.

My two duffels feel *very* small, suddenly.

We pull to a stop just behind the Escalade and I unbuckle my seat belt, but my parents do too.

"I can take it from here," I say quickly, leaning forward between the front seats.

"What? You don't want us to come inside?" Dad asks. He hasn't peeled his gaze away from the big doors. They're slightly open, and every few moments I can see a person sweep by, though only enough to make out their shape.

I wonder briefly if Pierce is standing there, or maybe his father. I don't remember seeing his mother very often; I wonder briefly if she's even alive. It would be very theatrical for her not to be. The golden boy with his eccentric father and loser brother and dead mother.

I shake my head—it's an asshole thought, what is going on with me?—and I clear my throat.

"No," I say. My mother opens her mouth to complain, but I anticipate her words. "That girl doesn't have her parents going in, demanding to speak with the adults. *I'm* the adult. I'm eighteen."

"Okay," Mom murmurs finally. Dad nods too.

I swallow back a squeal that's wholly unlike me, that probably stems from the part of me that belongs to Toni, and instead I leave smacking kisses on both my parents' cheeks.

"Thank you, thank you. I'll call when I can—"

"I don't *love* that there aren't phones," Mom says, lips pursed.

"I can't be distracted," I remind her, just like it said on the itinerary. "I'll tell you everything when I'm done."

I mean it. I want to memorize every piece of this moment, of this time, brand it to my brain stem so that it feels real and lived in, even decades later, instead of fuzzy around the edges like an old, ill-kept photograph. The moment that changed my life forever.

"You be good, Dina," Dad says.

"I will. I'll be the best," I promise.

I'll be twice as good, is what I mean, and they know it. They know I have to be, like they taught me. I wrench open the back door and climb out, tugging my duffels over my shoulders.

I leave behind our sedan and wonder if the girl still by the doors will turn around and look at me, but instead she sashays forward in her black Balenciaga sock sneakers that should only look good on Instagram, but that she makes work in real life. I bite my bottom lip as she slips between those front doors before I catch up to her.

This is the start.

I could do anything.

Be anything.

All I've ever needed is access, and finally . . . the doors are literally open.

When I enter the foyer, I expect to find myself amongst the eleven other girls. Instead, only the girl from outside and I are there. Briefly, I wonder if we're late. The girl doesn't seem too concerned, but she does finally notice me, and I notice her right back.

Her long glossy thick hair spills down her back in a river. The sharp jut of her chin is intimidating, and she's taller than me, even in her weirdo expensive sneakers.

The eyeliner on her eyelids is sharp, like she used a knife to apply the straight lines. There's something about her stance that makes me stand even stiffer and taller. She looks out of place here, but not in the way that I do.

"Oh, good. Someone who isn't the color of copy paper," she says in a stiff, almost British accent.

I drop my bags as I burst into a surprised round of laughter and her mouth twitches too before she turns to face forward, toward the sound of clicking heels. I just manage to smother my laugh as an unfamiliar figure appears on the grand staircase.

She moves with practiced grace, each step deliberate. Her strides aren't very wide, hindered by the tightness of her black pencil skirt, but she manages to make them feel like a power walk anyway. There are three strings of pearls of varying lengths dripping from her veiny neck, which is so thin and birdlike that her head looks in danger of falling off her shoulders. I wonder how long it takes her every morning to form the perfect blond waves that are swept over her right shoulder.

She has to be a Remington.

"Welcome to the Finish," she says, her voice deeper than I expected, and *very* New England. "You must be Liu Ruolan, and *you* must be Adina Walker."

"I go by Saint. It's easier," the girl says; the *for you* is heavily implied. "And you are?"

The woman doesn't answer, just looks each of us up and down, and I wonder if she finds us wanting. She circles us, her gaze picking apart every inch. Saint looks bored with it, but I squirm underneath the incisive gaze. It feels more cutting than the stares of my peers, like she can see my insides and knows them well. And then the woman stops directly in front of me. When I meet her gaze, I am nauseous with a familiar eagerness for this woman to like what she sees, of wanting to be up to standards.

"Interesting," she murmurs, like she's confirmed something with her own eyes.

I immediately feel lighter.

"My name is Dr. Leighton Remington," the woman says proudly, finally answering Saint's question. "I am Pierce's aunt. By marriage. I'll be the Game Mistress of this Finish."

It's an odd title to use. Game Mistress. Not coordinator or director or judge.

"Nice to meet you," I manage finally.

Dr. Remington doesn't seem upset by my hesitation. "You'll have a chance to change before we have a program rundown. Come this way. You're the last girls to show up, so you'll be rooming together. Don't worry, you'll see that you have an ample amount of space."

I glance over at Saint, wondering if she'll be upset with sharing a room, but her face is still coolly unaffected. I go to grab my duffels and Dr. Remington pauses on the stairs, as if she's sensed my movement.

"Leave your personal items, dear girl; someone will bring them up after you."

The moment she says it, three servants appear, each one in a crisp black uniform. One of the men grabs my bags while I follow her upstairs.

I can't keep my eyes off the walls. Everything is dark wood and cedar, the banisters gleaming so much, I can almost see my own shape reflected. I drag my fingers over the wood, wondering if they'll come away with polish, but they don't. It's as if it's brand-new. Above us are enormous two-story windows, and on each one the Remington crest is emblazoned in yellow and royal-purple Tiffany glass, a snake winding its way through the center, its mouth open wide to reveal the outside world, as if the snake is preparing to eat everything in sight.

Beyond the windows, the grounds look like they could swallow me whole too. The gardens are an explosion of multicolored flora, with winding paths leading to an enormous hedge maze that looks like something you'd find in a movie. The groundskeepers move about, clipping and trimming at the edges, making sure there isn't even a weed out of place.

"You'll grow quite familiar with the grounds soon enough," Dr. Remington says, her voice low and lilting, weirdly soothing.

I hum, curiosity piqued. I don't know what's in store for us, but I didn't imagine we'd have much time to fool around in the backyard like kids.

"This way," Dr. Remington calls, and I jump, realizing that she and Saint have already reached the second landing.

She continues down the hall, and I hurry after but I wonder what's up on the third and fourth floors.

Is it where the family lives? Does Pierce live up there?

"Did you go to Edgewater?"

Saint's question cuts through my own internal interrogation.

"I did. You didn't, though," I say needlessly. I shift a look at Dr. Remington's back, but she's not paying us much mind, or at least she's pretending not to.

"No," Saint agrees. "I went to a boarding school in Switzerland, but I'm from Beijing. I attended summer courses at Oxford with the oldest brother."

"Graham?" I ask, surprised.

"Is that his name?" Saint murmurs. "I couldn't remember. He didn't exactly make an impression beyond being high for the majority of the time. Good at chess, though."

"Really? I wouldn't have thought that," I manage.

"I suspect that this family is quite good at games," Saint murmurs, and there's an edge to her voice now. She doesn't say anything else, and I squint at her harder while we turn down a corridor with more tall, narrow double doors.

There are seven of them, three on one side and four on the other, all leading down to a tall window that points to the east side of the grounds. I stare, squinting, and see that far past the gardens there is a stable. Of course the Remingtons ride horses. Penthesilea is an equestrian. She probably rides with Pierce. A prince and princess on horseback.

I remember the feel of his mouth on my neck, and I cringe from the thought of both Penthesilea and what I've done. For now, it doesn't matter. She's not here. I can reckon with the morality of my decisions after I get back what's mine.

Dr. Remington raps her bony knuckles against the door that now belongs to Saint and me. Her long, thin fingers are devoid of any gold. No ring. Interesting.

"That room at the end of the hall is a common area. A place to mix and mingle. Ladies, I'd like to see you both there, dressed and readied, at one *sharp*. Dresses have been prepared for you, as we'll be taking a photo. Also, please bring your phones," she says. She doesn't seem the kind of person that will tolerate lateness.

I file the observation away for later, moving to press the door open as Dr. Remington walks away.

It's bigger than any bedroom I've ever seen in real life, even bigger than Esme's, where I was a guest more than once over the years. I swallow hard, staring at the two enormous four-poster beds, the tall ceilings and long windows filtering in bright summer light. There's a plush chaise at the end of one bed and a slightly harder-looking bench at the end of the other, though that bed has an extra nightstand that looks like it could've been handcrafted in the Baroque era. It probably was.

"I want this one," I insist firmly, claiming it and the extra nightstand by falling back onto the heavy brocade comforter. I sink into the plushness, turning my face into the silk pillows. Sitting up slightly, I look to the far wall, by the door that leads to what I can only assume is a bathroom. Lined up there are our bags. "How did they get them up here so fast?"

It couldn't have been easy to lug all of Saint's trunks up the stairs, and they didn't come up behind us.

Saint is too busy inspecting her own bed to answer. She picks up the throw at the bottom of the bed between two fingers, rubbing at it. She raises an eyebrow. "I think this is Shahtoosh."

"What?"

"Doesn't matter," Saint says, but she sounds impressed. She marches up to the wardrobe against the wall, flinging it open with abandon, and there, as Dr. Remington had promised, are two muslin garment bags. "There are tags. This one is yours."

I reluctantly leave the most comfortable bed I've ever sat on to go and take it from her. Just as she promised, there's my name in the same swirling script the writing on the invitation was in.

"How did they get my size?" I mutter. It feels almost . . . *creepy.*

"Market research," Saint jokes, looking at me, as if she expects for me to be in on it. When I don't crack a smile, she frowns. "Well . . . we don't want to be late, do we?"

The cotton dresses are old-fashioned, with lacy, high necks and shin-length hems. The nipped-in waist and tight sleeves look like they belong to an era one hundred years before, and the back is secured by tiny buttons that feel like *pearls*. The only saving grace is the fact that there isn't a dumb matching hat.

"I feel stupid," Saint says once dressed, giving voice to my own feelings. But while I feel uncomfortable, she sounds more put out than anything.

With a few minutes to spare, we leave our room, even though I could be happy spending the entire two weeks just exploring there. I cast it one more excited glance before we make our way to the common room.

Opening the door, I'm not sure what to expect—maybe solemnity—but instead, it's full to the brim with a gaggle of girls, all speaking loudly over one another, dressed in the same white cotton and lace.

"Adina? Adina!"

Penthesilea's freckled arms fold delicately around my shoulders. My arms go around her automatically, though I've never hugged Penthesilea in my entire life. She pulls back, beaming, her fiery red hair framing her face, complementing the angelic rose and cream of her skin.

"P-Penthesilea," I choke, because she's *here. Why is she here?*

Pierce's *girlfriend* is here, competing in the same competition that I am, and suddenly, it all feels very much like a setup.

"I've been looking for a friendly face. There are some girls from Edgewater, but not many. There's a girl from Nightingale-Bamford too. You know, the all-girls school?" Penthesilea says. She speaks to me as if we're friends, as if we've shared something more than a few friendly words and a Remington. Not that she can *ever* know that.

"Oh? Oh, really?" I stutter. I turn to examine the competition, which is easier than looking at Penthesilea.

There's a girl I recognize from the lacrosse team at a boarding school two towns over. Another girl or two who might be from the private country day school nearby. Other girls, girls who mean nothing, girls who might mean everything. Girls who don't need to be here as badly as I do.

And then, as if that all wasn't enough, there's Esme Alderidge, her signature diamond choker exchanged for a single rope of pearls, like that will make her seem more adult. Her little follower, Hawthorne, apparently has followed her even into the Finish, and lurks in her shadow.

Unsurprisingly, Saint and I are the only ones of color.

Esme notices me at the same time as I notice her and she sits up, her lips curling into a sneer too wide for her face, but the door edges open, and there is Dr. Remington again.

The giggles and whispers and gossip taper off at once, her presence creating the much more serious air I was expecting. Only Penthesilea seems unchanged.

"Oh, Aunt Leighton is here," she says, even letting out a soft little giggle. She latches on to my arm as we turn to her.

Aunt Leighton?

Dr. Remington moves through the room with purpose, cutting between two girls—one mousy and towheaded, the other a bony brunette. She stands next to the piano and plucks one key almost absently, and yet it feels so very practiced. The glass in her hand is filled with wine that's so richly red, it looks nearly black.

Somehow the whole effect is that she seems to darken the golden and blue parlor room even though she's smiling.

"Welcome," she says softly, and this time there's no comfort in her voice, "to the Finish."

CHAPTER

6

"TWELVE GIRLS STAND BEFORE ME—ALL EXCEP-
tional and bright, in your own ways." She takes a long sip of her
wine and turns swiftly on her heels, like she's relishing making us
wait. Her gaze flits over each of us, bouncing back and forth, to
and fro. "But each of you has arrived here unrefined and raw. We
will rectify this."

Penthesilea is still at my side. Saint is lounging on a chaise, her
posture bored though her face seems a little more alert now.

"Our family founded the great Edgewater Academy, some
two centuries ago, a boys' school with the mission of creating
a new and brighter generation of young men with each class.
The Finish was established fifty years after the foundations of
Edgewater were laid, in response to a question raised by one of
our very own, Matilda Remington," Aunt Leighton says. She
moves with a deliberateness that would be captured lovingly on
thirty-five-millimeter film.

Matilda Remington is not a name I know, but Penthesilea startles, sitting up taller. I follow her gaze to the oil portrait of a woman on the wall, amongst a plethora of other paintings. Matilda looks nothing like her descendants, except in the shape of her eyes and the way she holds her chin up, so that she has to look down her nose.

"Matilda Remington was an exceptional woman. Brilliant and shrewd with an eye for detail. She knew that she and many other women of her status were being underutilized by their families. That they had more to give. Her husband had seen that in her, and Matilda wanted to demonstrate to her sons that she was not an exception to the rule in her brilliance." Aunt Leighton waxes on poetically, a lecture that is so carefully constructed to have us hang off her every word. She is a storyteller, better than anyone I've ever seen or heard. "Matilda fashioned the Finish to uplift and mold young women in the same way Edgewater did young men, a representation of the Remingtons' generosity and commitment to the development of the future. Even after Edgewater was made coed in the last midcentury, we continued this tradition of the Finish, championing women in industries that are traditionally male dominated and committing ourselves to our mission of propelling them upward. For what are women if not the progenitors of the future?

"And here we are, six generations later. Your time in the Finish will teach you skills that are *vital* to your survival in this world. Girls with aimless ambition are the easiest to snuff out. But girls who learn to channel it become women who conquer. I should know. I was once in your very place."

Another sip brings a heavy pause, perfectly cultivated, and some of the girls break out in whispers.

"Aunt Leighton won the Finish the year Pierce's uncle graduated from Edgewater. They ended up attending Harvard together. Fell in love. Married," Penthesilea whispers in my ear, just in time for Leighton to lower her glass again, ending the gossip in a silencing wave.

"There will be three events, each with an opportunity for lessons and the cultivation of useful skills leading up to it. Those events are the Ride, the Raid, and the Royale. With each event, you will be ranked according to performance, and rewarded when you succeed. But with each event, there will be also be a . . . culling." There's a twist to her mouth that sets my teeth on edge.

The other girls titter, like they know what she means, but I look around, searching for the joke. My eyes catch on Penthesilea again as she sits upright in rapt attention, and my stomach sinks to the pit of my pelvis. I turn sharply in my seat, attempting to refocus even as her presence, her clear front-runner status, tugs at my confidence, unraveling it slowly.

"Between these events, you will have the opportunity to foster bonds with the family and each other through the Repartees. These cocktail evenings will be crucial to your advancement, with certain advantages or disadvantages being gained based on your performance during them," Leighton says. She finishes her glass of wine, then sets it atop the piano, as if it's not a Bösendorfer. She takes a step closer to Hawthorne, taking her delicate hand in both of her own. "I understand the pressure that you will all be under to perform. I want you to know that I am a trained psychiatrist, and I will *always* be there for you to speak to."

What could be so intense that we would we need a psychiatrist? A twang of *not-right* shoots up my spine.

"Now, I must ask of you . . . your phones." It's the first time I notice the little basket at her feet.

There's a beat, stiff with simmering tension. I look over at Saint. Her fingers clench around the sleek edges of her iPhone. I squeeze mine tighter between my thighs. The itinerary said phone use would be limited. They warned us. But I still don't feel prepared to hand over a piece of myself. No one moves—and then surprisingly Esme stands up, tugging Hawthorne to her feet.

She stalks forward, shoulders back, completely confident as she holds her phone in an outstretched hand. "Aunt Leighton, here you go." She drops her phone in like she hasn't been glued to it since the sixth grade. Hawthorne is shakier, but murmurs her assent too.

And then it's a melee, everyone fighting to not be the last to obey Leighton's request. That status falls to Saint, Penthesilea, and me.

Leighton smiles. "I do not take your phones to punish you," she says firmly. "You will need all your focus. When you agreed to come here, you made a commitment." She turns to address the room at large. "That means that you are to follow the rules of this house, as they are set by me. There will be no after-curfew wandering, no bothering the staff. No distractions, at all. These next two weeks will test your grit, your ambition, and your minds. You will either rise to the occasion or you will fall, but you must do it alone. Your future begins now."

She swoops down to pluck the basket from the floor, and no sooner does the door click behind her softly than everyone explodes into chatter again, that excited hum from before changing into something more frenetic.

Penthesilea slots into my line of sight and she seems to be gearing up to say something when I feel a tap on my shoulder. I sag with gratefulness when I meet Saint's eyes.

"Want to look around?" Saint asks.

"Are we allowed to do that?"

"Have we been told that we aren't?" Saint retorts, and I can't help but crack a smile. I nod my agreement, and look back over at Penthesilea but can't quite meet her eyes.

"I'll see you around," I murmur, and she nods, but there's something else there, something that crinkles at the corner of her eyes like confusion.

No one has ever rejected her, I think. Without Charles and Pierce, she seems almost . . . lonely.

As Saint and I move toward the door, I overhear Esme speaking to a small gaggle of the girls, "Come closer, Margaret. Let me tell you about our competition. *Some* are barely worth a breath but—"

I shut the door behind me and take a deep, noisy inhale.

"That seemed pointed," Saint murmurs.

I look up at her, forcing a smile. "Yeah, Esme and I . . . have a history."

"That's obvious," Saint says, but she shakes it off and looks around.

We don't wander with a destination in mind, but there's something to look at everywhere we go.

"So, how are you liking Massachusetts?" I ask awkwardly as I look closer at the Tiffany glass.

"It's very *green*," Saint expels, and it isn't a compliment. "I've never been on this coast of the States before." Her gaze drifts to the exit again as we march downstairs.

"She took our phones. . . . Why did she take our phones?" I ask, accidentally skipping the next step. I grab on to the banister hard to keep myself from pitching forward, and then Saint's arm—surprisingly strong—yanks me back, steadying me. "Oh, thanks."

"Don't make a habit of it," Saint warns. "I expected this. I don't like it, but I definitely expected it."

"Yeah, I guess I should have too. They're probably trying to make it even more intense by cutting us off. The Finish . . . is, like, super private. No one even knows what the requirements are to be invited. It's just . . . you suddenly get a letter out of nowhere. But it sounds different from what I'd expected so far. I thought it would be more . . . academic? I don't know."

"Oh, I'm sure we'll have to use our brains *somehow*," Saint explains. She gives me one of those looks, like I'm supposed to hear something else in what she's saying. But when I don't, her face falls and the look she gives me is almost pitying. I chafe at that, glaring forward.

"All I'm saying is, whatever it's going to be, I don't like giving my phone away," I insist. It's like she doesn't want to even examine the weirdness of it all. The way that suddenly the walls seem to be closing in. "Your phone . . . is like an extension of yourself, right? It has important parts of you on it. I don't like that someone else could potentially have access to it." The idea that they might actually go through my phone makes me squirm.

"Of course it bothers me." Saint shakes her head, wary. "I expected the possibility so I have nothing on there that would give much away, but having my phone steadied me. Gave me an out. Without it, I'll need to find another out."

The idea that it *does* bother her too makes me unwind. I'm not acting out of place. I'm not crazy for thinking that the air is off.

My curiosity gets the better of me. "An out?"

"Yeah, in case I decide that this is not for me."

I snort to myself. "So . . . you don't *need* to be here either. Figures."

"Do you?" she asks.

"Isn't it obvious?" I retort.

Saint doesn't apologize. Instead, she looks me up and down, not in a judgmental way, but assessing. "Yes, I suppose it is," she says simply.

Instantly, the edge sharpening in my chest dulls. There's something about her outright honesty that makes me like her instantly.

"You're all right, Saint," I decide.

Saint looks thoughtful again. "Yeah . . . so are you."

Another sharp ding of *not-right* zips up my spine and settles at the base of my skull, because in that moment, Saint sounds sad about it.

CHAPTER

7

"DO YOU NEED HELP WITH YOUR HAIR?"

"Does anyone have a red lipstick?"

"*Shit*, I broke a nail—"

"Wait, I have nail glue, here."

Each voice layered one upon the other grates against me. It's evening and all the girls are gathered in the same common room where we met. Instead of sitting prim and proper in white lace—the stupid dresses we took a group photo in around mid-afternoon—they're all frantically putting finishing touches to the canvases they've made of themselves.

For a moment, if I close my eyes, I see myself back in my bedroom with Toni urging me to get ready. When I feel a touch against my chin, I imagine it's Toni again, tilting my face up to inspect my makeup. It's calming, brings me focus in a way that I need now. But when I open my eyes, I flinch in a way that threatens to knock me off my feet.

"Not going to even say hello to your competition? Realized it isn't even worth trying?"

"Hello, Esme."

Damn. I was just on the verge of forgetting that she was here too.

"Adina *Walker*. Now, whose dick did you suck to get here?" she asks with a smile.

"No one's," I say through gritted teeth.

It's time to keep my head under the radar again. I bite my bottom lip and make eye contact with Hawthorne over Esme's shoulder, but she looks away. She *always* looks away when Esme starts something.

"You shouldn't touch people without permission." Relief sings through my veins as Saint slides in from God knows where. She looks stunning in a rich blue cocktail dress. Her long black hair swings behind her in a high ponytail, and she looks down at me. "Sorry I took so long. I couldn't get my hair right."

Esme looks displeased that I have someone in my corner already, but she doesn't let it stop her.

"I just *wonder*," Esme sings. "Every single one of us has been nominated to be here. I'm childhood friends with Pierce. Hawthorne is a champion archer. This is Jacqueline—she's the Northeast junior poker champion. Margaret—she goes to Rye Country Day—is a ranked debater. Even Saint is the daughter of a big-shot developer—"

And under her breath, I hear Saint mutter, "'Even Saint.' My father could buy your entire state."

"—but you. Who are *you*, Adina Walker, to merit a nomination?"

"I earned my place here, just like everyone else," I insist. I can't tell if I'm lying, not even to myself, but in that moment when I opened the box it felt true. I look over at the other girls with her. I doubt any of them has ever met Esme before today. She's their competition, yet just by the strength of her personality and will alone, she's established herself as their leader. Esme has always had an infuriating talent for command.

"I'm sure," Esme says softly, sticking her tongue into her cheek over and over again, crass and crude, yet supposedly *I'm* the one who's unworthy.

"Now, Esme . . ."

As if she's descended from the heavens, Penthesilea emerges from a break in the crowd. She turns to one girl, brushing a stray curl from her face, straightening the skirt of another, like some kind of queen mother in a gown of gold on her way over to us.

". . . must you pit everyone against each other before the events have even begun?" Penthesilea asks, and Esme's smugness curdles. Penthesilea never *sounds* disappointed, but she always manages to make you feel like she is, and there's nothing worse than disappointing Penthesilea Bonavich. It's her weirdly detached benevolence. It's like disappointing your favorite teacher. Impersonal but it hurts.

"I'm just being *polite*," Esme drawls. "Speaking with our former classmate."

"It doesn't sound very polite to me, especially when she was a friend. Not just a classmate," Penthesilea says firmly. She turns toward me and smiles. "You look pretty, Adina."

Despite Esme's snort, I don't doubt Penthesilea's sincerity, so I thank her.

But I do doubt the truth of her statement. I didn't think at all that these cocktail parties would be formal occasions. It's a contest, not a beauty pageant. I didn't think I'd need gowns like these girls are wearing, with jewels dripping from their skin. I feel stupid in my borrowed Mac Duggal, the one I thought I wouldn't even wear until the ending formal. It's nice and structured, but it's not couture.

"Thanks," I say softly, off balance. "I'm just—"

"I can do your makeup," Saint says firmly. She takes me by the wrist, tugging me away to a corner, where we're distanced from the other girls. She sits me on a settee and squats in front of me. "I'm actually really bad at doing makeup on other people, but I can do your eyeliner? And brows?"

"I can do my own eyeliner," I say defensively. "I . . . but yes to the brows. Please. Thanks." I breathe out. "Why'd you pull me away?"

Saint hums to herself as she goes through her little makeup pouch from her purse. She makes a sound of triumph when she pulls out a new brow gel.

"Close your eyes." She leans forward and her breath fans across my face—sweetly acidic like champagne.

I do as I'm told.

"The redhead. Penicillin—" I snort. "Don't move. I can see she makes you uncomfortable. I can't see why. She seems perfectly pleasant, unlike that *other* girl. The menace. Open your eyes, let me see what it looks like."

I blink again, watching Saint go from a blurry form to sharp features in relief. I glance over at Esme. "The menace" is ridiculously apt.

Esme lifts her ever-present bottle of Dior perfume, leaning forward, with a much kinder smile on her face than I've ever seen, which is how I know it's fake. "Just a dab at your pulse points and wrists. You'll smell *divine*. You should be honored that I'm sharing my scent with you, Margaret. The Finish can be really overwhelming, but I'll take care of you, all of you, I promise."

She used to spray me with her Dior too—she just never took care of me. She tore me apart instead.

Eat shit, Esme.

I roll my eyes, looking away, catching Saint's sly grin even though I haven't answered her question. "What?"

"You pretend that you have nothing to say, but I can tell you do. I bet you keep every bad word behind your teeth," Saint says like she understands. "But that's how you survive out there. You can't do that here."

"'If you don't have something nice to say, don't say it at all,'" I say, practically singing the kindergarten adage. One of the many lessons I learned from my mistake. My mouth—rumors—led to my downfall, and it's not like I had very far to fall.

"That won't work here. These girls make a game out of cruelty and they're here to win. They will hold nothing back. Learn the spoken and unspoken rules of the Finish. Quickly."

It sounds like both a warning and a threat.

I decide to heed both.

❦ ☠ ❦

The butler comes for us at 5:52 p.m.

"Ladies, if you would line up, single file," he says, plummy-voiced and severe.

Esme and her pack rush to form a line right up front. She sweeps to the head in a gown with sleeves that look like silver leaf.

"Thank you, Mr. Caine," Penthesilea says gently as he ambles down the line, making sure that each of us is in place.

I slip in behind her, followed by Saint and another girl—I think I heard her mention that she's from California, and she looks it, tanned and beachy and model-esque.

Mr. Caine nods at Penthesilea, something like affection in his gaze, which he lets harden over when he meets my eyes. He turns on the heels of his shiny Oxfords and marches forward. He means for it to be a dismissal, but it's a look that's familiar. I know I don't belong, but it only makes me want everything more.

"Onward, ladies, or you shall be late for dinner."

It feels a bit like a parade from then on. We march back down the hallway, heels sinking into the overplush Persian runner, and then clicking on the stairs.

"Careful not to scuff the wood," Mr. Caine barks when the girl just ahead of Penthesilea trips.

I pay close attention to the sloping walls. There is a lingering layer of dust motes on the windowsills that reminds me of the age of this place, a stately home that has stood for centuries now. Still, the house isn't as complicated as I previously thought. We're moving toward what I'm already starting to recognize as the heart of the estate, approaching a pair of tall, heavy wooden doors.

"Have a lovely dinner, ladies," Mr. Caine says, throwing them open.

We come to a stop in the doorway as I survey the Remington Family gathered inside as a whole.

Pierce Maxwell Remington III is a solid man, the kind whose hair might've once been blond but it is now more ash colored than anything else. It's slicked back, revealing a proud forehead and a sloping brow. The cut of his suit is expensive, tight against the lines of his body. One hand rests on his namesake's shoulder, and just looking at Pierce, it's easy to imagine what Mr. Remington looked like in his wonder years.

It's also easy to see how Pierce's conservative navy suit would look perfect next to Penthesilea's golden gown. Gold like she's already won.

I shake the thought away and turn to the last two members of the Remington Family.

Graham stands there looking bored, while Aunt Leighton looks pleased by something. She whispers something in Pierce's ear, but her gaze stays on us. Pierce smiles once, and nods at whatever she's saying. And then he steps forward, arms stretched open wide.

"Ladies . . . welcome to the Opening," Pierce declares.

He claps, still nodding, and leads us in applause that feels more for the Remingtons than for us, as they stand tall and powerful, basking in it all. Pierce steps back into the fold of his family, and for a moment they are a four-headed monster.

Then they scatter, leaving us to divide and conquer.

Margaret darts forward, smiling brightly. "Dr. Remington! Or should I call you Aunt Leighton?" she asks cheerfully.

"Pierce, darling, can I steal you for a second?" Esme drawls, stalking forward, her clique all falling over themselves to join her in speaking to the son of honor.

They leave Saint and me in the dust, and there's a brief moment of confusion as we're swept up in a sea of movement when at least five servants march between us, all balancing silver platters with bubbling champagne glasses.

"Look alive, Adina," Saint hisses, just as I'm trying to decide where to go. She's right. The competition starts now and I have to be smart about this. I grit my teeth, searching for my target. I've already met every other Remington. It's about time that I acquaint myself with the one I haven't.

"Let's talk to the father." I gesture. "He looks like he'd want to talk to us, right?"

Saint snorts. "Sure. He's probably drawn to the 'exotic.'"

I roll my eyes at her, so pointedly that she laughs behind her hands, but straightens as we near him.

"Mr. Remington, pleasure to see you," Saint says, and suddenly, she sounds older.

"Mr. Remington, it's good to meet you," I say, standing tall. I treat it like a college admissions interview. It's all the same. This is someone I need to impress. Someone I need to convince of my worthiness.

"*Roo*-lan, how *is* your father?"

He says her name strangely, without any of the care Leighton used. It sounds *wrong*, and he seems oddly proud of it despite himself.

"He's well, sir. And please, call me Saint," she answers delicately.

Mr. Remington nods. "Yes, yes, I do remember that you chose an English name. Cute. But I *can* pronounce your name, *Roo-lan*."

"I'd prefer if you didn't," Saint says through a pretty smile, full of teeth.

I hold my breath, waiting for Mr. Remington to snap back. Instead, he looks pleased. "Then . . . Saint," he says. "You've graduated, haven't you? Any idea of where you'll be going?"

"I'll be attending Princeton," Saint says, sounding rather put out by the fact. "I wanted to go to uni back home, but my parents believe that the Ivies will suffice."

"Princeton isn't Harvard, but not much else is," Mr. Remington says. "You know, I went to Harvard." *We all know he went to Harvard.*

We get it, Remingtons go to Harvard. "I rowed. What's your sport?"

"Fascinating." Saint somehow makes it sound true and like an insult all at once. "I'm afraid I don't play any sports."

"You must have padded that résumé somehow. After all, Asians don't really count as minorities anymore, do they? Do you play any instruments?" Mr. Remington asks. I wince. He's on his third glass of bourbon since we've entered the room. Each time he drains the glass in one swallow, a server is there to exchange the empty crystal for a fresh one. "Piano?"

Saint stares at Mr. Remington "No, I don't play any instruments. I'm not that sort of Asian," she says very coolly.

I expect Mr. Remington to blanch or turn red, but he does nothing of the sort. Instead, he laughs, like he's delighted by the casualness of his racism, and by the casualness of Saint's quick comeback.

"Oh?" he challenges.

"No. I understand that you selected some of these ladies based on skills like that, but I can't claim musicianship," Saint says loftily. "I don't have the time. I'm deeply invested in the success of my family's business."

"How so?" Mr. Remington interjects now.

"I've been attending meetings with my family's investors from the time when my nǎi nai still ran our company. We're in real estate development," Saint says with a proud smile. "So, no, I did not have time to learn my scales. I was in the business of learning the stock market instead."

"Oh. Very good," Mr. Remington says, and now he sounds

impressed. He licks his thin, dry lips like he's hungry, even greedy. "So, you'll know all about your father's stance on moving into the American market—"

"Ah, ah, Mr. Remington," Saint says with a placid smile. "That's insider information. For now." She turns and plucks two champagne flutes off a passing platter, then offers one to me.

I take it, knowing the bubbles will take off the edge that has me wary, but it's exactly that wariness that tells me I need my wits about me. I hold the flute close to my lips and mime taking a sip. I can taste the champagne on my tongue, but I don't swallow.

"And, Miss *Walker*," Mr. Remington begins, finally turning toward me. "Oh, I've heard about *you*."

"Have you?" I ask, my voice pitching higher with my rising discomfort.

Mr. Remington looks thoughtful. "Yes. My boy says that you were very kind to him at the bonfire, when you didn't have to be. You listened. Kindness is harder and harder to come by, the higher you ascend. Pierce knows that better than anyone. You must have made quite the impression."

"I didn't mean to," I lie.

Mr. Remington sees right through me. "You want to go to Yale. My other son goes to Yale. A . . . safe choice."

"Your son did say that Harvard was the better one of the two. I could be convinced by a well-structured argument," I say with a lipless smile.

"Could you?" he asks, raising an eyebrow. He puffs out his

chest, as if he means to do just that, when a striking figure of fire and gold catches all of our eyes. "Penthesilea!"

"Third!" Penthesilea sways between us, her dress spiraling around her. "Third" or Mr. Remington or *whoever* the fuck takes Penthesilea's hand and spins her under his arm. Penthesilea laughs, so pretty and delicate. "It's been ages."

"I was just telling your father that I haven't seen you in months. Pierce doesn't bring around his best influence much anymore," Mr. Remington says.

Penthesilea giggles. "He wanted there to be an even playing field. That's all."

"Is it? Even?"

Mr. Remington's smile flakes away, revealing a far grimmer expression as Graham swaggers up. His eyes aren't bloodshot, but he and his father have matching glasses, full of shimmering brown liquor, and it's clear he's been keeping pace.

"Yes. It is. We make the Finish as fair as possible. The girls are all presented with the same accommodations, the same goals," Mr. Remington says stiffly. "Graham, we've gone over this."

"Hello, Graham," Penthesilea greets him, but she isn't smiling anymore.

"Hey, Penny. Four's over there if you're looking for him," Graham says, barely sparing her a look. Instead, he inspects me. "Adina Walker," he declares, his voice just a little too loud, garnering attention from some of the others. "The good girl. That's . . . that's disappointing."

"Looks like I did have what it takes," I say pointedly.

Graham nods. "Maybe. But you still don't belong here."

It's the way he says it that sparks anger in me, that same anger that I felt in the woods.

"I don't need to be reminded," I say. He doesn't know me, but I know what I'm capable of, what I could be with the same opportunity as these girls.

"You are making our guests uncomfortable. Graham, if you would please remove yourself," Mr. Remington says through clenched teeth. Graham ignores his father with the practiced ease of someone who's been doing it for years.

"It's not an insult," Graham says. "It just means you have a soul."

Of course, he's one of *those*. A sad, disillusioned rich boy who thinks that money is dirty. He's only able to think that because he's had it all his life.

He leans in close, close enough that I can smell the whiskey on his breath. It's sweet and strong and hot against my cheek. "I hope you and that soul survive this," he confesses.

Then Mr. Remington wrenches him away from me. "Do you have any *goddamn* sense, Graham?" he demands, dragging him off.

They make it only a few steps before Graham shakes off his father's hand. Mr. Remington is taller and broader, but there's something in Graham's stance that makes him hesitate for a moment. It's just enough time for Graham to storm across the ballroom and open the balcony doors. Mr. Remington stares after him before stalking off toward his other son, jerking him away from the gaggle of girls, pointing violently after Graham.

"I'm so sorry for Graham," Penthesilea says in earnest.

"Why are you apologizing for him? He's not *your* brother," I retort, sharper than I intend.

Penthesilea seems surprised by the barbs in my words. I down the champagne and pass the empty glass off to the nearest server with a murmured thank you. I pinch the bridge of my nose as my stomach roils. I shouldn't have said that. I shouldn't have gotten so *aggressive* so suddenly. That's my problem. I have so very little patience left to give. I need to find some.

"I think I need . . . a moment," I murmur. "Excuse me."

"Adina, careful—" Saint begins, reaching for my wrist.

"Saint, it's fine. I'm fine. I just need to . . . *breathe*." I'm kinder as I finish, shedding my annoyance with my only ally in this before I ruin that, too. I slip away from her, and dart back through the ballroom doors.

Outside the ballroom, away from the crackling croon of the phonograph, my lungs still tighten with anxiety.

I look down at my black circle skirt and laugh breathlessly. Every time I close my eyes, I can picture the silk and velvet and taffeta cocktail dresses and gowns, each costing at least a grand. And here I stand in a borrowed black dress thinking I can win.

I still feel too exposed. My feet are moving before I can think of a plan or direction. Creeping down the hallway, I stick close to the wall then slip into the next room, pausing when I register it as an empty music room. It's eerie looking, with only the moon streaming through the long windows and a single glass door that leads out to a balcony. I plink out a high note on the baby grand as I scoot around a stray music stand, then I push the door open, letting the warm summer air wrap around me and hopefully start to loosen my lungs.

I shut the door behind me, flinching at the click that booms like thunder in the silence, before I settle and finally let out a heavy sigh. My chest does start to feel far more open, and I can register the ends of my limbs more now.

"Can't breathe in there, can you?"

"Fuck!" I yelp, looking for the source of the voice.

I realize my mistake. The balcony isn't a singular one but instead wraps around the entire back of the second floor, and there, just a few doors down, is Graham, sitting on the ground with his back to the brick wall, glass balanced on his knee.

"It's . . . it's . . ."—he hiccups—"so *much* in there. Loud as shit."

"You're pretty loud," I accuse.

"With the truth? I'm the only one who's going to tell it to you in this shithole," Graham says back.

"Somehow, I doubt that," I say dryly, moving closer so he'll stop yelling. "You made a scene. Penthesilea apologized for you."

Graham rolls his eyes. "Penny knows better than to apologize for my poor behavior."

"Yeah, well, she's . . . dating Pierce. I think she feels responsible for some reason," I say stiltedly, feeling bad still for snapping at her for that. "Then your dad said something to your brother."

Graham lets out another sharp laugh, which he drowns in his glass. "Yeah, of course he told Four. 'Call your brother, Four. Watch out for your brother, Four. Teach your brother right from wrong, Four.' As if I'm not the older one. As if I didn't practically raise that kid on my own."

I scoff. "You mean like the nannies didn't raise you both?"

"The nannies aren't the godsend they're meant to be, especially when your dad's fucking them," Graham says. He shakes his head. "I inherited all my bad traits, as you can see. Can't seem to shake them. Blood is thick and all that shit."

He salutes me with his glass.

"Sounds like you're just foisting blame off on someone else," I say. I look down at him and tilt my head. "You think you're so different from them? Why? Because you're 'self-aware'? I can promise you . . . you're not."

Graham laughs. "I'm not?"

"No," I say shortly. "I think you're kinda worse. Pretending that you're not morally bankrupt when you're sitting here in a custom suit drinking top-shelf liquor."

"Damn. Harsh," Graham drawls. "Maybe you're right. But so am I. You'll never be one of us. And you shouldn't want to be."

I squint at him. "I don't."

He thinks he has me all figured out. They all think that. They don't. They don't know anything about what it's like in Suburbia, where nothing moves and all the houses look the same. They can't comprehend that I don't want what they have either. That I want to make something that's mine, that has *my* reflection.

"Then why are you here?" Graham asks.

The words stick to my tongue. For some reason, this feels like a moment that matters. "To get back what I earned and all the potential that came with it," I say finally.

To even the playing field.

Graham frowns at me and, quiet and hushed like a confession, he says, "I would give every *single* cent of it away, the Remington money, if it were mine. All of it."

I stare at him, my observation from earlier confirmed, and can't help the laugh that bubbles out of my chest. He stares at me confused and he is so *innocent*, in a way. He thinks he's the main character. People like him *always* think they're the main character, because life tells them they are. They don't need a playlist to convince themselves.

"Graham Remington, without your money, you wouldn't last a day. You don't have what it takes."

Graham looks up at me and his eyes glint in the moonlight, but before he can answer, a scream shatters my triumph. I twist away from Graham as yet another flash of *not-right* hits me, swelteringly uncomfortable. What could cause a scream like that in a place as perfect as this? Graham stands sharply, that smug expression sliding off his face. I stalk past him, rushing through the double doors off the balcony, moving toward the commotion.

Margaret from Rye Country Day—on the debate team,

nationally ranked—is at the center of a small crowd in the ball-room. Her face is shiny and dark purple, like an overly ripe eggplant, with bloodshot eyes bulging from it cartoonishly. She lets out a horrible sound, like air leaking out of a balloon, and she claws at her arms, at her wrists, at her own neck. My stomach turns when I notice the harsh rashes along her forearms, now irritated red by the vicious tearing at her skin, blood welling there in lines.

I'm grabbing her by the hands before I even realize that I've crossed the room. As soon as I touch her, she collapses, and I drop with her.

"Are you okay? Margaret!" I shout. Sprawled across my lap, she convulses, her neck swelling up now. I look up, wild eyed and breathing fast. "Please! Somebody help her! I think she's dying. She's *dying*!"

And . . . no one moves.

"Oh, God," one girl—the beachy girl, the one who looks like a model—squeaks. There's the sour smell of urine somewhere underneath the tangy sweet scent of perfume and champagne, like someone's just pissed their fear away.

And yet they all just stare, different degrees of horror twisting their expressions. Hawthorne never blinks, even as her eyes grow shiny with tears. Esme is stone faced, like any expression at all is a weakness.

"HELP HER!" I shriek, my voice tangling in my throat, and then I look down at her.

Margaret doesn't struggle anymore. She just looks frightened. Her trembling swollen hand lifts to my face. I grab it and hold it tight, pressing it against my cheek, feeling how hot she is. I can smell the blood now, like old pennies, and Dior perfume.

"It's okay. You're going to be okay," I whisper to her, even though I can taste my own lie. Because in one clear, chilling moment, I realize . . . no one is coming to help. "I know . . . it's *okay*. Just . . . just rest, all right? You can stop."

Almost like I gave her permission, Margaret's eyes roll into the back of her head, and then she's still.

CHAPTER

8

MARGARET'S DEAD BODY IS WARM IN MY LAP AND I can't breathe.

No one in the ballroom is breathing. The phonograph plays until it ends in a record scratch.

My giggle is inappropriate, one that burbles up from my chest and strangles in my throat. I might be able to pass it off as a sob, except another follows, unbidden. I clap my hand over my mouth at the absurdity of it all, and then suddenly, I don't feel like laughing anymore.

I feel like screaming.

And then I am. *Screaming*, that is.

A hand clamps around my shoulder, hauling me up. Saint tugs me out from underneath the body, and Margaret's head thumps against the cold marble floor. I expect it to crack like an eggshell, for her to cry out like Humpty Dumpty.

But Margaret doesn't make a sound.

Another strong hand wraps around my wrists. Mousy, blond, quiet Hawthorne, who doesn't look mousy *or* quiet right now.

Pierce is the first Remington to move.

"Adina, are you all right?" he demands, even though underneath his gleaming tan, I can see a sheen of green. He watches me because he doesn't want to see *her*—Margaret.

I want to say he's asking the wrong person, but I still haven't stopped screaming.

"Not now, Pierce," Hawthorne says sharply, and I can just hear her over my own panicked yelps. "Come on, Adina. Come on, let's go, let's go."

And then Third looks at his sister-in-law and drawls, bored, "Clean up, won't you?"

Leighton spins into action. "Move her," she snaps at the servers, pointing at Margaret like she's trash, and then I'm being hauled from the ballroom, down the hallway, and up the stairs.

"She's dead. That girl's fucking *dead*. What the actual fuck?" I try to wheeze, but my harsh breaths slur my words and my vision starts to spot.

Is this a panic attack? It feels like a panic attack.

"Yes. She's dead," Hawthorne says. She looks over my head at Saint. "Your room or mine?"

"*Definitely* mine," Saint says, accusatory and snappish, like this is *Hawthorne's* fault. Like it could be someone's fault.

I blink and we're on the stairs. Another blink and we're in my room. With the door shut, I finally feel my knees give out, and I land halfway on the bench at the foot of my bed with a deafening thud.

"What the hell was that?" I demand breathlessly. "Margaret is dead, and nobody did anything! Nobody even moved! What kind of messed-up shit is that?"

I can imagine how I look, coming apart at the seams, but Hawthorne hums sympathetically, her arm coming around my shoulders. I sag into her willowy frame, recognizing it. I once craved this comfort, after the falling-out with Esme, but Hawthorne chose a side and it wasn't mine.

I don't realize that I'm shaking until Saint grabs my wrists and steadies my trembling hands.

"Just breathe, Adina. Breathe," Saint insists, pulling me back onto my feet, but it's hard to breathe when I know this is what Margaret must have felt, but a thousand times worse.

"You need to wash your hands in case the poison was still active on her skin," Hawthorne says gently, steering me into the en suite. "Come on, Adina."

Her words register thirty seconds too late.

"Poison?" I spit through chattering teeth.

"Yes, poison," Hawthorne says gently. She turns the water on and she grabs one of my arms from Saint, then begins scrubbing viciously at it. Saint does the same to the other, but I squirm in their grip.

"What do you mean poison? We ate all the same things! And that wasn't food poisoning."

"No, it definitely was not," Saint agrees. Her eyes are bright with fury. "You were closest to her, Adina. Did you smell anything?"

"Besides Esme's heinous Dior perfume—ow!" I shout as my skin raws under Hawthorne's continued scrubbing.

"Esme was wearing Chanel perfume tonight," Hawthorne whispers. She looks at me with big brown eyes, like she's trying to tell me something.

"Esme has never worn Chanel perfume in her life," I snarl. This I know.

And then my brain short-circuits.

Saint stills. "Now you know why. I knew she was a tricky one."

The implication of Saint's words doesn't go over my head. I jolt forward, turning to gag over the porcelain toilet bowl, jerking away so hard that both of them release me. My heaving echoes in the bathroom over the running water. Closing my eyes, I inhale once. Then exhale.

Standing tall again, hands gripping the sides of the sink, I say, "You think Esme *poisoned* her? Esme is a bitch. I will be the first one to tell you that, but this isn't a movie. People our age don't poison other people."

Saint frowns at me. "I suppose here they do." She sounds so blasé about it, but I can see the crease of worry at the downturned corners of her mouth. She shakes her head. "I thought the red-head, Pennywise, would make the first move."

Hawthorne laughs to herself softly. "Pen? No, Pen wants something, but not what everyone else does."

And what is that? I can't bring myself to ask.

"I didn't expect it to be so . . . underhanded. Though maybe I should've. I don't know any of you, but from what I've seen, Esme Alderidge is the kind of girl who inspires loyalty through fear. She is wealthy, smart, ruthless when she wants to be, charming when she has to be. So I guess it makes sense she wanted to make her dominance clear from the beginning."

"It's just girlhood warfare on another level." Hawthorne pushes. "Getting them before they get you is the only way to win."

"Stop!" I insist. Both Saint and Hawthorne look at me like *I'm* the crazy one. "The Finish is just a competition. We're doing shit like . . . etiquette and brownnosing and brainteaser shit. We are not combatants in a *war.*"

Hawthorne snorts. "Oh, *hell.*"

But Saint has that same expression from before on her face—pity. "You really don't know."

"What is there to know?" I retort, pushing back. I want them to say it, to hear how completely insane what they're alluding to sounds. How completely impossible it is for it to be the truth of this place, even though I can still smell hints of poisonous perfume.

Saint's defenses spring right back up, that mask of utter control returning, so well constructed that it makes sense that she's already involved in her family business. Business is just an ocean of sharks, and I see now that Saint is a shark, through and through.

"A lot. I did some digging before I came. In most years, the

Finish is a normal thing. Exactly what you said. A competition for power and influence. They take tests. They learn to be ladies—whatever that means in our day and age. They pick the girl who has the best future ahead of her. The one who will reflect well on the Remington name. Who, in interviews, will one day be asked—'Who was your greatest influence?' And her answer will be, 'The Remington Family; they've given me everything.' All perfect publicity to cover up that some years, very *specific* years . . ." Saint trails off, and then she looks over at Hawthorne as if waiting for confirmation.

Hawthorne nods and looks at me. "The Finish isn't about us, Adina. The Finish is about the Remingtons. The Remington men."

"Of course it's not about us. We're tax write-offs. That doesn't mean we go around *killing* people for their attention," I spit, the guttural rage in my chest making me sound unlike myself.

"When someone wants something badly enough, they'll do anything to get it," Hawthorne says, her voice going reedy.

I push past her weak insistence. "I get that Esme's entire family is probably already a step away from prison, but she didn't have to up the charge from tax evasion and embezzlement to first-degree murder."

Hawthorne arches her pale eyebrows. "That really isn't any of your business, is it?"

My terror transforms into venom. "Congratulations on missing the point, *Becky*." Hawthorne bristles but I continue my tirade. "Hawthorne, *what* is going on? And no talking around the real answer. Tell me the truth."

Hawthorne's eyes widen, bright like headlights. And then, after she chews on the words, she finally says, "The Finish is about the Remington men, because one of them is the prize. This is part of it. Proving that we'd die to have them. Proving that we'd *kill*."

She says it as if violence is an expectation, one fully accepted. When I look at Saint, she doesn't seem surprised either.

"How did you know?" I spit.

"I'm from the area. My family has been really close to the Remingtons for generations, just like the Bonaviches and the Alderidges. The girls who are invited to Finishes like this usually are close. Makes the whole thing . . . not cleaner, but easier. The risk is understood. But a Finish like this hasn't happened for a long time."

"A Finish like this?"

"The kind where a Remington heir turns eighteen and hosts the Finish, not to further a girl's opportunities, but to find a wife."

Her declaration cuts through clear, like a sudden break in the static friction of an old radio. The words sound foreign and they don't make sense, but also do. *A wife.*

Strangely enough, all I can think about is icy blond hair and hard eyes and the ringless finger of Dr. Leighton Remington.

"So . . . Leighton?" I whisper, but neither seems to hear me.

"I suspected," Saint adds. "But I didn't know. Not for sure. Hawthorne is right. It's kept really hushed. *Very* insular. I did research before I came. Like I said, most years—totally normal. But every year that a Remington heir graduated, no one ever talked about those years. I couldn't find any of the losers. Only the winner. And there was a pattern. She won. She became his *wife*."

I shake my head against Saint's casual theorizing, because it makes no sense. It can't.

"What *about* Leighton?" I demand, voice ringing through the bathroom.

Hawthorne sighs and confirms. "It was a Finish like this one." She levels a look at me, like she's waiting for me to break down again, so I hold my breath, steeling myself. "Dr. Remington . . . Leighton, she was a nobody. Her father was the stable master here. Her mother was a homemaker. She lived in town her entire life as *nobody*. But she had been around the Remingtons her whole life. She knew what they wanted for a Remington wife and she was smart, ambitious, ruthless. Everything Matilda Remington was. So she played their games and she won expertly. And by the end, Third's younger brother *wanted* to marry her. She'd made herself into his dream girl."

I open my mouth and then close it again when I can't manage any words. Every word from Hawthorne's mouth shatters the reality I've made for myself. Every plan means nothing now.

Because the Remingtons have their own plans. I will die. Or I will be a Remington. Every accomplishment I could ever have, any future, even if by some miracle I win, would always be second to being *Mrs. Remington*. Not Adina Walker. I wouldn't be regaining what's mine, because I wouldn't even be me. Not that that's even a possibility because—

Every girl would kill to be a Remington.

Except me.

"I can't be here. I'm leaving."

"This is why they took our phones," Saint reminds me, edge creeping into her voice again. Her hands slowly clench into fists. "This is the first real Finish since social media was created. They are in control now and we can't leave unless they let us."

"This is *illegal*," I say.

"They are the Remingtons," Hawthorne says. "They own this town. This state. All of New England. Nothing is illegal for them."

Suddenly, Graham's words ring true. "I hope you and that soul survive this," he'd said. He knew. He knew all about this and he didn't warn me. None of them warned me.

I'm alone here.

"This is a nightmare. I'm going to die," I realize.

Hawthorne shrugs once. "Maybe. Maybe not. It's different now."

"What's so different?"

"There are more girls from outside the usual circle. More

variables. There's *you*," Hawthorne says, but that doesn't reassure me. It just drives in the point again that Pierce didn't invite me here to save me. He invited me to *end* me.

"It's a new era, a new game. Get ready to play."

CHAPTER 9

I DON'T SLEEP THAT NIGHT.

I lie in the darkness, on my back, head turned toward the door, wondering if Esme will darken it at any moment with her poisoned perfume. Every time I think to close my eyes, I see Margaret's face as she clawed at her arms and her neck, like the pain would bring her back to life. My stomach turns, but there's nothing to throw up, not after that first time, when I spewed champagne into the toilet.

Saint called for a meal to be brought to our room. She ate it when I didn't. I sat against the chaise, knees tucked against my chest, staring straight ahead as Saint talked at me. Then she put me to bed.

With the moon pitched low in the sky, I feel my hackles rise, adrenaline thundering through my veins. I turn in my bed and look over at Saint. She's buried in the sheets, planted facedown, and finally a soft snore tells me all I need to know. I roll out of the bed without a second thought, gliding across the chilly floors, swinging a sweater around my shoulders and grabbing my Air Forces from my bag. I stuff my feet into them, tying the laces in a stranglehold around each ankle.

I don't want them to get loose when I start running.

The door hinges whine with age. I still, waiting for Saint to wake up, but she doesn't budge. I slip out, and leave the door open just a crack, wishing her well, this brilliant girl who figured out what she was walking into, who saved me from falling down the stairs, who washed poison from my skin. She's safer than I would be. Smarter.

And she has someone who can rain hellfire if she disappears.

I don't. There's no one who could fight for me if I disappeared. Not against the Remingtons. So, I have to disappear myself.

The house is so quiet that I don't dare to even breathe. Each shadow is a ghost of a girl, a warning of a man, all threatening and long, an all-consuming darkness. The silence gets louder and louder, and then I realize that it's half in my head.

The real world is not so quiet.

I hear them, closer than expected, in a room that I thought was an abandoned office when I explored earlier in the day with Saint but is very much occupied now.

". . . yourself together. Enough, Four, enough," a voice says gruffly. I don't know it well enough to immediately place it, but it's familiar in a way that I don't have to search my brain long for.

Mr. Remington. *Third,* my brain supplies.

"You want him to get himself together? He just watched a body get loaded into the freezer." An acerbic voice retorts. Graham.

"I'm fine, I'm fine. I just . . ." Pierce trails off.

Slowly, I creep closer, watching the thin line of light that beams from under the door. Crossing it feels dangerous, like they'd catch me, so I stay pressed into the shadows, listening to a conversation that I don't belong in.

"You're not fine," Graham says. "This is why we should have canceled it."

"You want your brother to be a disappointment like you?" Third asks snidely.

"Better a disappointment than making himself sick," Graham retorts.

"Things are supposed to be different. That's what you said, Graham," Pierce says, voice growing stronger with each word. "You said it was going to be less . . . *dire*."

"Your brother is a fool. There is tradition for a reason," Third snaps with impatience. I hear a shuffle of movement and then Third's voice rings out, much closer than before. "Why you listen to your brother, I don't know, but the fault lies in you, Pierce. You wanted women from outside our circle, wanted this to be different, fine, but then you invited that *girl* here."

"What girl?"

Me, of course.

"Adina Walker?" Pierce whispers. My name sounds loud in the silence. "She's just a—"

"She's not just anything. I don't know what games you're play-ing, but this isn't the one to experiment with," Third says, each word careful and measured. "Each of those young women was hand selected, some perfectly *bred,* even, with the purpose of join-ing this family, knowing if they didn't, we could keep them quiet about anything that occurred. And then you bring an outlier. An *inadequate* choice that—"

"Why?" Pierce barks. "Because she's not yours? Not Pen?"

"That we have no *leverage* on to keep quiet." Third's snarl rises over Pierce's voice, effectively silencing him. "You're the one who wanted the rules to shift, and now you've introduced an element that we've no idea how to handle other than how we always have."

It's veiled, but it's not hard to glean the meaning.

"May I remind you that a girl died," Graham interrupts. "A girl has *already* died and it had nothing to do with Adina."

There's a brief moment of silence. "I didn't think this would happen. Why is this happening?" Pierce whispers.

"I told you." Dr. Remington's voice joins, richer than all the others. Unemotional. "No matter your intention, there will be blood. That is the very nature of this game."

And then Graham again: "Dad is right about one thing. She changes the circumstances, because she's not one of us and she's not prepared. Just send her home before they eat her."

It sounds like a condemnation, but I remember what he said. *It just means you have a soul.*

I intend to keep it. I slide away from the room, going back the opposite way, toward the stairs. Only when I turn the corner do I feel comfortable running, sure that I'm far enough away that they won't hear me.

I rush down the hallway, down the main staircase, not daring to cast my gaze upward.

I creep along the front wall, not directly to the front door—no, that would be obvious—keeping an eye out for a security system. Going through the arch into the next room, I search for a side door, but I find myself in a sunroom, a place with wide windows that look out onto the manicured lawn and the iron gates that block my way to freedom. In the silence, there's a crackling sound that I only place when I think of things like *Mission: Impossible* and James Bond.

The crackle of a walkie-talkie.

"Saw some movement earlier, confirmed deer, but all is quiet out front." The voice is slightly distorted with him being outside and me being inside, but I can hear him as much as I can see him—just barely. He's a tall, broad man, his body subsumed by the matte black of what looks like tactical gear. I can see only his back and the dark bronze of his hair as he stands in front of the window, staring out at the gates, feet planted hard to the ground.

The man pauses, like he can sense my presence. And then he starts to turn around. There's no time to think—only react. I fall to the floor hard, my only saving grace the soft wool rug underneath the breakfast nook. I crawl beneath the table and peer through the tiny slit between the table and the end of the wooden bench.

The man—a security officer—frowns, the doughy mess of features creasing. His eyes flit back and forth as he squints into the dark room. The walkie-talkie crackles again, too tinny for me to make out the words.

"No, no," the man says. "Thought I saw . . . God, this house is creepy. No need to let Dr. Remington know that I saw a weird ghost in the morning report. Doc-tor Remington. She's hot, right? MILF material."

He chuckles and turns back around. My heart is so loud in my throat, I nearly choke on the sound of it.

"Are you crazy?" The whisper echoes like a firecracker in the stillness.

I stuff my fist in my mouth to keep from screaming.

Saint is crouched by the archway, just a few feet from the stairs, her teeth grinding together hard. She's holding herself tight, like she regrets even being down here.

"Come back here," she warns. "You're going to get yourself hurt."

I look back at the man standing outside, in front of the window, and my gaze trails down to the pistol sitting heavily against his thigh.

"He's not the only one, I can promise you that," Saint warns. "Crawl back over."

My body is still screaming to run—*Take your chances, trust no one*—but I fight back the terror. Instincts aren't always right, I tell myself. I kneel on the edge of the rug, knees pressing into the cold wooden floor, staring up at Saint, unable to keep my misery in.

"I'm not going to just wait for my own execution," I whisper, my voice cracking.

"That's not the only option," Saint whispers. "If you stay, you can *fight*."

She holds out her hand, strong and steady. I take it because I have nothing else to take, and I let Saint lead me upstairs, back to our room. I don't speak again and neither does she as she sets me on the edge of my bed and then slips into her own. I untie my laces, kick my shoes off, and curl under the covers. This time when I put my head down, exhaustion overwhelms the horror and drags me under, my body turned inside out.

☠

It feels like moments later that Saint's shaking me awake, the nearly summer sun piercing through the room, making everything look more golden than it should. It feels wrong when there's a dead girl's body somewhere in this colossus of a house.

"Come on," Saint insists. "Breakfast."

I wait as she turns on her heel and pulls a robe over her silk pajamas. "Aren't we gonna talk about last night?" I ask.

"Do you need to?" Saint asks.

"I don't want to," I confirm after a moment.

Saint shrugs. "Then we won't."

There's a rabbity knock on the door, rapid and timid all at once. I stiffen, casting a panicked look over at it. Saint stands up and her eyes narrow.

"Give me a hanger," Saint commands. I roll out of bed and cross to the wardrobe, tossing one of the heavy wooden hangers at her. She catches it easily, and with an overabundance of caution, she opens the door, revealing only Hawthorne in a sea-green sweat suit.

"Good morning," Hawthorne says pleasantly.

Saint doesn't lower the hanger.

"What do you want?" she asks, harsh enough that Hawthorne wilts just the tiniest bit.

"Would you like to walk down to breakfast together?" Hawthorne asks.

"Where's Esme?" I demand.

Hawthorne takes a deep whistling breath through her front teeth. "Esme's been . . . reprimanded by Aunt Leighton," Hawthorne says delicately. "She won't be allowed to join us for breakfast and training today. She's having a bit of a meltdown over it, but it won't reflect well on me if I stay with her."

It's strategic in an unexpected way for Hawthorne, who has always been so loyal to Esme.

"I can imagine." I slide out of bed, shivering the moment my feet touch the icy floors. I didn't think to bring slippers—I don't even own slippers. I hop like the floor is lava over to my duffel bag, digging through it in search of my thickest socks. Even through the plush cotton, even though it's June, I can feel the icy grip of the Remington Estate.

"I'm starving. Do you think they'll have noodles?" Saint asks. She doesn't seem to feel the cold in her yellow silk tank top.

"Like spaghetti?" Hawthorne asks, tilting her head.

"There's your answer," I mutter to Saint as we leave. "Hope you like eggs Benedict and avocado toast."

Saint gives a long-suffering sigh. "Even Swiss cuisine is better than that."

The halls don't look as menacing as they did in the night hours, but I still check every corner, peer out every window, searching for remnants of the security detail that was outside, not keeping us safe but keeping us trapped. I don't see any of them, though; they're all gone as if they were ghosts.

"What were you saying about training?" I ask distractedly.

"Aunt Leighton didn't say much, but the Ride is coming up first," Hawthorne says.

I purse my lips together to hold the sarcasm back behind my teeth. *Will it even* really *be a ride? Will there be obstacles? What happens if you win?*

What happens if you lose?

Going downstairs, I pass the front door again, and the ache of failure mocks me. I had a chance last night and I blew it, allowing Saint to convince me to follow her back to our room. Maybe she saved me from death, but I still didn't *try*. Not really.

I begin to hear the others, a cawing sound not unlike a murder of crows, as we move down the hall. When we come to another set of double doors—the only rooms I've found with a single door are our bedrooms and the bathrooms—I steel myself, ready to be faced with a room of girls all willing to do what Esme already has.

Saint throws the doors open and the dining room falls into silence. Saint ignores it perfectly well, swinging through the entryway, but it roars in my ears as we walk the entire length of the dining room to grab the only open seats, next to Penthesilea.

Hawthorne cringes under the weight of everyone's stares, but she doesn't pull away. She stands by my side.

"Ah . . . good morning," Penthesilea says, disrupting the stillness as we settle closest to the wide picture windows, light streaming in hard enough to make us squint.

"Morning," Hawthorne returns.

Slowly, the other girls go back to their conversations. When I count, I notice Margaret's chair is missing. So is Esme's.

"How did you sleep?" Penthesilea asks.

"It's *freezing* here," Saint declares. "And I say that as someone who has essentially grown up in the Swiss Alps."

"Yes, the Remington home is quite chilly, even in summer. I think it's because it's old, it doesn't have the proper ventilation built into the walls to maintain heat," Penthesilea explains. She turns to Hawthorne and smiles. "I hope you slept well."

"I did. Esme too. She slept like a baby," Hawthorne murmurs.

One of the girls—Jacqueline from Nightingale-Bamford—leans forward over her avocado toast and caviar and asks, "Your name is Adina, right?"

I freeze under the weight of her question. The other girls are watching, some more slyly than others.

"Yeah," I say quietly, giving her the benefit of the doubt. "Pass the bacon, please."

Wordlessly, Penthesilea passes the platter to me, and I dump at least six strips onto my plate. The spread is decadence: poached eggs, a porcelain bowl of caviar, a platter of lox and chives atop freshly baked bagels. Croissants that look so perfect, they have to be imported. My stomach snarls, reminding me of my missed dinner and the strength I'll need for today.

At least I'll be well fed, marching to my death. I help myself to each and every thing, trying things I've never been able to afford before. I don't care if I look like a starving urchin, or whatever Esme would call me. Decorum doesn't matter now, like Saint warned me. The rules are different. The first bite of the croissants is everything, steam rolling into my nose, the flaky layers melting like butter on my tongue. I can't help the pleased moan and Penthesilea smiles, amused. I half smile back at her.

"The caviar is good too," she says. "It's a bit fishy. A bit salty."

"Like ocean water," Hawthorne adds, eager to assist *someone* now that her supreme leader is out of commission.

I do as they bid, and wow. "Oh, you're right, it's very good," I mumble around a mouthful, following it up with the most fatty, perfectly salted bacon I've ever had in my life.

"How are your *accommodations*, Penthesilea?" Jacqueline asks, turning to her while I eat, self-consciously stroking the light acne scars on her cheek.

"Very nice. I face the rose garden," Penthesilea says pleasantly as she butters another piece of toast. She doesn't seem to catch the malice in Jacqueline's voice, or perhaps she *does* hear it, but she's not letting it bother her. "I used to take a lot of walks through the garden. It's lovely in first bloom."

"That's nice," Jacqueline says dismissively. "You have your room to yourself, don't you?"

Penthesilea's grip on her knife gets just a hair tighter. "Yes, I do. After . . . last night's tragedy."

I nearly drop my own fork. Penthesilea was *rooming* with Margaret? She seems barely affected by her murder, or at least she wants everyone to think she is. But the longer I look at her, *really* look at Penthesilea, past her hazy edges and frothy bliss, I can see the rigidity to her spine.

"Did you know Margaret?" Jacqueline asks. She leans in, looking at me again. "Adina, I mean."

"No, I didn't."

Jacqueline makes a face, like she doesn't understand. "Then why did you run to her?"

My stomach gurgles and I'm no longer hungry. I can feel my heart hardening to her, hardening to nearly all these girls who seem to lack basic empathy. The worst part of it all is how nothing feels like it's changed at all for them. Margaret's life was nothing but an inconvenient end to a pleasant evening.

"Why *didn't* you?" I retort. Jacqueline rears back.

She sniffs as if the question itself is offensive, and she looks at Penthesilea again, who must seem easier to deal with than me. "Well, what's done is done, I suppose. Penthesilea, I've found that I don't have *nearly* enough space," Jacqueline says, leaning forward with her shark smile. "Care to play a game?"

Penthesilea places her knife down and laughs. "Oh, so you're in the know—a bit early for a game, isn't it?"

In the know?

"'Early'? I don't know the meaning of the word," Jacqueline tosses back.

Penthesilea quirks an eyebrow. "Cards or dice?"

Before Jacqueline can decide, the doors are thrown open.

Leighton Remington stands in the doorway, dressed in a sleek sheath dress that makes each of us look sloppier by the second. She brushes back an imaginary flyaway, patting it into her perfectly coiffed blond hair.

"Ladies, finish your breakfasts in quick order. Once you do, you will return to your rooms to find today's attire spread and ironed. Your training begins now."

Everyone moves collectively. Jacqueline shovels the rest of her avocado toast into her mouth. Penthesilea slots a piece of buttered rye between her teeth, and they both get up.

"Come on. We were already late for breakfast," Saint mutters under her breath. She grabs my wrist, tugging me up after her.

"Miss Walker."

I jerk to a stop and turn on my heel, swallowing.

"Yes, Dr. Remington?" I mutter.

She tilts her head. "Before we begin, I'd like to see you in my office."

CHAPTER

 10

"DID I DO SOMETHING WRONG, DR. REMINGTON?"

"Do sit down, Miss Walker," Leighton says. She shuts the door behind her and walks past me in her crocodile pumps.

Her office is a grand space, with built-in bookshelves lined with tomes ranging from what looks like a collection of Dante's poetry to the latest edition of the DSM. The elegant jewel-tone wallpaper complements the panels of rich, dark wood. Her desk looks like it's carved from the same, old but gleaming with a fresh polish. I look to the red leather chair that I expect she wants me to sit in, but she takes the seat there, leaving only the velvet green couch that dominates the back wall.

I squirm. "Dr. Remington—"

"Please, Miss Walker," Leighton insists, in a way that makes it clear that she's no longer asking. I'm quick to do as she demands, surprised to find when I sit that it's hard, despite its plush appearance. "And do call me Aunt Leighton. Most of the girls do."

Leighton Remington is *not* going to be my aunt.

"What is this about?" I blurt.

I don't want to accuse her of anything or let her accuse me. While she has a glacial mask to the planes of her face, she doesn't look cold, just calm, like an undisturbed tundra.

"Last night a tragic event occurred. And where others stood still, you displayed a remarkable amount of compassion. In fact, I applaud you."

My worry stills. "Really?"

"Yes. Margaret must have been in a considerable amount of pain. You had no idea what was wrong with her, whether it was contagious, but you put that aside and wanted to help her," Leighton says. She leans forward in her seat, her hands folded over her knee. "It's commendable."

"Then, why . . . ?" I trail off. I shouldn't ask. I'm not meant to ask.

Leighton sighs and looks away. Her mask evaporates, and she lays her shame bare. Her shoulders sag and she moves even more deliberately, like it's the only thing holding her together. It's so honest that my stomach turns, unused to it from someone like them.

Except she wasn't like them. I remember. Not at first.

"Did you know that I was once in a Finish quite like this?" Leighton asks.

"Yes," I whisper.

"Then I'm sure you've already heard of my roots. Like you, I did not come from a family of means. We lived in town, but my summers were spent here, at the estate, helping the dearly departed Mrs. Remington in her garden. I attended Edgewater due to the generosity of the Remington Family. I was in the same year as my husband, but we didn't move in the same circles. Still, they saw my potential and invited me to participate," Leighton explains. She sounds almost wistful. I want to ask if this place has changed for her over the years. It must've. Just yesterday it felt like a fairy-tale castle. Now it feels like a tomb, a place of stale air and too many secrets. "Like you, I thought it was an opportunity to . . . 'level the playing field,' as Pierce loves to tout. I wished to reach my full potential. Instead, I learned that it was a game of quite . . . deadly proportions." Her face falls again and she looks more tired than anything else, the lines around her eyes deepening.

"Then *why* continue it?" I demand.

"Because much like you . . . I was powerless to stop it. Adina, I see myself in you."

"Do you?"

"Yes. A girl of not many means invited to a place that does not want her, and in which she does not fit," Leighton says.

"You look like you fit in pretty nicely," I say. Her story does hold an uncomfortable mirror up to my own life, except it's distorted by the fact that this woman looks exactly like them and nothing like me.

Leighton laughs, a rich sound that's more real than any word that she's spoken to me yet. "Well, if you win, one day I might say the same about you," she retorts, missing my point entirely, of course. She sits up taller. "Yes, I give off the appearance that I am a part of this family, I admit. But, Adina, as you well know, just a number of years in an institution doesn't give you power. They have leverage over all of us. I am not a true Game Mistress, I'm a pawn here too. The Remingtons have rules and I cannot change them simply because I want to. Neither can you."

"What does that mean?"

Leighton doesn't hesitate again. "I am aware that you left your room last night and attempted to leave the estate."

My heart crawls into my throat and stops. I don't breathe, bolted down in place, my fingers crushing into the velvet sofa beneath me.

"Adina," she says, sterner now, her voice demanding my attention. "From the beginning of our conversation, have I ever indicated that you are in trouble?"

"No . . ." I trail off, my voice ending in a horrified wheeze.

"Exactly," Leighton says. "You attempted to leave, and Miss Liu drew you back upstairs. This was the right thing for her to do. So ultimately no rules were broken. But if they *were*, broken rules result in consequences. For all of us."

"What kind of consequences?" I whisper.

Leighton looks far away again, like she's remembering something she'd prefer not to. "They would try to hurt you. The Finish can only exist this way because to be invited, one must volunteer information about herself and her family. To reveal assures mutual destruction between the families that have offered their daughters to compete and the Remingtons, if the results don't go their way. You have no secrets. But you do have people. People that you love."

Toni. My *parents*.

"No!" I declare, shaking my head. "No, no, *no*—"

"Adina, play by the rules, as I have done, and no harm will come to them. Keep your head down and remember you are not like them. They are cruel and vicious for cruelty's sake. This is just a game to them. But . . . not to you. Never for you," Leighton says swiftly, sliding forward in her chair and taking my clammy hand in her cool one. "Do you understand?"

"Yes," I whisper. "Yes, I understand."

"Good," Leighton says, and she smiles, so gentle that I try to smile back. It falters, and Leighton sighs again, shaking her head. "I am your ally. I will make sure that you get through this. I've done it before. I made it out alive and whole and with the world at my fingertips, not just a Remington husband. Will you trust me to help you?"

Finally, my vision clears and I feel the possibility of survival stir within me, stoked by the threat to my family. I will play by the rules to the best of my ability. I will get through this with my hands clean, with my conscience clear, with my family safe, maybe even, if Leighton is telling the truth, all that I desire. And I will because Leighton did. Whole. That must mean she didn't have to *hurt* anyone. If I win, it will not be because I was a game or an amusement for anyone. It will be because I am here for what is mine, like Leighton. Let the others fight over Pierce.

"Yes, I will, Dr. . . . Aunt Leighton," I confess.

Leighton leads me to the rotary phone on her desk and leans against it, her hand strong and reassuring on my shoulder. "Go on. Call your parents if you want reassurance."

I reach for the phone hungrily . . . before I let my hand drop to my side.

I want to make my mother proud. At graduation, she promised me that she was. But I could've made her prouder. I *should've* made her prouder. Now I have the chance.

All that veiled disappointment will go away, after this. Even though the stakes are now higher than I ever imagined, after everything my parents have sacrificed to get me here, in this position, I still might finally be able to deliver on that promise to be *better*, to have better. To be twice as good.

"No," I say, meeting Leighton's eyes, recognizing the test, and nervously I decide, "I . . . I'll play the game."

CHAPTER

 11

JODHPURS ARE THE MOST UNCOMFORTABLE PANTS in the history of existence. They cling tightly to my thighs and cut awkwardly into the skin at my ankles, and wearing them, even in just the mild summer air, I feel so hot.

"Have you ever ridden a horse before, Adina?" Leighton asks as we walk across the green toward the stables.

"Does one trail ride count?" I did that once, on one of my trips up to Esme's country house with the other girls. It was uncomfortable, not just being up on a horse, but also because I was the only one who didn't know how, and no one had thought to teach me. I vowed to never do it again.

Leighton laughs to herself. "Well, that's one area in which our backgrounds differ."

Another thrum of pride calms me. This woman—tall and blond and perfect—sees herself in me. Enough that she wants me to *win* this godforsaken competition. And wouldn't that just be cosmic justice, in the end?

"So . . . the Ride is literal, then?" I ask. I'm not sure if I'm pushing my luck, asking for information before it's given to the other girls, but Leighton has already made what feels like strange allowances.

"Yes, quite literal. And it's less of a ride and more of a race. But the Ride sounds far more elegant, doesn't it?" Leighton says.

Every answer turns into a question. Leighton is worthy of her medical license.

She says nothing else until we reach the stables. She stands taller the moment the other girls spot us, and I do the same, determined not to shrink into myself anymore even as I can feel their curiosity on me like jagged little knives. "Go and join the girls, Adina, dear."

Quick to follow her command, I walk ahead, and Saint steps to the side, allowing me to slot in next to her. Her fingers wrap around my wrist and she leans in, quick to hiss, "What did she want? Are you in trouble?"

"No. We were just talking about Margaret. That's all. She wanted to make sure I was okay," I whisper back.

"Does she know . . . ?" Saint trails off.

I bite my bottom lip. "Yes, but we're good," I hiss back.

Saint gives me a look, like she doesn't believe me. I look away at the other girls, hoping she won't ask anything else. Hawthorne is at the other end of the long arc, but she doesn't look my way. Some of the girls next to her are staring right back at me, though, curious and accusing in equal measure.

"Ladies, thank you for being so prompt," Leighton breathes. "Today marks the true beginning of your training. Here is the first lesson: Life will throw many obstacles at you. Don't allow them to unseat you. Keep dignity and grace, always. Three days from now, you will embark on the Ride, a horse race through many challenges. The winner will be ranked first, and will gain the special privileges that that rightly entails."

"Special privileges?" one girl asks.

Leighton hums and tilts her head. "Cocktails with the family and private dinners with the Remington heir to discuss . . . future career opportunities and otherwise."

Jacqueline straightens, and sharp inhales crackle with the tension that suddenly fills the stable.

Meals with Pierce Remington. An alleged advantage.

I may not want that particular prize, but having his ear would give me another ally in the house. This is allegedly all for him, after all. He picked *me* in the woods. *Me.* All because of the attention I paid him. I could do that again.

"If you have ridden before, step to the left. You will be instructed by Trainer Rogers. He will introduce you to your steeds and give you the proper equipment you will need," Leighton commands. A man in riding jeans steps out from around the corner in the stable and snaps his fingers.

"This way, ladies," Rogers says gruffly.

Penthesilea moves first. The knot in my throat throbs. Penthesilea is a decorated equestrian. She's clearly at an advantage here. Saint squeezes my wrist one more time before she gives me a meaningful look, one that tells me that she'll definitely interrogate me later, and then she's off with the other girls, because *of course* she's ridden. As they head off, I realize I'm alone except for that one girl who asked about special privileges.

I recognize her briefly as the beachy Californian model, though she looks different without her makeup. It's clear she works out, though. God, if I'd only known that all that time spent studying would've been better spent working *out,* of all things.

"Uh, hi, I'm Adina," I murmur.

The girl's nose wrinkles. "I know," she says dismissively, without introducing herself back.

Okay.

"Do be polite, Hannah G," Aunt Leighton warns, but turns to look at something.

"Hannah G?" I repeat.

Hannah G's sneer deepens. "Well, I'm clearly not Hannah R," she spits.

I can't remember who the hell Hannah R is.

But then Hannah G puts her hands on her hips and sidles closer to me, turning a more doe-eyed expression on just as Aunt Leighton turns back. She looks suitably unimpressed, thankfully.

"As the pair of you are novices, I have elected to go with a much more personal and aggressive approach for your training to put you at less of a disadvantage. You will be trained by my nephew," Leighton says, her voice dripping with a strange amount of distaste.

Hannah G straightens hopefully. "Pierce?"

"No, I'm the shorter, less impressive brother. Sorry to disappoint."

Graham. Hannah G deflates entirely, and she crosses her arms, cursing under her breath. Graham swans in from around the corner, dressed far more casually than I've ever seen a Remington. I don't think I've ever seen any of them in a pair of jeans. Even as a child, Pierce was perpetually dressed in chinos.

Leighton gives him a warning look. "Do your job, Graham. If they fail, there will be consequences."

"For who?" Graham retorts pointedly.

"I'm being serious, Graham. For once in your life, do as you're told," Leighton commands coldly. She turns to me and warms, just the tiniest bit. "Now I'm going to speak to Esme about last night. Good luck."

Graham groans, pinching the bridge of his nose, looking up at the vaulted ceiling.

"Okay, Graham, get it together. You volunteered for this job," he mutters under his breath.

"Do you even ride?" Hannah G asks. "I know your brother does."

Graham glares at her. "Every Remington rides. And I volunteered because I'm trying to minimize the amount of death here, in case last night didn't clue you in to what's at stake. And you *will* if you don't fix your attitude."

Hannah G opens her mouth and then closes it, more fish- than model-like now, and I choke on my own spit.

"The Ride is an obstacle course as much as a race," Graham explains. "You will be faced with hedge jumps, bank climbs, river swims, and mud pits. Horses have died on the Taxis Ditch jump."

"And girls?" Hannah G asks, her voice smaller. Suddenly, she looks young, quiet, and terrified. She looks like Margaret did, when she died in my arms, and I can tell for all her bravado that she's thinking of her too.

Graham folds his arms over his chest. "There have been what they call accidents. But beyond the jumps there's only one rule in the Ride—finish the obstacle course. Anything you do to ensure someone *doesn't* has historically been considered fair game. Though I very much hope that will not be the case this time."

I shiver. Graham shakes himself and looks away.

"Come on, let me get you familiar with the horses," he says.

Graham leads us deeper into the stable, going past a few empty stalls. Hannah G hangs back, staring through the slitted windows to where the other girls are already in the ring. I keep in step with Graham.

"I get the distinct impression that you aren't a fan of the Finish,"

I say coolly. But here he is participating, not stopping it. He really is no better than them.

"Oh, I'm not," Graham says, grinding his teeth together and rubbing at the patchy stubble on his jaw. He gives me a long side-eyed look, the kind that makes my skin tingle underneath it, but I refuse to look away. "I don't want to be here at all, but Four was . . . unsettled by last night. I want to make sure that everything else goes smoothly, fairly, and that there won't be any more . . . accidents. So, I'm here."

Accidents, like he said before. If I die, it will be an "accident."

"Is that what we're calling Margaret, too?" I ask.

Graham nods. "One thing you'll learn is that words have specific meaning here, and even though what happened . . . *happened* outside one of the events, it's best to call it an accident. Truth is what they say it is. So, it was an accident because that's all it can be. You understand?" he asks. And I don't know him, but I can hear the warning. It's not a threat, but it's clear that this has been drilled into him and will now be expected of us.

"So what happened to last night's . . . accident?" I ask, and then my stomach revolts at the very idea of calling Margaret's murder something so polite. There was nothing polite about what happened to her.

Graham grimaces. "Margaret's body was delivered to the coroner this morning. She'll be hidden in the morgue until . . . until it's over. I wrote the condolence letter to her family. I told them you tried to save her. I thought it was important that they know that someone . . . held her. That someone *cared*."

My heart twinges, and I can't look at him anymore, my vision blurring in front of me with tears for the first time since it all happened. It feels like a thousand years ago, but it was only twelve hours. Every minute here feels like a century.

"Thanks," I say roughly.

We stop in front of a stall, and Graham clears his throat awkwardly. He turns to face the pair of us. "Right. So, um, this is going to be a really weird lesson, because you two need to be able to not just ride but jump and whatever in three days. So, these mares are our best for beginners, Starlight and Princess—"

"I call Princess," Hannah G proclaims, darting over to the butternut-colored horse. She coos as she shoves into the stall, reaching forward to pat the side of the mare. "Oh, you're just so *pretty*."

I look over at Starlight, a dusky, gray-speckled mare that looks back at me with the same amount of wariness. Good, we're on the same level of caution. Strong building blocks for our new working relationship.

"Yeah, whatever. Anyway, Starlight and Princess are really good mares. Kind and reliable. They're definitely not, like, prize-winning thoroughbreds, but they're already trained for this sort of thing, so it's all about just earning their trust," Graham explains. He steps over to Starlight, and his smile is different from the one that he's been sporting this entire time. The bitterness slips away, and he leans into the horse's side, stroking Starlight's mane.

"Is she yours?" I ask.

Graham shakes his head. "No. She used to be my mother's."

I don't know a thing about Graham and Pierce's mother.

No. That's not true. Now I know she won the Finish.

"Are we going to ride now?" Hannah G interrupts.

Graham's expression hardens again. "No. You need to learn how to saddle a horse first."

He takes us through the motions, teaching us how to greet our horses, how to put the saddle on them, how to check if they're nervous or anything other than perfectly steady. He speaks with authority, and it's clear, no matter how he acts, Graham is still a Remington. This is all in his blood.

"Now that your horses are all tacked up, let's take them out to the practice ring. Come on," Graham commands.

I swallow hard, gripping Starlight's reins just a little too hard. The mare snorts and stomps a warning at me. "Sorry, sorry," I whisper. "Look . . . this is my second time with a horse, so, uh . . ." I stutter to a stop as Hannah G stalks out of her stall, leading Princess and effectively cutting me off.

"Jesus, Walker, you're so weird," Hannah G sneers, elbowing me as she leads Princess down the stable hall. "Which way, Graham?"

"To the right, first barn door."

I follow Hannah G, taking careful steps through hay and dirt.

"You're going to be fine," Graham says, leaning over to grab the mounting block.

"That's what *you* say," I sigh as we walk through the stable.

"It *is* what I say, since I'm your teacher," Graham says smugly. When we enter the ring, I realize how much bigger it is than the stall. But the Ride must be even bigger. The magnitude of what's going to happen in just three days is overwhelming.

"Hey, um, how long is the Ride?" I whisper softly.

"About four miles," Graham says solemnly.

"How big is this horse arena?"

Graham swallows. "*Much* smaller than that. You can go around this ring in about fifteen seconds. It takes an average of ten minutes to get through the Ride."

"Have you ever done the Ride?" I ask.

Graham doesn't meet my eyes when he says, "I have. But it wasn't really the Ride. It was just the path it's raced on. The jumps and ditches are one thing. With the other *riders* working against you, that's another."

I laugh hoarsely. "Right."

"Just learn how to mount your horse first," Graham says, trying to distract me with a more manageable step. I nod and he clears his throat. "Hey, Hannah—"

"Hannah *G*. I'm *not* Hannah R," she reminds us again.

What the fuck is so wrong with Hannah R that she doesn't want to be mistaken for her?

"Right," Graham mutters. "Come over so I can tell you how to mount—"

But Hannah G is already sliding one boot into her stirrup.

She places her free hand to the saddle and swings her leg over in a perfect mount. Then she sits primly on the top of the horse and stares directly at Graham.

"I did a campaign with Gucci on horseback," she says, like that's something everyone does.

"Of course you did," Graham says. He drops the mounting block right next to Starlight, then turns to me, offering one hand. "May I?"

I'm not stupid enough to not take the help. I grab his hand and immediately, the air in my lungs seems to dissipate. I shake the feeling away and pretend I don't feel the heat of his body right behind me.

Get a fucking grip, Adina. This isn't a period drama.

I will not let this Remington man distract me. I step up on the mounting block.

"Now, grab the reins tight. Slide your left foot into the stirrup. Good, just like that. Hand on the saddle. Then swing your right foot over."

His instructions echo in my ears and suddenly I'm off the ground.

"Yeah, uh . . . what now?" I ask.

Graham smiles, grabbing the reins from me. "Now we get you comfortable. Hannah G, you need any help?"

"Nope," Hannah G says with a pop on her *p*. She squeezes her thighs, and then Princess breaks into a clean trot around the arena. "I had ponies at my birthday parties every year until I was twelve."

Graham begins to lead me around the arena, and I lurch as suddenly I'm in motion through no choice of my own.

I'm not riding so much as following Graham around the ring. Hannah G is going in the opposite direction. Despite her anecdote about her ponies, she keeps shifting uncomfortably, and Princess doesn't seem particularly keen to obey her sharply squealed commands.

I refocus on Starlight, who has begun to wander like my attention.

"Easy," I mumble, and Starlight eases. The ambling trot beneath me starts to feel almost normal after a go or two around the ring. I sit taller, and I even manage to find a tiny smile for Graham when he finally passes me the reins and I loop them around my wrists. He returns that smile, but more absently, distracted as he looks away to the other ring.

I follow his gaze and see Penthesilea galloping around the circle, standing in her stirrups, leaning forward, her thighs engaged in her tight riding pants. I can't see her eyes beneath the brim of her riding helmet, but the power that she holds in her core is taut and I imagine they must be laser focused. She races forward ahead of the pack, and I think I hear her bark a command at the midnight black thoroughbred she's on as she nears a massive hurdle.

And then she soars over it, like she and her horse are one—like they're air.

"Graham . . . do I have to learn how to do that?" I whisper.

Graham doesn't answer, but his expression—the way the corners of his mouth turn downward and his shoulders stiffen—is answer enough.

CHAPTER

12

"JESUS, I'M STARVING," I PROCLAIM THE MOMENT I meet up with Saint at the barn entrance. My growling stomach has been waging war with my disgust and fear for hours, and finally, hunger is winning again.

"Same," Saint admits. "How was your lesson? I saw it was with the other Remington boy. I always forget his name."

"Graham," I remind her.

"Yes. Well, he doesn't make much of a lasting impression. At least, not compared to his brother," Saint declares.

I don't tell her that I'm starting to disagree.

"It was good. I'm trotting on my own. Galloped for a minute toward the end. It was really fast, and I was terrified, but Starlight's a good horse," I acknowledge. Saint nods, and she even looks at me with a bit of pride.

"That's good. We jumped a few times. I rode when I was *much* younger, but I remembered the basics quite easily," Saint says.

"Like a bike, yeah?"

Saint's brow furrows. "Is that . . . an American saying?"

"Oh . . . yes, I guess. I wonder, do they have an equivalent in Switzerland?" I ask.

Saint shrugs. "I don't know. I don't really like the Swiss."

I snort into my hand and we begin the trek back to the main house.

"Hey, Adina! Saint! Wait up!"

We don't exactly stop, but we slow down just enough that Hawthorne doesn't need to sprint to catch up. She arrives, stray blond flyaways sticking to her sweaty forehead and sliding down the bridge of her nose. She smiles brightly, her cheeks flushed a healthy pink.

"I've heard that there'll be a late lunch for us in the common room. Let's go ahead before the other girls get first pickings," Hawthorne says, walking briskly past us. She turns backward as she walks in, lively in a way that I've never seen her. "What are you two up to after lunch?"

"Lying on my stomach? My ass hurts. We just rode for, like, four hours," I retort.

Hawthorne waves it away like it's nothing. "You get used to it. Did you see us jumping? Those were hard. I've only ever ridden casually. Like trails in Vermont when we used to visit Esme's country house. Remember that, Adina?"

I wince. "Yeah . . . I do."

Hawthorne continues. "Maybe we'll go up for winter as a girls' trip. We'll be in college, but it's good to remember high school friends."

It's ridiculous on a number of levels. Esme's family probably sold that country house already. I'm not even going to college. Plus, we might not be alive, as she well knows.

"I don't really understand your attachment to this Esme," Saint says. "Adina seems to have severed that tie."

"Yeah, really quickly, I remember," Hawthorne says, and there's a bite in her voice that makes me actually turn to look her in the eye. But it's gone just as soon as it appeared, disappearing with Hawthorne's sigh. "We've been friends since we were kids. We were in the same playmate group and we just . . . she *gets* me more than anyone else."

There's something wild about her, outside Esme's overbearing presence, a restlessness that unsettles. Her eyes move like she's taking *everything* in so much faster than we are, and her smile is relaxed. Outside Esme's shadow, Hawthorne actually looks like a person, not a pale imitation of herself.

"You're all adults now. You can pick your own friends," Saint says dismissively.

Hawthorne blinks owlishly, like the thought has never even occurred to her.

We trudge up the stairs, and some of the girls peel off for a quick shower. One of them is visibly trembling with exhaustion, and for a moment I feel something like camaraderie with her—which ends as she turns to glower at me. I roll my eyes, cracking my neck as I lean heavily into the banister, my breath whistling. We're all competing and I don't want to show weakness, but my muscles ache, and I know, in the morning, I'll feel like I've been hit by a truck.

Despite how much I want to fall asleep, I know I can't. This is valuable time spent with these girls. Watching them. Learning them. Graham and Leighton have tried to be reassuring, that there's a difference between what *might* happen during the Finish separate from the *accident* that has definitely already occurred. But knowing that difference doesn't make learning to ride a horse in three days any easier, or make me trust these other girls any more.

The door to the common room is already open, and I stop short. Saint nearly collides with my back and Hawthorne actually rams my shoulder with hers as she stutters to a stop.

"Hello, girls."

Esme lounges across the chaise, an entire platter of finger sandwiches balanced on the table by her head. She plucks one up with her long acrylics and bites into it with far more relish than necessary. Her burgundy lips pull into a wide smile.

"Lunch is served," she announces with a flourish. Her gaze flits over the group and she clears her throat. "Jackie, Hannah G, Hannah R, come sit by me. I never finished telling you my story about my *fabulous* trip through Europe last summer."

Hawthorne has stopped breathing next to me. Esme didn't call for her.

There's a moment where the girls hesitate. They aren't sure

after what she's done. Her absence this morning, coupled with Hawthorne mentioning that she's been disciplined, seem to be confirmation of what she is capable of. They also know that whether or not Esme *did* hurt Margaret, she's the one who's still here, still in the running, having taken one of their competitors down. I can see the choice before they even make it.

The girls rush to her side, dogs to their master. Vassals to their liege.

I recognize each of them as enemies officially. At least I finally know what Hannah R looks like—very New York, the vibes definitely different from Hannah G, so I can see why she doesn't want to be mistaken for her.

"You weren't at breakfast this morning. Did you eat?" Hannah R says attentively.

"Aunt Leighton says that she spoke to you. Are you in trouble?" Hannah G asks.

"I did eat, Hannah R, thank you for asking. One of the maids brought me breakfast in bed," Esme says carefully. "And Aunt Leighton speaks to all the girls. The Finish is quite taxing on the mind, and as a licensed psychiatrist, she's most equipped in handling the emotional challenges that the Finish creates."

"You mean emotional challenges that *you* create." I don't regret speaking aloud for once. Now everything's in the open. It's useless to pretend.

Esme's cold gaze flits over to me. She slowly sits up on the chaise.

"Whatever do you mean, Adina?" she asks sweetly.

"You killed someone yesterday," I insist.

It's like I've spoken something unforgivable, the way they redirect their gazes to the floor. Hannah R swallows a sniffle and Esme casts her a warning look. Pretending is easier when it's something you've done all your life, and confronting the truth is too ugly for pretty girls. Margaret was a pretty girl too, and that did not serve her at all.

"What a *cruel* accusation," Esme simpers with a pout. "Hawthorne shares a room with me. If I wanted to hurt someone, wouldn't she have been an easier target? Right, Hawthorne?"

"Right," Hawthorne says weakly, but also with a touch of odd relief. Like she's been *waiting* to be addressed.

Hawthorne marches over to her without a backward glance. She sits gingerly on the chaise next to Esme and Esme giggles, leaning into her side.

"How was training?" she asks, just for Hawthorne. This is the Hawthorne I remember. The Hawthorne who was always Esme's friend first and never mine at all.

I stalk away, glaring down at the spread in front of me, the charcuterie of meats and cheeses and fruits becoming an abstract painting. A platter of dainty sandwiches swims in front of me.

"If you're going to go at her, go at her with a purpose," Saint hisses.

"She murdered a girl and no one was going to say a word to her. She thinks she got away with it and telling her she didn't *is* my purpose," I say, seething and piling my plate full of the rich meats and expensive cheeses.

"She's watching you," Saint warns. "She's pretending that she isn't, but she is. She *wants* you to get mad and come at her so no one will blink an eye if she does it to you."

Well. As usual, Esme's gotten her wish.

CHAPTER

13

I WAIT FOR ESME TO MAKE HER MOVE OVER THE next two days. She doesn't.

The day after our lunch altercation, she joins us for training. It's then that I realize that the real punishment, besides her morning "time-out," was having less time to prepare. Not that she needs it. She fits in effortlessly with the more advanced group, and as Graham rides beside Hannah and me, I catch glimpses of her. Esme's not as talented as Penthesilea, who rides like she's Artemis incarnate, but she's right behind her, out of sheer will. Whenever they race in groups of three, Esme leans forward in her saddle, her eyes narrowed into slits as she chases Penthesilea.

But she always comes in second. And it always enrages her.

The day after, I learn to jump for the first time. It terrifies me. Starlight knows what to do far more than I do, so I try to just trust her, but still, I fall off the first time. It doesn't hurt so much as shock the fuck out of me. But after I get back on and do it successfully, Graham calls it progress, and I see my ease and confidence building, even though it's slow. There's no way for me to feel ready in time—they don't *want* any of us to be ready, they want us frightened—but I gain a single-mindedness. It's only the first event. Winning for me will be getting through it alive.

After falling time and again through hedges and fences, I'm achy all over, but getting used to it. Graham recommends ice baths, but I'm too nervous to call Mr. Caine for the ice, so I take two freezing showers a day.

That night after the latest, my teeth chatter and I tug my robe tighter around my body where I sit with Saint, the cool air prickling my skin despite the warmth of the setting sun cutting through the glass windows. I briefly cast a cursory look over at the map we taped to the inside of the wardrobe. We found the map to the Ride sealed in a heavy cream envelope along with an invitation to this evening's Repartee, our first, when we came back from training.

"Come on now, Adina. Pay attention," Saint says sharply.

I jolt, flicking my eyes back over to her. She sits across from me, glaring, closely guarding her cards. I look down at my hand, refocusing on our game. "What's it called when I have three cards with the same suit? Is that three of a kind or does it have a special name?"

"Tā mā de, you can't tell me your hand!" Saint barks.

"I didn't!"

"What suit do you have? Hearts?"

"Maybe."

"See, you just did," Saint says, throwing her cards down. "God, you're terrible at card games. What's going to happen if Esme challenges you to a game tonight?"

I purse my lips. "The person challenged always picks the game, anyway. We'll play Old Maid or something."

"Okay, Adina, if you don't know how to play real card games, why do you have a deck?" Saint asks.

I swallow and slowly turn my head. I stare at her ear. "They belong to my best friend, Toni. She gave them to me to keep me occupied. . . ." I hiccup out a laugh, remembering when I thought there might be moments of boredom. "I was supposed to go to Yale, but something happened. She feels responsible. She's not, but . . . she encouraged me to come out of guilt and now . . ."

Saint flops back on her comforter and sighs, folding her hands over her belly. She stares up at the canopy of her bed, probably studying the stray patterns up there. I lie next to her, searching for whatever she's staring at. For a moment it feels like lying on the carpet with Toni, and I miss her like an amputated limb, a haunting.

"Well, if your friend is from Edgewater, it sounds a little like she might have set you up here," Saint says as she slips off the bed, jutting her chin at the wall clock—we've only an hour to get ready.

"No, she didn't. She's not like that. She . . . she was on the outside looking in too," I defend. Saint snorts and it incenses me, her dismissal. "She didn't know. She couldn't have known. She would've *never* told me to come here. . . ," but I trail off, startled to find I'm not sure even if I trust my own conviction. Not anymore. Charles is Pierce's *best* friend. Did he . . . ? No. I shake it off.

"Well, what are *you* doing here, then, if you knew what this was about?"

Saint turns to meet my gaze as she draws a garment bag out from her trunk. She tilts her head, examining the contents, and then tosses it aside. "My father wants to expand into the States. We're in real estate. The Remingtons have their fingers in every pie—petroleum, glass, energy, fiber. Things you need to build buildings. And I had this idea . . . that we should contract with them. We'd pay a reduced price for using them exclusively. And in turn, since it's a crowded market here, the Remingtons would help us make room. I'm here to lay groundwork. To force this contract and prove that I know what I'm *talking* about."

"It all sounds . . . dangerous," I mutter.

"Maybe. But I'm a survivor and I have leverage now, being here. Remington doesn't want to cross my family. I'm in control," Saint says. She believes it to be true. I'm not so sure.

I don't say anything. Instead, I move toward the wardrobe, reaching for my wrap dress, which I'm sure everyone will whisper about, when a knock on the door distracts me.

When I come to the door, Saint stands just behind it, lying in wait just in case. I crack it slightly.

"Yes?" I relax minutely when I see only the pale shape of Mr. Caine in his crisp suit.

"Miss Walker, if you would, the mistress of the house took the liberty of providing something suitable," he says, his eyebrow twitching with impatience, or maybe disapproval. I take a step back, squaring my feet as I open the door a little wider. He offers a garment bag.

The crisp white muslin is just another confirmation of Leighton's favor. She really *does* see us aligned in purpose, and it gives me some much-needed confidence going into another night of the unknown. This will be an even more formal night than the past few, and still I haven't seen a single other girl repeat an outfit except for our riding uniforms, in case a Remington showed their face during dinner. Of course, they never did.

I thank Mr. Caine and then shut the door. Immediately, I unzip the garment bag, revealing the semiformal dress. It's couture. Black, like my borrowed dress, with the same shape but now with a bustier bodice, sheer netting sleeves, and a black tulle ballerina skirt, all kept modest by its tea length.

"That's Oscar de la Renta. Classic," Saint murmurs, stroking the nylon top.

"It's beautiful," I whisper. I've never owned anything so beautiful. I bury my face into the fabric, breathing in. It smells strangely like Leighton, though I can tell it's new.

"You want to smell it or wear it?" Saint asks.

I roll my eyes at her sarcasm as I strip out of my robe. The bruises on the insides of my thighs are stark. I poke at the yellowing spots and Saint frowns, unconsciously rubbing her own shoulder, the one she fell on yesterday.

"You okay?" I ask.

"Yeah," she says. I don't quite believe her as she distractedly goes through another trunk before pulling out a turquoise silk number, the kind that will spill over every line of her body. "Do you have any gel?"

I snort. "Do I have *gel*?" I go to my second bag, the one full of my hair products. "Help yourself."

As Saint goes to the bathroom to get herself ready, I slip into my dress, gasping at the feel of the finery against my bare skin. I try to reach behind me to zip it up but only manage it halfway. Still, it's easily the best I've ever looked. Until I glance over at my casual blocky heels. They'll look terrible with the dress.

Saint is humming in the bathroom mirror, probably going through her massive jewelry collection, searching for those long dangly diamonds that'll look nice with the simplicity of the silk slip dress. At least, it's what I'd pick out for tonight. It's dramatic, the kind of look that you'd want to see in close-ups. I've spent all my life seeing girls dress that way for school dances and sweet sixteens, all working hard for the effortlessness that Saint actually achieves.

As she assembles an armor of makeup, slick black hair, and

YSL heels, I envy her just like I've envied the rest of them, all these years. But when I catch a glimpse of myself in the mirror, in this dress, I know that I *too* could be an object of envy. It feels like a costume, but I wonder—just for a *tiny* moment—what it would feel like if it weren't. But the memory of Margaret's purpling face and the soreness of bruised skin banishes the thought, and my confidence erodes. I need to get it back.

"We should go to the common room," I say, the thought sparking.

"Why?"

"Because that's where they'll be. And I want them to see me," I say firmly.

Saint's mouth twitches. "Risky, but could have good payoff if you want to unbalance Esme," she says. "And she needs some unbalancing."

"Agreed."

When we enter the common room, I push my shoulders back.

Esme is holding court, dressed like a queen in a red gown with a plunging neckline, with Hawthorne standing at her right hand. Hawthorne has always looked like a porcelain doll to me. Dainty, rose-cheeked, pale, and breakable. She looks even more so next to her best friend, in a sea-green dress that looks more suited for a sixties mod girl, her long blond hair spilling down her back to meet her short hem. But tonight, shockingly, she's the one in the diamond collar.

"—course is unwieldy, but hold to the right and stay in tight

142

formation and we'll make it through. Are we clear?" Esme says coldly, tapping on the map she has spread over the coffee table, the other girls, dripping in taffeta, all nodding seriously, like this is a war meeting.

Esme stops when she notices me in the doorway. "Walker, why are you dressed in this season's de la Renta? Aren't you poor?"

Aren't you about to be? I bite my tongue. There are other ways to challenge Esme, to demonstrate that I'm ahead of her in this game.

Instead, I smile sweetly. "Aunt Leighton noticed that I was . . . lacking in more formal wear. She just wanted to make sure I feel like I belong." *And I do.*

"You look like a pretender," Esme accuses.

"Leighton doesn't think so," I say. Esme has nothing to say to that, and I smile wider as I watch her flex her hands into fists, only smoothed out by Hawthorne's touch.

Saint cracks the tepid silence as she steps around me and sits in the armchair, tugging me along to squish into it together. Our backs are to the wall, giving us the widest vantage point. From here, I can see another group has formed outside of Esme's merry band of bloodthirsty bitches—a trio of girls, mousy brunettes, whose names I can't remember except for one—Reagan. They never speak above a whisper, so it's no wonder Esme hadn't found them threatening enough to recruit. She picks her battles a little more carefully now. She waits to see what's underneath before she comes for them. Strategic.

Saint leans in and whispers, "No sight of Pentatonic."

"Spoken too soon," I correct as the door cracks open.

Penthesilea draws every eye, but not a single greeting, as she enters the common room. Her pink dress flutters around her shins, dotted with lightly sparkling strawberries. She steps against the wall, smiling when I meet her eyes, wiggling her fingers in a wave. I give a half wave back and watch as she turns to look at Esme and her alliance. Jacqueline is staring at her intently. But no one dares approach.

There's a target on Penthesilea's back now, even if she acts like she doesn't feel it, a thin veil that separates her from the rest of us.

Finally, after what feels like a century too long, Mr. Caine opens the door. "The Repartee awaits." And we are shepherded off, all good little lambs brought to the slaughterhouse. No, wait, I guess that's tomorrow. *It doesn't have to be. It won't be. Get it together, Adina.*

On the walk down the hall, I track Hawthorne as she falls back from standing at Esme's side until she's right next to me. Saint shoots her a wary look over my head.

"Nicely done," Hawthorne decides, allowing herself to look mildly impressed.

Smugness tugs at my lips. "Thanks. I learned from the best," I say, keeping my eyes on Esme's back. Jacqueline has quickly wormed her way into Hawthorne's abandoned place, whispering to Esme. Esme doesn't even look at her; it's how I know she's seething.

I state the obvious: "Esme doesn't look happy."

"She doesn't want me talking to you. But *I* want to talk to you," Hawthorne says.

"Why?" I ask.

"Because . . . I don't like just talking to people that are afraid of Esme. Fearful people make boring conversationalists. And they don't talk to me. They talk to *her*," Hawthorne says plainly. Then her brow furrows. "She's too distracted to pay them attention, though. And these kinds of girls, they're needy for attention. That's how you can gain their loyalty. But if I'm here talking to you, instead, she's going to watch you all evening and spend the rest of the night asking me what we talked about, poring over every word."

"Why *do* you report to her?" I ask. "Is she holding something over you?"

Hawthorne barks a laugh that doesn't belong to her, a high-pitched sound that rings animalistic. Like a hyena. It's a pitch-for-pitch match with Esme's. A *not-right* tingle zips up my spine once more.

Hawthorne slaps her hand to her mouth and shakes her head. "I'll tell her you said that. She'll find it funny," she says inexplicably.

"Ladies," Mr. Caine calls again, far ahead of us. His impatience is obvious as he looks down at a slightly dented, glinting pocket watch. He snaps it shut.

No one speaks any more as we descend and pick up the pace. I grow tenser. Leighton has told us a few details as to what a Repartee is, but we know now not to take words at face value.

And then we're at the doors.

"Announcing the Ladies of the Finish," Mr. Caine says.

"Let the *games* begin," Saint taunts in my ear.

I square my shoulders. "Haven't they already?"

CHAPTER

14

THE PHONOGRAPH IS PLAYING LIVELIER MUSIC tonight, a big band record that's meant to make the room feel fuller but instead has the effect of sucking the air right out of the parlor. The room is slightly on the side of too warm, probably from the unseasonal fire roaring in the enormous fireplace, for ambiance and aesthetic over practicality. The chandelier overhead is lit with candles, like this is the seventeenth century. But the wood is warm and there's no gold filigree wallpaper or wide windows, just long slotted ones. This is a room that's used, and frequently.

Leighton and Third are a united front, giving off a surprisingly welcoming feel. She smiles proudly, looking at all of us, her eyes flitting around in search before she finally finds me—and nods her approval. Pierce stands to his father's right, like a good son. And Graham . . . well, Graham is harassing the bartender in the corner for another drink, despite the three servers standing at attention with trays of champagne.

"Ladies, welcome to the first Repartee," Leighton says, her husky voice reaching deep into my chest. "The Repartees—of which there are three—are timeless moments of the Finish, in which a young lady can further determine her fate through hard-won advantages. A Repartee is meant to reflect the skills required to conquer the challenge that she faces the next day. During my Finish, the first Repartee preceding my Ride was a round of charades. It was a moment in which the purpose of the Ride was further illuminated—a moment where our bodies had to speak louder than our voices. Our bodies, the strengths of them, were weapons. But as your Game Mistress, I have gone a different course. We will be playing *cards*. The cards, much like your horses, are a tool. It's what you do with that tool that determines your success. Let this night begin with light fare in anticipation for tomorrow."

No one moves toward the collection of card games waiting on the table. Instead, we surge forward, each of us vying for the attention of a Remington. Hawthorne tears herself from my side quickly to join Esme as she approaches Leighton, being sure to get there before I can. Jacqueline and the Hannahs are like puppies, clamoring for Pierce's eyes. Penthesilea is welcomed with an outstretched arm to join Third's side.

"I'm going to get a drink. Circle the room before I have my conversations. I'd advise you to do the same," Saint says with a nod toward Third, and suddenly, I'm alone amongst the wolves.

I walk slowly toward the games. It's not a wide variety. It's all cards, as promised. And yet I still feel the looming threat of a curveball, one shaped by violence. A server finds me, offering a glass of champagne.

I take it without the intention of drinking. The sharp scent of bubbles stings my nose and I clear my throat. I've never been good at standing alone. It makes me feel like I'm backed into the corner, like the only way out is by being wild, and I'm not supposed to be wild, not ever again.

"Adina Walker, as I live and *breathe*, you look like a goddamn funeral."

I glare at Graham, but the heat of it is gone. I'm not his biggest fan, but I can't forget that he is actually helping me.

"Thanks, it's mine. Scheduled for tomorrow evening. Hope you can make it."

Graham's smile slips. "That's not funny, Adina."

"I wasn't trying be," I admit, looking down at the champagne.

"I'll finish that off for you if you want," Graham says.

"Should you really be drinking more?" I ask.

Graham scoffs. "I'm not *drunk*."

"No, but you want to be," I retort.

Graham's entire demeanor stiffens. "I don't think you know me well enough yet to cast that kind of accusation."

"Probably not."

"You can't waste a hundred-dollar glass of champagne," Graham tries again.

I promptly throw the entire champagne back like it's a shot out of pure spite. It tingles on its way down and I regret my brashness. But I don't regret the look of sheer delight on Graham's face at my audacity.

I roll my eyes and look back over at Leighton. She looks bored with her conversation, despite her attentive nods. I can tell from the way her eyes glance over at Third every thirty seconds. It's the opening I need.

"Excuse me," I say brusquely, ignoring Graham's startled noise.

"Adina, wait, I wanted to tell you about—"

But nothing he could tell me is more important than Leighton's signal. I look for Saint and find her at the fringes, arms folded as she sips her champagne, smirking at the rest. I come up behind her, hooking my arm through hers and herd us toward Leighton.

"—could get a drink. We could continue by the bar," Esme says with the same smile she used to convince our precalc teacher to give her an A in our junior year.

"Aunt Leighton," I say before she can agree.

Leighton stands taller and looks briefly at Esme and Hawthorne once. "You may get *me* a drink," she says, and the dismissal is so loud and ringing, both girls melt backward, stunned. I come forward. "I knew you would look exquisite in this gown. Doesn't she look gorgeous?"

I'm not sure who she's asking. But both Third and Pierce turn from their own conversations. Penthesilea watches me with phoenix eyes, pleasant and even engaging, like she's unbothered by my interruption.

"Yes," Pierce agrees. I meet his gaze over Leighton's shoulder, ignoring Jacqueline's furious glare, and he flashes a boyish smile that I'm compelled to return.

Third's gaze is sharp and narrow on me, like he still finds me lacking. I remember what he and Graham said in that room, in a conversation half overheard. That I am an inadequate choice.

"Adina Walker, I'm told by my sister-in-law to expect great things from you," he says slowly, his lips curling. "A former acceptance to Yale. Anywhere else?"

"UChicago, Amherst, Bowdoin, Tufts. But Yale was my first choice," I admit, gaze sliding downward. I can feel his amusement; he knows that Yale *isn't* a choice any longer.

"And your acceptance to Yale was rescinded due to . . . violence at Edgewater. Correct?"

He knows the answer. He just wants me to say it. So I smile and through bared teeth I do. "My acceptance *everywhere* was rescinded. Sir."

"I see," Third says. "Well, maybe you do have the stomach for this."

I nod at this small, unkind victory, my head bobbing up and down. Saint carefully extracts herself from me.

"Mr. Remington," she says, "my father has always spoken so highly of you, and I can see why now. Thank you for your continued hospitality. . . ."

"You've been doing divinely, Adina," Leighton murmurs, keeping her voice low. "I knew you would. Continue doing so, and you *will* reap the benefits. I can feel it." This close I can see that her eyes are dark and rich, nearly mahogany in color, like even they have learned to blend in with their surroundings. "Miss Alderidge seems unsettled this evening."

"Does she? I hadn't noticed," I simper.

Leighton chuckles and another flash of pleasure rushes through me. I stand taller, lifting my chin just so, and Leighton pats my cheek. I beam up at her, basking in the pride in her voice.

"Penthesilea, did you know Miss Walker very well in school?" Third interrupts.

It's like a wash of cold water over me. Saint looks alarmed at the sudden shift in conversation—away from her father, their business, the secrets she means to tease out, and back to me. Penthesilea looks surprised too. She darts a look at Pierce as he tries to extricate himself from Jacqueline and the Hannahs, like she expects him to *save* her. From me or Third's line of questioning, I'm unsure, but neither seems to make sense.

"Not as well as I'd have liked to," Penthesilea says.

"Do you believe she would be a good fit?" Third asks.

A good fit for what? I want to ask. *I'm right here,* I want to say. But I don't.

Penthesilea stares at me for a long time before she says, "Better than she'd like to believe." She says it like she's been watching me. Not just for this evening, but for a long time, and I just never noticed.

Third smiles, letting his hand fall on her shoulder. "Penthesilea?"

"Yes, Third?"

"Go start a game," he says. Penthesilea's eyes go wide, but Third is already ignoring her reaction, arms stretched up like a grand ringmaster. "Yes, why don't we all play *games*. Isn't that what the Repartee is about?"

And we all laugh, as if we find him clever, when he is the least clever person in the room.

We don't move, though. None of us knows how or where to start. Not even Penthesilea.

Or maybe Jacqueline does. She breaks away from where Pierce isn't giving her attention, his gaze caught on Penthesilea and me, and she very deliberately steps into his line of sight, flashing a wide smile.

"Let's play a game, Penthesilea. We never did get to play the other day."

Jacqueline isn't shouting, but her words cut through the parlor like she is. She wants everyone's attention. I look over at the bar, at Esme, and I know this is part of her scheme. She'd never outright challenge Penthesilea herself, at least not this early on. Penthesilea is powerful, the front-runner considering she's already dating Pierce. She's the better equestrian, too, and it's not hard to presume that she'll win the Ride. Esme would find it safer for someone else to test her. And here, at a night of cards, of course, *Jacqueline* is the obvious choice.

"You want to play a game?" Penthesilea repeats. Her eyes are wide but her tone rings false suddenly. There's a playfulness to it that Jacqueline doesn't seem to hear. "With me?"

Jacqueline nods. "Yes, I want to play with you."

Penthesilea hums and she strokes the jut of her freckled chin for just a moment before she nods. "Yes, all right. Let's play a game."

Penthesilea crooks a finger at Jacqueline, and the two girls walk toward the coffee table. Neither of them sits in the offered chairs, choosing to kneel in front of the mess of card decks and the stacks of chips. Esme approaches, Hawthorne in tow, and they converge around Jacqueline.

"Gather round," Leighton commands, herding the rest of us forward to form a circle around the two of them "Miss Moriarty, as you challenged Miss Bonavich, she will be allowed to select the game."

Jacqueline nods. "So. What'll it be? Texas Hold 'Em? Omaha? Five-Card Draw? Five-Card Stud? I know the uncommon variants too."

Penthesilea picks up a deck and shuffles the fifty-two cards quickly, as if counting them.

"What do you want to play for?" Penthesilea asks instead of answering, in her soft, baby-queen voice. She leans forward as she does one of those complicated shuffles, the kind dealers do in movies set in casinos.

"Play for?" Jacqueline asks.

Penthesilea smiles. "Winners win things, Jacqueline. What do you want to win?"

"Your room, remember," Jacqueline says firmly. "I hate sharing."

Penthesilea laughs. "Well, all right," she agrees. "But . . . what do I get? If I win?"

Jacqueline rolls her eyes and cuts a glance back at the alliance of girls. They laugh at the very idea of Penthesilea winning. "I don't know. What do you want?" she asks, humoring her.

Penthesilea shrugs. "I'm not sure yet. We'll see," she declares. And Jacqueline is so confident, she doesn't object.

But then Penthesilea leans forward. "Let's play War."

Jacqueline blanches. "I . . . I don't know that poker variant."

"It's not poker. It's a card game," Penthesilea says.

"The kids' game?" Jacqueline blurts.

"I like War. It's a game of chance." Penthesilea drums her fingers against the table. She looks like a Monet.

"If you don't want to play poker, I know Blackjack or *literally*—"

"You challenged me, so I pick the game," Penthesilea practically sings. "And I've picked War. Let's play." She doesn't give Jacqueline another breath to push back. She begins to deal the cards, throwing each back and forth. "This game can get long, so let's not screw around. We throw down the cards. Unseen. A battle. If the value matches, we start a war. Highest valued card wins the lot. We check the unseen declarations for aces. When they're revealed, put them to the side—they're out of play. And then we shuffle. Whoever collects the most aces wins."

"Fine," Jacqueline says. She gathers her cards to her chest and makes an aborted move to look at her cards, only stopping when she remembers, this isn't the game she's used to. She sets them down and stares at Penthesilea with contempt that's meant to disguise her fear.

"Let's begin," Penthesilea says.

Within seconds, it's clear that while War is a child's game, the pair don't play as kids. They slam down cards one after the other. It goes on for five regular hands. Penthesilea seems to be at an advantage at first, having an overwhelming number of the face cards. She does snatch a win by collecting the first ace on the sixth hand, though—the ace of spades, having had it in her own deck. Jacqueline hisses at that.

And then there's a match.

Two nines. One is a spade. The other is a club.

"I. De. Clare. War," the pair call together.

And then Jacqueline slaps down a seven of diamonds. And Penthesilea—a six of clubs. Jacqueline pumps her fists, and Esme begins to clap, an applause that's swiftly joined in by her other lackeys. When I look back, Third looks amused. Pierce does *not*.

"It's a game of chance," I mutter, rolling my eyes. "It doesn't take much skill."

"Maybe," Saint says, eyes narrowing on the table, like she's searching for some hidden clue. "Maybe not."

"That pile's yours, then," Penthesilea sighs. "Check the cards for any aces."

Jacqueline flips them all overeagerly, and she gasps triumphantly when she finds the second ace. The ace of clubs is from Jacqueline's own hand.

"Better be careful, Pen. We're evenly matched now," Jacqueline crows as she sets it to the side, preening.

Penthesilea's mouth pulls into a taut smile. "Yes, it seems so. Shuffle your deck. Let's begin again."

She shuffles her deck and then there's only a brief moment before they're slapping cards down again, going back and forth, until finally—another match.

"I. De. Clare. War."

On the fourth card, Penthesilea lays down a queen of hearts. Jacqueline only has a four of clubs.

"Guess this round's mine, then," Penthesilea muses. She plucks the cards from Jacqueline's grasp before she can even react, and she shuffles through them, checking for an ace. There are none. "I haven't played this game since I was a little girl. I forgot how gratifying it is."

Jacqueline shuffles her deck again, and Penthesilea meets her. "Ready?"

And then they're slapping down cards fast and hard.

The match comes faster this time.

Two threes.

"Well, then," Penthesilea hums. "Jacqueline, I do wonder . . . how did you get here?"

"What?" Jacqueline snaps in frustration. She cracks her neck, a loud rippling sound that makes Hannah G cringe.

"Who nominated you?" Penthesilea asks.

"First, I'm the Northeast junior poker champion, that should earn a nomination by itself," Jacqueline mutters. "And as for *who* nominated me—I don't know for sure, but probably one of Mr. Remington and my father's mutual associates. My dad works at Goldman. He's one of the Remingtons' investment managers."

"Oh, of course," Penthesilea says placidly. "New money. Ready?"

Jacqueline jerks back in her outrage, but Penthesilea doesn't give her time to process.

"I. De. Clare. War."

"Damn it!" Jacqueline snarls.

Another match. Two kings.

"Oh. How *fascinating*," Penthesilea murmurs, like she actually means it. "You know, Jacqueline, to be invited to the Finish, one must be above reproach. One must be a young woman of grace. And talent. And ambition. Of the right stock, that's what they say."

"What are you getting at?" Jacqueline snarls.

"I'm only thinking aloud."

Another bout of War.

Penthesilea gathers her spoils after a win with a five over Jacqueline's two. She flips over her cards and lets out a shuddering gasp.

"Oh, I nearly gave you my ace of diamonds." She pauses, brushing her fingers over Jacqueline's cards. "I do thank you for losing."

"*Fuck* you," Jacqueline spits.

"Careful, Jacqueline. You don't have many cards left,"

Penthesilea says, dipping her head toward her hand. "And only the heart is in play. We're getting close."

Jacqueline throws down a card in answer. Penthesilea meets her.

The play slows now. Jacqueline measures each card.

Eventually the match comes. A pair of eights.

"Let's get this over with," Jacqueline says, lifting her small stack.

"By my count, I have two of the aces. That means we'll either draw or I'll win," Penthesilea says. I'm not sure if it's for Jacqueline's benefit or her enraptured audience's. She slides them to the side, all facing upward, all out of play. Club. Diamond. Jacqueline's spade. "And I think I know what I want now if I win."

"What?" Jacqueline demands. As she spirals, her voice gets deeper. Unhinged.

Penthesilea leans in. "I want your saddle."

Jacqueline falls back, eyes wide. "What?" Her question is repeated, but it's different now—lost.

"I want your saddle," Penthesilea repeats, folding her hands in her lap. "For the Ride. You know how we all get saddles. I want yours."

"But you *already* have one! They're all the same—"

"I don't care," Penthesilea says gently, fiddling with her skirts, smoothing them out over her thighs. "I don't want to *swap*. I want yours."

Jacqueline falls back, one hand over her mouth as she looks

up and over. The Remingtons are all staring at her with distaste. With pity.

She's been losing this whole time and at more than just a game of War.

"Fine," she whispers, gathering what's left of her dignity and her cards in her hand.

Penthesilea lifts her own hand, over her mouth, like she's hiding a smile. And then it begins.

I hold my breath, despite how *stupid* I feel. It's just cards.

"I. De. Clare. War."

They slap down their cards and Jacqueline is dealt a six of clubs.

And there, in front of Penthesilea, plain in white and red, is the ace of hearts.

Jacqueline flips over her hand, searching it, despite the ace of hearts being *right* there. Nothing can help. A six, a two, and two face cards, a jack and a king. It's over for her. Jacqueline jumps up and glares down at Penthesilea, who is still ethereal and smiling.

"You can deliver my saddle at the Ride," Penthesilea says. She gathers the cards together, neatly settling them in a stack and then sliding them back into the box before she gets to her feet. "Third, Aunt Leighton, I'm very tired. May I retire for the evening?"

Third smiles, self-satisfied, and strangely enough, he turns to Leighton as he says, "Have a good night, my dear."

Penthesilea walks past the Remingtons and stops in front of Pierce, looking up at him. She rocks up onto her toes and kisses him once, at the corner of his mouth. She whispers something in his ear, something that makes him wince, and then she slips from the room, which erupts into chatter the minute she leaves.

"Holy *shit*," Esme breathes, a wild look of exhilaration on her face. In contrast, Jacqueline looks devastated.

I turn to Saint. "She can't ride without a saddle," I hiss. "She's going to fall off and *hurt* herself. Or worse, die."

Saint swallows. "Yeah . . . I think that's the point."

It makes me look at Penthesilea in an entirely different way. It's when I realize—she's not above the game at all.

She's the most masterful player.

Jacqueline crumples at the tea table, her forehead pressed against the warm wood. Hannah G and Hannah R slide off their chairs, flanking her. But Esme stays on hers, Hawthorne tucked neatly against her, whispering in her ear, as she stares down at her pawn, utterly unimpressed.

Third and Leighton are still staring each other down. Leighton has lost somehow. And when Third looks at me and snorts, I know somehow *I've* lost this round too.

"Where are you going?" Saint calls. "Don't get involved."

"I'm not. I just want to know . . ." I trail off, and then I hurry from the room after Penthesilea as I call behind me, "Excuse me. Restroom."

Leighton doesn't lower herself to calling out my name, but I can feel her disapproval like a throbbing tattoo. I step out to find Penthesilea standing in the middle of the corridor, her long billowy sleeves trailing past her fingers. Her back is toward me, her head tilted up to the vaulted ceilings. I look up, wondering what she's staring at.

Slowly, I shut the door behind me, just loudly enough to alert her to my presence.

She turns, but she doesn't seem surprised to see me.

"Were you supposed to challenge me?" I ask, breathing heavily.

"I think that was Third's intention, yes," she says evenly.

"But you didn't. Why?" I demand.

Penthesilea shrugs. "Do *you* like being used?"

"*Am* I being used?" I challenge.

"Are you?"

Penthesilea's lips curl into a tiny smile that feels more danger-ous than anything else that just went down in that room. I sneer at her. She likes to answer questions with questions, and each time she does, she pretends like she doesn't know how *irritating* it is. But she knows. It's how she riled up Jacqueline so expertly. It makes me wonder if she learned this from Leighton, learned how a woman who might survive the Remingtons would behave.

"How did you win that?" I ask.

"What do you mean 'how'? It's a game of chance," Penthesilea says.

"You didn't play it like it was," I retort.

Penthesilea sighs. "You're right, I didn't."

"So how did you know you would win?"

I peel myself away from the door, shuffling closer until there's only a foot between us. Staring at her, away from Pierce, is just as

162

hard as it is looking at him—like staring into the sun for too long.

Penthesilea pulls at her skirts, tugging it until I see the slightest tear, neatly done, as if with a knife. She reaches inside and pulls forth a single card. An ace of hearts.

"You cheated," I breathe.

"Everyone does," Penthesilea says solemnly. She takes a step closer, leaning in to whisper into my ear. "I knew she would challenge me. That Esme would challenge me. Because I am Third's favorite. Because I am Pierce's girlfriend. Because I am going to win tomorrow."

"You're very sure," I rasp. I take note of her not claiming to be her own boyfriend's favorite.

"Do you think I just happen to be a champion equestrian? I've been training for this for my entire life. Esme's mistake . . . Jacqueline's mistake was in thinking that just because of that I am *above* cheating, which I am not," Penthesilea says. "Now, listen up, Adina. That dress, while you look lovely in it, has done nothing but paint a target on your back, just like mine. And not just for Esme. Before, they would have discounted you, kept you alive to pick off at the end. And now that they have another, easier target, they won't miss."

I flinch back. She acts like more "accidents" are all but guaranteed. But I force myself to focus on the other part of her statement. Leighton's favor came with caveats, ones I didn't foresee. I was so distracted by Penthesilea's obvious advantages, I didn't see them closing in on me, too.

"Don't pretend you're doing me a favor by telling me that," I say.

Penthesilea smiles, staring at me from under the fringes of her orange lashes, each one appearing golden in the day's dying light. "But it is a favor. A favor amongst the favorites, you could say. This is the last favor I'll do you, Adina. Save *yourself* next time."

The image of Third and Leighton's staring contest flashes before my eyes again. My mouth is dry as I watch her walk off, proud of what she's done, of the chaos she leaves behind. A chaos that I have to face again. It's hard turning my back on her when I want to interrogate her more, but the door behind me opens and I twist, already cringing at what I expect will be admonishment from Leighton or a snipe from Esme.

"Pen— *Adina.*" Pierce is backlit, his face cast in shadow. He looks behind his shoulder again and smiles. "Just a moment, ladies. Hannah G, I *do* look forward to hearing about your latest . . . shoot in Belize."

He shuts the door behind him.

"Belize?" I blurt out.

Pierce runs a hand over his face and rolls his eyes. "I don't know. I think she said Belize. Or Bolivia. I'll smooth it over," he says. He looks over my shoulder, frowning into the shadows. "Have you seen Pen?"

"She's going to bed. Big day tomorrow," I say lightly. "She didn't seem . . . upset with what happened, if that's what you're wondering."

Pierce snorts. "No, she was pretty pleased with herself, I'm sure," he says, his words more biting than I would have expected. I try to control my expression, but he catches sight of the question in it and sighs. "Pen is just . . . let's not talk about Pen."

"Shouldn't you be getting back inside?" I ask, torn.

I don't want to be his wife, especially not after he tricked me into coming here, and that's what he expects out of this. That's part of the prize, the biggest part to them, and it seems nonnegotiable. And yet, I want to win. I *need* to. So I need him to stay.

"All I said was that I didn't want to talk about Pen," Pierce says, taking a step forward. "I do want to talk to *you.*"

"Me?" I ask, mouth twitching.

"I've wanted to talk to you all evening. You look gorgeous, Adina. Truly stunning," he says, leaning in and smiling down at me.

"Thanks. I . . . I've never owned anything as pretty as this," I admit.

"Well, *you* make the dress. Not the other way around," Pierce declares, like that's absolute fact.

"You really know how to flatter a girl." I laugh awkwardly, rubbing at the back of my neck, tugging on one of my curls, bound at the nape of my neck. I suddenly regret going with a low puff. Maybe I should've *redone* my hair, though that would've been stupid—the Ride is tomorrow. What am I even thinking?

He's so charming, he dulls my sense. He makes me *stupid,* and I can't afford to be stupid, but I also can't afford to lose his favor.

"How are you feeling about everything?" Pierce asks.

He sounds like he *actually* wants to know. But the way he's smiling at me doesn't inspire truth. It doesn't make me forget what he didn't tell me or quell the way my stomach turns as I think about the river crossing or the jumps or the Taxis Ditch. It doesn't stop the haunting of Penthesilea's warnings in my ears—now that they have a target, they won't miss.

"Okay . . . I think," I say slowly, hedging.

Pierce leans in conspiratorially. "My aunt thinks you could win. She likes you. She doesn't really like anyone, so *that's* truly an achievement."

I notice that he says nothing about his father liking me. We both know who Third likes.

"Aunt Leighton has good taste," I say. "I'm a winner."

And I know I've played it right because Pierce looks *delighted*.

"You are a winner," Pierce says. "*I* want you to win tomorrow too." Pierce takes a step forward and grabs my hand. It's big and warm. "I have . . . Graham is going to give you something tomorrow to help. Take it. Please."

"Cryptic," I say slowly. I can't be too eager. "I think we both know the . . . *prize* at the end. Shouldn't you be giving this 'special gift' to Penthesilea? You know . . . your girlfriend?"

"I think Pen has made it *very* clear tonight that she doesn't need anyone's help, don't you?" Pierce says firmly. He takes another step closer, close enough that I'm forced to crane my neck, and in the dark, here, it feels like we're back in the woods. I know this boy's mouth. This boy's hands. "I don't want you to get hurt. I know what you must think after what happened the other night, but I swear what you said . . . about evening the playing field really resonated with me. Let me do that. Let me help you."

"I don't *need*—"

"Yes, you do," Pierce dismisses. "But also, I *want* to help you. Graham knows what I want. You're going to get through the Ride."

This is cheating. But Penthesilea says everyone does it. Everyone cheats. And is it really cheating if he's the one who makes the rules?

"I promise," he finishes.

"You promise," I murmur, doubtful. As if he has anything to do with whether or not nine girls decide to murder me or anyone else tomorrow in his name.

But he's so earnest when he nods, like he really believes it. Finally, he takes a step back and drops my hand, reaching back to push the door open. "Now, before anyone else tries to mess with you . . . do you want to play something with me? Your choice of game."

"Yeah," I say slowly, thinking of Saint. "Let's play Old Maid."

CHAPTER

15

THE DAY OF THE RIDE I'M UP BEFORE MORNING call, dressed in our uniform. I expect another pep talk but Saint doesn't speak to me at all. Instead, we stand side by side in the mirror, taming our hair back into stern ponytails. Saint reaches over, tucks one of my stray curls, and knocks her shoulder into mine. I knock her back and slide on my boots. I make sure they're tied tight. There's no room for mistakes today.

The danger feels heavier already, roiling like the thick fog that dusts the morning in dew.

"You ready for this?" Saint asks finally as we stand at our door, knowing that when we return to this room, nothing will be the same.

"Absolutely not," I say.

Saint huffs. "Well . . . let's get this over with."

"Bet," I agree, and then I throw the door open.

The other girls wait in the hallway this time, instead of in the common room. There's a nervous energy and not many of them are speaking. Esme is down the hall, by the window, Hawthorne at her right hand as always. Hannah G, Hannah R, and Jacqueline round out their clique. The other group of three girls, whom I still don't know very well, wait farther along, casting furtive glances at Esme—they're still afraid of her, but not enough to put themselves in closer proximity to her. Smart girls.

Smarter than me. This should've been played like a waiting game. Esme always would have come for me, but I showed my hand too soon, with the dress, to everyone else, and there's no going back for me now.

A few seconds later the door across the hall swings open.

Penthesilea appears, holding on to the doorframe, her fingers covered in black leather, just like the rest of her. She's traded in the cream uniform we were given for all black. She takes a step through and makes eye contact.

"Good luck, Adina," Penthesilea says quietly as she passes.

And then she turns sharply, just before Mr. Caine arrives with Leighton at his side, like she sensed them coming.

"Dr. Remington has arrived," Mr. Caine announces unnecessarily.

She claps her hands.

"Well, ladies. You have taken on the challenge of the Finish admirably thus far. You have demonstrated strength and commitment. Your hard work is commendable. Now it is time to put that work to the test," Leighton declares. "The Ride is a symbol for the journey you have ahead. Not in the Finish, but far beyond. Life will be a series of obstacles, some larger than others, and you will *always* be in competition with someone faster, stronger, and better. It is acknowledging your shortcomings and pushing forward past them that matters the most. Some will rise to the occasion. Some will fall. Here, we weed out the weak from the strong. Here, we see who finishes *first*. Let us begin."

She turns on her heel and descends, leading us to the grounds. Leading some of us to our potential deaths, whether at the obstacles or from our competitors. The sudden reminder of Penthesilea's warnings make me shake and the idea of any of the other girls being like Esme makes me almost retch, so that suddenly, I'm glad I was too nervous to eat breakfast.

I stick close to Saint's side and she to mine as we're led out of the Remington mansion. In the fresh air, away from the fortress-like walls, I entertain the idea of running again.

But these grounds are so open, and they go for miles. I know I wouldn't make it far.

In the stables, Saint pats my hand and then she disappears down the barn to find her own horse. I go into my stall with Starlight and Princess, ignoring Hannah G's incessant cooing.

"Hey, Starlight," I whisper, leaning in to press my head to her snout. She bumps me and I laugh. "You ready? We're gonna make it through, you and me. Promise." But I don't know if I'm promising her or asking her to promise me.

Suddenly, there's a quick rap on the stall wall, and I turn.

"Graham," I murmur, relieved.

"Graham," Hannah G says. She barely looks at him. He's not the important brother, and so as per usual, she gives him the bare minimum.

I wrap an arm over Starlight's back and smile weakly. "Here to wish me luck?"

"No. Here to make sure that you don't fucking die," Graham whispers. He grabs my saddle from the wall. "Come on." He's already walking down the stable, *past* Starlight. I slide into the next stall, and gape at the horse inside. He's enormous, so much bigger than Starlight, and so much more impressive. "We'll fake like Starlight is sick, okay, so no one will suspect you're being helped."

This, I realize, is Pierce's version of "help."

It doesn't surprise me that Pierce's horse is a white one.

"No," I whisper, shaking my head.

Graham acts as if he hasn't heard me, sliding the saddle onto the horse's back.

"What are you talking about? Widow Maker is a thorough-bred, trained to be the very best. He'll take you far," Graham insists. "Most importantly, he'll take over if you falter. He knows the way."

The name "Widow Maker" *does* surprise me.

"Maybe, but I've never ridden him. I . . . I can't," I say. Graham is about to buckle the saddle together, so I reach forward, grabbing his wrist, yanking him back. I must take him so much by surprise that he stumbles and nearly falls back into me.

"What do you mean, you can't?" he spits. "Are you taking this seriously? You could *die*."

"Yeah, so could anyone," I retort. "Jacqueline isn't even using a saddle."

"Jacqueline was stupid enough to think that Pen is a pushover," Graham says sharply. "*You're* not stupid." It feels like he's calling me stupid if I refuse, and that makes rage flare in my stomach.

"I'm not going to ride him. I'm going to ride Starlight," I insist. I grab the saddle from him, clutching it to my chest as my heart sinks. This is not the help I was hoping for. "Just . . . trust me."

"I *do* trust you. I don't trust the rest of those bloodthirsty creatures out there. They're going to eat you *alive*. I thought maybe some of them would be different, but they aren't. They will lie and steal and *kill*," Graham presses.

"How would you know? You didn't have a Finish."

Graham's eyes narrow. "I know the women in my family."

"Your aunt already wants me to win. She'd have given me this horse at the start if she thought it was best. I'm not your responsibility," I say simply.

Graham groans. "You're starting to feel like one."

I roll my eyes because I can't help it as I stalk out past him, rejoining Starlight to saddle her. I focus on her to calm my nerves, but Graham's claiming responsibility for me keeps creeping into my thoughts. Our relationship is based on his teaching me to ride. He's self-righteous and arrogant and none of it is charming, not like it might be on someone else. Sure, he's patient. And sure, he has actually helped me, even though he's an ass about it.

But he's the wrong brother. The other brother, I remind myself.

I shake it away. It doesn't matter now. I have to focus.

I step up into the stirrup and swing my foot over Starlight. I slide into the saddle and sit up taller. Graham stands against the far wall, watching me. He looks small from this angle, and he looks afraid. Somehow, seeing him afraid makes me feel less so.

"Hey, Adina," Graham says quietly.

"Yeah?"

"You should try to stay on the outside of the path."

I pause. "What?"

Graham presses his lips into a thin line. "The path is carved in a way that if you stay outside, it'll bring you closer to the jumps and make them easier to charge. And when you get to the fork in the road, take the right. I know the map doesn't show that there's a fork, but there *is* a fork. If you go to the right, it'll take you away from the Taxis Ditch."

The Taxis Ditch is the most dangerous obstacle, supposedly responsible for the death of more than one horse, and *definitely* more than one girl.

"Why are you telling me this now?" I ask. He could've told me before. But he didn't.

Another part of Pierce's help or . . .

Graham frowns at me. "I was trying to tell you last night but then you ran off to Leighton. And, well, especially if you aren't taking Widow Maker, you need to know. You're a shitty rider. . . . Good for a novice. But generally, shitty."

"Thanks. Asshole." Still, I smile. Just a little bit, grateful for the information that might actually help me get through this.

"And, Adina?"

"*What*, Graham?"

"Don't die."

I swallow. "I'll try."

I squeeze my thighs and Starlight shifts underneath me, beginning to walk.

I lead her down the hall, but instead of turning right into the ring like in practice, we join the others at the beginning of the road. I line up next to Saint.

Esme sits tall in her saddle, a look of complete intensity on her face. On one side of her is Hawthorne, at the ready. And on the other, Jacqueline stands next to her stud, saddle in her trembling hands.

Penthesilea stands in front of her, beatific smile on her face as she reaches out. When she kisses Jacqueline's cheek in thanks, it's a mark for death. Penthesilea passes the saddle along to Mr. Caine with purpose, then pushes up onto her horse, swinging a leg over the saddle and sitting there like she was born for it. And all Jacqueline can do is *watch*.

Jacqueline senses my gaze and her head snaps around to look at me, like a great bird of prey. She hisses something up at Esme, and when Esme looks over, her gaze narrows on something past me, her lips curling into a sneer. I try to read her lips and it looks like Esme whispers to Jacqueline—"See, he's helping—"

"Didn't take my offer, I see?"

I jump, startling Starlight, as I look down at Pierce Maxwell Remington IV. He smiles up at me. He looks dressed for a Saturday afternoon at the country club, not a morning race to our potential deaths.

"Widow Maker is beautiful, but . . . he's not mine," I say.

"Integrity. That's . . . different," Pierce says. He sounds caught between disappointment and dawning wonder, like he couldn't imagine anyone turning down anything from him. He mumbles the word to himself again as he continues past me, going to stand before all of us with his hands clasped behind his back. In an instant, he transforms, standing taller, looking surer as he addresses us. "I'm sure my aunt has relayed to you what this Ride means. It is a measure of your grit. Your intensity. Your passion. Your drive. How far will you go for what you want? I look forward to accompanying the winner tonight and lending her my ear to hear what other things she hopes to accomplish."

Pierce steps to the side, and I can hear some of the other girls shifting. I look down the row and Esme looks even more intense, and just past her, in a funereal swathe of black, Penthesilea allows her gaze to follow her boyfriend. A boyfriend who hasn't looked at her once.

I lean back on my mount to avoid crossing into the gutting line of her stare. But again the sudden intensity that I spy in Penthesilea goes just as quickly.

"Good luck," I say to Saint.

"You too," she whispers, shifting on top of her own horse.

Our plan is simple. *Survive.*

Beyond that, I won't be first. I'm not stupid enough to think I'll even be close. But I can't be last. Being last makes me weak, and if there's anything worse than being a favorite, it's not being able to live up to it. Being weak—like Margaret must have seemed to Esme. I can't afford weakness.

We look straight ahead at the path.

Immediately, I notice how it starts to narrow ahead of us, designed to push us closer. There'll be a clear leader of the pack right away.

I can see the first obstacle, too: two hedges, so closely spaced that they have to be jumped as one. I sit taller, closing my eyes once, and breathe. I know this course on paper, the basics of the obstacles. I've memorized it, like information for a test. So, I do what I've always done with tests at Edgewater, I compartmentalize everything else, ready myself for battle.

"READY! SET!"

The shot is fired.

There's the briefest beat where we all still hold our breath. All except for Penthesilea, who flies immediately down the dirt path on her tall midnight horse, kicking up dirt in her wake. We're just a moment behind her and my heart rattles in time with Starlight's gallops as we rush toward the first hedge. All of us crowding is dangerous enough as it is, but the first jump is just ahead and intimidating. I've only cleared the practice for it a handful of times with any sort of confidence during our training.

I rock up in my seat, tightening my hold on the reins like Graham taught me.

Penthesilea flies over the hedges and lands with a thud. Esme and Hawthorne swiftly follow her. One of the other girls—one of the ones I don't know—rushes past me, nearly clipping me, and I swerve Starlight out of the way, toward the outside of the path, while she lands clumsily on the other side, rocking dangerously in her saddle, almost careening forward.

"Let's go, Starlight," I urge as we come up on the jump, and then we're soaring. "YES!"

We land easily and continue on the path, flying forward.

One down, six more to go. Next is the single hedge, then there will be another double jump of a pair of fences, the mud pit, the ramp, the river, and finally the Taxis Ditch. I say them like a mantra, a reminder that soon it'll be all over.

The path narrows further, forcing us tighter and closer, and I gasp when I look up to my left and there are only inches between Saint and me. Saint looks over at me, equally surprised by how close we are. If either of us shifted the wrong way, the other would be thrown off her horse.

"Pull ahead!" I shout. "I'll pull back tight to the rear!"

The only sign that she's heard me is a sharp nod and the way she lurches up to stand in her stirrups, chirping at her steed with a click of her tongue.

I'm solidly in the middle, and when I chance a look back, I find the Hannahs coming up quick behind. I'd rather be closer to them than to Esme and Hawthorne, but the unhinged glint in Hannah G's eyes sets my teeth on edge. I urge Starlight faster, a controlled canter, as Graham would call it, as I brace for whatever they have planned. Hannah G comes up on the left side and then pulls even with me, ahead of Hannah R. I look to her, ready to be defensive. She reaches into her saddlebag and pulls out a fistful of something. She turns, a wild look on her face, suddenly far less put together than her model-esque pout from before. But the look isn't for me. She throws her fistful back at Hannah R.

There's a brief moment of nothing, and then Hannah R's horse stumbles, and suddenly, I realize what the small things are that sailed past me—*nails*.

I screech as Hannah R's horse bucks, trying to clear the nails, and she grapples to stay on, but it's too hard, and then Hannah R is *falling*—

I have to turn back sharply to look ahead, knowing we're coming up on the next hedge, so I don't see the impact, but the sickening crack echoes.

"Ha!" Hannah G squeals. "Guess who's the only Hannah now, *bitch*!"

Hannah G—well, *the only Hannah now, bitch*—jerks her reins

with a war cry and then she's pulling farther ahead of me, still cheering as she races off and makes it roughly over the next obstacle, the full green hedge.

I turn in my seat, facing forward again, shivering as I think about Hannah R's dark glassy eyes before she hit the ground. Almost too late, I take a half-seat jumping position, and then we're over the hedge too. But I feel my late start, and find myself slipping sideways, losing my bearings. My heart thuds harder in my throat as I feel Starlight startle at my weight redistributing, and I fling myself forward and flat, tightening my thighs to right myself.

"I'm sorry, I'm sorry," I gasp against her flickering ears.

Another obstacle cleared, clumsily this time, but done. Five more to go.

We're down to ten girls. But it's still too many to watch out for. Too many to keep off my back. What if Hannah G attacks *me*? What if someone else does something worse? Who else is going to die? *Am I going to die?*

Focus, Adina, I command myself.

We break into a gallop on our way to the next obstacle. Hannah G is too busy celebrating her victory to defend her position, so I take the opportunity to pull past her so she can't throw her nails in my path. We approach the double fences, and this time Starlight and I don't go over easily at all. It's an even rougher landing, so rough that I lurch forward and only throwing myself backward keeps me upright.

My brain goes hazy with fear as we come up on the next obstacle, the mud pit.

There's a horse waiting to the side, smothered in mud, watching its rider sink facedown in the muck. The terror of it being Saint wells inside me, but when I look back at the horse again, I realize it's not hers. Even as relief fills my chest, so does self-loathing because I don't look back again at the unmoving body, don't stop to help. Not like with Margaret, because now I know it's useless.

I don't know what I'm doing, but Starlight does, and we fly over the mud pit.

"Ramp time, buddy," I call, breathless.

Starlight doesn't pay me any mind, all her concentration focused on getting us through this alive. Shuffling up the ramp means that I have to shift back and forth, carefully finding my center to counterbalance the sliding that might occur. Starlight takes it slow and so do I, and when we're finally up the ramp, we find it's a slip and slide down the other side, which very nearly makes me soar over Starlight's head. I *just* manage to correct it.

The river is next, and there's no jumping over this one. I mourn my curls as the sound of rushing water gets closer and closer.

Starlight quivers beneath me, and I lean forward, burying my face in her mane, by her ear. "I'm sorry, Starlight. We're almost to the end," I whisper. I can feel what she feels—the exhaustion and fear that's setting in beneath the achy muscles, down to our marrow. As we get closer to the water, I urge her on faster, past both our limits. We have to keep up speed so the current doesn't sweep us up. I take the chance to look back once and my heart stutters and just for a second stops.

It's Jacqueline. She's kneeling on her horse's back, her arm looped through her reins to keep her steady. And in her out-stretched hand, she has . . . a gun.

I've never seen a gun before in real life. The cold dark metal looks foreign to me, unreal, like it's in a movie or television show. Threatening, but in a distant way. They use blanks in movies, though. I know just from looking at Jacqueline that she isn't using blanks. Those are live bullets and she intends to put them through my body.

Poison is such an abstract way to die. It happens on a chemical level. You don't see it happening so much as you see the after-effects. But a bullet. That burns through flesh, destroys sinew, and explodes outward, ending life. That bullet is real.

This gun wipes away my last shred of denial. This violence, this death-game *Finish* is real. *Real*-real.

"Come on, Starlight!"

I flatten myself to the saddle and urge her faster, frantic, into the rapid current ahead. The river is only twenty feet wide, but it's deep. Starlight stutters at the edge, and then she brays loudly at the sound of a gunshot over the water. Jacqueline curses at her poor shot, still too far away to properly nail me, but the gap is closing. I know only God will make Jacqueline miss a second time, so I can't give her an opportunity. I click my tongue in Starlight's ear, and for a moment she's wild, tossing her head back and forth, still grabbing her bearings. My breath comes quicker as I lean in, lips near her twitching ears, begging,

"*Please, Starlight*, move!" and thankfully she rushes forward, cutting a path into the river.

The sloshing water crashes over our heads as we enter the river, and I can't breathe. I'm drowning, water rushing up my nose and over my eyes. But just as suddenly, Starlight breaks through the surface again and I gasp, air returning. I try to clear my blurred vision as she powerfully starts to cross.

But Jacqueline's gaining on me. "I've got your number, *Walker*," she spits, lifting her gun again, close enough for me to touch, close enough that a shot at this range to the head would kill me instantly. Jacqueline is nearly breathing on my neck, and I almost feel the chill of gunmetal against the nape.

I don't second-guess my instincts. I turn in my seat, duck under the gun near my ear, and shove her hard in the chest with two hands. Jacqueline loses her balance and she crashes into the water, and for a second I think I might too as I lose my grip on the reins and slip on the wet saddle, inhaling another swallow of water. But I grasp for my reins again, and seconds later Starlight is already fighting her way onto the bank. I shouldn't but I pull her to a stop to let her catch her breath, as I catch my own, turning back to the river to watch for Jacqueline. I still feel like I'm drowning, coughing and sputtering all over myself, fresh water and spit slicking my chin.

Her horse keeps on moving steadily toward the bank, but Jacqueline doesn't burst from the water. I hold my breath, heart in my throat. *Did I . . . kill her?*

Hannah G is still on the opposite bank, screaming something that I can't hear over the water, and I wonder then if she saw it all. If she saw Jacqueline try to *murder* me and just watched and waited, until one of us finished the other off, and suddenly, my chest is tight again and I can't breathe, wondering if I did—but then a hand bursts out from the river. It's Jacqueline, fighting against the current, clinging to one of the jutting rocks. And while I can breathe again, any relief is short-lived, and the minute Hannah G sees her, alive, she and her nails start across the river too. I turn on Starlight, urging her forward again toward the last and most dangerous of obstacles—the Taxis Ditch.

As I ride away, I hear Jacqueline screech, *"FUCK, I GOT MY GUN WET."*

Graham's advice rings in my ears. *Stay on the outside of the path. Take the right in the fork.* If I stay to the outside of the path here, I might find a way around the two-meter-deep ditch hidden behind a tall hedge. The Taxis Ditch is meant to serve as both an illusion and an obstacle, something easy that hides the impossible. The Taxis Ditch is what kills people, the obstacle we couldn't even practice. Facing it when there's another way would just be stupid. But can I trust him?

Then I remember, Graham doesn't want me to win. Graham wants me to *live*, and that makes all the difference.

I take the right in the fork, and immediately crash through branches and brambles on a path that's clearly been carved through the forest but rarely taken. It's rockier and hillier than the racetrack so far, but through some of the breaks in the trees parallel, I can see the other girls racing toward the final obstacle, while I move freely, avoiding it.

There's a moment where I think I've been tricked—where I wonder if I won't come out the other side. But then I'm bursting free of the trees and merging onto the main path again. I don't know who's in front of me. Or who's left behind. I just keep going.

When I reach the finish line, only then do I start to cry.

CHAPTER 16

I DON'T DISMOUNT FROM STARLIGHT SO MUCH AS
slide off, collapsing to my knees in the hard-packed dirt, gasping
and wiping furiously at my cheeks with dirty hands. I bend over
my lap, wet matted curls falling over my face as I try to stop the
flow of tears, pressing the heels of my hands hard into my eyes.
My heart thunders in my chest and I jump wildly when something
touches my shoulders. I fall back, and only when I blink a few
times does the blur of white in front of me turn into the shape of
Saint.

"A towel," Saint says softly. She's not nearly as soaked as I am.
Her face is dry, but her hair is still in a wet ponytail at the nape of
her neck and she is wrapped in a robe. She holds a matching one
over one arm for me.

"Thanks," I rasp, voice sore from the screaming and rough
waters that I swallowed on my way across the river. I wipe the
towel over my face, hoping that the remaining dregs from the river

covered my tears. I take a deep breath, inhaling the scent of fresh laundry, before I finally let the towel fall into my lap and see who else made it.

Penthesilea is here, of course, standing next to Third, a bottle of water in hand like she's just finished a gentle warm-up. Saint is with me. Esme and Hawthorne are huddled farther down the grass. Esme can't even hide her disappointment to see me alive. Leighton is watching, approval in every line of her body, and then there's Graham. *Graham*, who stares at me with relief, and the urge to cry, *Thank you, thank you,* catches in my throat.

Saint holds out her hand to me and she pulls me up. She doesn't bother to ask me if I'm okay. She knows I'm not. *She's* not. I can see that for once she's almost shaken, and I wonder what it must have been like, caught in the thick of riders like Esme and Penthesilea.

I avoid having to say anything to her because the sound of hooves grows louder, confirming I didn't finish last, though the ranking barely seems to matter at the moment. I clench my hands into fists to stop the violent flinch that rockets up my spine. I turn on the defensive and watch as a waterlogged Hannah G enters. She looks satisfied for someone who's come in sixth, and I don't have to wonder why. She's the only Hannah now.

And then comes Jacqueline, lying flat on her horse's back, her face flushed bright red with exertion.

I take an unsteady step backward and then another, stumbling, my shoulder crashing into Saint's as Jacqueline slides from her horse, and she has the *gun* and it's pointed right at me. Her eyes are so wide that they're nearly bugging out of her face, and her bottom lip is split, the pink aftermath of blood staining her chin like cherries.

"YOU TRIED TO DROWN ME, I'LL FUCKING KILL YOU, WALKER," Jacqueline screeches, her voice distorting into something demonic.

Someone blurs past me, soft blue linen and perfectly curled blond hair, and Leighton grabs Jacqueline by the wrist and twists so hard that Jacqueline screams in pain, dropping the gun. Leighton releases her, just as quick, and Jacqueline stumbles back, cradling her wrist to her chest and whimpering.

"Miss Moriarty, you are *embarrassing* yourself," Leighton says coldly. "The Ride has finished."

Jacqueline lets out a cracked sob, eyes welling with tears. She looks around, first at Leighton and then at the other Remingtons, willing them to understand her rage, all this *rage*. Graham is still watching me, but Pierce looks at her, his upper lip curled, his nose wrinkled. It's an easy look to read—disgust.

"But she tried to *drown* me. She wanted to *kill* me," Jacqueline accuses, which is ironic given the gun she was brandishing. But Leighton lifts her chin, looks at me, and deliberately says, "Good girl."

I squeeze my eyes shut. I don't want to hear that. I don't want to look at her. I don't want to be called *good* for doing something so fucking awful that I never wanted to do.

After that, we wait in silence for the rest. Reagan Mikaelson comes across only five minutes later.

We wait twenty more minutes. No one else comes.

And I know what that means.

❧ ☠ ☙

The bruises along my side look like a bouquet of flowers, blooming roses and deep moon-purple carnations rippling along my skin. I never thought skin as deep brown as mine could bruise like this. My bruises have always been dark, violent things, but these bruises are almost beautiful. Like the *smell* of the Ride, floral and gore.

I hide them beneath satin, and suddenly, it's like they were never there in the first place. Except, with each ginger step, the pain zips over my skin, stinging and sending flashes in front of my eyes, and the aching exhaustion burns in the arches of my feet, stretched thinner by the heels I'm wearing.

Saint looks over at me, grim faced. All her good humor from before has drained away as she shifts back to stare into her vanity. She pops open a fluorescent bottle of painkillers, takes one dry, and flexes her hand again.

"How bad is it?" I ask, my voice a little too accusatory.

Saint doesn't look at me, focusing a little too hard on securing the brace on her wrist. "It's a sprain. Or something. This is just for the next day or so. Then it's Advil for me," Saint says. "We were getting close to the end. Hawthorne and Esme blocked me in. Spooked my horse. Esme swung a branch at my head.

Knocked me straight off but over the finish line. I don't think she foresaw that."

I can't say anything to make this better. To make her feel better. But I have to try.

"We just have to make it through dinner. And then we can pass out. We can *sleep*," I say, just as much for my benefit as for Saint's.

"Yeah. But sleep isn't going to fix . . ." Saint trails off, looking at her wrist, but then she shakes herself hard, as if she's trying to wake herself from a nightmare. "This was a calculated risk. A good risk. I knew what I was getting into, wading out front. I needed top three. I need face time with the family."

For a moment I think she's talking to me, before I realize that she's staring into her own reflection, reassuring herself that she's in control. I don't have the heart to tell her that she isn't anymore.

And then she deflates, and I realize that she already knows.

Saint declares. "I . . . I should've let you run. I should've run with you."

I want to leave too. I want to tell her, *Let's run now. Let's run when they don't expect it.* And then I think about the threat against my parents. Saint has money to protect her from the threat of ruin or retribution. I don't. My *parents* don't.

So instead, I try to smile.

"The day is almost over and we are so beat, we couldn't walk, let alone run. We'll try again tomorrow," I say, careful and measured.

Saint—dependable, never-bothered Saint—reaches for me this

time instead of the other way around. It's one thing to witness violence. It's another to be in the thick of it. I grab her hand and squeeze hard before I let go, leading us into the common room as the other girls hurriedly slip in as well. Esme pettily steps on our heels just to remind us that she's right behind us.

Leighton is already there.

"Ladies. Finally," Leighton says. Her calm smile contrasts horrifically with the tension that racks through each of us, a collage of exhaustion and pain. "Are we ready for lunch?" She doesn't wait for an answer. "All right. Line up in order of rank."

I bite my tongue to stop the vitriol I want to spit.

Instead, we do as we're told. Reagan Mikaelson heads to the tail of the line. She keeps her head down, in hopes of her dark brown hair covering the livid cut along her jaw, jagged and newly stitched, but it's clear as day. She's pathetically lonely without her allies—friends, maybe. From what I gather, one's facedown in a mud pit and the other lies broken in the Taxis Ditch. Gone, like Hannah R.

Jacqueline lines up right in front of her. Then Hannah G, myself, and Hawthorne.

I'm surprised when Esme is called third and not Saint. I guess she really did fly off ahead of her. Saint flinches when she's called for second place, like it has cost her something.

And finally, at the head of the line, having "demonstrated resilience and ambition," in the words of Leighton, or as I would put it, "years of experience as a horsewoman," is Penthesilea Bonavich.

The first-place prize is one that Penthesilea is long used to—private, one-on-one dinners with Pierce nightly until the Raid, when her ranking might shift. Second place comes with a private brunch with Pierce and prime seating during common meals. Third, to Esme's chagrin, comes with nothing but the pleasure of not being *dead*.

As we're shuffled along the halls, I keep my eyes on the back of Hawthorne's head. I find a strand of hair to focus on. I try to get myself to move on. My stomach feels hollow, but I know I need to eat. To act as if nothing has happened.

As if three more lives weren't suddenly snuffed out for the Remingtons' egos. I know not to ask about the dead girls this time. The definition of insanity is doing the same thing over and over again, expecting different results. I won't let them drive me crazy too.

We enter the dining room to Mr. Caine's self-important proclamation of "Dr. Leighton Remington and the Ladies of the Finish—"

Pierce is right next to Mr. Caine, and he offers his arm to Penthesilea with practiced ease. She takes it. For once, they look like a proper couple, heads tilted toward each other, whispered words passing back and forth between them. For once, Penthesilea looks *real* instead of the hazy version of herself that she's been since the start of the Finish.

He leads her to the seat immediately to the left of the head of the table, and we fill in behind.

Esme and Hawthorne sit next to Penthesilea. Saint sits *far* away from them, at the other end of the table, where Third sits, and I'm quick to find a place next to her. I try my best not to look directly at Graham, who sits beside me, or at Pierce. I will never put another target on my back.

The rest of the girls fill out the table to the end, Leighton placed somewhere in the middle.

Saint engages in conversation with Third immediately, like she's determined to make this matter.

"What a day," Saint says, smiling broadly. "Did you enjoy the race, sir?"

"It went better than I thought it would. You did well, Saint. I am impressed," Third compliments.

"Thank you. My father taught me how to ride," she says. "In the South of France, at a friend's villa."

"Oh? That wouldn't be Villeneuve, would it?" Third asks. That must mean something to Saint, something *good*, because she straightens, leaning in and nodding.

I look down at the table grain.

"You didn't want to sit with your father?" I ask Graham. Slowly, I look at him from the corner of my eye.

"He'd much rather speak to any one of you than me," Graham says with a shrug. He steeples his fingers, balances his chin on the joined tips of his fingers. "You did well today."

"Thanks. I don't feel like it," I say gruffly.

"Well, I do. That first jump was *clean*," Graham says.

"I had a good teacher and a good mount. It wasn't me at all," I say. I look down at the plate. Salad to start. I pick at it, shredding kale to pieces with my fork. When I finally do take a bite after staring for a long moment, the raspberry vinaigrette explodes on my tongue. It's delicious. It's also hard to make myself swallow. Graham doesn't say anything for a while, not even something smart-ass, and when I look over at him, he's watching me try to chew. "What?"

"I . . . nothing. Nothing," Graham says, shaking his head, sounding mesmerized by . . . *something.*

"I'm too tired to figure out what that 'nothing' is," I sigh wearily, not asking again.

Across the table, Pierce looks like he's falling in love with Penthesilea all over again. I frown at them. I don't understand them at all, which is odd, because looking at them, in this context, they make perfect sense. They match, but it's almost like . . . the shape of Penthesilea is different now.

"How was the Taxis Ditch?" Graham asks like he already knows my answer.

"Thank you for telling me," I say, looking at him hard. I choke over the words "Thank you," but I mean it. "I don't know what I would've . . . I couldn't . . . Reagan's friend died in the Taxis Ditch, and she actually knew how to ride. I wouldn't have . . ."

I trail off, the full force of what's happened and almost happened finally hitting me.

Graham leans in and I know we're too close for comfort. We look like we're conspiring, but I can't move away.

"I was *not* going to let you *die*, Adina," he says firmly. "You aren't built for this life, and I promise you, I'm not being self-righteous when I say that's a good thing. You don't want to be like us."

Us. Penthesilea and Pierce are a united front, smiling at Esme like she hasn't killed a girl. Jacqueline's chatting with Hannah G like she didn't have a gun trained on me an hour ago. Like I didn't almost drown her. Saint sits next to me, talking numbers and figures like her shoulder isn't swollen, like she didn't dry pop a painkiller before she slipped into a tight dress. Maybe he's right.

In my moment of dissociation, our salad is swapped out for the main course.

It looks delicious. Wood-smoked salmon, garlic-butter mush-rooms, broccolini, and rosemary. Everything fresh, properly cooked by a team of chefs. It's rich and decadent, the kind of food that I'm not used to, that I thought I could grow used to. But just the thought of eating any of it makes my stomach turn now. I push it around with my fork, cutting it into pieces to busy myself.

Graham leans over in his seat, his fingers brushing over the lace sleeve of my dress. I flinch and he immediately lifts his hands, showing them to me, demonstrating that he means no harm.

"Aren't you going to eat?" he asks.

"I don't like salmon." Another lie.

"What do you like to eat, then?"

"The rich." I glare, daring him to sneer.

Graham smiles, liplessly. "That's fair."

He's not being fair, though. His kindness is *unfair*.

"If you're not going to eat it, can I have it?" a voice interrupts.

I look across the table at Esme. She looks serious, unsmiling and unmocking, and it's a large enough change that I hear Saint's voice falter just the tiniest bit before she continues strong in her own conversation.

"I think I will eat it," I say, only because I don't want her to have it. I'd rather stuff myself to the point of vomiting than let Esme take something else from me.

Esme leans across the table, and with a sincerity I didn't know she was capable of, she says, "Good. My mother always told me not to play with your food." But then she smiles wide, too wide, the kind where if this were a nightmare, her mouth would split open to reveal a cavern. "That one . . . that one I'm still learning."

CHAPTER

17

EIGHTEEN HOURS ISN'T ENOUGH TIME TO RECOVER from the aches and pains of the Ride and the chilliness of our lunch.

Eighteen hours is all we get.

The rest of the day is spent in and out of ice baths, nursing our wounds and looking over our shoulders even more, while eating dainty sandwiches and caviar for dinner. The rich taste of the chef-prepared meals isn't wet and heavy in my belly anymore. When I realize that, midbite, everything begins to taste like ash.

Sleep doesn't come easy either. The memories come at inconvenient times throughout the night. On the edge of sleep, suddenly terror wells from somewhere primal and I hear the anxious whinny of a horse or Jacqueline's cries, and my heart rate rachets up so fast that I worry that the sound of it will wake Saint. And then I breathe through it, only for the moment to repeat itself, until exhaustion hits so absolutely that I pass out more than fall asleep.

The next morning, after breakfast, we're all finally allowed to call home.

Waiting feels like another challenge, but one of the mind. Leighton summons us to her office with little rhyme or reason to the order. Reagan goes and returns shiny eyed. Esme's next and returns with a dour look to her face. Saint excuses herself from a call. When it's finally my turn, it's the early afternoon and only Jacqueline is left, and she seems to take it personally as I leave the common room, already shuffling the lies I will tell to my mother on my tongue.

The phone in Leighton's office is old-fashioned, but stylish and shiny, with a rotary made of brass. We don't even *have* a landline at home.

"You'll have twenty minutes of conversation," Leighton instructs from behind her desk. She gives the appearance that she's not paying attention, carefully reading some kind of scholarly article, but I know better.

I dial my mom's cell. The steady clicks and shuffle as the rotary swings back into place feel ominous. When I lift the receiver to my ear, I can feel the ringing in my teeth. And then there's a soft click.

"Hello?"

My mother's voice makes my eyes sting and the knot in my chest loosen. She sounds confused, and I frown, wondering why, until I realize that she wouldn't have the Remington number saved in her phone and I'm breathing heavily like a serial killer.

"Oh . . . Mom? Mama?"

"Adina? Is that you?" she gasps excitedly.

"Yeah, Mama, it's me," I whisper.

"Oh, Adina, my darling. Your father went to the grocery store! Oh, shoot! Maybe I should call him back—"

"No!" I bark, probably too loud. I glance over at Leighton, but she just flips the page of her article. "Sorry, it's . . . I only have twenty minutes."

"Oh, wow, they're really working you hard, aren't they?"

I look down at the fading bruises underneath the fresh dark-plum marks on my thighs, where my shorts bisect them. "Yeah, they are," I confess. I swallow the excess saliva in my mouth, taking a deep, shuddering breath to dry it all out. "I miss you so much. Like, so much."

My mother laughs softly. "Already? You've only been gone a few days, Dina." She hasn't called me Dina since I was a kid; she misses me too.

"I know, but . . . it feels like millennia," I whisper into the phone.

It's been five days since she dropped me off, and everything has changed so much. *I've* changed, and I worry that she won't recognize me when I get out. If I get out.

"Are you okay, honey? You sound . . . off," Mom says.

I want to tell her. I want to tell her everything. I want to be back in my living room, choking on my own tears as I tell her this *terrible*, terrible story about dead girls and acceptance to a family, to a *society*, that I'm not even sure I want any part of anymore. The truth is gummy on the roof of my mouth, waiting to be spit out.

"I'm okay," I say instead. "I made a friend. Her name is Saint."

"Saint? What kind of name is that?" she asks.

"I think she named herself after Yves Saint Laurent. She's from China, but she went to school in Switzerland."

"Oooh, fancy. Tell me more."

I tell her what I can. I tell her about the other girls—the ones who are left. I tell her about the fancy dinners and the card games. I tell her about how beautiful the Remington Estate is, that it feels like a foreign, magical place. I tell her about learning to ride a horse.

I don't tell her about Graham. He's too wrapped up in the truth, and I know how far away I have to keep my parents from it.

"That sounds . . . that sounds amazing," my mother says, and I can tell that I've spun a tale of awe. She's properly impressed and I think even Leighton, who is "not" listening, is too. She won't ask any real questions. She'll be *safe*.

"It is," I whisper, trying to match her excitement. "It's hard too, though."

Leighton said my mother and father will be safe as long as I play by the rules. But one round in and I'm already exhausted.

"You just need to try your best, Adina, you hear me?" she says. "Try your best."

What does my best mean in a place like this?

"Hey, Mom, I have to go," I say quietly. I know that my twenty minutes aren't up yet, because Leighton twists to look at me, raising an eyebrow, but I can't keep this up.

"Oh, already? Man, your dad is going to be upset he missed you. When can you call again?" she asks.

"I'll be back before you know it," I say, forcing a smile into my voice and skirting the question. "Just another week."

It feels like another long eternity ahead.

"Well, all right, my dear, I'll—"

"Mom, wait," I stop her, realizing something. She stops and I swallow hard. I'm not stupid enough to not at least try to create an exit strategy. My parents can't help me, but I *do* have someone in my corner with resources. I don't look at Leighton as I say, "Can you tell Toni something for me?"

"Oh, sure. Toni was by here the other day, looking for one of her shirts. What is it?"

"I ran out of my Suburbia Sweet lotion from Bath & Body Works. Tell her to get me a new one while she's out?"

There are so few people I've ever talked to about my Suburbia feelings. Only Toni knows the extent of how much I wanted to leave it. Any mention of it while I'm in a place like this would confuse the hell out of her. It's not concrete but it's a first clue.

"What kind of nonsense is that?" Mom asks. "I've never heard of that scent."

I laugh. "She has. You'll tell her for me, won't you, Mom? Oh, and that I miss her. I know she misses me anyway."

My mother sighs. "Yes, Adina."

"Thanks, Mom. I love you."

"I love you too," she says warmly, like always, like nothing has changed.

The phone call ends with a sharp click, but I'm still breathing heavily into the receiver. I can't manage to put it down. My eyes sting but I blink away the feeling sharply. Steeling myself, I finally set the phone down and turn to Leighton.

She's stopped pretending that she wasn't listening. She leans forward, tilting her head, and I hold my breath, waiting for her to question my words, the code, meant for Toni. She doesn't. Instead, she asks, "What's changed?" That's when I know she sees that the blinders are off. There's no more pretending that the Ride wasn't set up to push us together, to create violence. There's no more pretending that death isn't going to happen in the Finish this time, that I won't have to kill or be killed to win. No denying that for the Remingtons, deaths are preferred, simpler, tidier, and baked into everything they've set up for us. "What's changed?" is a stupid question with a simple answer.

In short? *Everything.*

"Me," I say softly instead.

Leighton smiles a secret smile, and the way she looks at me is as if she's looking at a very fond memory. "Adina, do you know what happens when one applies pressure to carbon?"

"Yes. It turns to diamond," I say.

"It must be unpleasant for the carbon, but wouldn't you say it's worth it in the end?" Leighton posits, "Think of the Finish as a becoming, of sorts. What will you be when the end comes?" She doesn't expect an answer. Instead, she leans back in her seat and tilts her head to the door, dismissing me.

CHAPTER 18

AFTER MY PHONE CALL WITH MY MOTHER, I RETURN to my bedroom with a resolve to tell Saint we need to come up with a proper plan for the next event. But I return to a girl who doesn't look altogether whole. She lies back on the bed and stares up at the ceiling, letting out a long, shuddering sigh, the kind I feel in my rattling bones. "I'm so tired."

In that moment, that moment where she slips, she looks my age with all that entails. Young. Uncertain. Afraid. But then as usual, Saint seems to blink herself awake and she is steel wrapped in silk again, sharper than a knife's edge. She's so aware for someone higher than a kite.

"You should sleep more. Tomorrow's your brunch. Maybe Pierce will slip and tell you about the Raid," I suggest. Yesterday's Ride was draining on everyone. Even Penthesilea.

Saint closes her eyes, and I think she's fallen asleep when she says, "There are so few secrets when a person revels in their own wickedness." And then she really is asleep.

Let it not be said that Saint doesn't have a flair for the dramatic.

I settle in for the evening, curling up with a book I've stolen from the library, one I can barely find it in myself to pay attention to, my eyes sliding sightlessly over the words.

The silence makes time go by quickly, interrupted sparingly by giggles and soft chatter. Sometime around six, I hear a knock at the door, announcing that dinner has been brought to the common room for the evening. I don't move, listening instead as the other girls congregate and then disperse. It's nearly midnight before I decide it's safe enough to show my face without the company of my ally.

The common room is stuffed full with different games, ways to pass the time. A half-finished game of Go, a Monopoly board dominated by someone's little red hotels, and a game of Catan that someone has lost rather embarrassingly. Strategy games. As I thought, the games have resumed, mental warfare until the physical challenges start again with the Raid.

Esme and Hawthorne are in there alone. I know just how dangerous they can be without the eyes of others.

"I'll just—" I start to back out, unwilling to put myself in the belly of the beast.

"No, come in, Walker," Esme says. "You weren't at dinner."

"I was not," I acknowledge. I sway forward onto the balls of my feet and then rock back hard on my heels, unsure how to move further. My stomach answers, gurgling noisily.

Esme smirks. She wants me to submit.

But the Ride is still fresh in my mind, and Jacqueline tried to do something to me after, too. Leighton's condemnation of "The Ride has finished," as she put Jacqueline on her knees, rings. This room is not a place for violence. To be a coward would just be another way of *losing*, and I can't afford that.

I keep my chin high as I march forward to survey the buffet table. There's more than enough left, an excess of food for the number of girls that remain. A platter of golden gougères, a tray of buttery brioche smeared with pâté, and the bloodied filet mignon on crostini decorated with goat cheese and shallot are just a few of the dishes on offer.

"I recommend the stuffed mushrooms. They're to die for," Esme says, so close that I'm forced to look up at her to meet her eyes.

"If you're trying to intimidate me, you're not," I lie. "I know all your tricks. Remember we used to be friends." The trick about lying, though, is that you have to believe yourself for anyone else to believe you. I don't believe myself, and so neither does Esme.

"Were we?" Esme says flatly.

"I thought so," I say. "As much as you can be friends with anyone."

"Friends don't spread rumors about each other," Esme retorts.

I frown. "Friends don't torment each other for their success, either."

Esme grabs my arm, acrylics digging into brown skin.

"You humiliated me," she snarls, neck craning forward. This close, all her features no longer look pretty. She is jagged, like the edges of her diamonds. I reverse, the small of my back slamming into the table, jostling it. "You and Charles's bitch sister. After I took you in and *made* you somebody. Almost made you worth *knowing.*"

"You made me someone I didn't want to be," I say. *Violent.* I was violent that day.

Esme sneers. "That day you showed me exactly who you are. Disloyal. Conniving. Selfish. And you've shown that every fucking day since, Adina. You showed it at the bonfire, too."

I scoff. "What are you talking about?"

"Maybe you were too drunk to remember, but I wasn't. I remember something else I saw happening in the forest. *Slut.*"

She knows.

I go cold all over then. I jerk from her grip and look down at the four welts forming on my bicep. Esme doesn't back down, though. She stares at me, her lips curled back over her teeth.

"I know that's why he's helping you. He had you once and suddenly thinks that you might be worth something. But I know you; you're nothing," Esme whispers. "I've been his childhood friend for *years.* He knows me. All the good, the bad, and the ugly, and he knows we're the same. He'll soon understand."

I swallow hard, rubbing at the marks that Esme has left behind. "You think you're going to win and tell him about how your mommy stole money from her charity board, how Daddy has a few offshore accounts, how the *Feds* are after you, and he'll think you're worth the headache?" I shake my head in disbelief at the fairy tale that Esme is imagining. She's always been an asshole, but never so unrealistic.

"You forget who you're dealing with," Esme growls. "Nothing is a headache for the Remingtons. They can make *anything* happen. After all, the Finish has been going on for over a century. Girls, weak like Margaret, have been dying *forever*. And no one has stopped them yet. My family's shit is nothing. It's a wish and an email away from being turned to dust."

The claustrophobia that has haunted me from the moment I entered the house swells to a crescendo.

I refuse to break. I take Leighton's advice and let it turn me into a diamond. Unbreakable.

"Yeah, but you won't ask him for shit. Not unless you win, because if you ask now, you'd be begging," I spit. I glare at her. "That would require you to swallow your *big* ego. And you're not capable of it."

"You don't know *what* I'm capable of," Esme bites out. "Not yet."

"Unfortunately, Esme, I do," I sigh, skirting around her.

"No, you don't," Esme promises. "You don't know anything. Because while you're here to get back something *you* lost—I didn't take it from you, you lost it by being *sloppy*—I'm here because I have people to take care of. I have people *relying* on me."

From this angle, in this light, I can imagine her as the wicked girl that sprayed poison and sent someone off to her death easily.

So for a moment it doesn't really click that Esme's cruelty could be derived from something not wholly selfish. That she isn't only in it to protect her own reputation or spite me.

She's here for her family, I realize. Esme's unhinged look peels from her face like old paint. When she looks at me, she's far more focused and intense than anyone ever gives her credit for. She touches her fingers to her diamond collar. Outside here, she wears it to remind people of her wealth, of who she is. Here, tonight, it feels more like a reminder for herself.

"I offered to sell this," she says, "to pay for the lawyers' retainer. My father said no. He said that it was a gift. I just think that he was ashamed. When I win . . . he'll never have to feel ashamed again."

When she takes a step back, she looks oddly vulnerable. She didn't mean to reveal so much of herself, but I know why she did. It's easy to show your underbelly to someone you hate, because hatred is strong, personal. It bonds people closer than most things. Before she can reveal any more, she leaves the room, ducking under Hawthorne's outstretched hand, sending the room into a silence that feels like a funeral.

I stare down hard at the floor, fighting back the burning pressure in my eyes.

The silence is a heavy thing, suffocating.

"You should eat." Hawthorne makes a plate for me, picking a little of everything, before she shoves it into my hands. I fumble to catch it and she holds my wrists steady, looking at me from under translucent lashes. "Are you all right?"

"I'm never all right." I take the plate without thanks—it's

just reparations for not saving me from that fucking awful conversation. When I curl up on the couch, far away from where Hawthorne was sitting, she doesn't seem to take the hint and joins me.

"You make her so angry," Hawthorne says with a quiet sense of awe. "I don't think you realize how much you do."

"I think I'm well aware of the strength of her rage," I mumble around puff pastry.

"I don't think you are," says Hawthorne. "You unbalance her. Make her feel like she's out of control. There's nothing she hates more than being out of control."

Well, I suppose we have that in common.

"Why me? Why not . . . Penthesilea? She should be back by now, but she's *still* downstairs with him *right* now. She's winning. Not me," I insist.

Hawthorne purses her lips. "Come on now, Adina. You're both favorites. Pen's performing better in the Finish, but up until the Ride he's liked you better. We'll see if that holds," Hawthorne says with a quiet sigh. She squints down at the ground. "Pen's always been just . . . nice. Since we were kids. She never cried. She always shared. She was never 'it,' even when it was her turn during tag, because *Esme* liked to be 'it.'"

"More reason for Esme to focus on her instead of *me*. Penthesilea's a pushover," I say, and almost immediately, it doesn't feel right.

"I don't know. I've known her my whole life," Hawthorne says quietly. "But I don't *know* her, if you get me? I think only Pierce knows her. He's like a dragon, sometimes. Hoards his treasures."

"He's not scary like a dragon."

"Oh, give it time." Hawthorne laughs to herself, shaking her head. "There's nothing worse than a boy who is lovely and knows it."

I turn to stare at her, flattening my expression to hide my irritation. "Why are you here?"

"I thought I'd keep you company," Hawthorne tries.

I snort. "I meant in the Finish, but we both know in a choice between my company and Esme's, you'd choose Esme's. You always have."

"You're right," Hawthorne sighs. "But . . . Esme snores."

This is much easier to believe than Hawthorne choosing to spend time with me.

"I don't agree with everything Esme does, you know," Hawthorne says softly.

"Then why do you let her get away with all of it?" I ask. "What she did . . . what she's *doing*. What she's planning."

"Planning," Hawthorne scoffs.

"It has to be her. She told those girls that Pierce is helping me. That's why they're all after *me* when I didn't even know what this was days ago." It makes sense. I remember the way Jacqueline had stared so viciously at me at the start of the Ride, the poisonous words that Esme had probably whispered in her ear, just enough to make Jacqueline decide without having to be *told*.

"Maybe. But Esme doesn't plan. Everything she does is by

instinct. That's why she needs me. To stop her from falling off the edge of the cliff."

"She's getting *very* dangerously close to that cliff, Hawthorne. There's only *so* much bullshit that anyone can put up with, and only so many girls left," I snarl.

"I love her," Hawthorne says simply. "That's why I'm here."

That startles me right out of my rage, makes it dissipate into nothingness.

"Oh . . . like, you love her or . . . you *love* her?" I ask, hoping that my awkward emphasis is enough to communicate what I really mean.

Hawthorne presses a hand over her mouth to smother a giggle. "She's more than just my best friend. She's my soulmate. She *was* my first kiss; we practiced together so that we didn't come off inexperienced. She was there for my first boyfriend. She was there for my first heartbreak. She's fought people for me. I'd do anything for her. *Be* anything for her."

"I really doubt that she'd repay the favor," I say, my voice dripping with sarcasm.

Hawthorne squints, like she's searching for something. And then her expression smooths into a smile. "Esme and I used to attend Lake Bryn Mawr together when we were kids. It's an all-girls camp in Pennsylvania. When were eleven, we were sent to different cabins for the first time. Esme pitched a fit, but I . . . I didn't say anything at all. I've always been quieter."

"Does this have a point?" I ask, tired.

"God, you're impatient. I'm getting there," Hawthorne scolds. "The girls in my cabin didn't like Esme . . . or me by association. She's always been Esme. So they tormented me. Spilled paint in my bag, left frogs in my sheets, tripped me into the mud at the bottom of the cabin steps, *every* day. Once, they locked me in the equipment shed overnight. There was a storm. It was freezing. I was sick for a week. I didn't say anything. But Esme knew. And one day . . . I came back to the cabin and Esme was there. With the three other girls. And for a moment I thought they got her, too. But those girls got to their knees. They crawled to me. And I tried to accept their apologies, but Esme said, 'No, they're not done yet. Let them beg.' They begged all summer. I forgave them on the last day. They never bothered me again. We were *never* separated again."

Hawthorne smiles, like Esme did something sweet for her. And maybe she did. But all I can picture are three girls—maybe cruel, definitely stupid—*crawling* because Esme demanded it of them.

"And so you allow her to do whatever she wants?" I whisper.

"Esme has never made me feel weird or . . . out of place. You think she sees me as a follower, but I'm her *equal*. We're partners," Hawthorne murmurs. She isn't looking at me; instead, she's staring into the vaulted depths of the ceiling, then looking at the dark mouth of the door, beyond which there could be eight prowling monsters.

"If you were really partners, when I got into Yale . . . why did you let her talk to me that way? Why did you let her do that to me?" I ask, and I can't help the way my voice cracks. I finally turn to look her in the eye. "I thought we were friends."

Hawthorne is gracious enough to look ashamed. "Adina . . ."

"There's no defending what she did, Hawthorne. I know . . . I know I started the rumors. And that wasn't right. But you all . . . made me feel so *small*. Belittled my achievements. Made it seem like I got what I had because of what I am instead of what I've done. And then . . . when Esme thought it was Toni, you were both so *cruel*. She called her needy and nosy, and an 'uppity, social-climbing cunt,'" I insist, flinching as I repeat the moniker that still rings in my ears. "And because I defended us, you all lied and said I started the fight. Do you understand what that means, Hawthorne? I lost my *scholarships*. I lost my acceptance to *Yale*. The basis for my entire future."

Saying it out loud to Hawthorne, one of the few people who was actually there, makes everything feel so much more real. It makes it hurt all over again.

Hawthorne can't even look at me.

She stands up suddenly and sighs. "She should be cooled down now. Hopefully, she's asleep." Hawthorne tilts her head as she looks down at me. "We *were* friends, Adina. And I don't want you to get hurt any more than you have been. But that's it. That's all I can give you. I can't let you win. Esme has always protected me from my fears and I have to return the favor, because you . . . you terrify her."

"Everything I do is self-defense. Everyone says I'm such a

threat. I don't want to hurt anybody. All I *want* is to live through this and get back into school," I say.

Hawthorne smiles. "That's what makes you so dangerous, don't you know? You see all of this and you still *want*. When has a girl ever been allowed to want?"

CHAPTER

19

I NEVER QUITE MANAGE A DEEP SLEEP, BUT I DO GET some, I realize as sunlight wakes me up, unkind in how bright it is. Sinking into the overplushness of the bed, I stretch, my spine cracking and relieving pressure. I twist, looking over at Saint. She's sitting on top of her bed, cross-legged, staring down at a book. She doesn't look fragile anymore, even with the brace on her wrist.

"We need to talk," I groan into my pillow, pushing myself up halfway.

"I agree," Saint says. She closes her book with an audible thud. "I'm not going to win. I've always been aware of this."

"What?" I ask, raising an eyebrow.

"It's never been about winning this. It was about gaining leverage. *I'm* the leverage. And what I've experienced and what I know. I just have to make it out of here," Saint says firmly. She sounds so blasé about it, using her trauma as a linchpin in her plan. But her word won't be enough.

"It'll only work if you have someone who would corroborate. You want me to win," I say as I catch on. Saint nods once. I lean in. "Good, because I want to win too. I'm *going* to win."

It's something I've gone over—my exchanges with both Aunt Leighton and Hawthorne. Their pretty words turn over in my head even now, and for all their euphemisms and half answers, there is a simple truth to it all. Only one of us is meant to survive. And I meant what I said, I don't want to hurt anyone, but I do *want*. I want what was *stolen* from me. I want to make this worth something, before it's too late.

"We'll be the last two standing. I'll forfeit at the last possible moment," Saint says simply.

"Will they *let* you forfeit?" I ask.

"If not, I have the distinct feeling all you need to do is ask. Ask for them to let me live, and Pierce will let me. Then you'll get your future back, and I close a deal that will help make my family even more powerful than the Remingtons," Saint says, and there's a revitalization to her now. She looks brand-new after just a night, and I can't tell whether this confidence is felt or manufactured.

"Agreed," I say. There are things we'll need to do to get there. Things I might not be able to, but in this moment I feel bigger than I have since the Ride.

"You should go shower," Saint says coolly. "It's nearly ten. You have brunch with Pierce at ten."

"*Excuse* me?"

"Pierce doesn't have anything to offer me. But he has *everything* to offer you," Saint says. "You're never going to get his father to like you. He's a bigot. But you have Leighton and Graham. *Now* you have to keep Pierce on your side. All that time he spent with Penthesilea last night? You have to undo the work she might have put in."

Her words and the truth of them start to take shape in my mind. To the Remingtons, winning means securing Pierce's hand in marriage, as absurd as it sounds. The other girls—besides Esme and Hawthorne maybe—have their sights set on that. They want to be a Remington.

To me, winning Pierce is a means to an end. It means access. It means Yale, and the means to pay for it.

I'm not here for the right reasons, and Penthesilea could be reminding him of that.

"The other girls want Pierce, and he knows," Saint continues, echoing my thoughts. "But he's barely spared any of them a glance. He's interested in your success. In *you*. And they all notice. I suspect they'll come harder in the next event. Especially Jacqueline. She was humiliated by you and Leighton, and Pierce looked disgusted with her when she lost it. He was pleased when *you* made it and that you rose above. We use that to our advantage and show him you're just as interested in him as he wants you to be."

I hesitate. "But what about Penthesilea? They've been together so long."

"He has her already," Saint says sharply. She leans back on her hands, staring into my eyes. "All men like him are the same. They *want* the things they haven't had."

I know what Pierce wants. Pierce called me his choice in a roundabout way. He likes me. He likes what he sees. And most of all, he thinks choosing me makes him "good." Inviting me here gives him the chance to say that he's done something noble and benevolent, and it's my trump card. Because Pen doesn't "need" him the way he thinks I do.

"So, go to breakfast with him. Smile when he says you look nice. Laugh at his stupid jokes. You don't have to do much. He's been impressed with your dismal performance already," Saint drawls.

"Hey!" I snap.

Saint shrugs. "It's true. While you're doing very well for someone who is dreadfully underprepared, you've not done anything that particularly makes you stand out, and he still finds a reason to bend the rules for you. He wants to be a white knight. And you rejected him. I bet his dick is *so* hard."

"Jesus, Saint, it's, like, ten in the morning," I say, my face growing hot. I roll out of bed and stalk past her as she laughs, jackal-like.

I feel like a caricature of myself as I get ready, dressing up *pretty* for this boy that I feel nothing for beyond attraction. But that attraction is strong, and it has overwhelmed my sense in sharp, gutting moments of *want* before. I have to control it and use it, not let it control me.

Hawthorne's words from last night cut me all over again, and I shove all thoughts of want from my mind. I square my shoulders as I get dressed and make myself look as close to perfect as I can when I am a collage of bruises and exhaustion makes its mark under my eyes. When I finally emerge from our room, I make sure to look both ways before stepping out. I watch as Jacqueline slips into Esme's room, giggling, and keep still, so as not to draw her eyes. Then I fly down the empty corridor as soon as the door shuts, scurrying down the stairs before someone can see me slipping away, dressed well enough to garner suspicion about where I'm going, though I realize I don't know which room I am meant to be going to anyway.

"Miss Walker?"

I jerk on the second landing, looking up to find Mr. Caine. He moves with the silence of a shadow. He looks at me like I've done something wrong, or been seen somewhere I shouldn't be.

"I'm . . . I have brunch with Pierce," I say. "Do you know where he is?"

Mr. Caine raises an eyebrow. "He's expecting Miss Liu."

"Miss Liu is still recovering. She asked me to take her place," I say, forcing a smile. Mr. Caine nods slowly, and then he stands at attention again, like now that I have *permission*, he'll lend his assistance.

"This way, miss," Mr. Caine says, and then he turns like he's in the military and marches back up the stairs, leading me down a new corridor, to a wing of the Remington Estate that

I've only been to once. The night I meant to escape.

As we walk along the red carpet, still beautiful, even though it should be dingy with centuries of tread, I think about a group of children running through these halls. I think of them playing tag, Esme always "it," Penthesilea always strategizing, training for this moment without even knowing it. There are more dire consequences to the games we play now.

We stop in front of a door I recognize. This is the room where I overheard the Remingtons' conversation.

"He'll be in his study," Mr. Caine says, gesturing to a closed door. "Have a delightful brunch . . . ma'am." He tries the word out, the one he's only ever called Leighton and Penthesilea. It means that he's been paying attention, that he *sees* how three-fourths of the family treats me. I feel surer of our plan by the minute.

With confidence, I rap my knuckles on the door and open it to find Pierce sitting by the window, buttering his toast. He's staring out at the gardens, a strained expression on his face. Even with a frown, he is unfairly handsome. Each glimpse reveals something new about him. This time, I find the tiniest scar on his upper lip.

I tasted that scar, I think, though it's suddenly hard to remember what happened in the dark. I lick my lips, trying to recall, but all I can summon is the flickering of flames and the look on Esme's face as I confronted her. Besides, I don't want to be thinking about that now. Drawing myself back into the moment, I stare at Pierce, waiting to be addressed.

He shifts, like he's just realized the door opened, and turns absent-mindedly.

"Saint, thank you for— Adina."

"Good morning, Pierce," I say. I have the oddest urge to call him "Four," like his brother does.

"Good morning." Pierce jumps up from his seat, a genuine smile now on his face. The study is similar to Leighton's office, except for touches of moneyed youth. Old photos of a playgroup of children on the desk—even though they are young in the photo, I recognize Esme's devilish smile and the pale shadow that was Hawthorne. Prints of him and Pen in various exotic locales line the wall. A receipt from Prada, with a note from Charles scrawled across it that I can't read, pinned to a cork-board. A framed photo of him and his brother on the bookshelf, both of them in riding gear. "Come, sit. Caine laid out a spread for us."

The table of choice is a heavy wooden one, set up in the round of a reading nook. It's like a diner booth, designed to bring us close.

"You look lovely," Pierce says. He sounds genuine.

"You always say that," I say with a smile as I slide into the reading nook. I lean over the table. "I'm sure you're surprised by . . . well, me."

"Yes, but it's a good surprise, I promise," Pierce says, with what I once might have seen as an empty charming smile. Now there's more to him—that smile means favor. He sighs, suddenly looking far looser. "To be honest, it's the best surprise."

"Oh?" I ask carefully. "Why is that?"

"You know . . . before the Ride I asked to add a prize for the one second ranked, because I thought that you'd choose to ride Widow Maker. I didn't think you'd beat Pen, but everyone else would've been in the dust," Pierce says with a rueful smile. He shakes his head. "Anyone else would have taken Widow Maker out, but you didn't. You had too much integrity."

That word again. "Integrity." He says it now like he's decided it's a good thing, not a blow to his ego. He doesn't know I've decided to throw that away, just in a different way.

But I let him believe what he wants to believe about me.

"Why do you want me to win so badly?" I ask with a tiny smile. "You have a girlfriend competing."

Pierce's smile drops just a little. He busies himself with buttering his toast again and then seems to decide that he doesn't want it. He sets it aside and pushes a bowl toward me. An açai bowl, the kind you order from a fancy breakfast place, because who *makes* açai bowls at home?

"Our chef made it. She's gotten quite good at it," Pierce says, confusing my disbelief for awe. "She knows I really like it."

"Pierce . . . ," I start. "Are you going to answer my question?"

"I . . . I don't *want* to," he says, strangely petulant about it, but he gets past it, realizing how he sounds. "Fine. My aunt Leighton was going to go to community college before she won the Finish. But, when she did win, and my uncle began to court her, his gift to her was a place at Harvard with him. My father did the same for my mother. My father wants Pen there with me. Pen may be great, but no one has asked what I want."

"He wants her to win," I say, forcing a smirk and laugh, but it rings false even to my own ears. "Should I start writing my last will and testament then?"

"Don't even *joke*," Pierce warns, looking thoroughly unamused. He sighs to himself, shaking his head. "But, yes. He wants her to win. By any means possible."

"So, he buys into it, then. The whole 'there can only be one' thing?" I ask.

"It's not just him. It's how the Finish is designed. You know, the Repartees change, but the events—the Ride, the Raid, the Royale—they never do. They're exactly as Matilda designed it. And they're designed so that there *can* only be one at the end, the most worthy. God, I can see why my mother hated this shit," Pierce murmurs. It's the first time I've ever heard him curse. He feels just a little less shiny now. "It isn't how I want it, though. What's happened so far has been . . . a tragic accident. I'm trying to make sure that there are no more."

Accidents again. At least two of those deaths weren't accidents.

"But you just said they were designed to do this," I say. "How are you trying?"

"Giving you all training, for one. That was never a thing," Pierce says earnestly. "And . . . broadening the circle of girls to include people who weren't raised planning to kill each other. My brother came up with that one."

My heart sinks. Neither of those plans has made any difference, but Pierce doesn't seem to see the flaw in his brother's *glorious* logic, instead turning back to the subject of Pen.

"My father thinks he can stop us changing it and choose the winner because he's head of the family. But these things evolve, and it's my life. *I* picked you," Pierce says with a small smile. He looks down at his plate. "You were a decision I made on my own. Unlike Pen." His smile drops again.

It's in this moment that I realize that Pierce actually takes this seriously. That he sees me as a potential wife. My fingers curl into fists in my lap, nails cutting into the soft flesh of my palm. The sting grounds me. "So, what about Penthesilea attending Harvard bothers you that doesn't bother you about *me*?"

It's easier for me to frame it this way—confronting a future, not a marriage.

Pierce's eyes widen and he looks out the window, his lower lip jutting just the slightest bit. "I'm not *bothered*."

"You clearly are," I snort. "So, is the issue her or your father?"

Pierce huffs dramatically. "I've never wanted to be part of *that* couple coming out of high school. The couple that goes to college together, that never grows outside of their partner."

"Did you tell her that?"

"I told her that they're holding a spot at Harvard and it's not meant for *her* but for the winner. I broke up with her so the competition would be fair, and she responded quite *reactively* to that." With each word, his voice sounds different, more distorted by a frustration that seems far too large for a petty argument between a former couple. All my pretend amusement drains from me. And then Pierce seems to realize how he sounds. He takes a deep breath, and suddenly, he looks kind again. "I'm sorry. I shouldn't get into this with *you*."

"Why?" I say quietly.

"I told you. I want it to be you," he says with a small smile. "You're not fake like the other girls. You like *me*. And you're not . . . overwhelming like Pen is. I feel like she's always smothering me. Keeping me small."

His cockiness, assuming he knows what I like, is rich, but for the first time, I have the odd thought that maybe we *aren't* so different. I know what it is to feel small. But then I look at this house. This place, and I can't imagine feeling small in a place where you can stretch out and be enormous. Still, true or not, it's a victory.

He broke up with her. Whatever Third may want, this is *my* game to lose. Not Pen's. It was never Pen's.

And then like he can hear my thoughts, he says: "You'll beat the Raid."

The statement forces me upright again, brings me back to the dual layers of my plan. To get to the endgame there are still two more tasks, and I need as much information as possible.

"We start lessons today. But I don't know anything about it," I say, stirring my açai bowl but not eating it. I gnaw at my own tongue, worriedly, but try not to show it.

Pierce leans forward, a smile playing on his lips, like he's keeping a secret. "I'm not *supposed* to say. But . . . I want you to know. I'd like to be good to you, Adina," Pierce explains. "And I was *going* to tell Saint, you know. Truly."

I don't believe him.

"You won't get in trouble?" I pretend to demur, eyes wide. Imploring. This moment has to be calculated, more so than all the rest. It has to be his idea.

Pierce clears his throat. "It's . . . it's a hunt. The Raid is about making choices in the maze of life. Good choices lead to something real, fulfilling your desires. Bad ones lead to trouble, dead ends, the death of your dreams. You go through the hedge maze; make the right choices and you find the object of the Raid."

He makes it sound uncomplicated, but I know there's a trick. There's going to be *something* that makes the game that much deadlier.

"What about the girls who don't find it?" I ask dryly.

"Well, just like in life, someone always wants to take what you have away. So, then you have to get out without giving it up. You fight them off to keep possession of the object. With . . . whatever's on hand," Pierce says slowly.

"Could you be *clear*, Pierce?" I say, words dripping with sugared honey.

Pierce sighs, drawn like a fly. "Well . . . in *some* years past, hopefully not this year, mind you, some of the girls get . . . enthusiastic about being the ones to get the object or keep it away from others. It used to be that only the top three were armed as an advantage, but I've decided that perhaps arming you all keeps it fairer so you can defend yourselves."

I stare at him. "Do you see why that doesn't make sense?"

Pierce's brow furrows. "I . . ."

"If you arm us, then we'll be *better* equipped to hurt one another. And you said you didn't want anyone to get hurt," I say slowly.

Pierce is silent for a long moment, and I watch as he forces that charming smile onto his face. He's going to say something meant to placate me, and I know no matter how much he believes in me, those words will be empty. Still, when he looks up at me again smiling, he seems paler.

"I don't think *you* will," he says, finally. He doesn't say it, but I know he has more "help" planned; it's in the veiled turn of his words, the way he leans forward, conspiratorial, like it's nothing but a joke.

"But . . . it's not just about me," I say quietly. "It's about Saint and Hawthorne and Pen and the others. If you don't stop it, you're endorsing it."

"But I told Aunt Leighton and everyone I didn't want violence. I can't help it if they don't listen. At least I'm leveling the playing field," Pierce says steadily, refusing to look away. "That's what we talked about. Right?"

I can't bear to look at him so I look out at the maze instead. It's vast, probably full of dead ends and traps, and around every turn of hedge, there might be a girl, waiting there to end it all for me. All of us searching for something that we don't know or understand. Life indeed.

"I . . . I'm not hungry anymore," I whisper, all the fight from this morning draining from me, my bones drooping in my skin.

Pierce's golden eyebrows arch, his mouth parting. "You've only had a few bites of your açai bowl," he insists.

"I don't think açai agrees with me," I mutter as I stand, shoving back from my seat. Pierce jumps to his feet, reaching for me, and I clear my throat, stepping back. Immediately I regret it and reach for him, brushing my fingers over his knuckles. "Thank you for trying to help me. I want to win as much as you want me to. I better start preparing."

"Are you mad . . . ?" Pierce trails off, shaking his head. "Of course. I'll keep helping you."

I turn on my heel and leave the room without another look back, my heart rattling in my chest.

❧☠☙

Fifteen minutes later as I walk the halls, Pierce's charming smile still flits across my mind, something slightly unsettling about it. I never found him unsettling before the Finish, not at Edgewater and not in the forest. It doesn't take much work for me to convince myself that it's *this*—the Finish—that sets me on edge, that makes me want to grind my own teeth to powder.

I'm so lost in thought trying to figure it out that I don't realize

I've wandered so far, I now also can't place where I am in the estate.

"Miss, are you all right?"

I startle. "I'm sorry?"

It's the security guard from the first night, with the red hair and doughy face. He's dressed differently, though, no tactical gear in sight, just a cheap navy polyester jumpsuit that makes him look more like a janitor than an armed guard. It would almost work if it wasn't for the wire coiled around the shell of his ear.

"Are you all right? You seem lost," he says.

I could ask how to get back. But I don't want to go back to Saint just yet and tell her what I just learned we have to survive. Not when I don't have any idea how to make that sound doable yet. I don't want to get upstairs and potentially be found out by the other girls. And I definitely don't want to run into Third.

"D-do you know where the kitchen is?"

Congratulations on not stuttering, Adina.

"The West Kitchen is just at the end of the hall and down the servants' stairs," he recites.

West Kitchen. Servants' stairs. It sounds like something out of a fucking period drama.

"Right. Got it. Thanks," I blurt before I take off down the hallway again. I look left and right for another set of stairs, and it takes me a moment to realize that the narrow, arched door half hidden behind a tapestry leads to a set of rickety steps.

I take one step down the stairs and hear them creak horribly underneath my feet. Another hesitant step, another creak. I turn, expecting someone to be staring at me in disapproval. But when no one comes, I rush my way down until I'm in the warmest room that I've seen yet in the Remington Estate.

It's cozier than I was expecting, creamy and yellow with white cabinets and marble countertops. The lighting hangs low and intimate. But I startle when I notice I'm not alone. Graham sits at the enormous island in the center of the kitchen. Trading one brother for another. Great.

"Uh . . . hello," Graham says with a nod.

"Hey." I walk deeper into the kitchen. "Did you know only rich people have servants' stairs?"

"Yeah, well . . . can't imagine why we do, then," Graham says sarcastically.

"Do they go through the entire house?"

"Yup. At each end of the house, there are servants' stairs that lead up and down so they could move without being seen back in the old days. Sometimes Third gets into moods and makes them use them. My grandfather used to do it a lot more, though," Graham says, distaste coloring his voice.

I look around for something that isn't him. It's funny. He's not the golden boy. He's not the sun. But it's getting harder to look at him. His nose has a bump at the bridge, like it's been broken before. *Real.*

"And you have an island," I say almost reverently.

"What's so great about a kitchen bar?" Graham asks.

"Island," I correct. "And it's more about the countertops.

Marble. Only rich people have marble countertops. I know. I've collected all the substantial evidence proving this theory correct. All the houses in my neighborhood are the same. Granite. The workingman's marble."

"Yeah, I can imagine you have. You've known a lot of rich people in your life," Graham says. He's eating cornflakes. I crave the simple taste of it, soggy and thick on my tongue, and tasting faintly of cardboard. I'd rather have that than an açai bowl I ordered someone to make. I'd rather have something that I know, that's familiar, that I've put together myself with my own hands. And that is a confusing thought, because I never thought I'd want cornflakes over caviar, over freshly baked croissants, over toast already buttered for me.

"Unfortunately," I say, and creep closer, leaning on the edge of the island. "Anyway. Your brother told me about the Raid."

"Did he?" Graham asks, doubtful. "Did he tell you how to survive it?"

"Not exactly. Isn't that *cheating*?" I drawl.

Graham huffs. "I think we're long past cheating, don't you? I told you about the Ride."

He was the one to give me real help. Not a horse I didn't know how to ride at the last minute like Pierce or half answers and half explanations like Leighton. Not a bland, "I want you to win, because *I* will it so." He wants me to win because he just wants me to *live*. And that shouldn't be enough to make me like him, that should just be standard decency, but in this moment it's enough. Suddenly, I can't look away from him at all.

"There's something different about you," he says. He swivels in his seat to follow me, holding his bowl with one hand, letting cereal and milk drip from his spoon, a splash landing on the knee of his jeans.

I hop up onto the island, right next to him. Slowly, he sets his bowl down and looks up at me. "Is it my hair?"

"No, but it does look good," he says.

I haven't washed my hair in a week. "Flatterer," I accuse. "Is it the skirt?"

"No, but that's nice too," Graham says, tilting his head as his gaze catches on my bare thighs. I roll my eyes. Graham's eyes flicker back up to my face. He's fighting a smile. "You look . . . well rested."

"Now I know you're lying."

Graham laughs.

"Tell me more about the Raid," I demand.

He shrugs. "You know . . . I really thought you were a good girl. Yet here you are, demanding I spill family secrets to you. You're doing well in this game."

The somberness in my belly rises to the surface again. "This isn't a game," I correct. "And I am a good girl. I just have to win, too."

"I wouldn't fault you, you know, if you *weren't* being good. Integrity doesn't mean much to the dead," he says. He pauses, thinking. "The maze . . . is hollow."

"What?" I blurt out.

"You can push through some parts of the hedge wall. We used to hide in the walls a lot when we were playing, and it grew back *around* the dead spots," Graham explains.

I mean to push off the kitchen island, now that I have actually helpful info I can take to Saint. Instead, I take his bowl from him and set it to the side. I grab his wrist and pull him until he stands, frowning at me. Hooking one leg around the back of his thigh, I draw him closer. He's not that tall. Like this, we're nearly the same height. I can feel he wants something from me, but that he won't ask or assume, not like Pierce. It makes me feel powerful and I grow heady off that feeling; it's been so long since I've felt anything but afraid.

"What are you doing, Adina?" Graham whispers. I can count every dark lash that sweeps across the freckled skin of his cheeks. Beneath that scruff, he certainly inherited the Remington cheekbones. I rub my fingers against the grain, feeling it scratch pleasantly at my skin.

What would it feel like against my lips?

"I don't know," I whisper. "I'm exhausted, Graham."

"Not so well rested, then," he murmurs. He tries to lean back, and I lash out, grabbing at his threadbare T-shirt.

His hands land on my thighs, big and warm.

I feel out of body. Out of my *mind*.

And I crave closeness, intimacy, not having to pretend, in this space that feels like a war zone, with violence thrumming through the air. I want something to ground me and he's here, and I can see it in his eyes. That he wants me.

I reel him in, licking my way into his mouth before he can say another *smart-ass* thing.

Kissing Graham is very different from kissing his brother. Pierce's fingers dug into my scalp as he tilted my head *just* so. But Graham waits. Graham waits for me to tug him between my thighs and he only ever keeps his hands on my legs. His stubble rubs against my cheeks, the feeling foreign and welcome. His lips are thinner, his hands are bigger, and he takes it *slow*. Everything with Pierce was hard and fast, and this . . . this is molasses.

This is pleasure and it's real, and it's *far* more terrifying.

"Shit, Adina," he whispers into my mouth. He tastes like cornflakes. He tastes like *Suburbia*, and for the first time, I miss it, my chest concave with how much I yearn for the familiarity, this feeling of home.

"Do you use Bath & Body Works?" I murmur into his mouth.

"What the *fuck* is that?" he asks.

I breathe heavily, breaking apart as I slowly drag my fingers over his jaw and close my eyes. "You're nearly perfect," I whisper.

"My father would beg to differ," Graham laughs hoarsely.

And suddenly, all the threats, the powerlessness, return as I realize what I'm risking, doing this with the wrong Remington.

And suddenly, I don't want this anymore. I can't want anything to do with him.

"*Don't* tell Pierce," I say, letting him go.

Graham jerks away, staring at me as if I was the accomplice to the worst crime.

"Adina," he says, and then he stops like he doesn't know what else to say to that.

"This . . . can't happen again," I decide.

"No, it cannot," he agrees.

I slip off the kitchen island before I can give in again, and I leave him wanting, because boys are allowed to want.

CHAPTER 20

"THE RAID . . . IS A METAPHOR." LEIGHTON PACES IN front of us, the dichotomy between the eight of us and her starker than ever. She is in her silk and satin, and we are in black military-grade fatigues. "Life is about searching for something worth living for. Searching for reason. Searching for purpose. We can spend all our days searching aimlessly. But you, young ladies, are not aimless. Life is made of decisions that will take you closer to or further from your goal. You are always constantly looking for the right direction . . . left or right? And if you *don't* make that right decision, you can't double back, as there will always be someone on your heels, ready to slit your throat and take *everything* from you. That is the Raid."

It doesn't sound like a metaphor.

Leighton's gaze flashes over to me like she can read my thoughts. I redirect my stare at the ground, nudging my boot into the grass. I'm already sweltering, sticky sweat frizzing up my hair out of its gelled-down state.

"Pierce," Leighton calls, raising her voice suddenly, and that changes everything.

The girls straighten up, all exploding into whispers, as the Remington in question jogs down the steps and across the grounds, dressed in blinding whites, like he's about to step onto a tennis court. When he arrives in front of us, he claps his hands together and smiles brightly, eyes flitting over each of us. When our eyes meet, his grin widens.

"As my aunt has explained to you, the Raid is metaphor for obstacles you may face in the future. But we, as Remingtons, do not go into that future unprepared," Pierce says, and then he leans forward to look Hannah G in the eye. Her lashes flutter, cheeks pinkening. "And neither should you." He winks, and then turns away like he has no idea what he's done to her. *He's enjoying this.*

"In prior years, only the top three ranked were allowed to select defenses. Everyone else had to rely on their cleverness. However, this Finish is different. My nephew is . . . different," Leighton says, weighing that *word* on her tongue. "My nephew will be the one to arm you. As the winner of the Ride, Penthesilea, you will be the first. In continued practice of rewarding those who succeed, you will be assigned two."

Penthesilea steps forward, looking at ease even in battle fatigues. Lifting her chin, she meets Pierce's gaze easily and he steps close into her personal space, a comfortableness that only time can create. He doesn't smile as he reaches for a delicate butterfly knife, flipping it open and then closed again before he turns it handle first. She takes it from him, fingers brushing over his knuckles.

"And?" she prompts.

Pierce's eyes narrow, like he finds a thousand meanings in that one word. He reaches past her toward the table and holds up a machete. This one he offers blade first. Penthesilea's smile widens.

"Thank you," she murmurs, and then she steps back into place, nodding her thanks also to Leighton for graciously allowing her to be gifted two *fucking* knives.

"Very good," Leighton says, sounding impressed, which is also alarming. "Now, Saint."

Pierce smiles politely at her as he alternates between a broadsword and a rapier-and-dagger set. He tilts his head as he looks between the weapons and her, and then he says, "You strike me as sneaky."

"I have that air about me," Saint deadpans. Pierce does not seem to find her nearly as funny as I do, frowning as he passes her the rapier and dagger.

Esme is next and Pierce is quick to give her a large hunting knife, as threatening as her smile. Hawthorne is given a crossbow that she throws back over her shoulder. A pit forms in my belly as I suddenly remember that Hawthorne is a *prizewinning* archer.

What is Pierce thinking?

I catalog the table quickly, looking for anything that remains usable. Jacqueline and Hannah G are eyeing the very sharp *battle-ax*. Each weapon I see is more intense than the last. A broadsword, a spear, nunchaku. My survey is cut off as Pierce finally steps in front of me. He holds out a hand to me, full of expectation.

Everyone is watching. There is already a target on my back. This will make it worse.

I take it anyway. Pierce grins as he tugs me forward, out of line.

"You think you have me figured out yet?" I ask.

"Nope. But I do know *exactly* what suits you," Pierce says. He reaches for a slim black case with a handle. I frown at it—black, hard plastic that I don't recognize. It's unintimidating. And then Pierce flips it open, like a box of jewelry, and I force myself not to retreat.

This weapon feels more violent than the rest—a row of shiny bronze bullets to go with the slim, sleek gun. It is the one that Jacqueline pointed at me, and now I know where she stole it from. Touching it feels forbidden. I can hear Jacqueline's bloodcurdling screams, can see her staggering toward me, drenched and burning with fury, gun in stretched-out hand.

When Pierce sees me hesitate, he pulls the gun from the case and sets the case aside before he steps back into my space with an unearned intimacy. The barrel of the gun brushes my stomach before he spins it on his finger, offering the handle toward me. He's not even looking at me, I realize. His blue gaze cuts deep into Jacqueline's twisted expression. He's punishing her, as much as rewarding me.

It's her face that makes me take it. I want to make her feel every bit of fear that swelled deep inside me and never left. I grab the grip and point the empty gun directly at Jacqueline, and I can't help the sick flare of satisfaction when she staggers back, hands held up over her face.

"Pew, pew," I say, voice flat, before I turn back to Pierce.

I do not like this smile of his. Everything is too wide, his mouth, his eyes. My own momentary victory is dulled under the scream of my hindbrain. He doesn't look like the kind of person *anyone* could make feel small.

"Pierce," Leighton prompts, settling a hand on her nephew's shoulder.

Pierce schools his expression again, looking apologetic toward me. "Um . . . ," he says, blinking rapidly, resetting mentally. "Hannah G?"

Hannah G receives a fairly innocuous staff. For Jacqueline, there is the battle-ax, but to my relief it is *almost* too heavy for her. It'll slow her down. And finally, to Reagan goes a baseball bat.

When Jacqueline scoffs, Pierce smiles and says, "Reagan is a softball player. I think she knows her way around a bat."

And for the first time in days, Reagan *smiles*, stretching the cut on her face.

Leighton nods her approval at Pierce. "Very good," she agrees, and where we might have preened under her praise, Pierce disregards it altogether, barely blinking. "To prevent any undue accidents, each of your weapons will need to be checked out through the proper channels for practice. Now come closer, we will begin to lay out your training routine over the next few days."

We are meant to huddle closer, but as the other girls squirm in front of me, I fall back to survey them all.

"I've always thought guns to be dishonorable." Esme's voice is a hiss in my ear as she sidles closer. I reach to my left, toward Saint, without taking my eyes from Leighton's hands as she describes our schedule. Saint grabs my wrist, assurance that she's here. Pierce sees nothing; he's watching over Leighton's shoulder, politely disinterested. He'll be there just for today's practice, but none of the rest. "It puts distance between you and the target. With a gun, you don't even have to have the courtesy of looking them in the eye. Knives are more personal."

I flicker a look at her from the corner of my eye. Esme shakes her black bob out and her shoulders wobble; she's laughing silently though I have no idea why. She leans into my space, and the scent of her perfume turns my stomach. It's the Chanel perfume, hints of lavender and sandalwood. Not the Dior that killed Margaret. Plausible deniability and all that.

"It's . . . it's just, he *really* wants you to win," Esme says, answering my silent question. "He's not even trying to hide it anymore. And neither are you."

"What's the point of hiding?" I ask.

"You're right. There is none. Pierce wants you to win. So does Leighton. Probably Graham, too, but who knows what he wants underneath his constant need for vodka. All it does is make everyone want to take you down even more than I do, though. Just because you have the tools doesn't mean you have the stomach. *I* do. I have to."

"He knows you've fucked me over. He won't pick you," I warn. "If Penthesilea can't win, you certainly can't."

Esme snorts. "Pierce, in the grand scheme of things, can be convinced about what he wants, because he's just like the rest of them—bored," Esme drawls. She shrugs and shakes her head. "But I can't afford to be bored. Don't pretend you're special, Adina Walker. You're not the only one here for the wrong reasons."

When we turn to look forward again, we stay there, shoulder to shoulder, eyes trained on our next obstacle—the maze. We do not look away.

CHAPTER

21

I PREFER TO TRAIN AT DAWN.

The other girls are still sleeping at that time, even Saint, who burrows deeper into slumber when I rise in the early hours of the morning. I dress slowly, ignoring my Raid fatigues in favor of leggings and a T-shirt. Like I'm at Edgewater's gym again, pretending to work out with Toni, but really taking photos of her lounging across various gym equipment for her Instagram.

Wandering the halls of the Remington Estate, I feel lonelier than ever, despite the ghosts haunting every corridor.

All the weapons are locked up in the hunting parlor, each with a little name tag, meant to be checked out like they're library books. It's to prevent what had happened during the Ride, when Jacqueline got access to a gun she wasn't supposed to have. It feels like a moot point right before we are all meant to murder one another.

When I arrive, there is only one guard. The housekeeper.

"Can I get the pistol? It's under my name," I ask.

The housekeeper—a brown lady with gorgeous dark eyes and lashes that I envy—looks up. She's younger than most of the other staff members I've seen around, dressed in bland khakis, armed with a massive set of keys around her wrist and a bottle of ammonia. My eyes catch on the key ring.

She probably has the key to every door in this house. Including the front.

"Ah," the housekeeper says, before she purses her lips and shakes her head, as if to say, *Not my business*. I get it, lady. "Your name, miss?"

She sounds impatient. I'd be impatient if I were her too. There's a lot of house, and I haven't seen any other housekeeper around except for her. I don't count the chef, who only comes to prep and cook our food before she sees herself out.

"Adina Walker," I say. This woman is more like me than I'm like anyone else in this competition. But she doesn't look at me that way. She looks at me like I am part of the other, and given what I've just requested, how can I think she's wrong? It's like I can't breathe, each inhale coming sharp and jagged enough that it hurts.

"All right. Gimme a minute," she says.

The woman putters toward the lockboxes set in the cradle beneath the enormous coffee table. She unlocks the box with my name on it, printed in perfect Arial, and then she pulls the case out, passing it over.

"Thank you, ma'am," I say sincerely. The woman blinks her surprise, and I leave the hunting room and head out one of the side doors, onto the grounds. I avoid the path down to the stables, moving toward the range, set up right by the maze. Leighton has arranged this space for everyone with long-range weapons, from throwing knives to the magazine of bullets that I carry with me. It's simpler than the kind that you'd see in one of those procedural shows, just a few targets pinned to bales of hay, with a table to lay out our wares.

The maze is vast, stretching far on either side of me. The foliage is so bright, it looks fake, and I can practically smell the chlorophyll. Slowly, I set the gun case onto the table and step around, squinting harder, trying to make sense of it, trying to formulate a plan. And then, before I can take another step forward, someone walks across the yawning entrance, patrolling from the inside, a figure in black, a gun at his hip. In the weak morning light, his hair looks copper.

I turn on my heel swiftly. Of course they wouldn't leave it unattended.

I unpack the gun safely. The first thing that I was taught yesterday was gun safety. The irony of being taught how to carefully handle, put together, and take apart a gun did not escape me.

"Fancy seeing you out here, this early in the morning."

I can't quite fight the smile that threatens to tear itself across my mouth at the sound of his voice. Drumming my knuckles against the table, I take a deep breath.

"Well, I'm trying not to die, Graham. As you instructed."

He slides into my range of vision, leaning back against the table. "Sweetheart, we'll all die one day."

Sweetheart. My stomach twists. I busy myself with the gun, sliding the jigsaw puzzle together, each individual bullet pressed into its proper place.

"My day will hopefully *not* be Thursday," I retort. Three days to learn how to aim and shoot. Fine. I learned how to ride a horse in three days; clearly, I thrive under pressure. I just have to not think about what I'll be aiming at.

Graham leans in, grabbing my chin gently. My breath catches in the space between my lungs and the back of my throat. It's almost like he's asking for permission. I don't move, and he takes the chance, tilting my face up toward his.

"I want to kiss you again," he says.

"That would be a bad idea," I acknowledge. The windows are large and wide, and while the sun is still rising, anyone could be awake.

Graham concedes my point by stepping back and I breathe easier.

"Do you want to kiss me again?" he asks.

I roll my eyes. It's not a *no.* He takes it as such and grins.

"Why are you here, anyway?" I pick up the gun and goggles and step up to the end of the lane, checking my stance awkwardly. The gun feels too heavy in my hands.

I remember Leighton's instructions from yesterday—*good stance, firmly planted feet, straight shoulders, aim, shoot.* I follow through them, pulling the safety off, and then fire. Almost immediately, my arms are ripped up and back by the kickback, and I stumble, cursing *loudly.*

"Mother*f*—"

"To help you learn how to shoot."

I pause and look back at Graham. His mouth is pressed into a thin line.

"Don't *laugh* at me," I snap.

"I'm not laughing!" he protests. He bites down harder on his bottom lip. *I know what that lip tastes like.*

"You want to," I accuse, and that's what breaks him. He snorts into his arm, making a quiet keening sound.

"You're very bad at shooting. Worse than your riding," Graham says plainly.

"All you ever have to say is how bad I am at things. Maybe I should ask Pierce to help me," I taunt. I regret the mention of his brother almost immediately. Graham does too, from the way he gives a full-body twitch that takes him a second to control.

"Pierce is a terrible shot. I'm not," Graham continues. "So, I'm here to help. If you'd like me to."

"You know I *need* your help," I say impatiently. "'Like' has nothing to do with it."

Graham's lips twitch and he shrugs. "Yeah, I guess. Now, first things first: You're way too stiff. Loosen up."

"Leighton said—"

"'Leighton said,'" he mocks, voice scooping into a shrill, pointed, know-it-all voice.

"I don't sound like that."

"Oh?" Graham asks, raising a single eyebrow. I roll my eyes as he steps up, his large hands falling onto my shoulders, gently massaging the tension out. "Leighton only knows how to shoot like she's at a range; she preferred a more close-range weapon in her Finish. I know you don't want to use it, but if you *have* to, in the maze, you'll be on the run. You'll need to be as loose as possible."

"How can I be loose when I'll be trying to put a bullet in someone's head?" I demand.

"You won't be," Graham says patiently. "You'll be aiming for the leg, because you're good and kind and not a raging murderer. Now, come on, loosen up."

I relax under his fingers, the weight of them familiar now.

"Breathe in." I inhale sharply as he leans in. "Breathe out." I exhale, and then something finally comes loose inside me and my muscles relax.

"You're really good at this," I murmur.

"Good at what? Getting you to relax? I've been known to do so," Graham says flirtatiously.

"No, I mean rich-boy things," I explain. "Horseback riding. Hunting. It's very WASPy for someone who's always seen as not fitting in with his family."

Graham groans. "God, don't say *that*."

"Well, it is!" I laugh, shaking my head.

Graham lets out a messy sigh and steps in close again. "At least it's finally proving useful." He presses his chest against my back and guides my wrist back toward the target. His fingers wrap tightly over mine, the weight daunting on the trigger.

"So, you're going to do what I said. Relax. Breathe. Center yourself, but *relax*," Graham repeats. I inhale and exhale. "Good. Now, aim with your dominant eye. Arms aren't *straight* out, but slightly bent. Nowhere near your face."

Each line of Graham is pressed close to me, and saliva pools on my tongue as I follow his guiding motions into a much looser and comfortable version of what Leighton showed me on the first day.

"Just . . . like . . . that," he whispers, the scrape of his stubble against the shape of my ear, and I bite my bottom lip hard. His hands over mine guide the pistol up, and I squint at the target, not too far, just far enough, the length of a lane in the maze, according to Leighton.

I steel myself over as I guide the safety back until I hear the softest of clicks. And then I pull the trigger.

I barely feel the kickback as Graham holds me in place, and I stare at the damage.

A perfect bullet hole in the chest of the target.

My eyes sting and I slowly lower the gun, clicking the safety back into place. I turn in Graham's arms, groping for the side table. I drop the gun there, never shifting my gaze from Graham's face.

"Good shot," he whispers.

"I have a good teacher," I say, and then I deliberately take a step to the side, attempting to escape his gravity. And yet it still feels too intimate. I look back at the target, paper shredded in a tight circle.

In a person, that bullet would explode, ricochet off bone and muscle, turning them into mincemeat from the inside out. I close my eyes and inhale deeply, staving off the light-headedness. This is what they all want. What they all expect from me. Except one.

"How are you the un-favorite?" I blurt out, but sober quickly when I realize what I've asked.

"It's fine," Graham insists, shaking his head. He runs a hand through his short black curls. "I taught myself to be good at these things. The riding and the shooting and the biting wit. I taught myself because I have *always* been the un-favorite."

I can't imagine a time where Graham might want Third to look at him like Third looks at Pierce—the heavy weight of legacy in the pinprick pupil of his eye.

Graham grabs at the table edge, anchoring him there. "My father very purposefully didn't give me his name, because from the moment I was born, he decided that I wasn't Remington enough for it. It was how my mother reacted to my birth. She was distant. I know now that it was postpartum depression, but what kid understands that?" Graham asks softly, and he's sinking. I can see it happening, watching him vanish into memory. "I don't remember it. But the body keeps the score, right? Even now, when my parents touch me, it feels . . . unfamiliar."

"Graham," I call quietly, and he is not back with me, not exactly, but he seems a little more awake.

"And then Pierce was born," he says sharply, and the light in his eye grows. "I can't remember my life without him. There's a picture of me holding him soon after he was born. I'm, almost two, maybe? It was like my mother had gone to a board meeting at Edgewater, and she came back with something for *me*. That's the first picture I have with my mother, too. She came alive again. We all came alive. So, it makes sense that he got the name. And that I would make sure he only got the *right* things. The happiness that he brought back to our family.

"So, I became good at the things that a Remington was meant to, because I needed to teach *him* to be good at them," Graham says fiercely. "I taught him to be better so that my father would never regret giving him that name. And he hasn't. Pierce needed to have an eye for business, so I pretended I didn't. Pierce needed to charm at parties, so I would be disinterested. He had to seem sophisticated, so I was unrefined. For Pierce to seem simply *confident*, I had to be arrogant."

And with each word, his voice shakes more and more and he is shaking apart, and it is terrifying to watch.

"I didn't go to Harvard because he has to go to *Harvard*," Graham says, and he grabs my gunpowdered hands, trying to make me understand. "For my father and now for Pierce, tradition is *everything*. It's what makes someone special. And Pierce is the special one."

"Tradition" is such a heavy word.

"Traditions . . . like the Finish?" I ask.

Graham's gaze hardens. "That was the one tradition I tried to get him to break from, to follow in my footsteps. I draw the line at . . . at the Finish."

"You didn't have one? A Finish like this one?" I press.

"Yeah, I locked myself away in London and went on a bender and refused to come home. Refusing to do it kinda solidified me being . . . you know. The un-favorite."

"Did Pierce know why you didn't?" I ask. "Did he know what—"

"He knew what it was supposed to be," Graham admits. "But he wanted to make it different. I didn't think it was possible, but he wants to create new traditions from the old. That whole thing about evening the playing field. He really believes it. He wants to do good. That's why he invited girls from outside our circle. Girls like . . . you."

There are no girls like me. There is only me.

Pierce might've *wanted* to change things, but how hard did he try? I remember his glossing over my objections, the ways in which he thinks he has tried to help me, in his not-helpful way. He knew all along how this could go; he weighed out the gains and losses accordingly, and let tradition win.

Graham is still insisting that he can imagine what I'm think-ing. "I know how it sounds, but my mom went through this type of Finish too, and it seems like it . . . kinda broke something in her. She got better after Pierce was born, but she was lost in her own head sometimes, especially when the Finish was held. The old Finish . . . there was no preparation. No rest. It was just one week of the most vicious things you could imagine. I think Pierce wanted to make something new especially for her."

I hesitate again. "Your . . . mom? Is she . . . ?" I trail off.

Graham stares at me with narrowed eyes, confusion tightening the line of his mouth. And then: "Oh, no, she's not dead. She's at a health spa in Aspen."

"Oh, I . . . does she do that often?" I ask.

"Yeah, I mean, when she's stressed. The Finish stresses her out," Graham explains.

"It stresses *me* out," I press, and all those warm feelings from before are starting to dissipate. My hand clenches tighter around the gun. "This is not 'something new' because we're training and getting a few days' rest. This is still barbaric. I'm learning how to *shoot* people?"

Graham groans, stepping away. "Adina, please—"

"'Tradition.' You all love to throw that word around, but it's not *my* tradition. I didn't ask to have any part of it," I insist, closing in on him, dragging my fingers over his skin, over the soft fabric of his T-shirt that probably cost three hundred dollars, to remind myself that he's real, that all of this is real when it should be just a nightmare.

"Didn't you?" Graham says, tone nasty. "You didn't mind the invitation, I remember."

I let him go like I've been burned. Wounded.

"Don't even try to throw this back in my face," I hiss.

Graham shakes his head. "I warned you. I told you that you didn't have what it takes."

"You didn't tell me what that meant! What I had to *do*. What I'm expected to do." My voice cracks and I don't want to cry. I can't cry now. "You didn't tell me your brother would give me a gun or that your aunt would expect me to *kill* someone to win. Do you understand that?"

"I do," Graham says. "But you're here now. I don't want you to kill anyone, but I want you to *live*. I want you to win."

"Why? I understand you gave everything to Pierce to make sure that he never felt expendable like you did, but I'm not something to give, Graham."

And there it is—the truth of what winning means. I'm as unready to confront it as Graham is, our mutual bewilderment digging deep to compete with mutual anguish. The idea of marrying into this family makes cold sweat bead high on my forehead, frizzing my hairline. And Graham looks revolted by the very idea, his fingers flexing like he needs to grab something. We both look to the house, as if expecting to see Pierce in the window, his presence felt so heavily that it's almost like he's sitting on my chest, and all the air whistles out of me, wasted.

"Adina, I can't," he says. "I can't . . . I don't know what to do."

He sounds so sincere.

And it doesn't mean a fucking thing.

Two Remington boys, both proclaiming how much they *want* to help but, in the end, never doing anything at all.

"You're a coward." I'm not sure who I mean—Pierce or Graham.

Graham doesn't flinch at my accusation. He smiles instead. "I know. But I'm a coward who is at least going to make sure you can shoot."

"I hate you," I whisper.

I don't believe it. Neither does he.

"I'm sorry," he says. "But I'd rather you hate me than you be dead. Now . . . pick up your gun, point it at the target, and pull the trigger. Because I'm not letting you die, Adina Walker."

CHAPTER

22

I SPEND THE ENTIRE MORNING PUTTING BULLETS into paper targets, long after Graham leaves, still tender from our confrontation. I can sense the way the other girls feel, seeing me there early, training, and the way they react to Leighton smiling and remarking on my initiative and dedication to bettering myself. Still, I sponge her praise, parched for some acknowledgment or reminder that she sees herself in me, when I see it less and less when I look in the mirror. She is a reminder that I can do this. That I *have* to do this.

All throughout morning practice, Jacqueline stares at me and the gun now in *my* hands. I feel a thrill at her attention. She's angry and afraid, and it'll make her sloppy, exactly like I need her to be. I cut a look to her again and again, almost mocking, and it's enough that Jacqueline begs to speak with Leighton over our lunch break, crumpling into petulant fury.

I expect her to return still fuming, reminded of how

disappointing she is by Leighton, but when Jacqueline walks into the parlor after, she is all smiles, a certain level of calmness that has been missing the past few days returning. She immediately joins her clique of girls, joking softly, and for a moment I can see the ghost of who she might actually be, not the exaggerated fun-house aggression that she's adopted here.

Then she looks at me and her expression flattens. "She's asking for you, Walker," she says primly.

I don't quite pause in my game of Solitaire—I'm losing. Badly.

After lunch the games were laid out for us to pick from—the same games that I've seen before: Go, Monopoly, Catan—and an added stack of cards. Decision-making games, specifically. I chose to go back to a deck of cards. Solitaire seemed right, since I could do it solo, but I've already lost twice, made too many shitty decisions.

Saint looks up from her own deck, frowning over at me. "Since when did you have a meeting with her?"

"I don't," I say absently.

"Well, don't keep Aunt Leighton waiting," Jacqueline says sharply, finally shaking me out of my game. She twists back to smile toothily at Esme.

"Wish me luck," I say to Saint.

"You think you need luck?" Saint asks.

"No," I say with a tight smile. Whatever Leighton wants, I'm sure it'll be good. It's close to the Raid and I haven't spoken to her privately yet. She'll have something for me, something that'll help

Saint and me. "Protect my game. I'm going to finish it when I'm done."

I stand and pretend that I don't feel everyone else's eyes on me. At least I've gotten a lot better about acting like it doesn't affect me. I ascend the stairs, then walk down the hallway, moving as quietly as a breeze, my bare feet sliding across the wood.

I probably should have stopped to put on shoes, I think as I approach.

I mean to knock the second I reach her door, but in a mockery of the night I tried to escape, I hear that *same* voice first.

". . . indifferent. Do you understand why that's a problem?" Third demands.

"I fail to see how it's *my* problem. Third, you need to leave. I have one of the girls coming to speak with me," Leighton says. It's strange, hearing the pair of them speak. She sounds caught between exhaustion and the kind of coldness that women get when they want someone like him to leave them alone and he doesn't get the hint.

"About?"

"Does it matter?"

"It's that girl. You're *plotting*—" Third accuses.

"No one's plotting anything. You're paranoid," Leighton says carefully. And then, in her lilting voice, she asks, "Are you frightened, Third?"

"Of what?" Third snarls.

"Your eldest son is a failure. And your heir . . . well, he's not doing as he's told. Yes, I know you've had the winner of this Finish handpicked from youth. Penthesilea Bonavich is perfect on paper," Leighton drawls. "But the heart wants what the heart wants, and he wants . . . what was it you called me all those years ago? 'Working-class gar—'"

"Now you listen to me," Third says, his voice so quiet, I have to strain to hear. Leighton falls silent with a sharp inhale. "You were never my first choice for my little brother. I would've rather you ended in the gutter with the rest of your kind in that disgusting little town. But you are one of us now. Barely. But you are. Even after the death of my brother, I allow you to live here, year after year, leading the Finish. But make no mistake, it is only because I allow it. And I will *not* extend the same to her. She doesn't have the mettle. This is what happens when we let diversity lead our decisions."

Great. I'm the *diversity* pick.

I expect her to stick up for me, but Leighton doesn't say anything. I swallow. Perfect Leighton, with her beautifully curled blond hair, her sloping nose, her defined jaw. Gutter trash. Working-class garbage.

And then she says: "Come in, Adina."

I take a step back, stunned. There are two heavy steps and then the door is thrown open.

Third looms above me, his expression so cold, my lungs freeze.

"Little girls shouldn't be privy to conversations between their betters," Third says carefully as I walk in. "Eavesdropper." It's almost childish.

"Classist." The word drops from my mouth before I can stop it, and I slap my hand to my lips.

Third sneers. For a moment he looks like he might actually try to attack me, and then Leighton is there. But she's not looking at Third. She's looking at *me*.

"What is wrong with you, Miss Walker? You are a guest," she condemns.

I look at her, shocked. I thought she'd be pleased with my quip, defending us both, but she stares at me with none of the same pride from before. Third stares for one more moment and then exits, shutting the door quickly. Somehow, it feels like he's stealing the last word.

"Miss Walker," Leighton says, waving toward the seats. I swallow hard as I enter what feels like a confessional that I am too restless for.

"Aunt Leighton." I shuffle closer, sliding onto the velvet couch. She doesn't sit in the adjacent chair today, just leans against her enormous wooden desk, a glass of wine in hand despite the early afternoon sun filtering through her half-shuttered windows.

"Are you ready to behave?" Leighton asks.

I nod slowly, even though it seems an absurd question. Something's different. Whatever just *happened* has made it different.

"Well, then, my dear, how *are* you?" Leighton asks as if it isn't, but "my dear" has never sounded so damning.

"I'm not sure," I answer honestly.

Leighton purses her lips and lets out one of her deep laughs, the ones that sound like dark chocolate, rich and bitter.

"You are *quite* the popular character, I'll have you know. You've made an impression," she says, wanting me aware that every one of the other girls has me on her tongue. Like I don't already know.

"The Raid is almost here," I murmur, staring out at the maze that dominates the grounds. It's the kind of thing that belongs to fairy tales. But eight-foot-tall hedges full of dangers don't promise childlike dreams.

"Yes. I hope you feel ready, Miss Walker," Leighton says like a command after a sip of red stains her tongue purple.

"Does anyone ever feel ready for danger?" I sigh.

Leighton raises an eyebrow. "Do you *feel* like you're in danger, Adina?"

"I haven't stopped feeling like I am in danger since the moment I stepped through those front doors," I admit, my fingers digging into the fabric of my leggings. "And that's gotten worse in the past few minutes. Did I do something wrong?"

Leighton straightens, slowly setting her wine down. "My dear, do you feel as if you did?"

"Don't call me 'my dear' or answer my question with a question," I say, dropping all pretense. I evaluate her soft blond waves, the plushness of her purple-painted mouth, the way the skin of her throat looks thinner than it should. She is physically perfect, kept that way by the wealth she's acquired, that she'd do anything to hold on to. "I'm not stupid, you know. Or . . . or so blinded by the prize that I don't know that I'm being used as a pawn. Your pawn.

You only like me or help me when I say or do what you demand. I didn't react the way you wanted me to with Third."

"He needs to like you," Leighton says flatly.

"He won't ever like me," I say just as flatly, tugging at the knee of my leggings, pinkie finger digging deep. I can feel the fabric giving against the sharp edge of my nail. "You heard him. And I don't want him to. He's too . . . amused. Like this is a gladiator competition and we are all here to serve as his entertainment."

"Every gladiator wants glory," Leighton says.

"Not me," I whisper.

"Don't you?" Leighton challenges. "From our first conversation, you were clear on what you desire. You want power. You want this *life*."

"I don't want your stupid name," I insist. "I want Yale. I want what's mine and that's it."

Leighton looks delighted. "What's yours?" she challenges.

My slip exposes me, making me feel naked. I flex my hands into fists on my knees. "Didn't you always think of it as yours?" *Even though he called you gutter trash.*

"I think so. I had always been here. It had always been close enough for me to touch," Leighton says to herself. She sounds fond of her past this time, like it belongs to someone else. I can't picture her in polyester and 95 percent cotton. She's made for silk and wool and the scent of sandalwood and the slight oak taste of wine. "I looked at my competition and thought, *You have never fought for anything in your entire life. Not like I have. And* then I realized, *We all bleed the same.* So I made them bleed."

"Am I supposed to make them bleed?" I ask quietly.

Leighton meets my eyes, dropping her pretense too. "Without question and without prejudice."

She is everything I am supposed to aspire to be. She's made something of herself here. She just had to kill to do it. This is what she has been telling me all along. It is louder now, directly from her mouth, the inevitability that I would be required to make myself into something I never wanted to be to achieve the thing I always wanted, and the thought makes my throat close up.

Every one of us is lacking in Leighton's eyes. That's what she said in the very beginning. Every one of us had something that needed to be stamped out or polished. This was mine. I had to want it enough, like her. Everything that's happened, every interaction with her since Margaret died in my arms, has been designed to push me, to make me prove I still do want it. I can picture metal heating up in my hand, feel the kickback of the gun, and that's what makes me sick, how far my want has already taken me. But at a certain point, it won't just be self-defense anymore, not like I've been telling myself.

"Do you want to make Third bleed?" I ask quietly.

Leighton's eyes flash. "Every day."

My breath catches. This woman, cold-blooded and monstrous, sees herself in me, but looking at her now, I don't see myself in her. Not the person I want to be. No matter what she achieves, she is still not free of this, and even if I won, I never would be either.

I think of Third's threat and suddenly it's clear, I don't need Leighton *at all*. Her favor means nothing here. I jump to my feet. "I do not have your appetite," I say firmly.

Leighton laughs. "Don't you? You are *starving*. You are greedy. You would gorge yourself on whichever offers you most rather than have scraps of nothing."

She's talking about the Remington boys. She knows how they've helped me, how I've encouraged them to help. She knows that I don't feel guilty about it. She doesn't know that it's so much more complicated than that, that Graham makes me feel safe, that Pierce makes me feel powerful. And I'm not going to explain it to her.

"I'm done with this conversation," I say, turning away.

"I'm *not*," Leighton says. She downs the rest of her wine and sets the delicate glass down with a too-heavy hand. "You are playing a dangerous game and you will lose."

I shake my head, disgust swollen on my tongue, and stalk toward the door.

"Be very careful not to vex me, Adina," Leighton warns. "I am not one to be vexed. People get hurt when I am. Your parents. *You.*"

Fucking rich people.

"Don't you dare touch my parents," I hiss.

Leighton smiles at her victory.

"Then tread carefully," she retorts. "I have been a very good ally to have in this place, Adina. Do not threaten the very small amount of affection I have for you with this . . . nonsense. Don't get soft on me now."

I squash my rage, taking a deep breath, thinking of my parents. How far I'll go isn't my choice anymore. It never really was.

Softly I whisper, "I won't."

"Good girl," Leighton says, her voice molasses-warm again. I stare at the door once more, my fingers tightening around the knob. Leighton's every step feels like a whisper, and she settles a long hand on my shoulder. I look down and can see her engagement ring, the diamond unnaturally large; she didn't wear it the first night, but now she does. Like she needs to remind herself, and maybe the rest of us too. "See? You almost put them in danger for no reason. This is why I push you to be sharper. Harder. Unyielding. But also careful. You are not careful. With your parents. With my nephews. With my brother-in-law. With the other girls. You make yourself *vulnerable*, and I will stamp that out of you so you never will be again."

CHAPTER

23

THE SECOND REPARTEE SHOULD FEEL LIKE CHILD'S play compared to the Ride, but it doesn't. Expectations loom larger now. This is all mind games, but it's just as daunting.

It won't be card games this time, I know, as we're led downstairs in that single-file kindergarten line. The Remingtons don't seem the type for repetition. Maybe it's Chutes and Ladders, or Sorry!, or a hilariously ironic game of Life.

I'm disappointed to find that it's nothing of the sort.

"Chess," Hawthorne says, voicing my distaste.

"Blitz chess," Pierce corrects cheerfully. He's more casual for this Repartee, if one could call Vineyard Vines "casual." He's wearing boat shoes, unironically. It's as if he's stepped off a Cape Cod pier right into the parlor.

Leighton stares down her nose at us. "The Repartees are—as I have said—opportunities to demonstrate the less physical skills necessary to navigate the upcoming challenge within the Finish, and outside of it, in life."

Pierce steps forward, almost in front of Leighton. She stops short and breathes slowly, as if she meant to pause, but I know she's been interrupted. Pierce doesn't seem to notice the subtle shift in her mood as he says, "Chess is a game of strategy above all other things. But blitz chess requires one to make these strategic decisions on a dime, as you will be encouraged to do during the Raid. Come closer, so I can explain the rules."

Reagan, Jacqueline, and Hannah G scurry forward with abandon, eager to be in Pierce's line of sight, and Penthesilea looks vaguely curious. Saint and I take our time, casing the room. This is the third parlor I've been in, and it looks just as grand and majestic as the last, but it's getting old. Slowly but surely, the way the light flickers against the gilded walls makes it feel more and more ghoulish.

"We should stay out of this, if we can," Saint murmurs. "No need to draw attention to us or do anything to betray our strategy."

Our plan for the Raid is a simple one. Stick to the walls. Stay out of sight. *Don't* go for the prize at the center of the chaos. Being ranked first or second would only make the target on our backs larger, and it's obvious by now that the rankings don't really matter in the end. Hopefully, with how bloodthirsty the girls remaining are, they'll pick one another off and make it easier for when we get to the final challenge—the mysterious *Royale*.

"They'll notice if we don't engage," I warn.

Pierce is already noticing. Even as he tries to focus on his task of explaining, he looks over his shoulder at me. I manage a half-hearted smile and Hannah G sneers at me.

Saint shrugs. "Let them notice. They notice us anyway."

Saint is right in that aspect, but I can't help but think that it's the wrong move here. I've always followed her lead, tried never to set myself apart in any meaningful way, but her parents aren't being threatened, and doesn't this set us apart more? I hear Leighton in my ear, warning me. *Don't go soft.* Pressure turns carbon into diamond. She will be watching after our talk just as she's watched me in training these past three days.

Hawthorne and Jacqueline sit at the first chess table, Pierce smiling warm and encouraging as Leighton looks on with cold approval. Then there's Penthesilea and Reagan, and there's something pitiful about this, the girl at the top playing with the girl at the bottom. There is no competition here. This is sympathy, and Penthesilea shows dominance in her compassion.

But I am the favorite now. Tomorrow we'll play it safe, but tonight I'll act the part as Leighton and Pierce expect. Holding back is soft. I can't hold back.

Maybe that's what makes me move forward, into the thick of things. My eyes catch on Esme, standing over Hawthorne and Jacqueline as they play together, wearing a halter dress that dips low, and now that she's not wearing her choker, I can see three raised scars, waxy with new skin.

Scars take years to fade, and it's only been three months since I gave her these.

They are long, the width of three fingers. I knotted my fingers in her hair first, trying to pull her face away from me. But I pulled too hard and tore a chunk free, my fingers catching on the pale skin at the nape of her neck, and suddenly there was blood caked under my fingernails, blood staining her collar.

She turns like she can sense me looking at them.

"What are you doing?" Esme asks.

"Admiring my handiwork."

Esme pulls back like she's been slapped, but I look down at the game. There's a timer for both girls. After every move, a girl slaps the buzzer and it ticks down toward her opponent's doom—ten seconds per move.

Jacqueline is at a disadvantage. She's a poker player. They take their time. They're careful. Hawthorne is reckless, sacrificing knights and executing bishops, but soon it becomes clear it's all so that she may cross a pawn into position as queen. And then she is without mercy.

"Three queens all against Jacqueline's little army of pawns," I say, looking at Hawthorne's ivory army. "What did you bet?"

"Nothing," Hawthorne says simply. "Jacqueline has nothing to offer me."

"Taking a lot of *L*s there, aren't you, Jacqueline?" I dig at her.

Jacqueline looks up at me and says nothing, sniffing. She's still too mellow to rile up.

Esme's mouth twitches. "Careful, Walker. In here it's all fun and games, playing in front of those who would protect you. But, tomorrow, out there in the maze—"

Her amusement digs at me, but I turn my gaze back to the endgame.

"Check," Hawthorne says. She has Jacqueline's king surrounded by two queens, leading to a loss no matter the direction it moves in, except forward, which ensures a knight will check her.

Jacqueline tips her king in submission to the knight.

"Checkmate," Hawthorne says, and she giggles as Jacqueline huffs and slams her fist down. Leighton's head snaps around like a bird of prey, and Jacqueline inhales sharply before she exhales slowly and calms again. Hawthorne looks up at me. "Fancy a friendly game, Adina?"

She actually is beginning to *look* friendly, amongst all the other sharks. I prepare to take her challenge. I have nothing to offer her. She's ranked above me. It's the right move—but then Esme slips around the table and sinks onto the edge next to Hawthorne. Hawthorne moves over but makes no move to stand.

"Play me, Walker," Esme says.

I can only imagine what Esme would ask for. "No thanks."

"Bawk, bawk," Esme clucks.

"Are you three years old?" I demand. "Are you really calling me a chicken?"

"I am," Esme says loftily. "Are you, Walker?"

270

I look over my shoulder. Saint is glaring at me, jerking her head back toward the bar.

"Are you going to play her?" Pierce asks eagerly, too close for comfort. He looks over at Esme, words dry as he says, "Don't think about asking for her gun. I'll just give it back."

Esme doesn't pretend to look surprised. "Yeah, yeah, we get it, Pierce. This isn't actually about you, though."

"It's not *what*?" Pierce sniffs, offended.

"I'm asking you, Walker. Do you want to play a game?" Esme asks.

"Not with you," I decide, taking a step around her to look over Penthesilea's shoulder. She's losing to Reagan, but I can't tell if she's doing it because she feels bad for her or if it's an honest loss. Looking at Penthesilea's face discerns nothing.

"You don't get to walk away from me," Esme says, dogging my steps. "I'm not letting this go. I'm not letting *you* go."

"Why do I take up so much space in your head, Esme? I'm practically living there rent-free."

"That's good, then, seeing as that's all you and your parents can afford."

The mention of my parents stops me short. It doesn't sting, but it reminds me again of Leighton. Leighton, who is *looking* at me. Leighton would play her. Leighton would win. I'm sure she did just that in her Finish, challenging girls, being as aggressive as possible. Now she expects that of me.

Still, there's a difference between being soft and being stupid.

But there's something about Esme that makes me stupid. That makes me *angry*.

And Pierce is watching, he is close, and him being close applies pressure. I can hear the unanswered question of *Why her?* from the other girls, mirroring my own question of *Why me?*

"Budge," I command Jacqueline, practically ensuring that she'll try to smother me in my sleep. I slide into the seat across from Hawthorne and Esme.

"Since I challenged you, what do you win, if you win?" Esme asks.

"We avoid each other in the maze," I say. "If you see me or Saint . . . well, no, you didn't."

Esme smiles. "Are you *that* afraid of me?"

"No, you're basically a cult leader. I'm afraid of your sycophants. No offense," I say with full offense, looking up at Hannah G.

"Fine," Esme says with a light shrug as we begin to set up the board. "And if I win . . ."

"What, I just keel over?" I say.

Esme shakes her head slowly. "You don't sleep in your room tonight. You don't sleep on your bed. You sleep in the hallway. On the floor."

It sounds inane. Silly.

Chess hasn't ever been something I've concerned myself with. I was already on questionable social ground being in yearbook and the fucking student council. Chess club would have done me in. But even if I lose, it's just a night on the floor. I've slept in the back of my parents' car before, trapped between two suitcases and a duffel bag. And if I win, it's exactly the advantage Saint and I need.

"Fine. Let's begin."

CHAPTER

24

"THE CURRENT RANKING STANDS AS SUCH: IN FIRST, we have Penthesilea. Then Saint, Esme, Hawthorne, Adina, Hannah G, Jacqueline, and Reagan." Leighton's voice booms across the grounds, as bright and high as the noon sun. The heat is stifling, my hair an unholy halo of frizz despite my best attempts to tame it this morning.

I do my best to mask my yawn, my body dripping with soreness from a night spent on a cold, hard floor. Each flex of my neck is a victory for Esme.

I hadn't just lost. It was a bloodbath. Esme's Cheshire grin widened more and more until it was practically a Glasgow as she made move after move. She didn't have a strategy or a plan, which made it impossible to counter her. It was what the game was intended to demonstrate. Instead, she got lucky in her first ten moves and preyed on my franticness with each move thereafter. I knew I'd lost by move seven.

And I further incensed Jacqueline and Hannah G when instead of turning away from me in disgust, Pierce spent the rest of the night asking me if I was okay, as if I'd been punched in the face rather than just humiliated.

I tossed and turned in the cold hallway all night with just a throw from the common room and a hard decorative pillow. But Esme's cruelty had called for more than humiliation. Each creak of the house was a girl coming to kill me. Sleep did not come easy—it barely came at all. The residual soreness from the Ride has returned with a vengeance and the foggy headache from the lack of sleep claims all my attention.

So I'm surer than ever that Saint and I need to stick to the plan. If we run into trouble, I'm useless. The coffee I guzzled down this morning has only caused my heart to race with adrenaline, and I feel no closer to beating back the exhaustion.

"Are you okay?" Pierce asks again, and for just a moment I picture myself with my hands around his throat, asking, *Are you?*

But I shake it away. "I'm *fine*," I spit once more, rolling my eyes.

"You look . . . tired," Pierce says, unsure.

It takes me a moment to realize what he's unsure about, and then the panic sets in deeper. I've never spoken to him like this before. This is how I speak to Graham. Graham, who is watching absolutely unblinkingly. I force a smile that hides the way I want to vomit the dredges of coffee from breakfast right onto Pierce's suede loafers.

"Thank you for asking," I say softer. "I really am just fine. And I think . . . we are holding up the Raid."

Pierce smiles sheepishly and nods, stepping back into the fold of his family. His smile drops as he ignores whatever heinous thing Third is probably whispering about me. They walk away together, Graham skulking in their shadow.

Shifting uncomfortably in my black fatigues, I rub my hands over my thighs, up over the holster at my waist. I tighten it again, the gun heavy at my side despite being so compact and small. I know how to use it. I might have to use it. I still can't imagine using it.

"The Raid is a test of your mettle and your quick decision-making skills, all while maintaining focus on the goal: at the center of this maze, you will find a prize in a small black box, atop a pedestal. The moment the prize is lifted from the sensor plate, an alarm will sound. That will be your signal," Leighton says crisply. I know immediately what she means—our signal to herd toward the possessor of the prize and to take it from her by any means necessary. "You will enter the maze in rank order in forty-five-second increments to the sound of the gunshot. Pierce will do the honors."

The Remingtons are far away now, on their raised observation deck, full of crisp champagne and summer charcuterie, and just a little farther—a surveillance deck with monitors, all attached to a generator the size of an old computer tower.

Third isn't paying attention; instead, he's typing away on his phone. I wonder if he ever calls his wife, wonder what she thought when she was standing in the same spot that I am. Pierce has the starting pistol in his hand. And Graham is watching intently. He's watching me.

Our eyes meet and he nods once in acknowledgment. I nod in return before I turn back to the mouth of the maze.

"Remember, ladies, trust your instincts, make good choices, and . . . accept our challenge." I can practically hear the wry twist to Leighton's mouth, and I wonder if she finds humor or *joy* in doing what was done to her, if it gives her back the control that she might've lost the day she realized that she would have to kill to come out alive.

I don't have any more time to consider the thought, though, as the first blank is fired, and Penthesilea runs into the maze, immediately turning to the right at the first break.

Saint turns to me and looks me in the eye, her irritation at my bravado from the night before now exchanged for focus. She'll be mad at me after. "Remember," she says from the corner of her mouth. "Remember our plan." I nod, and then the second blank is fired. She rushes off to the left and I swallow hard and wait, anticipation building in my gut.

At the third blank, Esme surprises me by taking a moment to reach around Jacqueline and take Hawthorne's hand in hers. She squeezes hard, and then she takes off, already unsheathing her hunting knife from the thigh holster. With the fourth blank, Hawthorne runs, crossbow hanging over her shoulder, following as always after Esme.

Suddenly, I can't breathe. I can barely think.

I'm five feet off the ground, waiting for the Ride to start. I'm underwater. I'm on the cold wooden floor. I have a gun in my hand. I'm—

The fifth blank is fired and there is no time to calm down; I'm running, my feet pounding against the wet dirt beneath me until I enter the maze. The hedges are all-consuming, blocking out every other part of the estate except for the high sun, beating down a white tattoo of heat. I try to steady myself.

I have a plan. There is a plan. There's no reason to be afra—

A hand wraps around my wrist, jerking me to the left. I swallow back a scream. Saint's unimpressed face is only inches from mine.

"Are you good?" she asks. I shake my head, blinking hard, attempting to reorient myself. Saint pats my face roughly. "Come on, Adina. Get it together."

"I'm together. I'm sorry. I just—" I cut myself off, shaking my head. "Let's go."

Saint tugs out the dagger Pierce selected, holding it up threateningly. "I've got your back. Do you have mine?" she asks.

I look at Saint—the girl who has never treated me like deadweight, the girl who has patiently helped me learn, but never babied me.

"Until the end," I whisper.

Saint lets out a tiny huff, her gaze averting from my sincerity even as she fights a tiny smile. "Don't get dramatic on me," she mutters. She jerks into motion when we hear another gunshot.

Hannah G is in the maze now.

"We have to get moving," I say, shuffling with Saint down the path. "Esme definitely is having her little group meet up somewhere, and it's going to turn into a hunt for us just as much as for the prize."

I hear a shrill cry of girls, bloodcurdling like a skulk of foxes, accompanying the next gunshot because Jacqueline finally joins the maze, and their pack is complete.

"We have to move *fast*. All four of them are in now," Saint murmurs, and then we run.

❧☠❧

The sun is steady on, not budging out of the cloudless sky to grant us even the littlest bit of relief. I wipe the sweat from my forehead with the back of my hand and look over at Saint as we take another turn toward the outside and meet another dead end.

"Damn," Saint mumbles. We turn back and go past two openings, then turn right this time instead of left. We're forced to go up farther into the maze, and when we try to make another right to correct, it's a dead end again.

And that would be fine—the dead ends—considering we're biding our time until the prize is found and the others get out or, worse, ahead of us, but with each turn into the middle, the sounds of Esme's pack screech louder, cutting through the obscene silences.

The third dead end is when I have to stop pretending it's fine.

Frustrated, I groan as we once again double back. Every false turn feels like a chance to run into the others, for my nerve to be tested.

"How far into the maze do you think we are?" I murmur.

Saint squints around. "I can't really tell. I think we're still on the outer edges, but we keep getting stuck, which makes me think . . . we're being forced to surge forward, to the middle. To the prize."

"To a confrontation, I suspect," and Saint nods, agreeing with my suspicions. "I'd even guess the exit is near the entrance, not on the opposite side, so the first to the prize has to make their way back through everyone. I don't think we're meant to get out until we've gone through the middle."

Our tense silence is shattered again by an uproar—one that sounds far away but not far enough. This time the shrill screams that stutter out don't sound like joy, and there's a barking of orders, then silence. I exchange another glance with Saint.

"Whatever that was, I want no part in it," Saints says firmly. "Not until we're sure they have the prize and are focused on that."

"Agreed," I mutter. We force our way forward, pacing slowly as exhaustion begins to weigh on us.

When we turn the next corner, I nearly collide with someone.

On instinct, I tear the gun from its holster and train it on the girl.

Hawthorne raises her hands, crossbow tilted toward the air. Her face is tinged pink and she's looking behind her like terror is gripping her by the throat. "It's me! It's me!" she wheezes, before she doubles over, breathing hard.

"And that's supposed to reassure us, why?" Saint growls,

unsheathing her rapier. She looks behind Hawthorne, searching. "Where's Esme?"

"I'm not with her," Hawthorne insists. She huffs and I stare her down, refusing to tear my gaze away from her.

"You're *always* with her," I say coldly. Hawthorne knows that while I don't understand her, I know *who* motivates her.

"We got . . . we got separated," Hawthorne gasps, holding up her hands frantically. She is wide-eyed bliss and sweetness. She lets her crossbow drop to her feet, making herself as vulnerable as she can under our wary eyes.

"How?" I demand, keeping the pistol trained on her, holding myself in the exact stance that Graham taught me.

"Pierce was right. Reagan Mikaelson really does know how to use a bat," Hawthorne says with a wry smile. "She busted Jacqueline's two front teeth and definitely broke Hannah G's nose."

"Good," I say, and I can see the look Saint gives me from the corner of my eye, like she's surprised by my venom. It feels at home in my chest, like that's where it belongs now, like that's what this game has turned me into. "So you all split. But why should I trust that you're not scouting for Esme?"

"Because Esme has her eyes on the prize."

"And you *don't*?" I demand.

"You know why I'm here, Adina. Why she's here. I'm only *trying* to get Esme through without her getting hurt. It's Jacqueline who has a bone to pick with you," Hawthorne says firmly.

I scoff. It doesn't matter who wants what. They're still together.

That's an alliance, and everyone has an axe to grind with me, for one reason or another.

"We can't stand around too long. They aren't the only ones in here," Saint warns me. "What do you want to do?"

I look along both ends of the green corridor. No sign of Penthesilea yet.

"Let me stick with you. Three on three. We'll run the opposite way of them," Hawthorne insists. She slowly bends forward, reaching for her crossbow. I tense more, but I don't pull back the safety. Not yet. "No one else has to get hurt during this. I haven't hurt you yet, have I? I've had the chance."

This is a lie. I know the truth. People have to die.

But I let the pistol drop, just the tiniest bit. I square my shoulders. "Fine, you run with us. But don't think we trust you."

Hawthorne nods her agreement, and then we're marching through the green maze. With every step, the hedges rustle around us. Saint takes the lead, scoping out the next turn, and Hawthorne covers her while I keep an eye on our tail and Hawthorne, making sure she doesn't aim a bolt at the nape of Saint's neck.

The longer we wander, with the heat beating over us, the more I realize that the elements are part of this test. The constant terror that makes every rustle of a breeze a gunshot is the threat. Confirming our theory, each right we make toward the edges forces us to turn back inward at some point, until eventually we're nearing the beating heart of the maze. My pulse thunders in my ears, a dull roar outpaced only by my breathing.

Our path converges with three others in the center of the maze, and my eyes are drawn to the pedestal right in the middle. It's unassuming, made of smooth white stone, with a steel plate on its center. There is a small black box atop it. As promised.

"You've got to be shitting me," I whisper, looking closer. It's a jewelry box.

"*How* did we get here first?" Saint asks.

Hawthorne frowns, eyes darting around. "Who says we have?" She looks over at me. "Are you going to take it?"

"Why me? Are *you*?" I say with more than enough snark.

Hawthorne's lips pull into that weird thin smile again, the unhinged one. "*Maybe.*"

Rolling my eyes, I walk up to it, never breaking my stride. The opportunity is in front of me; it'd be stupid not to at least peek into it. I open it, careful to keep it on the platform, and look down at the mysterious prize. A startled yelp of a laugh escapes my throat, and Saint cranes her neck to look while still watching my back.

"A ring," she says flatly. "They are so—"

She doesn't get a chance to finish her sentence before they descend.

Hannah G comes up from the left lane while Jacqueline barrels down the center, both of them beelining toward us. Hannah G's nose is a mess of cakey blood, drying dark and crooked in her otherwise perfect California face. I can already see the dark smudges of bruises beginning to develop under her eyes. Blood streams down Jacqueline's chin and she turns to spit frothy pink. I can just see the hollow darkness of missing teeth.

And then Esme comes in from the right, still pristine.

I take a step back, my shoulder colliding with a bird-bone chest and I look back at Hawthorne blocking my exit from the way we came. Damn.

"Adina *Walker*, welcome to my party," Esme crows.

I glower at Hawthorne. "You're so full of shit."

Esme's lips curl into a Cheshire smile, and she lifts her hunting knife, but then she falters. "Hawthorne. Standing a little far from me, aren't you?"

"No, I'm right where I need to be," Hawthorne says, her voice tight. She lifts her crossbow and aims it at Jacqueline, just to Esme's left. I rear back. "Esme, we don't have to do this. The prize is right there. Let's just grab it and get out."

"It's called the Raid for a reason, Hawthorne," Esme says stubbornly.

"It was a meta—" I start, just to be a little shit.

"It wasn't a fucking metaphor, Walker," Esme interrupts, and she takes a step forward. "Between Walker and me, one of us is not getting out of here alive. And, Thorny, my love, *I'm* not dying."

"What if it was me?" Hawthorne demands. "You'd kill me?"

"Never," Esme swears. "But that's because you get it. You understand that I need to win. That *I* deserve this more than anyone. You're not standing in my way."

I can see now the flaw in Esme's plan. There's a chink in the armor of her faction. My hand tightens around the black box, and I look at Hannah G and Jacqueline, both of them staring at Esme now with unblinking contempt.

"*You* deserve this?" I repeat, loud and mocking, dragging their attention to me as I hold up the ring I've pulled from the box. I smile at Esme, wide. "*Your* way? Then what about these two? Do they 'get it'? Only one can survive at the end. None of us is making it out alive except one, because he can only have one of us, Esme. If I remember correctly, polygamy is illegal in Massachusetts."

My manipulation is too direct, but I can feel the crawl of time, the moment of escape slipping further and further away. The fractures in the alliance need to turn to a chasm, now.

"What *about* us?" Hannah G finally speaks up, sounding frantic, turning to look at Esme suspiciously. Esme raises a dark eyebrow. "I deserve to win just as much as you do. I want to be a Remington. I'd be practically a *princess*. Maybe you're *both* getting in my way."

Jacqueline opens her mouth, as if to agree, and then she closes it again, remembering that she has two missing front teeth. It doesn't stop her from shooting a nasty look at Esme, which Esme rolls her eyes at.

"Calm down. *Pierce* is no prince. I promise," Esme drawls.

"You sure seem to think he's worth killing for, though. You gonna kill me next, Esme?" Hannah G challenges.

Saint takes a step back, grabbing me by my wrist, as chaos begins to brew and unfold, deflecting the attention off of us.

"Don't listen to her. I told you. You can have anything you want *after* I win," Esme warns. "Stay focused, Hannah G."

"Don't!" Hannah G shrieks, and then her voice softens dangerously. "Call. Me. Hannah G. I'm the *only* Hannah now."

She shifts into a more combative stance now, holding her staff at Esme.

"Don't you *dare*—" Esme warns.

"I'm the *only* Hannah. I made *sure* of it!" Hannah G screams, animalistic, and just when she's about to lunge, there's a click and whistle.

Hannah G stumbles back, blinking her surprise, and I gasp when I see the bolt buried in her chest, black and solid. I turn to look at Hawthorne, who slowly loads another bolt, shoving past me, turning her gaze onto Jacqueline. But Jacqueline doesn't back down; she bares her open maw and then she lunges, lifting the heavy battle-ax over her head.

I jerk the gun out of my holster and shatter the silence with three gunshots that force everyone to clap their hands to their ears, eradicating all remnants of my exhaustion that haven't been cleared away by adrenaline. My ears ring and my vision doubles for a moment, but everything stops as intended. They all look at me, and for a split second I doubt my instincts as they turn their fury to me, but I have to commit. "Esme. Catch."

I lift the ring box and launch it at Esme. She fumbles for it as the alarm sounds incredibly loud.

I can hear Jacqueline lisp, "Wait, *stop*," her eyes darting between me and Esme, who is now holding the black box, and Hawthorne turns her attention back to Jacqueline while Esme bares her teeth at me.

"Run," Saint hisses in my ear.

We take off up through the middle, deeper into the maze again. Esme shouts behind us, and I don't need to look back to know she's chasing us. Even with the prize in hand, she would always chase me. There's an excuse here. Here, her bloodlust is more than allowed. It's encouraged. I pump my arms harder, running as fast as I can, taking another turn without even thinking which way it's headed.

"Left!" Saint barks at the next, and I can hear Esme, screaming my name as Saint and I run down the next long corridor.

When we reach the next wall, I feel Saint twist, but I register the direction too late. She goes left and for some reason—maybe because I'm scared of being stabbed or maybe because I slept on the floor the night before—I run right.

CHAPTER

 25

MY ONLY SAVING GRACE IS THAT ESME DOESN'T SEE
which way either of us has gone.

"WALKER! Walker, where are you?" she roars from the fork
in the hedge, and just beneath the sound, I can hear Hawthorne
pleading, probably reaching for her and trying to talk sense into
her friend. But we're long past sense. Sense doesn't belong here;
that's a thing of Suburbia.

My heart rate skyrockets as I creep forward, looking back and
forth. I whisper, "Saint," hoping she's found a path that will double
back this way, but there's no answer.

I scurry along, keeping tight against the walls, hoping maybe
Esme will just storm past me, blinded by her rage. And yet, inevi-
tably, her voice and steps grow louder. I can even start to make out
Hawthorne's words.

". . . mean anything. Margaret was the only . . . no more."

There's a brief moment of silence, where I think they're gone, and then I hear Esme's voice as if she's right next to me, booming in my ear with its rage: "I have to get this *right*, Hawthorne. This needs to go right or it'll all go to shit. I'll be a failure just like my father—"

"You're not a failure, Esme. *I* won't fail," Hawthorne promises. "You just need to trust that I know what I'm doing. We can do this."

That "we" says everything. I almost fell for it again, but they've always been a "we."

Esme's derision rings out in the form of a snort, and then Hawthorne whispers more placating words. But it won't be enough. Esme's patience has definitely run out.

I fumble with my gun, tugging it out of the holster again, my fingers shaking as I prepare myself for what's next.

If I shoot Esme, there's no doubt that I'll find an arrow in my chest a second later. If I don't, I'll find a knife in my chest.

"Don't get soft," I whisper to myself through gritted teeth.

Just as I am about to click off the safety, two freckled arms stretch from the maze walls and tug me deep into the green flesh. I open my mouth to scream, but that same hand, deceptively strong for its size, slaps over my mouth, muffling me. I hear her voice, gentle and insistent in my ear.

"Be quiet. Shhh."

I fall silent as I become one with the hedge wall, and I shut my eyes tight, feeling the length of her pressed against my back. The branches and leaves scratch at my cheeks and eyelids as

Esme and Hawthorne stalk past, presumably bickering over the value of my life.

I forgot Graham's warning about the walls after being angry with him, and I feel even more stupid and even irrationally angrier at him for distracting me—or allowing myself to be distracted.

I don't dare to breathe any louder than shallow hisses until minutes pass. And then, finally, those strong arms release me and I fall from the hedges, collapsing to my knees and wheezing.

Penthesilea slips out after me, pink scratches across her cheeks and neck and the back of her hands. She shakes it off and stares down at me, her expression impassive until she finally offers a hand. I take it and she tugs me up.

"Are you all right?" Penthesilea asks.

"Ye—" I vomit my breakfast onto the dirt path. Oatmeal and strawberries. How sexy.

"Guess that's a 'no,'" Penthesilea says dryly. And with a care I didn't expect from her, she reaches forward and, with her sleeve, wipes away my spittle. "You'll be okay. We've got to keep moving."

"I . . . I can't. Saint—"

"Did you and Saint have a plan if you got separated?" Penthesilea challenges.

I nod. I proposed it. "Yes. Keep moving." All that mattered was getting out.

"Then that's what we're going to do. Keep moving. And next time, don't hesitate."

Penthesilea doesn't say another word as she neatly steps over my vomit and starts down the maze after Esme and Hawthorne. I chase after her, not daring to shout.

"How did you *find* me?" I demand when I catch up.

"I wasn't *looking* for you. I was going through the walls. I have this," Penthesilea says, offering the machete up for inspection.

I stare down at it unblinkingly. Pierce gave her that. For all his complaints about his supposed ex-girlfriend, he's given her the perfect tool. The machete is an excellent choice to cut through lines and walls, to get yourself into places that you'd ordinarily be shut out of. *Like privilege.*

"Maybe it *is* a metaphor," I whisper to myself.

"You have a gun in your hand; of course it's not," Penthesilea says cheerfully. "Come on. We've got to keep moving. Esme is probably moving toward the exit, but she's not going to pass up killing you here if she can swing it."

"She should get out, she already has the stupid prize," I mutter. "It's a ring, by the way. Looked about your size."

Penthesilea sighs. "I'm sure Esme's convinced it belongs to you, actually. Pierce is making a show of you since the Ride." She lets out a private chuckle. Somewhere in there is a joke that only she understands the punch line of.

"No, *you're* the biggest threat," I counter, even though I'm not sure that's so true anymore. "Look at you. You were hiding in the fucking hedges like some weird, sexy Lara Croft. I knew that some of the hedges were hollow, but I was too stupid or tired to remember."

Penthesilea hesitates for just a moment and she looks over her shoulder. "'Sexy'?"

I sputter. "'Weird' was the operative word. And that's all you got out of that?"

Penthesilea snorts and turns back around, marching forward. "It doesn't matter what I can do with a machete. To Pierce, I'm a . . . nonfactor now."

"Then . . . why are you still here? You're a Bonavich. You don't *need* anything from the Remingtons," I point out. And then I stop, looking at her. "Wait. He said he broke up with you. Why did you even join the Finish if he *broke up* with you?"

It's the first time that I really think about it. The Remingtons are royalty in New England, but . . . so are the Bonaviches. Penthesilea is descended from people who came off the fucking *Mayflower*. Her father trades stock as a hobby. Her mother raises horses as a side hustle. There's no reason for Penthesilea to be here other than a *stupid* place at Harvard, and she could get that herself. Is she really that desperate to get him back?

Penthesilea's face does a complicated thing. It crumples, almost peeling away, and then she takes a deep breath and smooths it back out.

"Ask me again when we get out of here," she says quietly.

"I will," I insist. We jog for what feels like a long time and I squint over at her. "Do you know where we're going?"

"Yes. We all used to play hide-and-seek in this maze. It's why Esme and Hawthorne know it so well too. It's why I know that you can cut through the hedges. Now we make this left and—"

She's interrupted by the shrill piercing cry of, "Where's the box? Saint didn't have it! You have to have it!"

Reagan Mikaelson launches her entire body at us, a bat in her hands. The corner of her mouth is torn up toward her cheek, blood smeared down her neck, but it's a clean slice. Like it was made with a knife.

Or a rapier.

She swings with all her might, and I clumsily crash halfway through the hedges in an effort to avoid her.

Penthesilea, in contrast, ducks under the expert swing, sheathing her machete and drawing her butterfly knife in the same move. She springs forward and I catch a glimpse of the shiny glint of metal in her grip before she sinks it deep into the softness of Reagan's belly, cutting through the thick cotton to flesh and muscle. Reagan jerks, coughing wetly.

Penthesilea's expression never shifts as she rips the knife out and then stabs Reagan again straight in the heart. There's an unexpected tenderness to the way Penthesilea bumps her forehead with Reagan's before she rips the knife out. Penthesilea finally lets her face soften, and then she catches Reagan as she falls, letting out a tired whimper.

"You're okay. You're okay," she whispers. "Close your eyes. *Sleep.*"

Reagan dies much quicker than Margaret. And when she does, Penthesilea looks up to meet my eyes.

"We have to keep moving," she says, like nothing happened and nothing could touch her, and it makes me realize—Penthesilea Bonavich has never been bland or unaffected. She is *lethal* and always has been.

"I don't know if I should be going anywhere with you," I whisper.

Penthesilea's eyes narrow, "Are you going to try to kill me, Adina?"

"No."

"Then I have no reason to do what I did to Reagan to you. Let's go," Penthesilea says, turning and abandoning Reagan's body. She grabs my arm, and I follow her because I don't want to stay with Reagan's corpse and I don't know where to go.

Again and again Penthesilea slices through the hedges, drawing her machete back and forth. Everything is a blaze of green and red, and then we finally come to a path where I see an open mouth of white at the end. I find it alien and yet recognizable—we're to exit where we entered. An endless cycle, another metaphor. Penthesilea chases it without fear, but I lag behind, terrified to my bones of what awaits on the other side. If I stay here, in the maze, I won't need to go to the next round. I won't have to be confronted with any more broken girl corpses or the way terror has sewn itself to my soul.

But there is still as much danger in here as out there, so when Penthesilea walks into the sunlight and disappears, I force myself to follow.

When I emerge from the maze, my hands fall to my knees and I heave, but there's nothing left in my stomach, not after earlier. I hear the sound of applause and I look up.

The Remingtons and their staff are standing up on the deck, clapping politely, like it's a fucking golf match. The family even *grins*, huddled by the surveillance station. Third looks grudgingly approving, Leighton is smug, and Pierce beams.

Graham isn't there at all.

My eyes keep searching for him as I'm swept up in the bright orange of a shock blanket by one of the staff, but he's nowhere to be found.

"Your weapon, Miss Walker," Mr. Caine says plumly, offering the open gun case. I stare at him stupidly, then my hand flies to the holster, not to give it back but to secure it to me just a second longer. The weight of it in my hand means that it isn't in someone else's. "*Miss* Walker." His brow arches, voice growing higher with irritation, enough to call attention both to the Remingtons and to my common sense.

I unwrap the holster from around my waist, drop the gun into the case. I never want to see it again, even though I can still feel the shape of it in my palm.

He leads me over to the seating area below the Remingtons.

"Admirable performance," Third allows, and he casts a warning glance at Pierce, who is beaming, as if to say, *Don't start*.

Leighton murmurs, "Well done, Miss Walker." She is watching me, looking for something—blood or gunpowder or anything that would indicate that I've done what she intended me to. She finds nothing.

I glance quickly at the group sitting on wrought-iron patio furniture. Penthesilea's gaze cuts over to Pierce, but he isn't looking at her. He looks at me and he smiles, sticking up a thumb. When I look down at Penthesilea again, she's looking at the maze almost wistfully.

"Lucky, lucky," Esme tuts from her own shock-blanket burrito. She shivers hard as she comes down from the high, tucked against Hawthorne, the only other two to emerge so far. Blood drains from my face.

"Where's Saint?" I whisper hoarsely. "If you *hurt* her, I'll kill you."

Hawthorne squints up at me. "She didn't touch her."

"I was *convinced* that you both weren't worth it, not when I already had the prize and could get out in first," Esme says through chattering teeth, still managing to sound like a bitch. She lifts her hand, displaying the diamond ring that fits too tightly, only going past the first knuckle. She looks at me slyly. "Reagan, though—"

I flinch.

"I took care of it," Penthesilea says dully. "Sit down, Adina. Now we wait."

And so we do.

We wait for a long time, the sun beating harshly on us. We receive the finest treatment, offers of grapes and strawberries and sparkling waters like any of it could make this better. Esme requests a bottle of Moët. She doesn't share, of course, just takes swigs from the bottle like she *means* to be drunk. Like she *has* to be drunk after the maze. Her gaze never wavers from the entrance, like she can't look away. She looks . . . fragile, despite her talk. I have never seen her like that. To me, she is like the diamond on her finger. But now she looks like glass.

With Hawthorne's arm threaded through hers, they look like kintsugi, broken pottery mended with liquid gold, a formerly shattered piece made whole again.

Finally, thankfully, Saint emerges from the maze, looking wild in a way that I've never seen her. She stumbles and then she collapses to her knees and very visibly swallows back a scream. The moment she looks at me, I know.

She's finished.

CHAPTER

 26

IMMEDIATELY AFTER THE RAID, I EXPECT A RUN-down. A declaration of our ranks and what it means to win this particular challenge.

Again, Leighton surprises me and does nothing of the sort. Instead, she declares that we will have a day of rest before the final Repartee, and then the Royale thereafter. There is to be no advance warning or training. Presumably, we have nothing left to learn, and that is a signal to us all.

This is the endgame.

She dismisses us like she doesn't have any more time, and we are too tired to protest. We are marched upstairs to a gluttonous feast in the common room that none of us is up to eating.

Instead, I sleep. There's no time or room to continue my inter-rogation of Penthesilea or to hear Esme's crowing about her first placement around her yawns, or even to ask Saint what happened to her. I put her, trembling, exhausted, to bed—and then myself.

I sleep a long time, through the night and into the morning, without dreams. No nightmares, no sugar-spun fantasies. And when I wake up, there's a moment, just one, where I forget what I've been through. In that moment, between waking and the world, I am just a girl, in a beautiful room, in a soft bed, on a summer morning. Then the stale scent of old sweat and terror rises from where it's stuck to my bed, and I feel the urge to scream.

When I finally find the will to turn over in bed, Saint is awake, staring at the ceiling too. We ignore the comings and goings in the corridor of the only three other girls left. Only when I've had enough of my own stench do I get up.

Breakfast has been delivered, sitting outside the door, but I'm not all that hungry.

I spend an hour in the shower. The first twenty minutes I use to sob, the sounds of my grief overpowered by the pounding of the four shower jets, water swirling down the drain with the rest of the sweat and grime on my body. I weep for what feels like forever, without a single tear falling from my eyes. The rest I spend washing my hair.

First, I detangle, dragging a brush through the matted hair, working each curl until they hang stringy straight in a halo around my face, then I shampoo slowly, lovingly, slathering my scalp, scratching the grit up with my bare fingernails. I wash everything out. Finally, I deep condition and I stand in the steam, staring at nothing until I go hot and woozy and have to force myself out.

With nothing to do, we are discarded dolls in the prettiest of dollhouses, and that feels like another mind game—we are without use until a Remington picks us up and decides to play a game. When I step out of the bathroom, I see Saint has pulled herself free from her cocoon, but not particularly far. She's now crouched by her bed, near her trunks, talking to herself in murmured Mandarin interwoven with the odd English or French curse word.

I kneel in front of her, holding my towel tight to my body, and grab her hand. "Saint?" I whisper. "Breakfast is here?" My nose wrinkles at the congealed oatmeal, long gone cold, the soupy yogurt that looks half melted, and the curling leaves on the fresh strawberries.

She doesn't respond, at least not to me, but her whispering grows louder. It's like she doesn't hear me, doesn't even see me. It's too painful to look at confident, untouchable Saint like this, so I give her space and go to work on my curls, applying the pudding and gel in a methodical fashion. It's been years since I taught myself to do this; now I don't even have to think about it, which is good because I can't think about anything. I'm halfway through when there's a knock on the door.

Uncaring about my state of undress, or anything at all anymore, I stalk toward the door and wrench it open with a snarled

"What?" Fear is such a constant now, I barely feel it.

Pierce holds up his hands in surrender. He is so perfect looking, so absolutely golden, but his joy dims into what I'm sure he thinks is *honest* concern. "I'm sorry. Are you all right?"

Again, he asks. I laugh viciously and don't bother with answering because I'm past being able to lie. My hand tightens around the top of my towel, and Pierce's gaze drags down, over the top of my breasts, and then flits up again, like he's been caught.

"Do you need something, Pierce? I'd like to keep my peace for the rest of the day, before the Repartee," I say. There's nothing about his perfectly coiffed hair or his perfect smile that can muster up anything other than thinly veiled contempt anymore. Resentment is a hell of a relationship builder, and we don't even have foundations.

"Oh, I'm sorry, I'm supposed to have lunch with Esme," Pierce says, his nose wrinkling with distaste at the thought, "but I wanted to see how you were doing."

I squint at him. "How . . . do you think I'm doing?" I ask. An awkward beat of silence passes between us, where he doesn't even try to answer. "If there's nothing else—"

"Wait, I also brought you something for tonight. Here," Pierce says, and I finally realize that he has a garment bag slung over his shoulder. I take the offering and lean against the doorframe, looking up at him, waiting for the other shoe to drop, but he just says, "You were brilliant. With the Esme bit, turning the others against her."

"So you were watching," I say with a sigh, because I'm over the flattery. That's what it's always been. *Empty* flattery, meant to placate me into continuing.

"Of course," Pierce says.

"Was Graham?" I ask.

Pierce frowns like *why* am I asking about his brother when he is standing right in front of me.

"I only wonder because he wasn't there, at the end." I say quickly.

"I mean . . . not at first, but then he said something about how he's not a coward, and then . . . I don't know, maybe he *was* because he walked away."

"Well," I say, reverting back to the Raid because I don't know what to make of that. "You saw that your girlfriend saved my ass. So you should save the compliments for her."

Pierce's expression darkens. "Don't call her that. But, really, Adina, you've performed . . . beautifully in your own right. You're, ah, beautiful," he says awkwardly.

I am expected to be pleased. But it's as if he has nothing else to say to me. Just *that*. "Thanks. I have to . . ."

"Right. I'll see you at the Repartee tonight," Pierce says. He takes a step back, drinking me in again. "Save me a dance?"

"If you'd like," I say softly before I shut the door.

I wait for Saint to say something, but she only gives me a quick look before she's talking to herself again. I restart the task of my hair, trying not to think about the garment bag or what might be inside or the way Pierce's eyes traced my frame, every curve and divot and bruise. I try not to think of how I suddenly miss stubble and big hands, the same ones that helped me onto the back of a horse, that showed me how to shoot, that sat heavy on my thighs. He felt unpolished. *Real,* in a way Pierce isn't.

After the Raid I feel just a little more plastic. Hardened and hollow. I wonder if someone could look at me and see the way I'm cracking up inside. See that I'm being forced into shapes that aren't by my design. As Graham feels more real, I feel less than, and maybe that's why he wasn't there.

He couldn't muster a fake smile for me.

☙☠☙

The final Repartee feels monumental in a way that the others didn't. The feeling is sudden, swarming unease. The day is spent in meandering silence, and that in and of itself feels like psychological warfare. There isn't a whisper of movement in the halls. There are no giggles or laughter; there wouldn't be. There are only five of us left. It started with one dead girl, and now there are seven. All *gone,* for a boy who barely paid attention to them in the first place.

The feeling does not ease when plain white hatboxes wrapped with navy-blue silk ribbons are delivered, along with instructions to be ready in three hours.

Inside is a mask, delicate and beautiful, a marble cast of a woman's face with crystals laid painstakingly around the eyeholes, and painted silver lips. Silver filigree encrusts the face, swirling up into what resembles a tiara.

I glance over at Saint. She has a half mask, which looks vaguely like the Venetian carnival masks that we learned about once in seventh-grade World Cultures.

"Every day this feels more and more like a cult," I murmur to myself. I don't bother hoping for a response from Saint. She hasn't answered me directly since before the Raid. She doesn't look like the girl I saw when I first got here at all, and again I wonder what happened with her and Reagan after we were separated in the maze.

My thoughts grow so loud that I start to get ready early. I haven't looked at the dress that Pierce gave me since he visited just a few hours earlier. It didn't seem to matter in the moment, but now it feels like expectations. It's another way for Pierce to demonstrate his favor, favor I want less and less as the prize solidifies in my head.

I take my time unzipping the garment bag and reveal a dark, shimmering, emerald-green fabric.

"That's a Fletcher. Very avant-garde."

I jump, nearly dropping it, and spin to glare at Saint.

She sits straight up, her spine like iron, her mouth pressed into a thin line, and finally I recognize her. With grace, she stands from her bed and crosses the room, joining me. Her hair is mussed and she smells like outside, like the maze. Her nose wrinkles like she finally realizes it.

"Aren't you trapped at the bottom of a spiral?"

"I climbed out," Saint says coolly. Her expression doesn't soften when our eyes meet, but she does grab my shoulder and squeeze soundly. "He wants you to wear an emerging designer. Fletcher's whole deal is taking classic silhouettes and modernizing them. Bringing heritage into a new century. Rather heavy-handed. I bet he's going to wear something with matching accents."

"I'm beginning to think he's delusional," I mutter.

"You've only just realized?" Saint sighs. "Our plan failed."

"It did," I mumble.

"I didn't anticipate being herded toward the center. I should've. It was supposed to be a bloodbath. Bring it down to two or three," Saint says, echoing what's been cycling through my own head. Three girls died in the Raid, but that probably wasn't enough. "And we both survived. They definitely don't like that."

I swallow hard. "Probably not."

"I was wrong about our final-two plan too. They're going to want you to kill me," Saint whispers.

"Stop stating the obvious," I bite out furiously. "If you don't have a plan—"

"I'm working on one," Saint interrupts. "Now, turn around so I can zip you into this dress."

She helps me into it, covering the new marks on my body. I crave the reminder of the older scars that were made in childhood. The gathering of scar tissue at my knee from when I fell while roller-skating my first time with the girls—when Esme had still pretended to love me. The dark burn mark on my inner pinkie from searing bacon on the stove the morning after a sleepover with Toni. But then my eye is drawn to the pink from a knife pressed too close to my body, to the mark on my shoulder from when I fell off Starlight before our first jump.

I am reminded that I do not inhabit the same body that I had before I came to the Remington Estate. I can't believe that before, I thought I was broken.

The Finish is aptly named, I see now, because they are finishing us here, using our weaknesses and breaking down our needs to harden us into cartilage. I mourn us all.

Hawthorne, and her undying loyalty.

Saint, and her resolve.

Even Esme, and her relentlessness.

And of course Penthesilea for . . .

"I . . . I need to see Penthesilea," I say suddenly.

"Pentecostal?" Saint asks, the same tired joke that doesn't sound so funny anymore, now that she does it listlessly, like she's trying for normalcy and failing. "Why?"

"She saved me in the maze. From Reagan. She killed her. And she saved me from Esme. And I want to know why. She told me . . . to ask afterward why she's here. Because it's true: she *doesn't* need to be here, but she is," I whisper quietly.

Saint scoffs. "I didn't need to be here either." Then she grows quieter, and her forehead falls against the nape of my neck, her fingers lingering over the hook at the top of my zipper.

"But I know why you *did* come here—"

"I came here because I had something to prove," Saint interrupts. She's embarrassed, not looking at me. "My father didn't send me here. They don't even know. I told them I got an internship in New York at some hedge fund. And then, instead, I came here. I really did suggest teaming up with them, but Father turned them down last minute. And they were offended so they . . . cut off all our prospects here. And then they sent the invitation to the Finish as a way to offend my father further in retaliation. That solidified to him that it was a bad deal, but I was so sure that the Remingtons were our only way of breaking into the market, I came here. I thought I could outsmart them, blackmail them. I thought I'd . . . prove myself capable and ready."

She wasn't. She *isn't*, but my heart twinges for her.

"I'm sorry," I say quietly. Saint shakes it off, even though the words rub her raw. "Maybe that's true, but it's also true that you're still okay. And the only reason that they're okay and *still alive* is because you are not a *monster*—"

"Oh, I can be," Saint warns.

It's a promise.

I nod, my words getting caught in my throat. At least I know that if I don't make it but Saint does, she will find a way to ruin this family. And I want her to almost as much as I want to do it myself. I look away and step back, barefoot.

"I still need to talk to Penthesilea," I repeat, and Saint nods slowly again.

I wander out of our room and don't knock on her door, choosing to just walk in. Her room is like mine and Saint's, but not. The dying sun breaks through her windows, turning the gold wallpaper into hazy pinks and the burn of fire. This room hasn't lost its charm yet. It still looks like an illustrated storybook, a room for princesses. Or Remington wives. Whichever.

When I see her, of course she's put together, ever the fairy queen, ethereal in a way that I have only ever dreamed about being.

"Why are you here, Penthesilea?" I ask sans greeting.

Penthesilea doesn't shift from where she sits before the vanity, carefully applying a shiny pink gloss to her lips. She sets the wand down, smacking her lips and leaning back. She takes a deep breath, her palms biting into the edge of the wood, and squints at her own reflection. Her fingers drum for a moment before she takes up her brush, dragging it down her hair in precise strokes.

"I'd hoped you'd forget to ask," Penthesilea says thoughtfully.

"I couldn't possibly. Is this about Harvard?" I whisper. "You want the free spot so you can get back together with him?"

Penthesilea blinks at me, and then she laughs. "Is *that* what he told you?" She giggles. "I suppose it's true. In a manner of speaking. No, I'm not here for Harvard. Not really. I'm here because it is expected and I *have* to be perfect."

"I'm sorry?" I say, questioning.

"I have to be perfect. And Pierce is perfect. And we *will* be perfectly perfect together." Penthesilea sets down her brush, sitting up sharper. She exchanges it for a blush compact. She dusts pink to her face, painting life to her cheeks. She meets my eye in the reflection of the mirror. "I know that you tried to fuck my boy-friend, Adina."

I flinch, nearly tripping backward over the edge of the Persian rug. Penthesilea lets out another huff of a laugh that is so devoid of humor, it's nearly a sob. My tongue feels swollen in my mouth.

"I—I—"

"Don't bother with apologies. I've heard so many of them throughout my life that they all sound the same," Penthesilea says gently. Her gaze never wavers from me and I can't look away; it would feel like the ultimate disrespect. Cowardice. I can't afford that.

"When did you know?" I ask instead.

"When you appeared in front of your friend, defending her from Esme, I saw the way that he looked at you," Penthesilea mur-murs. "He's never looked at me like that."

"I'm sure he has—"

"I didn't say that was a bad thing," Penthesilea snaps. She slams her compact closed, shoots to her feet, and turns around.

"And I don't want you to think that it means something that Pierce says he cares about you. Pierce doesn't care about you. If he did, he would've gotten you out of this *hellhole*," she says. That word flies from her mouth with derision. "Don't let him trick you into thinking he couldn't. He could. No, Pierce doesn't care about anyone but himself. He looks at you like you're an *ending*. You're the 'happily ever after.' He would take your come-up story and make it loud and make it his. Class-crossed lovers. Traversing boundaries to be together. Third has big plans for his son. Governor, I think, and a governor needs a story."

Every word comes out like cracked porcelain. And all of it and none of it makes sense with what I know about Pierce. Pierce, who picked me because he believed in me, who wanted to help me but found himself trapped. Pierce, who was simple-minded and really did believe in his whole "level the playing field" schtick. Pierce, who put clothes on me that I would never wear and told me again and again that I was something that I'm not. Pierce, who, for all he talks about being different, is just like his father in a different font.

"That's not—"

"I know he gave you that dress, too," Penthesilea continues. "Or did he send Graham to do it? Always doing what his beloved little brother, Four, asks. If Four asked him to let you die, he would, you know. It would hurt, but he would do it."

Penthesilea says all of this clinically, like it means nothing to her that she's devastating the small oasis of peace I've found in a world that is trying to kill me.

"He wouldn't. He—"

"Graham would. I know him. Just like I know Pierce and all

the worst parts of him. There's a lot of them. That boy is *rotten*," Penthesilea says.

"Why are you here, then?" I demand.

Penthesilea's smile breaks for the first time. "Because . . . I have nothing else," she whispers. "You have your dreams. Your future you want restored. I have Pierce. I have *this*. This is what I was bred for. To grow up, get a liberal arts degree, marry well, elevate my family to new heights with that marriage, smile and shake hands, have babies, and pick out the fine china. Be a good influence on the wretched Remington boy. Lead *him* to success, not yourself. Keep *him* from doing harm or damaging his reputation. The family reputation. Our class's reputation. 'Shrink yourself, Penthesilea, so that he never looks small. So that he never feels wrong.' That's what they've told me all my life. *This* is what I've always had. I can't go back now. There would be nothing to go back to."

And finally, I get her. What makes her uncanny and strange.

Penthesilea is not nice. Penthesilea is not sweet.

She is seething. In the gaps between her teeth, she holds bitterness and rage, the kind that has built with resentment for years. Penthesilea is not the rays of the sun. She is a moon, tethered forever to a planet that she does not want anything to do with but can't exist without.

Penthesilea has found purpose at an altar, and it is made of Pierce's skin, his hair, his eyes. She adores him, but wants to destroy him, one kiss at a time.

"Pierce wants a girl who's finished. One who's broken, that's why he keeps you here. And he will break you," Penthesilea whispers, staring at the ceiling. "What he *needs* is someone who cannot be broken by him."

"What is . . . *so* awful about him?" I ask, voice catching in my throat.

Penthesilea smiles. "Adina . . . have you ever said no to him?"

I still. "What?"

"Have you *ever* said no to him?" she asks. When I don't answer, she continues, "Try saying no and see what he does. *That's* what's wrong with him."

I don't think I've ever said no. Not meaningfully or forcefully. Even the no to Widow Maker was spun into a choice that he'd like. "Integrity," he called it. So he wouldn't feel rejected.

"They want to make you a killer because that's what being a Remington is about. Kill to keep what you have. Kill to keep others from having it. Kill to keep the status quo. Kill to keep it perfect. Kill others. Kill yourself. All to keep them from harm, even of their own making. And we can call it a metaphor, and maybe it is, out there, but in here, it's real," Penthesilea says, her tone severe. "And if he chooses you, you won't be able to do it. You won't be able to do what needs to be done to keep things perfect. But I have sacrificed everything to make sure that I can. So I've kept you alive to placate him, but if I need to put you down to keep him in check—to keep it perfect—I will."

Every word is one I need to hear, because it makes my future very clear. It makes everything clear for me, especially the fact that I can't do what they call necessary.

But Penthesilea smiles at being the source of this revelation, like she's being compassionate. Then in that same sweet voice she finally whispers, "Now get out."

CHAPTER

27

"LADIES, TONIGHT IS YOUR DEBUT. WELCOME TO the final Repartee." Any other day Leighton Remington would be met with applause. But it is not any other day. It is today, when we are all brought so low that any moment could be shattered by a hard edge. Leighton continues as if she is unbothered by the atmosphere.

She looks otherworldly, her hair curled to perfection, burnished gold in the light of the fireplace. She smells wealthy and she looks it too, wearing couture like she was born into it. She doesn't have her glass of wine tonight, but leaning against the piano, she brings me back to the day of our arrival, all of us dressed up in white Edwardian lace for that group photo.

Now there are only five of us in the common room.

It feels too big. Saint and I sit on the love seat pressed against the far wall, our masks in our laps. Hawthorne and Esme are opposite us, on the piano bench. And finally, Penthesilea, in the middle, sits alone.

"Put on your masks and form a single-file line," Leighton commands. "Who you were no longer matters. Who you will become is all there is."

We do as she bids, because we are conditioned now. I secure the mask over my face with silver ribbons.

"This is weird," I mumble, my voice muffled by the porcelain.

Saint casts me a pointed look as she secures her own half mask. "Is it weirder than the death games?"

"Almost."

We fall in line, and even Esme seems too tired to say something caustic or snide, instead quietly allowing Hawthorne to secure her mask before we're whisked from the room.

Tonight there are no eerie shadows. Everything is cast in so much light that even the dark wood looks alien. The stale smell that I've grown used to has been replaced by the smell of Pine-Sol and the unique scent of burning wax. The carpet looks like it's been gone over with a vacuum about a dozen times, though I can't recall having heard it. There are whispers in the walls, and if I didn't know better, I might believe they were ghosts.

In the moment before we enter the ballroom, I steel myself for what feels like the millionth time. I remind myself that this isn't the Royale yet. I have survived a deadly horse race and a combat treasure hunt. The Remingtons—despite what they stand for—should not scare me more than that.

But when the doors open, all my thoughts are wiped away as we're met with thunderous applause. The only reason I don't turn away is the sharp bite of Hawthorne's nails at my wrist, stilling me.

The Remingtons have invited *guests*. There are at least two dozen people here, and for a moment I am lighter than air, choking on my giddiness. There are *people* here. People who don't know anything about all of this. People who will believe me if I tell them what's been done to us, if I show them the still-healing bruises on my sides and my thighs. If I tell them about the girls who were here, who are all now gone.

And then I begin to put names to faces. One of the senators of Massachusetts is here, along with his wife. The headmaster of Edgewater Academy, with a glass of brandy in hand. The CFO of one of those charitable foundations that partners with Edgewater's community service department; it's the same foundation that our senior class had to work and volunteer with for twenty-five hours to graduate. The kind of people the Remingtons call to give keynotes at the Edgewater fundraisers every year, whenever we need a new but unnecessary update to the chem labs or the library.

They all know.

I try not to cry beneath my mask as Esme marches forward, leading us around and into the crowd, which parts like the Red Sea. As we approach the Remington Family, Pierce is brimming with pride, his smile bright, while his brother fights off a grimace, strain tightening the lines around his eyes.

"Congratulations," Leighton murmurs, passing down the line, drawing each of us into a chilly hug. As she reaches me, I stiffen in her hold.

Leighton steps back and then moves to hug Saint, who extricates herself from the embrace as soon as she finds herself in it. When Leighton turns from us, I expect her to address the room at large, but she melts back into the circle of the Remingtons, and it's Third who steps forward. *Of course.*

"My dear *friends*," he begins, with far more enthusiasm than he's ever shown any of us. "Tonight we celebrate the penultimate night of the Finish. The Finish is a long-standing tradition, and a mighty one, in which we determine the mettle of the ladies in our modern society. In certain years—the best years—we go a step further, searching the cream of the crop for a diamond. A new member of the family to bring forth its next generation. It is an important moment for us, to bring someone into the fold, and we treat it with the utmost sincerity and seriousness, as do these young women. Some ladies are sacrificed in this noble pursuit, and though we think fondly of them, we come together to celebrate those who remain." What a nice way to say that girls have died under their watch. "May your evening be merry, my friends. Let the games continue."

He toasts them with a half-finished glass of bourbon. And everyone raises a drink with a monotone *Salut.* I twist in disgust and turn to Saint.

"There are so many people. Why are there so many people?" I whisper. This changes things. This changes everything. I didn't expect any more curveballs to be thrown, but the Remingtons, as always, love to show their winning hand right before they summarily beat you into submission.

"Just . . . smile and nod if anyone speaks to you," Saint murmurs. "We should try to avoid accepting anyone's challenges. Even without knowing what the Royale is, there's nothing left to gain. I'm going to get a drink. You want anything?"

I almost decline, but I am tired and bone-achy and angry. "Yeah. Liquor."

"There we go," Saint says without humor, and prowls through a crowd that parts for her.

I can read the intense scrutiny from the horde of the rich. They don't bother with being discreet, staring at my curls, at the shadow of bruises hidden underneath foundation on my shoulders, at the brown of my skin. They know who *I* am, at least, which brings it down to four—*Who are the four other girls?* they wonder. Only one is brave enough to approach me.

"I miss the black dress," Graham says.

"Good for you," I say bitterly, Penthesilea's words still ringing loudly in my ears. "Nice speech from your dad."

Graham scoffs, rubbing over his jaw. "Yes, it was very much his brand. Self-congratulating. Self-important. Self-obsessive. An unholy glorification of the Remington name."

"Your name." I can't help the jab.

Graham stills. "Did I . . . do something wrong?"

It's not what he's done, per se, but what he might do. I sidestep the question, unwilling to get into it here.

"There's a senator," I observe, looking at him covertly as Third schmoozes him, all smirks and smiles. The Bonaviches are across the room with someone I might've seen in the news once or twice. Maybe something to do with oil. Esme's parents are at the periphery of their little group. The rumors have clearly made their way to the adults, too.

The senator most definitely isn't the only political piece they have in their stranglehold, ensuring their secrets are kept. Graham nods like he can hear my every thought. He whistles to himself. "This is fuck—"

"Graham, give us a moment."

It's like we're being visited by goddamn Apollo. He swings out of whatever conversation he's having, his lips pulled into his permanent smile. But all I can think is, *Penthesilea calls him a monster.*

When Graham gives him his full attention, my mood sours entirely.

"We were talking," I say roughly.

Pierce looks back at me, wounded, like I've honestly hurt his feelings.

"You said you would save me a dance," he says quietly. His tie is the same emerald as my gown, proving Saint right. Everyone's eyes track him, making the connection. There's a new sense of curiosity now, divorced from a *Who is she?* Now it's *Who will she be?* I look down at his offered hand, then past him at Penthesilea where she stands, tall and frigid, between Leighton and Third.

She looks like she belongs. But she doesn't have the same indulgent expression as Pierce's father. Penthesilea is still as a sentry. A jail guard that is *allowing* her prisoner a privilege.

"You should dance with him," Graham says, subdued. He's so easily dismissed by his brother, like he can't help but give him *everything*, like I'm something *to* give, and it makes me resent him, too.

"Don't dismiss people like that, Pierce. And ask nicely," I insist. Pierce smiles, suddenly delighted again. It's *exhausting*.

"May I have this dance?" he asks, bowing with a flourish, like I expect ostentation. Like I want the show, for everyone to see me take his hand, when I just wanted him to be fucking *polite*, like a normal human being.

But still, I take his hand and let him draw me onto the dance floor.

My silk skirts are made for dancing, swirling around my shins as we whip across the floor to the waltz, a dance that I don't know but that he guides me through, one hand low on my back, the other holding my limp hand tight.

"Thank you," he murmurs, leaning in with a teasing smile. I don't feel up to smiling, but I force out laughter, suddenly grateful for the mask. "You do look really lovely in that dress. Green is your color."

"Looks like it's yours, too," I point out.

Pierce nods. "Do you like it?"

I stare hard at Pierce, tilting my head. "Pierce, you have been very kind to me throughout this entire . . . journey," I begin, unsure of another word to describe it. Pierce nods, like he's agreeing. "You've given me clues and assistance and *answers*. May I ask another question?"

"Always."

"Why did you want a Finish?" I ask slowly.

Pierce stares down at me, blinking owlishly. "What do you mean?"

"Your brother didn't have a Finish, did he?" I insist. "But you wanted one. Everyone has told me why you did. But I want to know from you. Why did you have one?"

Pierce sighs deeply. "Tradition is a hard thing to break, you see. It is baked into the fabric of a space. A house. This house. My face is tradition. I have my father's face. My name is tradition. I have my father's name. I couldn't do what Graham does and disappoint them." He says it so easily. He has no idea what Graham has done to give Pierce the life he has as the *golden* son. "So I *had* to have a Finish . . . but I wanted it to be mine. Every moment of it. It's my future, after all. So I'm making my own traditions. My own happily ever after."

It's that turn of phrase that haunts me, sitting low in my belly.

"How?" I force out through a clenched jaw.

"I expanded the definition of what a potential Remington wife might be. That's not how it's usually done. My father would select candidates from our circle, with the winner all but predetermined, but I wanted a *real* competition, like Matilda intended, not just a show that Pen would skate through. And then . . . I saw *you*. I'd heard of you. You were the girl who turned Esme into a monster, and showed her a monster right back, so I suspected you had it in you. And then you said that thing about evening the playing field, and I *knew*. You had to be here. It was a calculated risk, inviting you. But I knew Leighton would understand, would relate to you," he says.

"But then . . . didn't you predetermine your own winner?" I ask quietly. Every justification is met by contradiction. He widened the circle to keep the violence at bay. Violence is inherent to the nature of this competition, and he's always known that. It's been a consequence that he is willing to wade through, because consequence does not touch him. *That* is his truth.

Pierce shakes his head. "No. Well, yes. I just . . . wanted to produce my own ending. I want you to win, though you haven't made it very easy, have you? I've had to help you because you're . . . well, you need it, don't you? You couldn't possibly make it through without me, and I need you to. I *do*. Because . . . I'm evening the playing field. *That* will be my Remington legacy. And won't it mean so much more after we've really earned it? Our own love story where you beat the odds, winning the Finish transformed. You'll be perfect. We'll be perfect."

I freeze, and Pierce startles when he tries to spin me and I don't move at all, an island in this desert of opulence. He frowns down at me and his lips move but I can't hear him over the rushing of my own blood. I think he's asking me what's wrong. I stare up at this guileless, *stupid* boy.

"Let me go," I think I say, hoarse.

"What?" he asks. "We're dancing."

"I don't want to dance. Let me *go*," I insist, louder this time. It feels like I'm in the bathroom again, like Esme's voice is growing louder in my head as she spits vile, poisonous shit. About how she's made me. About how I'm nothing without her. He wants to *make* me. For him.

"Adina, what are you even doing?" Pierce hisses. "You're making a scene. Dance with—"

"*No.*"

It happens before I can even convince myself not to, or remember that the stakes are too high.

I slap him and his head snaps to the side. He raises a shivering hand to his cheek. He looks around, for anyone who saw. Thankfully, few did. But the ones who did elbow the others, whispering to one another. The quartet is still performing.

"You . . . you slapped me," he says obviously.

"I would do it again," I say, shaking with my fury, too late to turn back now. "This isn't evening the playing field, you utter *asshole*. I'll kill you." I don't sound like myself, my voice deeper, rawer than I've ever heard it.

It's the same thing I said to Esme before I launched myself at her, all those months ago. But this time, I think I might mean it.

I *do* mean it.

Pierce's eyes narrow, and suddenly he doesn't look so beautiful. He looks like his father. "You can't do anything to me, you little—"

Before it can escalate further, Penthesilea is suddenly there, stepping between us, her back to me. She stares up into Pierce's face.

"Pierce, darling, look at me," she commands, voice hard. Pierce keeps glaring over her shoulder at me, but Penthesilea grabs his face, redirecting his rage toward her. "Pierce, come on. It's not that serious. Please, look at me?"

Pierce's hands wrap around her wrists and squeeze down, hard. "You don't tell me—"

"I understand, my love. It's all right. She just . . . doesn't get it. Your intentions. You are so well intentioned. Some people just aren't grateful for it. I was always grateful, wasn't I?" Penthesilea corrects. She sounds so soft-spoken, but there is something in her that's completely in control.

But Pierce does not want to be controlled. He draws himself up and I am reminded of how tall he is.

"Let's play a game," he says, voice ringing out. He looks sharply over his shoulder. "Aunt Leighton! We're playing a game now!" He jerks out of Penthesilea's hold, stalking over and disrupting whatever conversation Leighton was in.

"What's going on?" I whisper, shaking, looking at Penthesilea.

She breathes slowly and draws her shoulders back. "You're finding out what I warned you about. The problem with saying no to him . . . is that he always retaliates. He's petty that way."

Pierce leans in to Third and Leighton, his hands growing more agitated with every moment. Third pulls away, grim.

"Attention!" Third calls, voice booming. He sounds far less jovial now.

The pinkness in Pierce's face could be attributed to health, but

I know that I've left my mark, and I feel a savage sort of triumph that soothes the roiling ache of fear. Leighton has a hand on his shoulder, but as her gaze falls to me, it sparks with amusement instead of the condemnation I expect. She likes that I've put him in his place, even if it means not winning—and just like that I know it was never about me at all.

"We have come to the game portion of the evening. For those who are attending their first closing Repartee, the rules are simple. A game is chosen that mirrors the next task and its goals. Tomorrow the final girl's goal will be to become a Remington. That is, to be a cut above the rest. To demonstrate leadership but also to know . . . when to follow," Third says, and he is a conductor to this orchestra of chaos. Each of them hangs off his every word, sycophants to the very last breath. "We present . . . our girls. In first after the Raid, we have Esme Alderidge."

Esme tears off her mask and they all applaud. Her parents are louder than the rest. Esme stares out, proudly, and when her gaze flits over her father's face, I can see her resolve return. She holds up her hand and gives a princess wave, flashing the prize on her finger, the diamond ring that still won't go past her second knuckle.

"In second, we have Hawthorne Harding." Hawthorne pulls her mask down to hang around her neck, and she curtsies.

As I look around, I can see the expressions of some people—those without personal stakes, there for the pomp and circumstance and blood—grow brighter.

"In third, we have our very own Penthesilea Bonavich."

Our very own.

"In fourth, Miss Adina Walker."

I swallow hard as I unmask, and suddenly, the world looks sharper and more terrible. I'm so overwhelmed by it, I don't hear Saint's introduction.

"—night's game is one we are all familiar with from our youths. A game of the schoolyard. Simon Says," Leighton says with a delicate laugh.

The rest of the room titters with her, and I have to bite my tongue to keep my jaw from dropping.

"She must be joking," whispers Saint from the corner of her mouth.

But no one is joking.

They clear the dance floor for us, all of them pushing to the outskirts of the room, except for the Remingtons. Pierce and Third sit in gleaming wooden chairs, like judges. It's like we're an exhibit to them. No, we are circus animals.

"The outcome of this game will determine the advantages and disadvantages going into the Royale. This is how it has been. This is how it will be," Leighton says as she walks along the line of us, looking each of us up and down before she turns to the attendees with her mysterious smile. "Who will be our first 'Simon' then?"

No one seems to want to volunteer. Then the senator does. He claps Third on the shoulder before he spins to look at the room, grinning broadly, backing toward us.

"I'll try my hand, won't I?" he asks, like he's at a fucking reelection rally.

And they *laugh*, like he is being funny. Like this is all so funny.

"So . . . basic rules of Simon Says?" the senator asks.

"The basic rules," Leighton affirms, backing away, her hands clasped behind her back.

The senator grins, his shiny skin so red that it looks like I could peel the first layer off, help him shed his snake skin. "This will be a fun game, girls, yes? Low pressure," he says. He means to be reassuring. "Okay, let's . . . Simon says . . . jump up and down."

For a minute all of us look at one another, exchanging hesitant looks. *Are you fucking kidding me?*

And then Esme starts jumping up and down in her Louboutin heels. Penthesilea follows suit almost immediately, and then Hawthorne, and then there I am, jumping up and down in ugly block heels like an asshole.

If I get out of here, I'm going to make it my life's work to see the junior senator of Massachusetts exposed for some heinous shit. Not because of his association with the Remingtons, but because he's here, making me look stupid.

"Good girls!" he says. *Infantilizing.* "Ah . . . Simon says, clap your hands."

And so it goes. Inane command after command. Give a thumbs-up. Stomp your feet. Nod your head. Flap your arms.

Then a new "Simon" takes over. Younger. She is crueler, faster.

"Simon says, sit down." "Simon says, stand up." "Smile." "Simon says, scream until I say stop."

It's the last one that makes Saint bow out first. She shakes her head, lips pressed in a thin line, even while I scream, loud. Louder than all the others, so loud that it starts to sound like white noise in my ears. I want to scream, *What are you doing?* to her, but I can't.

Saint steps back again and again, and then she's shoving past the crowd by the bar, reaching over past the bartender for a plastic bag that she heaves into. My stomach revolts in sympathy, but I turn back to the Simon. Saint is out. Saint will remain ranked last, with who knows what disadvantages. That's not good.

It's down to four.

When it's time for a new "Simon" again, Pierce speaks. "Charles. You should be 'Simon.'"

Charles. I don't know how I missed him before. He's the only Black person here besides me, tall and careful to display the gaudy watch on his wrist so no one thinks that he's the help. He looks on edge now and vaguely green, fiddling with his cuff links nervously. I see Toni in the shape of his eyes.

Toni, I think. And there's a spark of hope born.

"What? No, man. No," Charles stammers.

Pierce frowns. "Why not?" he asks.

"This is not my idea of fun, Pierce. No," Charles repeats, voice just a bit harder, and Pierce sighs long-sufferingly.

Instead, another "Simon" is chosen. A man I recognize. I see

Esme in the narrowness of his forehead, the widow's peak that dips down, the tilt of his chin. Her father lets every look of disdain or intrigue slide off him like oil as he steps forward, his wife on his arm. She doesn't wear a diamond collar, but she has donned pearls, fat and thick like they're straight from the oyster shells. Another layer of mind games, for once not directed at me. I look over at Esme and I see her throat move as she sets her jaw.

"Simon says, jump," he says. His voice is careful. Not nearly as unhinged as Esme's. So the similarities end with appearance and maybe the intense look in their eyes. "Simon says, stop. Simon says, hop on your left foot. Simon says, right foot. Simon says, about-face. Simon says, spin in a circle. Simon says, *stop*—"

We all freeze, all but for Hawthorne, who stutters in her movements.

"Miss Harding," Leighton says, her voice strained, "you're out." Leighton doesn't look well. She looks like she's unraveling and winding herself up again over and over in a painful cycle.

Hawthorne's nostrils flare, and she presses her lips together hard, making a loud sound, almost like a shriek, that shocks me. But then she swallows it slowly, letting it all melt away. She leans forward, whispering something in Esme's ear before she backs away, nodding reassuringly at her.

And then there were three.

"Simon Says . . . don't blink."

It sounds ridiculous. Basic in the face of Mr. Alderidge's ranted list before. But five seconds turns into ten turns into twenty, and my eyes begin to burn. I let out a whistling breath, forcing my eyes wider as they start to dry out and tears begin to swell.

It's only when he looks bored and troubled by our own mental fortitude that he says, "Simon Says, blink."

I blink so hard that tears fall free, clinging to my lashes, blurring my vision. I rub furiously at my eyes and look over at Saint. She's leaning against the bar, everyone giving her a wide berth except for Hawthorne. Saint nods at me—*Keep going.*

"Simon Says, slap each other," says Mr. Alderidge.

I'm just turning away from Saint when a blow comes across my jaw, enough to make me stumble, one knee buckling. Someone gasps, and I grab my jaw, looking up. Esme is unrepentant, staring at me with a wide smile. She's been waiting for that one for a while. I straighten slowly, never taking my eyes off her. One step forward. Another.

But Penthesilea is faster. Penthesilea backhands Esme so hard, it makes her spit blood right onto the gleaming tiled floor. And then Penthesilea turns, presenting her cheek to me.

I pat her deliberately, firm enough to count but not a slap. And then I smile at Esme, defiant. When we're back in line, Mr. Alderidge's expression has soured more and he stares even *harder* at his own daughter.

"Simon says . . . stab yourself with a fork."

"A . . . fork," Penthesilea says. Her voice sounds hoarse from the screaming. She clears her throat. "You want us to stab ourselves?"

"Simon Says. Isn't that right?" Mr. Alderidge challenges.

I bite my bottom lip. "Aunt Leighton?" I ask uncertainly. Leighton stares, her expression waning, her face more colorless than usual. "Aunt *Leighton*."

"The game is Simon Says," Third declares. "Alderidge is Simon, not Leighton, so you do what—"

"I know the rules," I say fiercely. Third's eyes widen at being interrupted in front of his guests. The entire room is holding their breath. "I don't care. I'm out." They move as if they expected me to quit, like I don't have what it takes, and for the first time that feels good.

I mean to make my way to Saint's side, to hear her reassurances, but someone else catches my eyes first. The only person who looks like me, attempting to fade into the background. Charles looks as if he wants to be here about as much as me. He takes a step back when he sees me, edging away, but I won't let him escape me.

"Charles, stop," I say, following him to the edges of the ball-room, close to the balcony doors. The moment we're in each other's company, it's like the eyes of the New England elite glaze over, slipping past us, focusing again on the game. I am used to making myself a background set piece when I need to, from being in yearbook, being Esme's friend, from being Black, and that serves me well now. "It's me—"

"I know it's you, Adina. I literally see you," Charles says sharply. He holds himself so brittle that a sharp wind would snap him. "Are you all right?"

"Of course," I say, because this is nothing. This is humiliating.

But this doesn't hurt. My jaw smarts, but it'll be gone by the morning.

"That didn't look okay," Charles says, shaking his head. "That looked . . . that was . . . has that been going on all this time? The . . . sick games? Girls getting lost?"

"Dying. And yes." He looks at me for more, but I say nothing. It doesn't seem like it should require any further explanation for him to believe what he's just seen, what Third said.

"What the fuck?" Charles says. "I've heard about the Finish all my life, but it's not supposed to be like *this*. If I knew that this . . . I wouldn't have . . ." He sounds shaken by the revelation, like it ruins the way he looks at the world. I don't have time for it.

I reach for his sleeve and hold tight so he doesn't run. "You have to get me out of here."

Charles's eyes widen. "Adina—"

"Charles, please, they're going to kill me. If you don't . . . if I don't . . . ," I stammer, shaking my head. I steel myself over, looking across the ballroom. Saint is watching me, sincere and serious and, above all, worried. "If you won't, tell Toni I need her."

Charles looks sick. "Adina, you want me to get her involv—"

A scream.

It's not any of the girls—I recognize all their screams now. It's a woman, in response to what she's just seen.

Penthesilea has bowed out. I knew she would. Even she knows that self-inflicted violence for spectacle is a step too far.

But Esme. There Esme stands, still with blood on her lips, and now a fork hanging by the tines from her fucking palm, the points tearing open her skin, leaving blood dripping down her wrist.

"I win?" she asks, her voice tiny.

Leighton shakes herself out of her reverie, eyes focusing on Esme again. "You win, Miss Alderidge. You continue to be first."

There is something lost about Esme amongst the arms of her parents, as they swarm in, kissing their pride to her temple. The room applauds, but Esme is staring at something no one else can see, her brow furrowed. It's like something has left her that she can't find again, and she misses it, desperately, more than anything.

In that moment she looks like the girl who was my friend, once, and more than ever, I know that tomorrow, in the Royale, I won't be able to kill anyone, not even her, because she'll always look like the girl who might have been my friend.

CHAPTER

28

CHARLES USES THE COMMOTION TO BREAK AWAY, and because I have nowhere else to go, I stay. I stay through the dancing and laughing, pressed up against the wall, with Saint at my side. We watch as Pierce makes his turns about the room, speaking to each important person like he's known them for years, confident in his ability to communicate on their level. Once or twice, I catch wind of his ambitions when he's close enough.

"Political science. Then an internship, hopefully with you, Senator. That'll certainly lead me on my way to governor one day," he explains when the senator asks him what he's going to major in, what his plans are, what his future is. He is so sure.

When someone thanks him for the invitation—not Third, not Leighton, but *him*—Pierce smiles and says, "There'll be plenty more social events here. My mother is not one for a full social calendar, but I certainly am."

Penthesilea works the room just as well, but with her, now that I know what she's really like, I can see how each movement is calculated. She is following Pierce. At a distance, but still. She speaks to every single person that he speaks to, cementing her place.

Esme and Hawthorne are huddled together, sitting with Esme's parents and another set of parents that I have to assume are Hawthorne's. Hawthorne has wrapped a table napkin around Esme's palm and their heads are bent together, ignoring everything around them.

No one makes an effort to speak to us and we don't make an effort to speak to anyone else, even when Leighton swoops by us on her second turn around the room. She glowers, jerking her chin at the old money of Massachusetts, making it very clear what she expects from me. I stare back at her, stony faced.

"I think . . . ," Leighton declares, and she lets it linger, waiting for her words to carry enough that attention is turned toward her. "It is high time for the girls to get to bed. They have a *very* big morning ahead of them."

"A big day tomorrow, Pierce," someone calls, and there's a crackle of laughter that no one finds inappropriate.

"Come along, ladies," Leighton prompts.

I push off the wall and take one more sweeping look around the room. Graham is no longer here—shocker. Charles skulks in the back now and I try to meet his eye, but he won't even look at me. Saint tugs me along, and we're just nearly out of the room before fingers slip into my free hand, stopping me where I am.

When I turn, I snatch back my hand immediately. I want to

say something terrible to Pierce, but I can't think where to start.

"Good night, Adina," Pierce says, and he sounds kind again. He leans in and presses a kiss to my cheek and I flinch so hard, I crash into Saint. Pierce pulls back and smiles, satisfied that I have learned my lesson. Determined to resume our story.

Saint tugs me away, looping her arm through mine, sneering at Pierce as we walk out of the room. Leighton stops just in front of the doors, looking at us as we cluster closer together. I can feel Esme right behind me, and I don't even mind. At least she's between me and the jackals still inside.

"Tomorrow morning it will only be us. It is important that the Royale remain one of our closest held secrets. So at eleven, you will present yourself in the hunting parlor in your finest," Leighton says. She takes a deep breath. "You have all played an admirable game. But tomorrow, it will all come to an end. Thank you. Good night."

Leighton doesn't tell us what the Royale is, but she doesn't need to. I know the definition—an event in which a number of combatants fight it out until there's one left standing.

She steps around us and walks back into the ballroom, shutting the doors behind us, leaving us in darkness. There is nothing to say between the five of us. Hawthorne nods once, gingerly holding Esme's injured hand in hers. They walk down the corridor toward the left. Penthesilea takes off to the right.

Saint and I take the long way, walking down toward the main staircase and ascending.

No matter how far we walk, I can still hear the echoes of music and laughter and, if I try hard enough, imagine the sound of clinking crystal. A toast to the Remingtons. To the rich. To the continued impoverishment of everyone who's not them. Meanwhile, our way is lit only by the stray candelabra on the walls, like this is some manor in some shitty budget eighties Gothic film.

My life *is* a horror movie.

Go figure.

But it's almost peaceful, knowing that tomorrow is the day that I'll die. I laugh to myself, my own voice echoing eerily through the halls.

Because even if I die tomorrow, I want to haunt these halls long after I'm gone. I want the Remingtons to *remember* me. *Witness* me. Never be free of me.

I open our door, content with this commitment.

Saint walks in and immediately drops her dress, tearing it off her body, the zipper popping. She kicks it off, standing there in her underwear. And then she stalks toward the wardrobe and tears it open, throwing aside the white lace dress from the first day in favor of the black fatigues Mr. Caine hasn't taken back yet.

I shut the door behind me.

"Saint . . . Saint, what are you doing?" I ask, weighing each word carefully. She pulls her hair back in a ponytail, so tight that her eyebrows arch unnaturally.

Saint hops into the pants, breathing noisily, nostrils flaring.

Then she tugs the jacket on and zips it up to her chin, like she wants to choke herself with the collar.

"I've seen enough. I've heard enough," Saint says. "I've had enough. I'm done."

I sober swiftly. I'm suddenly far too cold.

"What do you mean you're done?" I rush to her side and grab her hands, trying to unfold her arms. She doesn't resist, letting me grab them and squeeze as I look up at her.

"I'm going home," Saint says decidedly. She nods, like it's as simple as walking through the door, like me when I first tried to escape, no matter that she's dressed for war. "I can't be here anymore."

I drop her hands, wounded. "You can't . . . you can't *leave* me," I yelp. I look at her, wide eyed.

"I won't," Saint says firmly. "You're coming with me."

The words don't make sense, they scramble in my brain.

"I . . . w-we can't," I stutter. Immediately, all the obstacles leap into my head in the form of a helpful itemized list. "One: there are guards. Two: we don't know the grounds at night. Three: Leighton threatened my parents—"

"They can't touch your parents," Saint insists.

"And how do you know that?" I only realize that I've shouted when Saint takes a hesitant step back. I glance back at the door, terrified that Mr. Caine will show up. Or worse—Leighton. Lowering my voice to barely a whisper, I say, "I don't have the same resources as you, Saint. My parents work at the school that *they* own. My parents are all I have, but they have nothing to protect them."

"Not anymore. You have me," Saint corrects.

I do have her. And . . . I might have someone else.

"You know that boy I was talking to at the Repartee? The Black boy?" I ask quietly.

Saint nods immediately. "Yes. What about him?"

"His name is Charles. He's Pierce's best friend," I say, and I watch Saint's transformation, the way her entire expression turns to the steel edge of a blade. I shake my head, waving my hands. "No, that's not the important part. He's my best friend Toni's twin brother."

Saint straightens, and she's too smart to not figure out where this is going. "What were you two talking about?"

"When I called my mother, I asked her to give Toni a message. I told her this thing about Bath & Body Works and Suburbia. It's shit I don't talk about. Shit I would only talk about if I was uncomfortable," I whisper, cautious of being overheard. "It means that something's wrong. That I'm stuck. But it must've been too vague. So I told Charles to . . . to help me. To tell Toni that I need *help*. She'll come and we can go to her family first. Figure things out from there. They're not like my parents. They're rich. Not like the Remingtons, but still."

Saint hesitates.

"You just said he's Pierce's best friend," she reminds me.

"But Charles doesn't like this either. I could tell. He was

scared, but he couldn't do anything while he was here. When he gets back, though . . . ," I insist.

He'd tell Toni, but I realize that doesn't mean anything. He'd have to convince her first. And then, he's less impulsive than her. He'd stop her from returning without a plan. If he let her come at all. It would take time. Time we don't have.

"If it weren't for your parents, would you leave here?" Saint asks, interrupting my train of thought. "Can you honestly tell me another reason you wouldn't?"

Once there might have been. Here, there is a promise of a future. Of rich foods and bubbly champagne. Of Ivy educations and long-standing careers. Power over everyone and anyone that could ever try to hurt me again.

Apply pressure, Leighton's voice says. *Become a diamond.*

But it's all fake. Rotten, just like Penthesilea said. It's gaslighting and manipulation and casual racism and classism and never-ending total *bullshit*. Not to mention murder.

So, if my parents weren't a concern, of course I would try to run again. There's nothing to lose that I won't lose more certainly tomorrow, nothing tethering me here. My loyalty is to Saint alone. Hawthorne will never change as long as Esme is around. Penthesilea is desperate. Graham is spineless. And Pierce is dangerous.

"No," I whisper finally.

"Then we have to leave," Saint insists. "I will protect them. My family can protect them. And Yale. You want to go to Yale? I'll try to make that happen for you. I'll even pay for it out of my trust fund."

"Why?" I ask, but I think I already know the answer.

"Because we've gone through hell together in two weeks, and you got me through it. You have pushed me and taken care of me and made me feel like I wasn't going crazy. You saw exactly what *I* saw. A family of psycho, power-hungry assholes," Saint says plainly. "We both know that the Royale tomorrow is going to be winner takes all. And I don't think we'll survive it. At least, I won't. These white people won't pay for what they've done to us. America will protect them. So we need to go."

"Do you have a plan?" I ask.

Saint nods once. "Yes. Not a good one. But it's better odds than staying."

She grabs my hand and squeezes. "If I can just get to a phone outside of this place, I can end all of them. I can. I just need a phone and the closest bank. I can't get out alone, though. Are you coming with me, Adina?"

I can't go through another night like this. The humiliation. The complete loss of control. They made me compliant. I will not be again.

I squeeze her hand. It's not even a question anymore. There's no other answer.

"Let's get out of this shithole."

CHAPTER 29

WE MOVE UNDER THE COVER OF NIGHT. WE'VE BOTH abandoned everything, deciding that it can all be replaced. Dressing in our Raid fatigues makes it easier to slip from shadow to shadow. We don't speak, either. Both of us know the plan. It's the same as it's always been—stick together and survive.

Once, we have to press flat against the wall to avoid a maid slipping through the dark.

When we're on the move again, I don't take the time to catalog the spaces that I aim to leave behind. They'll be burned on my retinas anyway, the dark wood and the oil paintings and the gleaming gold of the candelabras.

We treat this like it's the Ride. Each security guard stationed is another obstacle to be avoided, and we slip from shadow to shadow, twisting around a sharp corner or ducking behind a door. Then it's like the Raid, searching for a way, hunting hallways that are unoccupied, moving through this maze of a house until we find one that leads out the back door and lets us slip into the gardens, by the stables. Out in the fresh air, we breathe a little easier. The security guards are stationed near the front tonight, by the gate and the garage, escorting the last lingering guests of the third Repartee off the grounds. I look at Saint from the corner of my eye. Her mouth is curved into a half-moon, giddiness tugging at the corner of her lips.

"We're out. We're getting out," she says, holding her hand out to me.

I take it and squeeze, letting out a tiny sigh. "Yeah, we're getting out."

We slip quickly into the stables. We've agreed to go through the two arenas and run the way back down the path of the Ride, hopefully breaking out into someone else's land, or at least losing security until the morning.

I want to suggest taking the horses for speed, but I know that they'll be loud and make us an easier target to see.

"We'll go—" I start.

"Go where?"

Both of us turn toward the entrance as one.

Esme leans against the doorway of the stable, arms folded over her chest. She hasn't bothered to change out of her silk pajamas, like she wanted to look as expensive as possible when she confronted us. Her left hand has been lovingly wrapped with gauze, medical tape painstakingly placed.

"Mind your business," Saint says coldly.

Esme has the audacity to look amused, fighting a smirk.

"You should go back to your room, before security finds you," I say carefully.

Esme nods slowly, eyes disdainfully wide. "You're *right*. We can all walk back together," Esme agrees. "Isn't that where you were going? Back to your room?"

Neither Saint nor I say anything as Esme taps her chin. Easing back, I grab Saint's arm, tugging her along with me as Esme stalks forward, eyes wide with curiosity.

"Because if you weren't, I'd have to say that it'll only be minutes before security decides to check the stables. They already know you're missing," Esme says dryly.

"And . . . and how would they know that?" I ask.

Esme smiles. "I'm not stupid. I saw your faces at the Repartee. You're done, aren't you?"

Looking at Esme, I wonder how she's *not*.

"I mean, isn't that what you want? Just . . . just let us leave," I insist. I take another step back, tripping over a beam of wood laying haphazardly in the hay. "If we leave, you'll win even more easily. It'll just be you against Penthesilea, and Hawthorne will help you—"

"No," Esme barks. And then she stops, like she's confused about what she's saying. She looks up at us, trembling, darkness tearing across her face. "If I can't leave . . . you can't either. If I'm gonna die here, I'm not gonna be the only one. Not after all I've sacrificed."

Her voice is deep and guttural. Esme has never acknowledged her own mortality in all the years that I've known her. She's caustic and cocky and cruel. She's still all those things, but now she's scared, too. She's human.

"This isn't worth it," I whisper gently. "If you don't wanna die, come with—"

"NO!"

There's a beat of silence, louder than all the rest, and then Esme turns, ready to run, to scream where we are. But Saint launches herself at Esme, tackling her to the ground. She tries to secure her there with a knee between her shoulder blades, but Esme flips and headbutts Saint in the nose. Saint falls back, gasping, blood spurting from her nostrils and splashing across the front of Esme's nightshirt.

Esme rolls over and crawls forward, fighting her way to her feet. "I have fought and *fought* all this time. I have humiliated myself again and again. I'm not going anywhere with you. I'm going to see this through until the end." The wound on her hand has started to bleed again, pinpricks of red spreading across stark white gauze. "And so are you."

Saint turns and spits blood on the ground, glaring at Esme's back. "You're not doing this for your family, Esme Alderidge. You just don't know who you are without diamonds around your neck. And you're too scared to find out."

"I'll kill you," Esme promises. She takes a step back, and I can believe it. I can see it happening, can see her wrapping her long fingers around Saint's neck and choking the life out of her. Saint would fight it, but in the end, Esme would win because she stinks of desperation.

"Don't do this, Esme. . . ," I warn. "I don't want to hurt you."

And it's true. This may look like that day with Toni, like a fun-house mirror, the two of us facing each other, both poised for violence, but this time the consequences would be deadly.

Esme looks at me for a brief moment, like she remembers too. And like she remembers before that. The years we were friends. That we used to go to her country house, that we went roller-skating together, that we used to eat lunch together. That we used to just *be*, a group of friends, a group of girls.

She remembers and . . . decides that it's not enough.

Esme launches herself at Saint, her acrylic nails curled over, and I move before I can even think, swinging the beam of wood with all my might at her back, intending to knock her over.

There's a hard crack, and for a moment Esme almost floats in the air, frozen. A trickle of blood slips from her scalp down the back of her neck, staining the clasp of her necklace rose gold. And then she falls into a heap and doesn't move. I can't even scream. The sound freezes in my chest.

Saint barely reacts. She is already grabbing me, tugging me back from Esme. *Esme*, who is not moving.

"We have to go. Come on, Adina. Come *on*," Saint insists, her voice wispy in my ear.

"She's not moving," I say, too loud. "Is she breathing?"

The sounds of security get closer, the static of their radios, the barking of orders. I jerk out of Saint's hold and rush back to Esme, collapsing to my knees in the hay. I press a hand to the back of her head, and it comes away wet, the blood so dark in the moonlight, it looks black, like something out of a fairy tale. Saint is still pulling at my shoulder, trying to get me to my feet.

"I can't . . . I didn't . . . I couldn't've," I stutter in starts and finishes. And then I grab Saint by the face with two hands, smearing a bloody handprint on her cheek. "I have to stay. She needs help, I can't leave her. You need . . ."

Saint shakes her head. "No, we've done this together—"

"Saint," I interrupt. The men are getting louder. *"Run."*

She looks terrified. But finally, finally, she turns and does as I command, running into the night, as fast as she can through the back of the stables, over the fence of the outdoor ring and gone.

"Okay . . . *okay*, Esme," I whisper, voice gone feathery with panic. I reach for her and turn her over onto her back, looking down at her. I cringe. Blood is spilling down her forehead. I put my hand to her lips, to her chest, but there is no movement. "You're okay, Esme. You're okay."

I punctuate my insistence as I press my hands to her chest, doing compressions. I've no idea if the rhythm is right or the form, all my knowledge gleaned from TV, but it's all I have. It has to be enough, because if it isn't—

"The stable!" a voice shouts.

I press harder, leaning down to press my lips to hers, feeling her lungs inflate. When I pull away, my mouth tastes like pennies. I press down harder, and I shiver, even though I'm not cold. This is Esme.

Esme, who is cruel and ambitious and forceful. Esme, who is here for her family, and yes, also herself.

Esme, who was my friend.

Esme, who was my enemy.

Esme, who might be dead.

Because of me.

The voices grow louder and louder, and security creeps closer.

"In here!" they call from just outside the door.

I slowly raise my hands in surrender, but then I'm jerked backward, a large hand flying over my mouth. I fight against the forearm wrapped around my stomach as I'm yanked back and then I try to slam my head back against the face of my captor.

"Stop," Graham's voice comes low and urgent. "Come with me or they're going to shoot."

I gasp and immediately fall limp in his arms as he tugs me back into the nearest empty stall. We collapse against the hay, then peer through the crack between the stall door and the wall, right where we can see Esme's body, her blood glittering. She'd appreciate the aesthetic if she could see it. The heinous thought makes me want to laugh and vomit.

Security guards finally spill through the door, and I press my own fist into my mouth and bite down *hard* to keep from making a sound as I catalog their rifles and Kevlar.

"Jesus," the man in front says, looking down at Esme's form.

"Get out of my *way*—"

"Oh no," I hiss into my fist. Security is shoved aside, revealing Leighton Remington, and at her side . . . Hawthorne.

Leighton's mouth pinches and she sighs. "Oh my,"

Hawthorne doesn't make a single sound. She stares down at Esme and then slowly sinks to her knees, head tilting like she can't quite make sense of what she's seeing. She crawls forward, dragging herself through the puddle of blood, until she's kneeling right where I was, her fingers searching for the wound.

"Hawthorne, please," Leighton begins.

And then Hawthorne *wails*, bloodcurdling and grievous and *sad*. Leighton winces.

Amidst the screams someone's radio crackles. And then: "The Asian girl—by the forest."

Saint.

"Shut her up!" the man barks as Hawthorne still screams. One of the other guards tries to drag Hawthorne away, but she throws herself over Esme's body.

Leighton steps up and there's the glint of something silver in grip, and then she's plunging a needle straight into Hawthorne's neck. Hawthorne goes limp in seconds.

"She's sedated," Leighton says coldly. "Bring her back to her room and lock the door. She needs to be well rested for the Royale. And be sure to clean up your mess. I don't want the girls disturbed with your presence in the morning."

"Yes, ma'am," a guard says. He hesitates. "The Asian?"

Leighton doesn't blink. "She is here because of Mr. Remington's *pride*. Her family is dangerous to our interests and do not know she's here. She can't get out."

"So?" the guard asks uncertainly.

Leighton rolls her eyes and stops pretending. "Kill her, obviously."

The guard lifts the radio to his mouth.

I shake my head, chanting no into my fist. Graham's hands are shaking on my shoulders, like he's trying to keep me back, like I might chase after them.

"Kill the girl," the man relays.

We all fall silent. I close my eyes.

Boom.

CHAPTER 30

"WHY DIDN'T YOU LET THEM CATCH ME? WHY DIDN'T you let them *see*? They wanted me to kill. Well, now I have." I don't let him answer, turning instead to inspect the room that he's dragged me into. "Where the fuck am I?"

"My room," Graham says, raising his hands placatingly. He leans heavily against the door. He looks like he's coming down from coke, his eyes bloodshot, his hands shaking. "Just . . . stay here—"

"Why?"

"I'm trying to keep you alive through the rest of the night. For that to happen, you need to *stay* in this house and make them think you never left, that you were with me, not her," Graham snaps.

When I exhale, all the air leaves the room and I let out a keening sound. The exhaustion doesn't creep this time; instead, it crashes straight through my chest and my knees buckle. Graham dives for me but doesn't make it to my side in time. I land heavily on the carpet and bury my face in my hands.

"Don't cry . . . don't cry . . . ," Graham whispers.

That, out of everything else, enrages me.

"*Fuck* you," I bite out. "I can cry if I want to." *I am always crying.*

"Yes," he says, placatingly. "Yes, you can." Graham clears his throat and presses a hesitant hand to my shoulder. He means to be comforting, but it just feels like a weight, holding me down underwater. "Adina, you had to—"

"I didn't *have* to do anything," I say roughly, remembering that split-second terror. I roll away from his touch when it starts to sting. He doesn't even have the decency to look wounded, just understanding. "Just . . . leave me alone. Why can't you just leave me alone?"

"You know why I can't," Graham says severely, like the way he's looking at me should mean something, like I should feel it too.

"Do you know what I went through tonight while you left like a *coward*?" I demand. "While you were getting high or whatever, I lost a demonic game of Simon Says and was humiliated by Pierce and your father's minions."

Graham's mouth goes slack. "Holy shit. What did Third—"

"It's not about Third! Pay attention," I shout. "We had to slap each other. Esme slapped me so hard, I'm shocked she didn't knock a tooth out."

"Why would they do that?" Graham whispers to himself. "Who—"

"Who? Your precious Four," I ask and answer, and even the mention of him fills me with fury. "You know, I hooked up with him," I snarl, because I want him to feel like I do. I watch the words land, and see his expression twist and I feel righteous. "I hooked up with your brother in the woods, at the bonfire."

Graham gives a sad smile. "I know," he says quietly. "But Four doesn't have anything to do with this."

"He has everything to do with this," I accuse.

"Don't say that," he protests, his voice small. He sounds young. He sounds naïve. He wants to not know so badly. I wanted to not know everything I know now. Mercy has long run out for me, and I hear Penthesilea loud in my ear. She was right about Pierce.

But Graham . . .

"If Pierce told you to let me die, would you?"

Graham stares at me like I'm crazy. "What the fuck kind of question is that?"

"I'm being serious," I insist. I swallow hard as I take a step closer, jutting a finger in his face. "You've made it very clear that you would do whatever Pierce told you to do. Even though I *expressly* told you that I am not something to give. So, I'm going to ask you again and I want an answer: if Pierce told you to let me die, would you?"

"Fuck no," Graham says. "And he wouldn't want that."

"I'm not so sure. And I'd rather die on my own terms than his," I bite out.

"You don't want to die. If you did, you would've let Esme get you, and you didn't."

Esme's blood has dried a dusty red on my hands now, and my skin feels tight underneath. I scratch at it, bringing it up in flakes, my nails leaving red welts in its place. "Get it off, get it off, get it off," I chant to myself, and Graham jumps to his feet, tugging me into the bathroom.

It feels like the first night all over again, like Hawthorne washing Esme's poison from my skin. Hawthorne. Her howl still echoes in my ear, feral and mournful. I open my mouth in a soundless wail, wanting to swallow the sound of it, but I can't manage it.

"Why didn't you save Saint?" I accuse as he lathers my hands with too-expensive soap and carefully washes away Esme's blood. The flakes swirl down the porcelain sink, sliding down the drain like they never existed in the first place.

"Besides the obvious, she had a better chance of getting away than you did."

Graham judges my hands clean, reaching for a hand towel, but I see there's still blood under my fingernails. I don't say anything about it, though, as he shuffles me from the bathroom back into the dark expanse of his bedroom. He pushes me to sit down on the edge of his bed as he turns on the light on the side table and goes to his dresser, searching through it for something.

"I saved you because you weren't going to save yourself. Not in that moment. Because you believed that whatever they did to you, you deserved. Which you don't," Graham explains. He makes a quiet sound of triumph in the back of his throat as he finally pulls out pajamas.

"Not because you care about tradition?" I drawl that word out like Pierce and Leighton and Third.

Graham kneels in front of me and I stare down at him, frowning.

"Fuck the Finish," Graham says quietly as he passes me a T-shirt and a pair of flannel pants that are just a little too big.

"That's easy for you to say," I whisper. "It's all so easy for you, isn't it? You've been telling yourself that for a long time. 'Fuck the Finish.' Saying you're helping me. Without doing anything *about* the Finish. If you're not going to stop bad things from happening, then you should have the decency to watch it, eyes *open*." Each word hits like a punch and each flinch is an earned victory.

Graham's face is pale in the low light.

"Adina, I couldn't—"

"You could," I insist. "But you didn't. You can't see that your brother is just as bad as the rest of them, because if you do, you have to admit that all you taught him was that he can have whatever he wants because of his name. You'd have to admit that you did nothing because decency means *nothing* to you. You are a coward, and worst of all, you are *selfish*."

Graham shoves the lent pajamas into my hands and I hold them loosely, a flannel pants leg dragging on the floor. "Adina—"

"You don't want to stop this because it means standing up for something. And you are only considering it now because of me.

You would've never tried this hard for Saint. Or Pen. Or . . . or *Esme*," and my voice cracks on her name.

"You know why. If there's anyone in this house who doesn't deserve to be dead, it's you, Adina Walker."

No one deserves to be dead, I want to scream. Not Margaret. Not Reagan. Not even Esme. None of us deserves to be dead.

"Why me?"

"Because I *love* you, Adina," he spits, exasperated.

I squint at Graham for a very long time, my brain slipping offline as I try to compute his statement. I don't realize that I've started to giggle until I register the resignation on his face. I slap a hand over my mouth, trying to smother my disbelief.

"Adina, please," he begins.

"No, I'm sorry, I—do you hear yourself?" I ask, and shake my head, trying to get myself in check again, all these emotions radioactive and reactionary, bringing me close to explosion. "It's just . . . you don't even know me enough to say that, Graham."

"I *could* love you. I know I could," he amends, though he sounds less sure now. When I just stare at him, waiting, he drags a hand over his face. "We should sleep. *You* should sleep."

And I know that's the end of the argument for Graham because he's still afraid. He's afraid, not of his family but of the truth of how he's still a part of it. That he, too, plays their games.

CHAPTER 31

GRAHAM ISN'T EXACTLY BEAUTIFUL. NOT LIKE HIS brother. But he does look softer, and even more so in sleep. I misjudged them, when they stood side by side, in the woods. Graham was more difficult and so I dismissed him. I mistook his acerbic nature for cruelty and was stupidly charmed by a low laugh and good bone structure. But I know better now. My fingers brush over his skin, and he turns in to the warmth of my touch, but he doesn't wake. Not yet. Good.

I slip from the bed.

In the daylight, his room looks very much like him. It is messy, clothes strewn about. A knocked-over bottle of cologne lies on his dresser. A baggie of weed is next to it, haphazardly out for the world—and the maid—to see. There is a photo of him and his brother on the side table, but none of anyone else. That makes sense too.

I pad over to the first door that doesn't lead out to the hallway.

I expect to find the bathroom, but it's a closet instead. I throw a glance backward, checking if he's still asleep. Graham turns on his side toward the window, burrowing deeper, so I can't help but snoop.

The closet is a walk-in, filled to the brim with oversized sweaters and expensive flannels. A rack full of different utility boots, each more expensive than the next, next to a pair of Aimé Leon Dore New Balances and another pair of sneakers, ratty Converses. And then toward the back are his suits, all dark except for one.

The last looks smaller than the rest. Gray plaid. I take it off the rack, pulling it in front of me and looking down. It's too big for me, but I take it anyway. I slip out of the closet and walk back toward the bed. I press my hand lightly against his back, between his shoulder blades, just to feel his heartbeat one last time, to feel that he's alive.

Graham, the un-favorite. Graham, who saved me, but also didn't. Graham, who still bleeds blue.

This time, moving through the Remington Estate, I take it all in.

My room is hollow without Saint. But there are signs of her everywhere. Her trunks are still open. Her bed is unmade. Her toothbrush is still in the bathroom. I can even still smell her perfume. She's everywhere.

Except, she's not. It still doesn't make sense. She's dead, but it doesn't feel real.

None of this feels real.

It doesn't reconcile with the girl I saw when I first arrived. Saint seemed a cut above the rest, solid Teflon and completely in control. But she isn't—*wasn't*—any of those things.

There's a dress laid out for me on my bed. It's beautiful. Blue. Extravagant.

Fuck the dress.

I reach for the suit that I took from Graham's room. Checkered and gray and just a little too large, but it's going to be more me than the dress. I tear into Saint's trunk, searching for something—*anything*—that will remind me of her—and then, there it is. A yellow silk tank top. She wore it at breakfast, the morning after Margaret died.

I take it and lay it out on the bed next to the suit.

I wash my hair again, stripping it of the oils and creams and the grimness of last night until I no longer smell the copper of Esme's blood clinging to my coils.

I'm going to start all over again. I have always had my routine getting ready for the school day. It looked nothing like this, but I'm resetting. I feel the broken bits of me, the pieces that are gone, stolen. I replace them with pieces of others.

Graham's suit. Saint's silk. Toni's eyeliner.

I feel Toni there as I apply it. She isn't coming—I can't afford to hope anyone will come to save me with only an hour until it's time—but I feel her anyway, sitting next to me, the weight of her hand on my shoulder. A perfect line and a flick at the end.

I want to make myself look like me for the final game. I go into my bag, searching for my comb, and pause when I see what began it all—the invitation. I read it over again. This letter I once thought held the answer to my predicament. Each handwritten curlicue a promise. *In pursuit of the furthering of women's education and placement in society,* my ass. These aren't promises. They're lies. Everything's a lie.

If you choose to accept . . .

A lie . . . and a challenge.

My heart skips and I can't help the way my lips twitch into a smile as I crush the letter in my fist and shove it into my pocket.

A challenge is just another word for a game, at least it is here. I've come to favor card games, in my time here, mostly because there are so many different sets of rules, the players can decide which ones to heed.

In a deck of cards, there are only three face cards, and I am none of them. If Third is the king and Leighton is the queen and Pierce is the jack, I would've once called myself an eight of clubs. Insignificant. *Random.*

But now I realize I'm the joker.

The joker is an unassuming card. In some games it has little function. In others, it's the highest trump.

In this game, it will be the wild one. The card that will finish them all. It has to be.

I sit before the vanity with purpose now and begin to part my hair, sectioning it into four areas. I never wore braids once I started at Edgewater. I never even wore them in summers in Suburbia, too afraid of being too much.

I know how, though; it's an ingrained practice that began at my mother's feet as she tugged a bristle brush through the coarseness of my curls, the scent of Blue Magic stinging my nose. I don't have any of that now, but I have gel and conditioner and my two good hands.

I cornrow my hair, and when I look at myself, I look like me. Finally.

Today is the Royale, I acknowledge, brushing mousse over my hair, dragging gel over my baby hairs with a toothbrush. There are two other girls out there, waiting. The Remingtons are out there, waiting. But I will not be dying today, I decide. I will not be quiet or swallow anything. I follow no one.

I will never think about this place after today, one way or another, I tell myself. I will not Finish here. My new life just began here, and no one remembers their birth.

I'm tired of their games and I hate the rules.

So. I'll change them.

When a handwritten letter arrives in lieu of an escort, I realize that the Remingtons mean for us to walk to our own potential deaths alone. Yet another metaphor, I'm sure. I clomp down the hallway in my ratty old Air Force 1s. There are no signs of life here, like they don't want anyone to witness the slaughter but them. Unlike last night.

I enter the hunting parlor.

Everyone else is already there. Even Graham.

It's a pretty picture, the Remingtons standing by the enormous floor-to-ceiling windows that show the gorgeous maze, the rose garden, the well-groomed paths along their grounds. They're backlit so that their faces are in shadow, but I can make out every expensive thread and detail of their silk and wool. Hawthorne and Penthesilea stand on either side, both dressed in their gowns. I fill out the apex of the triangle.

Pierce is wearing navy blue, the same color as the dress that was laid out for me, like he wanted to make a matched set of us again. An offer of forgiveness to me for saying no. He still thought that there was potential for us, as long as I paid for my mistakes. He frowns heavily, gaze flitting over my suit, like he's trying to place it. Graham doesn't take long to do so, surprise flickering over his face as he takes me in before he schools his expression into neutral. I can tell from the curl of her upper lip that Leighton recognizes it too.

"Thank you for . . . joining us, Miss Walker," Leighton says severely, making it sound like both an admonishment and a threat. She knows I had something to do with Saint running and what happened to Esme. But there's no evidence.

"Thank you for having me, Dr. Remington," I say back, imitating her tone beat for beat.

I look over at Penthesilea in her perfectly pink glory, like the princess that she is. She dips her head at me in greeting, but she doesn't exactly look at me. Instead, she's staring straight across at

Hawthorne. I follow the line of her stare and Hawthorne is staring right back, her eyes wide, nostrils flaring, a demented air to her I've never seen, despite how perfectly polished she is dressed.

Around her neck is Esme's thick diamond collar. If I squint hard enough, I can see specks of pink in between the tiny diamonds. I close my eyes to what I've done, looking over her sea-green dress instead, the embroidery of the flowers on her bodice. She reminds me of Ophelia, buried in a river in Denmark.

"Welcome to the Royale." Third's voice booms through the space, interrupting our strange standoff and drawing our attention back to him. Leighton opens her mouth to speak, but Third steps forward, effectively cutting her off. "Today is the finale of the Finish. You have proven to us that the young women of today, for how much they lack polish, are amenable to being formed and completed. Do you feel complete?"

He doesn't mean for us to answer. So we don't.

Instead, Leighton takes advantage of the silence, wresting back control, noticeably perturbed by Third's takeover. "After last night's . . . events, the rankings have shifted. In first place, we have Penthesilea Bonavich. In second, we have Hawthorne Harding. And finally, in last, the *incomparable* Miss Adina Walker."

Leighton's lips curl around my name, her favor evaporated, but I stand taller, refusing to flinch under the glacial weight of her stare.

"I will not sugarcoat this," Leighton says. "The Royale is . . . a game of Assassin."

A game for elementary school students. It's insulting and infantilizing and exactly right.

"The aim of the game is for players to track down and subdue their targets, by any means necessary. You may defend yourself, by any means necessary. When a player eliminates her target, she will continue and acquire her victim's target. When one player remains standing, the game is over," Leighton says carefully. "As the Game Mistress, I will assign each of you a target. Hawthorne, you are assigned Adina."

Hawthorne is breathing so slowly that it's almost like she's not breathing at all, like a predator that is *so* close to her feast.

"Adina, your target will be Penthesilea," Leighton continues. "And finally, Penthesilea, you are assigned Hawthorne."

It doesn't take a genius to see past Leighton's veiled language.

"Pierce, anything else you'd like to say?" Third prompts.

Pierce claps his hands together. "Not anything particularly. I did want to thank you for your participation. And I wish you the very best luck."

Leighton nods. "Very good. I will now count down from ten. Ten, nine—" I can't look away from Pierce and that small half smile, the forlorn look in his eyes like he regrets this. It is *practiced*, fake, exactly like that smile in the woods, and those words at breakfast, and everything about him.

"No," I say, remembering my plan.

"'No'?" Third repeats as if he doesn't understand the meaning of a two-letter word.

"I said no," I continue. "I have . . . something important to say. To all of you."

"Miss Walker, this is very irregular, but I'll allow it," Leighton prompts in spite of Third's outrage.

I take a deep shuddering breath.

"We can't begin, because not everyone who's supposed to be playing is playing."

CHAPTER

 32

MY DECLARATION IS DEFINITIVE AND DAMNING. Graham looks confused. Pierce is watching me with that stare that I can't discern, like either he'd like me dead after rejecting him a second time with the dress or he wants me to live, to see what I will do next.

The tension in the hunting parlor can be cut with a knife, so stiff and muffling that I would've once suffocated on the taste of it.

"What do you mean, Miss Walker, when you say that not everyone is playing?" Leighton asks. Leighton is looking for clarity, but not for herself. I know that she knows exactly what I mean. She casts a quick look over at Third, whose gaze doesn't waver from my face as he moves to sit down in the winged armchair. I bare my teeth in a grin.

"The Finish is essentially . . . a game, is it not?"

"No, it is a time-honored tradition," Third growls, "begun

with my great-great-great-grandfather, at the dawn of Edgewater's founding—"

"First, didn't a woman start it? Matilda Remington or whoever? Second, it's a competitive event that is played according to rules and decided by skill, strength, and luck," I insist. "That's a game. You've all been making snide little references about it the whole time."

Leighton takes a sip of her mimosa, long enough to nearly finish it, except for the tiniest pool of topaz at the bottom of the glass. "It's a game," she agrees flatly, impatient for me to get on with it. She looks back at Penthesilea and Hawthorne, who have now both moved to stand behind me, pressed up against the wall to better witness.

"In every Repartee, the person who is challenged picks the game. That's the rule, right?"

"Yes, it's the rule," Leighton agrees, and she leans in, swaying closer, eager.

"Well . . . then we should pick the game. We should set the rules. Because Pen and Hawthorne didn't challenge me and *I* didn't challenge them. *We* were challenged . . . ," I say. I glance back at the two girls. Hawthorne is holding herself taut, any kindness, any soft border gone. Penthesilea stares back, a peculiar tilt to her mouth. I turn back to the group. "By you. The Remingtons. But you're not playing. It's our game and *you* have to play."

My words waver in the air and then Third lets out a barking laugh. "Us? You can't be serious."

"Mr. Remington, I've never been more serious in my entire life." The laughter stops after I say that.

"How *dare* you?" Third booms, his voice thunderous as he squints at me through narrowed eyes. I nearly take a step back. "Little girl, do you know who you're playing with?"

"Do you?" I shoot back. "Are you afraid, Mr. Remington?"

He scoffs, unconvincingly.

"I thought you were all about rules, Third. I know I'm not your 'choice,' but I've made it this far. By playing by the *rules*. Your rules," I say, smirking at the Remington patriarch. I turn back to Leighton, who looks thoughtful. "But it should always have been our game. *My* game. And we can play Assassin, but you have to play too. No set targets. Two ways to win: you're the last one standing."

"Or?" Leighton asks, quirking an eyebrow.

Third sits up taller. "You can't be seriously considering this, Leighton."

"I'm the Game Mistress," she warns.

"I am the patriarch of this family," Third says. His jaw clenches so hard that I hear it crack on each word.

"And I won the *right* to this title. I shed blood for this title. You would never understand what that means. What it is to be in their places. So I will hear her rules and *I* will determine if we accept," Leighton says, and when she looks back at me, she is considering again. "The other way to win?"

"You get out that front door. After that, you leave us alone.

No money. No connections. No nothing. We walk away, and we never see each other again. We won't talk. No one will ever know. You never come after us. Accept the rules or don't. I'm playing the game this way anyway, and at least this time . . . the playing field will *actually* be even." I look at Pierce now, and he stares back, his face full of horror at the reality of what he's claimed to want.

"No," Pierce finally blurts out. He shakes his head frantically. "Aunt Leighton, you can't be serious. This is . . . this is absurd. Tradition states—"

"I thought you didn't like tradition, Pierce," I say, voice flat.

"Tradition *states*," he says, his voice rising higher and louder, "that the Royale will take place amongst the remaining girls. I— *we* are not competing."

"Aren't we?" And finally, Graham *speaks*. For once, he doesn't just let Four have his way. He has an enigmatic smile stretching across his face, crinkling the corners of his eyes. "This is our doing. Our family's doing. We've been making them fight over us and our fucking money for . . . Dad calls it tradition? I call it entertainment."

Pierce shakes his head stubbornly. "It's not for *entertainment*. It's to prove themselves worthy of marrying—"

"Why do they have to prove themselves? Did we ever have to prove ourselves?" Graham barks back, and Pierce looks at his brother like he's never seen him before. "Four, what did *we* do to prove that we deserve the money and power we have?"

"Our ancestors—"

"Exactly. *We* didn't do shit," Graham says, gesturing between the two of them. Then he jerks a thumb back at Third. "He didn't either."

"You watch your tone," Third roars. But then he takes a deep breath and he is startlingly calm. He leans forward, legs spread wide, powerful. Even sitting, he seems larger than anyone else I've ever met before. "Miss Walker, who are you doing this for? You can't think that you will win this. There is only one of you against all of us."

I'm doing it for Margaret. For Esme.

I'm doing it for Saint.

I'm doing it for *me*.

For all the other girls, even Penthesilea and Hawthorne. So I have to ask . . . "Penthesilea, Hawthorne. Are you part of their 'us'?"

They weren't expecting me to ask their opinion. We haven't been asked what *we* want to do in all this time.

"You were there when Esme . . . I know you were," Hawthorne says, her voice bristling and careful. She's staring at me with increasingly narrowed eyes, until all I can see is the blown black of her pupils. "She's dead now. Because of you."

"Hawthorne," I start. "Every minute we've been here, they've been pitting us against one another. Trying to get us to *hurt* each other—" But Hawthorne isn't done.

"She's dead now, because of all of *you*," she says, and her voice trembles on that last word. An accusation. A death sentence. She's looking directly at Third. "I won't let any of you out of here. I'll rip you all limb from *limb*."

"This is madness," Third says. His mouth is pinched and he slides farther back in his chair, pinned by Hawthorne's gaze.

"Penthesilea?" I ask again.

Penthesilea is humming to herself, barely paying any attention. That's answer enough. And finally, I turn back to Leighton.

"The Remingtons initiated a challenge. We accepted. You participate in the game. The game is Assassin," I say, never looking away from those cold, cold eyes. "Make it out the front door. Or die. Those are the rules. Shall we begin?" I extend a hand.

Do you want to make Third bleed? I asked her.

I very much doubt the answer has changed. I'm counting on that.

Leighton strides forward and grabs my hand in her iron fist. "Done."

"No, this isn't done. The Finish is for young women of standing," Third insists, standing up harshly. "I *object* to this heinous bastardization of Remington tradition. You're not even a blood Remington, Leighton. You're only—"

"Leighton, count down," I command.

Every second that Third figures he's still in control, he gets easier to ignore.

"Wait, wait, we haven't all even agreed to your terms! Just Leighton, and she's not even really a Remington; she doesn't count!" Pierce protests. He's cringing as he looks at me, like he doesn't recognize me, like I'm not worth the shit his racehorse Widow Maker steps in every day, and neither is his aunt.

My nose wrinkles. "That really *is* such a fucked-up thing to say."

"Count down," Penthesilea murmurs.

She slowly tilts her chin down, taking a step to the right and then another. I can see her eyes now. They're focused. There's opportunity, she smells. And after opportunity, the promise of cutting out the poison in her life, every obligation and compulsion to be perfection.

Almost immediately, Hawthorne sweeps over for the crossbow and bolts mounted on the wall. I rush toward the closest long-range weapon, the broadsword. Getting the handgun and bullets together out of the safe would take too long.

I expect Penthesilea to grab the machete or a knife again, but she takes up Reagan's bat, tucked haphazardly against the mantel, like it was forgotten there after a game of softball. She leans up against the wall.

"Seriously, Penthesilea?" I ask.

Penthesilea stares at me. "Time to play," she says firmly.

Leighton starts the countdown. I heft the broadsword up in two hands, my eyes darting around the room. The Remingtons haven't moved to arm themselves. Third is frozen in place, shocked at what Leighton has just agreed to. Pierce doesn't look like he believes it. Graham . . . Graham is watching me. When I raise an eyebrow, he smiles. And Leighton is still counting, steady as always.

"Five . . . four . . . three . . . two . . . one."

None of us moves for a moment.

"No! I refuse. I'm the Remington patriarch. I have conducted the Finish, year after year. This is Pierce's time. His rising. I will not allow you to ruin—" Third shouts.

Leighton sheds all manner of civility. She lunges forward, wrapping her long fingers around Third's throat. The chair falls over with a steady thump and the man thrashes underneath her. The muscles in Leighton's neck strain as she gets a hold on his chin and his neck and twists.

There's a deafening *crack*.

And just like that, Pierce Maxwell Remington III is dead.

Leighton sits atop him, a lioness above her prey, as she stares down the Remington boys.

She sneers at them as her glacial exterior shatters. Ruffled and undone, a run in her pantyhose, her silk shirt untucked, she stalks toward them. "I promised . . . there would be blood."

CHAPTER

33

"DAD! YOU KILLED MY *DAD*, YOU CRAZY BITCH!"
Pierce shouts, ducking behind the sofa as Leighton runs across the
room, snatching the hunting rifle from the wall, loading it with
an expertise that speaks to memory. Memories resurfaced for her
last night during Simon Says, and I've used the chaos it unleashed
in her to my advantage.

From the corner of my eye, I see a swish of sea green and blond
and I *just* swing out of the way of Hawthorne bringing her crossbow up. The arrow hits the floor with a thud, right where I was,
and then Hawthorne brings the bow back again, aiming at me.
Fuck.

I throw my shoulder forward, hitting hers. Graham snags me
by the wrist and then he tugs me straight out of the parlor.

"Let's get the hell out of here!" Graham insists. His bottom lip
trembles and he aborts a move to look back at his father. Instead,
he flinches when there's the sound of a gunshot. Leighton.

I start running faster, the broadsword heavy in my hand, slowing me down just the tiniest bit. "Yeah, I'm ahead of you there, Graham!" I shout, skidding around the corner. The hunting parlor is on the first floor and the door is close.

"Not so fast, Miss Walker." A shot is fired and we duck as the bullet slams through the front door, a single little circle of white piercing through the wood. I lift my sword defensively, but what is steel to a bullet? "The game has only just begun."

There's a click of another bullet being loaded and I duck again, yelping when my ankle twists underneath me and instantly starts throbbing.

Leighton aims the hunting rifle at the pair of us, her lips curling, but I'm surprised to see her tilt it at Graham.

"You were always so disappointing, Graham," she sighs, like it's no big deal that she's pointing a rifle at his head.

For a moment I imagine abandoning him here. I can make it out the door without him. But he came for me last night. He'd agreed to play, finally stood up to Pierce. I won't leave him until I have to.

"Upstairs! Upstairs!" I screech, and start hobbling sideways, tugging Graham along this time.

Leighton fires another shot and it whistles to the side of him.

"Fuck! Why is she aiming for me?" Graham yells as we scramble up the stairs, practically tripping over each step, rushing up past the second floor, up to the third, farther from the freedom I am so desperate for. My ankle twinges again and I fall hard on the last step, but I shove myself back up.

"Because killing Miss Walker is a privilege I'd like to savor. You are a Remington, and thus, a chore," Leighton says, her voice finally, after all these carefully controlled weeks, rising into a roar. She's coming closer, the click of her heels growing louder as she ascends at a steady pace, like she's savoring this moment. "Miss Walker, I really am saddened by this turn of events. I thought you were here for the right reasons."

Graham and I try door handles frantically but they're all locked. The sound of the bolts rattling in the frames sounds mocking and my heart sinks. We rush back to the stairs to ascend to the next floor, just as Leighton appears.

"I came here for *your* right reasons—because I thought I wasn't enough. But I'd rather die than be turned into some weird shiny smoothed-over version of myself that self-medicates with wine and becomes some fucker's puppet," I say viciously, lifting the sword again. "I'm good. Thanks."

Leighton loads the rifle again and lifts it to aim. "Well, I can oblige," she says.

I back myself up the steps to the fourth floor, my ankle stepping it up from a twinge to a steady throb, and I know I won't make it. I squeeze my eyes shut, but then I feel Graham throw himself in front of me, shoving me back and causing me to lose my grip on the sword, like he's going to take the *bullet* for me. But no shot sounds.

No pain blooms across my chest. Slowly, I open my eyes.

Leighton stands there, her eyes open wide with a childlike sense of wonder. She looks down at her blue silk top, and it begins to darken to a big purple splotch in the middle of her chest. She drops the rifle and it fires into the ceiling. And then she falls backward, sliding down the steps, revealing Penthesilea on the third-floor landing, hand outstretched, like she's just thrown something. Leighton's body rolls, and there, in her back, is the smallest black handle of a knife.

Penthesilea tears her attention away from Leighton and takes a step upstairs, like she's ready to pursue a new target. Graham drags me back to my feet. I reach for the sword on the landing, where it fell, but Penthesilea steps hard on the flat of the blade and slides it behind her, out of reach.

"Pen—" he starts.

"I thought you took the bat," I say.

"Come on now, Adina. You know I always have something in my pocket," Penthesilea says, and then she lifts her bat, holding it like she's goddamn Babe Ruth. But then a voice shouts:

"ADINA WALKER IS MINE."

Penthesilea doesn't say a word, she simply steps to the side and darts back the way she came, clearly deciding to let Hawthorne deal with us. Coming down from the fourth floor, Hawthorne has us cornered, her crossbow aimed at us. We'll be dead before we even think of diving down the long flight of stairs.

"Hawthorne, come on. Third . . . ," Graham swallows heavily. He shakes his head like a wet dog clearing its ears. "Third is dead. Leighton is dead. We could all just leave—"

"No," Hawthorne warns. "Esme didn't get to leave. So neither does *she*."

"Hawthorne, please. *Please*," I whisper. I try to take a step forward, but my ankle pops again. Graham holds me up, as we slowly back away against the wall, out of the corner of the third-floor landing, as Hawthorne walks down the stairs, never lowering her crossbow.

"You *killed* Esme. You murdered her," Hawthorne says, her voice cracking. "Give me one good reason I shouldn't kill you right here. Right *now*."

"She was going to kill Saint. She . . . she killed Margaret—"

"Adina, smell me," Hawthorne commands.

For a moment my fear freezes in the pit of my belly, and confusion is the far more overwhelming, more complicated emotion.

"Did she . . . just ask you to smell her?" Graham asks. He is about to make a move to look behind his shoulder at me, before he recognizes that it's probably a bad idea to turn his back on the girl with a crossbow.

"I wasn't asking," Hawthorne spits. "*Smell* me, Adina Walker."

I duck under Graham's outstretched arm, limping closer until there's only a foot of space between Hawthorne and me.

And then I smell her.

Dior. Not the sandalwood and lavender Chanel perfume Esme took to wearing here. But the floral one that was her signature.

It's the perfume that killed Margaret.

"You're wearing Esme's perfume," I whisper quietly, confused.

"No," says Hawthorne. "I'm wearing *my* perfume. Esme has always borrowed *my* perfume, not the other way around."

The world stops turning on its axis, just for a moment. My mouth goes dry.

"No, it was Esme," I say simply. "Esme . . ."

"What aren't you getting?" Hawthorne drops her crossbow to her side, nearly cracking it in half against the landing. There's a horrible plea in her voice as she tries to force me to understand, to see what she's been hiding all this time. *Look at the monster I can be.* "*I* killed Margaret!"

I try to speak but choke on it.

"Didn't see that coming," Graham murmurs.

"No, you didn't kill her," I say, shaking my head at her. "You couldn't've—"

"Why?" Hawthorne spits. "Because I'm quiet? I killed Margaret and Hannah G and Jacqueline, *too.* Esme's my best friend and she needs me. She has to win and can't do what has to be done."

My heart cracks; Hawthorne is talking about her like she's still here.

Hawthorne's voice grows higher again. "I'm not *afraid of her.* I'm not a coward. I *protected* her. I *helped* her. I got the rest out of the way to make it easier for Esme. She couldn't do it. She didn't hate them like she hated you. *You,* she could kill. So I cleared the rest out. I cleared them out and kept you alive so she could do what she needed to. You were never her friend.

She realized it. *I* realized it. You just used her. And then you humiliated her. You don't do that to friends. So now I'm gonna kill you for her," Hawthorne screeches, and then she's aiming the crossbow again.

I drag Graham down and the bolt buries itself in the wall. I yank the bolt out as Hawthorne rushes to load another. But she is shaking with rage and she fumbles. Graham seizes the opportunity and tackles her, trying to wrench the crossbow away from her.

But Hawthorne swings the crossbow up hard. With a thump, it collides with Graham's head and he tumbles into the wall.

As Hawthorne tries to right herself, I lunge, thrusting the bolt up, and I feel it find its mark, sliding between her ribs.

Hawthorne gasps, her fingers loosening, and the crossbow falls. I hear something snap.

She staggers back, her blond hair loose around her face, making her look ragged and small and above all, so *damn* young. She stares at me as she stumbles past, looking around in a daze as her breathing grows labored, and then she slides to the floor.

"Don't pull it out," I whisper. "Or you'll bleed out and die. It's not your time to join her yet. She'd want more for you. And despite everything, so do I."

Hawthorne blinks at me owlishly and doesn't say anything.

I grab Graham by the arm, hoisting him up. "I think I've made up for all the times you've saved me. So get up and stop throwing yourself in front of projectile objects for me," I say sharply.

Graham gives me a side-eye, rubbing his temple. "I'm pretty

sure if we survive this that I'm going to have a goddamn con-cussion," he mutters, and he looks back at Hawthorne. "She'll be okay, right?"

"I don't know. Come on," I say. I rush down the stairs, ignor-ing my throbbing ankle. But then I stop, Hawthorne's words still ringing in my ears, and Graham nearly crashes into me. Slowly, I look back at her, as she watches from one story up, unable to pursue. She looks tired. "No, wait. Enough of your 'woe is me' monologue. I'm not the villain of your story, Hawthorne. I feel bad for killing Esme. I do. She didn't deserve to die, but she was an ass. She was classist and kinda racist sometimes and she was coming to kill me. So, no, I'm not going to nobly accept the part you're trying to cast me in for your revenge fantasy. It's not that kind of movie."

CHAPTER 34

"BE ON THE LOOKOUT," I SAY TO GRAHAM AS WE limp down the stairs. "Penthesilea is still here. Pierce is still here."

"Don't worry about them. Four would never hurt anyone. And Pen . . . Penny will calm down," Graham insists. He somehow still sounds so sure of himself, of the people around him.

I wonder what that's like. I don't think I'll ever be sure of anything again. I won't be able to trust anything but my two eyes ever again, and even those have betrayed me over and over again.

Margaret. Saint. Esme. Hawthorne. Margaret. Saint. Esme. Hawthorne.

Those names are as good as burned into my flesh now.

"Oh, Adina, you were so close."

I'm brought back to now, gasping sharply when I realize that I've lost the past ten seconds. I blink hard, bringing Penthesilea into focus.

She's leaning against the wall on the first-floor landing, arms folded over her chest, eyes closed. When Graham says her name, she opens them, revealing sharp blue.

"Penthesilea?" Graham says, like a question.

"I can't let you go now," Penthesilea says quietly, answering it.

"I thought you weren't here to hurt anyone. You just . . . wanted to keep Pierce in line," I say, and I can't stop my voice from shaking, because she's right. I am so close and she's one of the last things standing between me and the door.

"What do you mean, keep Four in line? He hasn't done anything," says Graham, furious at the disparagement of his brother's character. "He's just . . . *brainwashed*."

Penthesilea smiles blankly.

"Is he?" Penthesilea asks softly. "Open your eyes, Graham. Pierce always knew that this was how it would end. He wanted this, Graham. He *orchestrated* this. He decided he wanted *her* to be the one to live probably thirty seconds after he invited her."

Graham frowns. "No, he didn't. He wanted to change the Finish. He wanted to even the playing field. He . . . he tried to change what he could."

Penthesilea shakes her head and finally pushes off the wall, tapping the bat against the floor over and over again, like it's matching her heartbeat.

"No, he didn't. He changed what he didn't like. What was convenient to the narrative he'd had in his head. Third wanted it to be me, but that didn't work for Pierce. Pierce wanted a girl who'd *realize* that she'd kill for him. Pierce found me boring because he knew I would. I was already finished, and Pierce likes a *project*," says Penthesilea, cutting her eyes to me and then back to Graham again. Graham looks at me, and then her again, trapped between two people telling him over and over again that he has failed in making his brother a decent human being. Penthesilea scoffs. "Your brother is a psychopath. You're just blind."

"Is that what you think of me, Pen?" Penthesilea looks up, past us, her gaze catching on the golden boy himself. Pierce slowly walks down the steps, staring at Penthesilea with the most wounded expression on his face, like his heart is actually breaking. "You think I'm crazy?"

"I think you're a narcissistic asshole," Penthesilea says gently, almost kindly. "I think that you ruin everything you touch, that you want to devour everything you see."

"You're not, Four," Graham insists. He is so desperate to believe the lie. Even now, even after throwing himself in front of me, he's still a coward in the face of his brother. "She doesn't *know* you—"

"I. Know. Him!" Penthesilea snaps. Then she tugs back the bitterness, trying to bottle it back up, but her expression grows frantic as she can't quite manage it, like she's about to burst at the seams with resentment. "I know that he *knew*. He knew that all these girls were going to come here, fighting for opportunity, dying for his affection. How do you think the ones not from Edgewater found out what it really was? Why do you think only Adina was left in the dark? He thought it would be too expected if I won, like a subpar season finale. Poor, innocent Adina has the better *story*."

Pierce shakes his head, tutting to himself.

"I love you, Pen. I've always loved you," Pierce says. He's talking to her like a wild animal and creeping close to us, like he means to defend us against her.

Penthesilea chokes on a laugh. "You don't love anything but your—"

The sound of a gunshot never gets familiar, especially at close range. It booms, so loud that for a moment all I hear is white noise, and then I find the source: that small handgun that I had in the Raid, aimed right at Penthesilea, is cradled in Pierce's hand.

Penthesilea makes a gurgling sound in the back of her throat and then she collapses, blood already pooling beneath her.

"Pierce!" Graham gasps, head thumping back against the wall. "You . . . you shot her!"

Hot rage fills my chest, so hot that it feels like the blood in my veins is fueled by that fury. I shove Pierce hard and he bangs into the opposite banister, surprised by my sudden move. I wrench the gun from his hand and take aim, pressing the muzzle against his chest.

"How could you?" I demand.

And Pierce stares at me with those wide, guileless eyes, like he can't *possibly* comprehend why I'm angry or what he's done wrong.

And suddenly, I have the words for what Penthesilea has shielded the world from. This is a boy who has never met a consequence in his life. This is a boy who has been told that he is to die for, to kill for.

This is a dangerous boy poised to become an even more dangerous man.

"She was going to hurt you! I told you, Adina, that you were my choice," he says insistently. "I knew from the night in the woods that you'd win. You're smart, you're talented, why else would you be at Edgewater when you can't afford it"—*fucking dick*—"but you were also biting and ambitious and *surprising*. My mother doesn't surprise my father. Until today, Leighton never surprised anyone either. Pen wouldn't surprise me. Pen wouldn't push me. Pen was predictable. People expected Pen. They always expect people like Pen and me to be together. But the world would see you and me and think that we are so different that we work. You were just a little rough around the edges. You weren't hungry enough. And Yale really isn't the place for you. You'll like Cambridge, I promise. But I knew that the Finish would fix that. And now you're complete. You changed the game like I changed it. Look at what you've done. Esme is dead. Hawthorne . . . well, don't worry, we'll finish that up. Everyone who's wronged you . . . this is what being a Remington is. They've made you perfect. *I've* made you perfect." He cups my face in his hands, rubbing his thumbs over the apples of my cheeks, smiling, like I don't have a gun pressed against his chest.

Complete. Perfect. A finished girl.

"Pen was right," I whisper, voice cracking. "You do need to be kept in check."

I cock the gun.

"Wait, wait, Adina, please—"

I look at Graham, and he's watching me, tears rolling down his cheeks. He looks so heartbreakingly sad, this boy who loved his younger brother so much that he was willing to do anything for him.

I turn back to Pierce, but he's not looking at me anymore; instead, he's staring down the stairs, confusion creasing his brow, his mouth dropping into a pout.

"Pen?" he asks.

Penthesilea stands there, one hand grabbing at her bleeding shoulder, the bodice of her dress soaked crimson with blood.

"You've always been a terrible shot, you fucking asshole," she snarls, her face pulled into a grimace.

Pierce takes a wary step down the stairs. My gun is still trained on him and he pauses, to look up at me and smile. "Let me tie up some loose ends, darling."

Before I can react, he leaps down the rest of the steps, and his beautiful face becomes something ugly and cruel. He growls and raises his hands, wrapping long fingers around Penthesilea's slim, freckled neck and squeezing tight.

It's only for a moment though, because then Penthesilea swings her bat at him, knocking him away. Pierce stumbles back so hard that his legs hit the foot of the stairs, and then he cracks his head on the edge of the steps as he falls back. He looks up at her and she stands between his legs, lifting her bat over her head, tall and powerful.

"Pen, what are you doing?" Pierce shrieks.

"What needs to be done," Penthesilea snarls. "Do you know what you do to a rabid animal, Pierce? You put it down."

She swings her bat, making a deep guttural sound, and it collides with the hard cartilage of Pierce's knee with a sickening crack. Then she raises her bat up high and I know there will be no stopping her.

"My entire life, I've been trapped by your family." She brings the bat down on his shoulder and Pierce grunts, rolling. Graham lunges forward with a cry, but I grab him, wrenching him back, with no care for my ankle. Penthesilea kicks Pierce until he's on his side. "By your promises." She brings the bat down again on his stomach. "By you!" His hip. "By everyone's *fucked-up* expectations." His wrist as he reaches out for Graham. Graham jerks in my hold but I shove him against the stairs, and I ignore the betrayal carved into his face, turning back to Penthesilea. "You have made my life into blood sport!" She brings the bat down on his head. "Never again, Pierce. *I'm tired, I'm tired, I'm tired!*" She chants over again, punctuating each repetition with another hit. Her roars swell into a terrible sound until finally she looks at the gore covering her wood, and then at the caved-in face of Pierce Maxwell Remington IV, and she sobs. Snot and tears fall from her face, mixing into Pierce's blood as she collapses.

For a moment I don't know what to do. And then Graham makes a wretched sound too, and he slides down the steps, nearly careening into the wall. He grabs Pierce's body, and I can just make out his cry: *"Four!"*

I take one step down the stairs, groaning when I feel my ankle nearly give. I grab harder at the banister, keeping a steady grip on the gun. Another step. Again. Until I'm past Graham mourning his monster of a brother. I near Penthesilea and she blinks, finally turning toward me. She lifts her bat again, still weeping, arms shaking.

Before she can land a hit, I grab the bat, fingers squishing through hot blood, holding tight. Penthesilea makes a shuddery sound of surprise. I tear the wood from her grip and toss it down the staircase. The bat clatters on the hardwood floor and rolls to a stop in the middle of the foyer, right in front of the door. I grab Penthesilea by the face, dragging her close, pressing her forehead to mine. She stares at me with glassy eyes, and I can feel the heat of her breath against my mouth.

"I . . . I . . . I . . . What did I do? I have nothing left," Penthesilea weeps.

I tremble, feeling her clammy cheeks under my fingertips. I want to shake her. I want to reassure her. I want to make this never have happened.

And all I can say is: "You win."

Penthesilea shatters.

I let her go and continue down the stairs.

I give Penthesilea Bonavich one last look, committing her to memory. She is the final shot of a beautiful film, as she falls to her knees with a heavy thud and crawls toward Graham and Pierce. She tugs the bloody mess of Pierce's corpse from Graham's weak arms and holds him to her chest, wailing, the delicious pink of her dress now drenched in blood. He is the worst person in her life. But for a long time he was one of the only people in her life. He was probably the first boy she ever loved. He was her future, even if that future was a prison, and I think that might be what she grieves. Now, both our futures end in a question mark. For her sake, I hope she finds an answer, but I know she won't in the body of her dead, emotionally abusive boyfriend.

I don't look at Graham, because if I do, I'll have to look at Pierce, and I refuse to feel sad when looking at someone like him.

And then I run, flying through the door on my messed-up ankle, stuttering over the front steps, tripping over them, until I practically crawl across the driveway, toward the lawn.

Stumbling onto the grass, I fall to my knees.

Free.

I kneel in the grass for God knows how long, pressing my face into the green, wheezing. I sit up on my haunches, staring up into the sky and gasping for fresh air, unsure of what to do next. The sky seems bluer now. The world seems quieter. I want to sleep for a thousand years. There is only me, and no one else.

A hand lands on my shoulder, making that a lie. I wrench

myself away and something painful tears its way from my throat. I look up at Graham Remington and he's not staring at me—he's staring at the gun in my hand. And in that moment I don't see him or the way he doesn't resemble his father or his brother.

I see every way that he *does*.

I tremble, my teeth chattering, and I can't stop making that sound, a scream that swells up deep and guttural and warlike from the darkest part of me—the part of me that's still trapped in that nightmare of a house and always will be.

"Adina . . . ," he starts, hands held up in surrender.

"No," I snarl, scrambling back. "Don't . . . don't touch me. Don't fucking *touch* me!"

"Adina, please—"

"ADINA!"

That voice. It makes me drop the gun in the grass and turn, my ankle rolling painfully underneath me.

There's a familiar BMW driving up the long driveway.

The car screeches to a stop and then, and *then*—

"Toni!" I cry out, and I'm crawling toward her. It takes me a second to realize she's not alone. I don't scream her name, but when I see her climbing out of the passenger seat, alive and whole, it feels like a miracle. *Saint.*

Toni fights her way out of the car too and then she's running to me. I blink, and then Toni and Saint are kneeling in front of me, throwing their arms around me, reeling me in tight, while

Graham backs away. I press my face into their neck—familiar and perfect and safe and *real*—and I *weep*.

"I'm here," Toni promises.

She's here, I think.

And then it hits me—I am too. *I'm still here.*

EPILOGUE

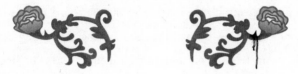

I WAKE UP WITH A START TO THE SMELL OF BACON and coffee. As I've had to for the past three weeks, I have to take a moment to remind myself of where I am.

I catalog my room—the old Super 8, my white armoire, waxy photos of Toni and me. All of it is mine. Sitting up in my bed, I turn over my phone—it's new, I never found where Leighton had tucked away mine—and look down at the lock screen. There's a message from Mom, promising that they'll be back soon, which answers who's downstairs.

There are about ten text messages telling me their ETA back to the house while they run their errands. They're still anxious about leaving me. My parents talk about pressing charges. But in my mind, there is no one really left to press charges against.

My parents talk about *therapy*. But I think about Leighton when I hear the word.

When I think about Leighton, I think about the Remingtons.

And then when I dream, I find myself back at the Remington Estate.

The bruises have begun to go away over the past couple of weeks. The nightmares don't. They get worse.

I tear away my blankets and slip out of bed. I trudge downstairs, rubbing at my eyes and tugging on the ends of my braids.

"Can you rebraid my hair today, Toni?" I ask, in lieu of a greeting.

"Good *morning*, Adina," Toni says with a wide smile, standing by the stove top. I didn't know she could cook. "Your parents said good morning too. They tried to wake you before they left, but you were out. They let me in."

"Where'd they go?" I ask, eyes flitting around to the window, the front door, the back door, checking twice that each one is closed before I finally ease into a seat at the kitchen table. I look down to find a stack of mail.

"Supermarket, but I'm sure they'll be back soon." Toni flips the bacon with a flick of her wrist. The edges are burnt—so not much has changed while I was gone. Except me. "I can rebraid your hair after breakfast. Are you sure you don't want to do anything different? We can pick up one of my wigs from the house. Or I can do twists? You can take them out in a few days."

"No, not yet," I say, sharper than I should, leaning back in my chair, staring up at the ceiling.

"Charles . . . Charles said to say hi," Toni says after a deep breath. She still hesitates on her brother's name, left over from her fury at how it took him twelve hours to decide to tell her what he had seen at the Remington Estate. She'll forgive him eventually—I already have.

When I got settled in her house, I waited for their explanation. Saint was businesslike in her recounting—it was dark, their shots had missed, she wasn't afraid of diving through the mud, and they must have been too terrified to tell the Remingtons she had gotten away. She had run as long and hard as she could until she'd reached the main road. From there, she had walked and walked, until she'd gotten to a gas station and an attendant had lent her his phone. Being rich pays, and from there it hadn't been hard to find out who Charles—and by association Toni—were and where they lived.

As Saint talked and Toni tended to my wounds, Charles lingered worriedly in the doorway, asking if I was okay, then wanting to know what'd happened, why Pierce wasn't picking up his phone, why no one was *picking up the phone*. Saint nearly bullied him away, until I looked up at him and said, "Hi, Charles. Thank you." I'd sounded like myself in that moment, apparently.

"Good for him," I say. Then I sigh. "Tell Charles I said hi."

"The . . . funeral was this morning," Toni says hesitantly, wringing her hands.

Three weeks to the day. A strangely long time.

I don't say anything for a moment. And then: "Who went?"

"It was really private. For once, no one wants anything to do with the Remingtons. Charles said the police showed up to the estate and, like, not Lenox police. State police. And the Feds," Toni explains. "Charles said their mom was there, though. She's distraught."

"You didn't go with him?" I ask.

"Fuck those people," Toni says coldly, and even now, after everything, it surprises me how people can switch on a dime, how underneath the façade of kindliness, there's always something lurking. "Penthesilea didn't go either, apparently. She's free while they investigate or whatever. Her doctor said she could've gone for 'closure,' and she laughed in his face."

"And Hawthorne?"

Toni's expression falls. "Still not awake. The infection was pretty bad." She shifts uncomfortably. "Charles told me that there was a lot of media waiting outside, though. They were . . . asking about the Finish. And the other girls."

The dead ones.

I hear the click of the front door unlocking, and I stand up suddenly enough that I have to fumble to catch the chair before it tumbles to the floor.

"We're home," Mom sings as she walks down the hall. "Hey, get this bag for me, babe. Oh, you're awake! Good."

Mom tries to be cheerful. She's always attempting to be cheerful, but she's stiff in it. There's always a strain to her throat. It's mostly because of what I've gone through, but I know that there's also some due to her quitting her tenured job at Edgewater because of me. *For* me. That, I don't feel guilty for. I don't think she would want me to.

"I'm awake," I say. Very carefully, I sit back down, spreading my hands wide over the kitchen table, attempting to ignore my father's very worried stare. He never hides his worry.

"Slept all right?" he asks.

"Well enough," I say shortly. "Had a nightmare—"

"Yeah, we heard," Mom says. She clears her throat. "And you're sure you don't want to talk to—"

"I called Saint. We talked," I say firmly. Mom doesn't approve of Saint as my version of therapy. But she's the only person who understands, fully, and she's not *here*. She's never coming back.

"I'm never going back to America, Adina. Never again," Saint promised in the dark last night. She'd called me from Beijing. It was noon for her, midnight for me. We call at least twice a day, because someone always needs to be awake to save the other from a nightmare.

"But what about Princeton?" I whispered into the phone.

"I can't, Adina. Not now. Not ever. I think I will go to the Sorbonne. But you will come visit me?" she asked. I'd thought she'd just want to forget about me, but she'd been forceful when she'd said that she didn't. She never wants to forget about me, and I don't think I'll ever be able to forget her.

"Yeah," I agreed softly. *If I can ever afford it.*

It's easy to slip in and out of memories now, and I dig my

fingers into my thighs to take me back into the now. My parents are patient, watching me find my words. They probably think I'm having another flashback. My mom is probably hoping that I'll actually share the details of them with her, let her in.

Instead, I say, "Toni is going to rebraid my hair. It looks bad."

"You said it, not me," Dad tries to joke.

Mom raises an eyebrow at me, mouth twitching as she and Dad go to unload groceries in the kitchen. "You've been watching this bacon, Toni?"

"Yes, ma'am," Toni says as I turn my attention to the mail. It's easier to shuffle through trashy catalogs and weird pizza flyers than to think about how the majority of the Remington Family is being buried in their overpriced mausoleum at their personal family cemetery.

I toss them all to the side, one by one, and then hesitate.

Because there's a letter. A white envelope with my address and my *name* painstakingly written in calligraphy, but no stamp. It was hand delivered.

Just like the letter that started this mess.

"What is it?" Toni asks, taking a sip of her coffee as she tries to slide the bacon onto a platter along with the quickly cooling eggs.

"I think . . . the Remingtons sent me a letter."

"What?" Mom asks, voice loud and edging on righteous anger. "Let me see that."

Toni jerks away from the stove. She finishes dumping the bacon haphazardly, and turns off the fire, then slides into the chair next to me, placing a hesitant hand on my shoulder.

"You don't have to open that," Toni says gently, reaching for the letter.

"*Don't* touch my shit," I warn, not raising my voice, but making every word heavy with a promise.

Toni falls back immediately, wounded. She's just worried. I know that. But I can't help the habits I picked up while I was there. Everything I said had to be a warning, everything had to have retribution attached.

"Language," Mom warns.

"Sorry," I mutter, turning the letter over in my hands. It weighs nothing, but it still feels heavy in my hands. I tear it open quickly before I can think about it more, and several newspaper clippings fall out.

The first week after, there was nothing. And then, when word of the dead Remingtons got out, the whispers started. *What is the Finish? Who started the Finish? What happens during the Finish? What happened to the girls?* I faced the questions myself, the one time that the police came to question me. They absolved me halfway through, after some call from whoever was in charge. I thought that would be the end of it—Lenox police were always in the Remingtons' pocket, and they wouldn't want that known.

But then the gossip and questions grew louder and more specific.

It happened so fast. The day after my interview, the world spun with the whispers of what the Remingtons had done to girls every year that a Remington boy turned eighteen. That they took girls and ruined them and broke them, until the one who was the most broken, but still alive, was ready to be dressed in white.

I expected it was the Alderidges. Esme was dead and they were still being investigated for embezzlement. They had nothing more to lose by accusing the Remingtons, and everything to gain. With the Remingtons on the chopping block, eyes would turn away from them. Maybe they'd even sue, get some of their money back.

But now I know it wasn't the Alderidges at all.

"'Sole-Surviving Remington Son Speaks Out: A Generational Tragedy,'" I read, unable to help my mockery. "'The Edgewater Horror. Remington Family Expected to Be Sued for Damages Due to Deaths of Girls.' 'The Finish of an American Family: The Remingtons Get Their Due.'"

And then I start to laugh quietly as I look at the last clipping.

"What is all that?" Dad asks.

"These are headlines for what happened. The truth is really coming out. The police were called, but they would've been quiet if they'd been told to be. Graham snitched."

Graham, who talked the talk but did nothing for so long, driven to do something now that they're all gone and he has nothing left to lose except the money he supposedly never wanted. I wonder if he would have still done it if any of them had lived.

I read the rest of the first article until I hit the last bit of news: "He turned himself in. He's been expelled from Yale and he's being charged as an accessory because everyone else is dead. Criminal and civil, because the other girls' parents are suing. Any of the money that he doesn't have to give to the families because of damages, he's pledged to give it away."

Six billion dollars of wealth *redistributed*. After this, he and his mother won't ever be able to afford the upkeep of the Remington Estate. They won't be able to pay for the maids or the butlers or the groundskeepers. Barely even the fucking *water* bill. And that bit about Yale is rich with irony.

"Graham? That's . . . that *boy's* older brother. Always skipping class," Mom says severely. She can't say Pierce's name. I throw it around freely, always with an added "fucking" as a prefix. *Fucking Pierce.*

"A menace of a young man," Dad adds. "He . . . admitted to all of it?"

"Are we really talking about *Graham Remington*?" Toni asks, because she knows Graham, the disappointing son, the pothead son.

But I know him differently.

The boy who taught me and helped me survive. The boy who kissed me. The boy I kissed. The boy whom *I* saved. The kind one. The coward. The one who had made me feel sane in an insane world. The only one whom I had trusted at all and who still chose his brother in the end.

"Yeah, Graham Remington," I murmur softly, sliding the clipping away delicately, promising myself to read them again later. I pull out the last two pieces of paper, clipped together . . . and promptly choke.

To Adina the Unfinished,

You're right. I was a coward. And I didn't know you. Not at all. But, one day, I would like to. Here's my number, if you're ever ready. (If I'm not in prison.) And if you're not, especially if you're not, know that I am always on your side.

Graham the Un-Favorite

P.S. Sorry I couldn't get you back into Yale. I tried. The Remington name doesn't mean much these days.

His phone number is printed painstakingly underneath his name. And then I see the second piece of paper.

"Oh. Holy *shit*," Toni whispers. "Adina, that's . . . that's six zeroes after the one, isn't it? That's a million dollars."

"What?" Mom asks, abandoning the groceries to my father. She stalks over. "A million *what*?"

"Yes. It is," I whisper. "He gave me a million dollars."

"Oh my God," Mom whispers.

"What are you gonna do with it? That's so much. You can go anywhere. Be anything," Toni breathes, trembling with her excitement. It's more than enough to do that. Toni grabs my hand, squeezing hard, looking at me with bright hope in her eyes.

I could probably buy my way back into Yale myself.

But I realize, then, for the first time . . . I don't want Yale. Not anymore. Not ever. Because it will come with conditions and expectations. Another world I would always be fighting to be accepted in, that would never really be mine.

I don't know what I do want, but it's not the rose-colored world of upper-class New England, and it's not Suburbia, either. I missed it, Suburbia. I missed my home and how simple and mine it all was. I had dismissed these houses that all looked the same, that felt small, but now I realized that each had an inside, unknown and glorious, a tiny kingdom. But it is not my kingdom anymore, and neither is the Remington Estate. All of it fits rough, if it ever fit at all.

All of it belongs to someone else. Other people's values and other people's dreams that have been pasted to me. I need to find my own. I just wish I hadn't had to learn it this way.

"You can't keep it," Dad says. "Can you?"

"I earned this money," I say quietly. I stop, trying to find the words. My parents are still, but Toni nods, encouraging, waiting for me to finish. "The things I had to do. What I saw. I earned this. Actually, I earned more, but I'll take this."

I sit back in my chair, closing my eyes.

I don't know if I'll ever call Graham. Even to thank him. I still think of the way I escaped and how when I looked at him, I saw his last name first, even with how much he helped me. Maybe even cared about me. I'm not sure if I want to know if I could care about him out here.

I don't know if I'll ever be okay. Maybe I'll always have nightmares, thinking back to that house, to that maze, to the stables, to everything.

I played a game, a bloody one, and I was made into someone new. But I was *not* finished. If I was made once, I can be remade. There will always be someone new to become, with each turn of a day, of a life. There's still more to see. Still more to be and grow. Still more to *do*. Maybe in New York. Maybe in California. Maybe I'll go to Lagos. Definitely Paris—Saint will be my first stop. So I'll take the money, and I'll go. Even with the terror that has made a home in my body, I'll go and *be*.

I'll live my life.

Because I'm not finished with it yet.

ACKNOWLEDGMENTS

WRITING IS SOLITARY. PUTTING TOGETHER A BOOK is not. This is a group project. I want to thank my agent, Quressa Robinson, for advocating for me and being my number one cheerleader here. You have always been so encouraging and have pushed me and my work in ways that I couldn't imagine. Thank you, Jenny Meyer, for advocating for my book abroad.

Thank you to my amazing editor, Alexa Pastor, at Simon and Schuster Children's. I can't imagine this journey with anyone else. I can't imagine working on this book with anyone else. It would not have been the book I wanted it to be with anyone else. You get it and you get me. Thank you so much! I want to thank all my friends at S&S, and I want to be clear that there are more names than I can even count because everyone has been going so hard for me and this book. But I would be remiss in not listing a few names: Alma Gomez Martinez, Dorothy Gribbin, Sara Berko, Laura Eckes, Justin Chanda, Kendra Levin, Lynn

Kavanaugh, Karen Sherman, and Cienna Smith. Thank you.

Thank you to my team in the UK! You have been absolutely fabulous to me. Thank you, Tom Rawlinson, my amazing editor and advocate over there. Thank you to Harriet Venn and Michael Bedo.

To my high school English teachers, Mr. Weisberg and especially Ms. Tramontin, thank you for showing me the power of the written word. I have never forgotten the words that you both told me over and over again during my four years—don't stop writing. I hold them dear.

To both loving sets of grandparents (and by extension my family), thank you for supporting me!

I want to thank specifically my aunt Daniella for always believing in me, promising to read all my work, and actually doing so when audio editions are available.

I want to thank some of my friends—Camryn Garrett, Shelly Romero, Molly X Chang, Racquel Marie, Jake Maia Arlow, and Christina Li. Thank you for being so supportive and always having my back. I love y'all so much!

To the Clown Clan (and all other variations of who we are)— Circe Moskowitz, Ashia Monet, and Joel Rochester—I love you. Thank you for not letting me minimize my success or talent. Thank you for reminding me that this wasn't just luck, I earned this.

To Selina Mao, you are the best writer I have ever met. Every day, I am thankful that we had our first poetry class together. The most humbling experience to meet someone so much better than me. The most amazing experience to meet someone who also was unabashedly into the same things as me. Thank you for pushing me and my craft.

To Alexandra Young, you are my person. I really do feel like that's all there is to say.

To Sarah DeSouza. Sarah, Sarah, Sarah, whom I love so so deeply and dearly. You are my very best friend. Thank you for reading every draft. Thank you for hearing every doubt and every anxiety. Thank you for refusing to let me pretend that this isn't a big deal, because this is a big deal. Thank you for being.

I want to thank my parents for reading me three books every single night from the time I was a newborn until I'd decided I could read myself to sleep. Mommy, I'm sorry I'm a little creep who likes writing about creepy little things, but you shouldn't have let me pick all my own books when I was seven. Dad, thanks for being a nerd and raising me to be a little nerd. I wish you were into zombies—this book has nothing to do with zombies, but I still wish you were into them.

Finally, I thank my sister, Alyssa. I still remember every shadow puppet show.